Staff Sergeant Corey Yarv
Basic Reconnaissance Course. ...
horror, but he can't remember those events. Battling severe PTSD, Corey's drinking is growing out of control.

Sean Chandler walks into a dive bar, and into Corey's life. An actor and a musician, Sean has the empathy and compassion to sooth Corey's pain, and the strength to support him as he struggles to heal.

Corey's lost memories are pivotal to a civilian murder, and a military investigation. Remembering could mean salvation, or destruction. Will the truth be too much for Sean to handle?

Featuring a roll call of some of the best writers of gay erotica and mysteries today!

Derek Adams	Z. Allora	Maura Anderson
Simone Anderson	Victor J. Banis	Laura Baumbach
Helen Beattie	Ally Blue	J.P. Bowie
Barry Brennessel	Nowell Briscoe	Jade Buchanan
James Buchanan	TA Chase	Charlie Cochrane
Karenna Colcroft	Michael G. Cornelius	Jamie Craig
Ethan Day	Diana DeRicci	Vivien Dean
Taylor V. Donovan	S.J. Frost	Kimberly Gardner
Kaje Harper	Alex Ironrod	DC Juris
Jambrea Jo Jones	AC Katt	Thomas Kearnes
Sasha Keegan	Kiernan Kelly	K-lee Klein
Geoffrey Knight	Christopher Koehler	Matthew Lang
J.L. Langley	Vincent Lardo	Cameron Lawton
Anna Lee	Elizabeth Lister	Clare London
William Maltese	Z.A. Maxfield	Timothy McGivney
Kendall McKenna	AKM Miles	Robert Moore
Jet Mykles	N.J. Nielsen	Cherie Noel
Gregory L. Norris	Willa Okati	Erica Pike
Neil S. Plakcy	Rick R. Reed	AJ Rose
Rob Rosen	George Seaton	Riley Shane
Jardonn Smith	DH Starr	Richard Stevenson
Christopher Stone	Liz Strange	Marshall Thornton
Lex Valentine	Haley Walsh	Mia Watts
Lynley Wayne	Missy Welsh	Ryal Woods
Stevie Woods	Sara York	Lance Zarimba
Mark Zubro		

Check out titles, both available and forthcoming, at
www.mlrpress.com

THE
FINAL LINE

The Recon Diaries

KENDALL MCKENNA

mlrpress
www.mlrpress.com

Copyright 2013 by Kendall McKenna

Published by
MLR Press, LLC
3052 Gaines Waterport Rd.
Albion, NY 14411

Visit ManLoveRomance Press, LLC on the Internet:
www.mlrpress.com

Cover Art by Jared Rackler
Editing by Kris Jacen

Print format: ISBN# 978-1-60820-875-3
ebook format also available

Issued 2013

DEDICATION

First and foremost, for Portia de Moncur, who wrote the first ever review of *Brothers In Arms*. She also holds the dubious honor of being the first to demand Corey Yarwood be given his own story. Her encouragement is why Jonah, Kellan and Corey live in more stories.

For Stephanie G. for her help with all things Rx related.

As always, for Agnieszka, I am so happy and proud that you are following your own dream.

To every reader, reviewer, and friend who fell in love with the men of *Brothers In Arms*. Special thanks to those who saw something special in Corey Yarwood that I had no idea I'd put there, and called for more to be written about him. This one is for you.

Chapter One

It was Tuesday night and Corey needed a drink. He hadn't needed a drink like this in more than two years, when he'd been deployed to Afghanistan. He sat on the foot of his narrow bed in the Bachelor's Enlisted Quarters and tried not to think of the bottle stashed in the ceiling of his room. The last time he'd needed a drink this bad was just after the cluster-fuck in Diyala, Iraq. It had damn near gotten good men killed, including Corey.

He scrubbed both hands roughly over his face and sat for a moment with his eyes closed. What Corey really needed was sleep, but sleep usually meant dreams, and he couldn't relive that shit one more time.

Fuck it. He stood up on his bed, pushed the ceiling panel upward and retrieved the black-labeled bottle he'd stashed there. He was a decorated Staff Sergeant now, he didn't have to hide his stash as well as he had when he'd been a boot PFC. Corey broke the seal and unscrewed the cap, bringing the neck of the bottle to his lips and swallowing greedily.

Whiskey always burned on the first swallow. It probably burned on the second and third swallows, but the first one always stole his breath so he couldn't think of anything else for several minutes. There was a trail of fire from Corey's mouth to his gut and it helped him not to think. If he drank the whole bottle he'd probably sleep without dreams. At least he might be too drunk to wake up from them and remember.

Corey was halfway through the bottle when the warmth began to spread. He should stop now, hide the bottle again and get some sleep. He knew he wouldn't stop. This was his ritual every night. It had been the same since he'd come back from Afghanistan and taken the instructor position at the Basic Recon Course.

Glancing at the bottle, Corey realized if he showed up on the course tomorrow with so much as bleary eyes and no record of having left base, someone might get the idea to toss his barracks room with some intent and efficiency.

Grabbing his cell phone, he called his usual cab company and arranged a pick up outside the front gate. He changed clothes, put his cell and his wallet in the pocket of his jeans, and headed out on foot.

Corey nodded at the young Marine staffing the gate and climbed into his waiting cab. He considered which bar address to give the driver. He liked that dive bar in Bonsal but that was a long drive. He wanted to still be drunk when he got back to base. Corey told the driver the address of a little place on the way to San Marcos. It was slightly more upscale than he preferred, but was usually quiet on Tuesdays.

He intended to drink and had no interest in talking. In fact, his buzz was fading so it was definitely time to pick up where he'd left off.

The bartender, Linda, he thought her name was, gave him a nod of recognition as he took a stool at the far end of the bar. He ordered a shot and a beer. A steady stream of those should dull his senses nicely.

His seat at the bar gave him a clear view of both exits and all of the occupied tables, not that there were many. Corey relaxed slightly. If things stayed like this, he could drink for several hours, make it back to base for a few hours of sleep, and be at the pool early to fish out wannabe Recon Marines before they drowned.

He was starting on his second drink, just beginning to slump over the bar, when a woman stumbled through the front door. Corey took stock of her. At first, he thought she was already drunk. When she sat heavily on a barstool and ordered a rum and coke, he realized she'd been crying.

So, not drunk, just upset and looking to drown her sorrows. Corey could respect that. He made sure to avoid eye contact, though. Usually, the thing that had a woman publicly upset was a man, and Corey had no desire to be tagged as a possible rebound fuck.

Many years ago, Corey had found himself a rebound fuck to help him forget Kathryn. Trouble was, his rebound fuck had been another man and Corey hadn't been with a woman since. There was no chance of turning back now.

Time passed, Corey drank, and some of the tables emptied out. Everyone left was getting steadily drunker. Corey knew the moment when the men around the bar realized they all only had one shot at getting laid tonight.

"Hey, what's your name, honey?" one of the men called down the bar.

The woman sat sipping her drink, spinning her cell phone on top of the bar.

"Hey, I said, what's your name?" he called a little louder.

The woman heaved a sigh. "I don't want to be rude, but I'm just here to drink. I don't want to talk."

"Only one reason a woman comes to a bar alone to drink, and it ain't to get drunk," the man growled, his tone becoming decidedly aggressive.

Corey pushed his unfinished drink away. He knew that was bullshit. He never understood why straight men had so much trouble taking no for an answer. Alcohol mixed with testosterone never helped.

The woman thumbed the screen of her phone and put it to her ear. "Are you awake? Yeah, I know that's why I called you… Can you come get me? I've been drinking…We broke up…The same reasons we always break up. He's just not the one."

As she hung up her phone, Corey hoped the woman's girlfriend hurried. All three drunken men at the bar were now trying to engage her in conversation. She glanced surreptitiously at Corey, probably trying to determine why he wasn't harassing her, too. When their eyes met, Corey recognized pain and loneliness. He'd worn that same look for a couple of years after Kathryn had dumped him. He probably still did, only now it shared space with haunting memories.

Linda tried to calm the men down but had little success. They were growing more rowdy and abusive, probably the whole group hysteria thing. Corey didn't want to have to intervene, but a good Marine wouldn't let a woman be treated with disrespect. A good man wouldn't allow it. Corey tried hard to be both.

The front door creaked open and Corey turned, expecting to see the woman's girlfriend enter. Instead, Corey's heart slammed against his ribs and his mouth fell open slightly. A tall, broad shouldered man with the sexiest ski-jump nose Corey had ever seen strode into the bar. He was lightly tanned and had pale eyes that weren't blue, like Corey's. Hazel colored, maybe? His biceps nearly burst the sleeves of his T-shirt and Corey could see every ripple of his muscles beneath the thin fabric.

"Hey, Sean, what brings you here tonight?" Linda greeted him.

Nodding toward the woman seated at the bar, Sean replied, "Picking up my friend."

"You got here just in time," Linda said. "Things were getting a little heated."

Sean's eyes darted to Corey, which made sense, given that Corey was seated closest to his friend. Corey tried to appear disinterested, but he was far from it. Women usually turned to their girlfriends after a break up. Unless one of their guy friends was gay.

Linda shook her head. "Nah, the Marine's on his best behavior." She lifted her chin toward the other end of the bar.

Sean's expression hardened. "We should go, then," he said, laying a hand gently on his friend's shoulder.

"You're here this weekend, right?" Linda asked.

"Me and my guitar, Thursday through Saturday," Sean answered. "I'll see you then."

Corey had no idea what kind of music Sean played but he suspected he'd be stopping by to find out.

"What'd ya call the fag for, honey? You know you came here

lookin' for a real man," one of the drunks slurred, rising from his stool.

"Carl, sit down and finish your drink," Linda said sharply.

Sean acted as though he hadn't heard. He helped his friend to stand and started to lead her toward the door.

"Slut came in here looking to get fucked and now she's leaving with the faggot," Carl shouted, his two drunken friends grunting their agreement.

"I'm not a slut and I didn't come here to get laid," Sean's friend screeched, turning back on the men unsteadily. Sean continued to try to get her out the door.

Corey sat up straight, one foot on the floor. Things were going to shit fast and he was going to have to do something. He had no idea if Sean's muscles were for show or if he knew how to throw down.

"No other reason a woman comes to a bar alone," Carl rounded the bar, approaching Sean and his friend.

Sean turned on Carl, squaring off and putting his body between his friend and the drunk. "And what the fuck do you come here for? You sit here night after night, hoping someone will come in here, either pathetic enough or stupid enough to finally suck your dick. Why the fuck is that okay for you and not for her?"

Corey came off of his stool and crossed the room in a few strides. He pushed past Sean and slammed a hand into Carl's chest. "Back off, old man," he said, using the same tone he'd used in Afghanistan, when he'd faced an unruly crowd. "This is a nice place and you don't want to cause trouble." With his free hand, Corey made a flicking gesture behind his own back, encouraging Sean to take his friend and go.

Carl looked up at Corey, gaze blurry and expression belligerent. "This ain't your fuckin' business," Carl shouted, his breath sour with the smell of too much alcohol.

Corey realized he was seeing his own future if he didn't get himself squared away.

"Carl, you don't want to mess with him," Linda said from behind the bar. "He's twenty years younger than you and the government taught him how to kill people in foreign countries."

Carl shuffled back a few steps when Corey pushed at his chest. The creak of the door told him Sean and his friend had made their getaway. Carl retreated only as far as the corner of the bar. It was far enough.

Corey turned to Linda. "Thank you for your good service this evening, ma'am," he said, inclining his head slightly. He'd paid cash as he drank so there was no tab to settle. Corey backed his way toward the door, pulling out his cell phone as he did.

In the parking lot, Corey tried to ignore Sean's rounded ass as he helped his friend get settled in the passenger seat of a small SUV. Sean turned and saw him.

"Hey," he called, closing the door and approaching Corey. "I wanted to say thanks."

Corey paused in the act of dialing the cab company. Sean came to stand several inches away from him. He was slightly shorter than Corey's six foot one. His features were sharply angled, except for that upturned nose. He was very handsome and this close, Corey could smell his cologne. He liked it.

"No problem," Corey answered, clenching his jaw and swallowing down his sudden rush of desire. "Those guys are drunk assholes and I hate to see good people victimized. Is your friend okay?"

Sean buried his hands in the front pockets of his jeans like he didn't know what to do with them. "Aimee's fine. She just had a lot to drink and is upset over another breakup. She'll sleep it off."

"Good. Okay." Corey awkwardly glanced at his phone, his stomach knotting as he tried to think of something to say. He thumbed the screen, pulling up the cab company's phone number.

"I'm Sean, by the way." He abruptly pulled a hand from his pocket and stuck it out. "Sean Chandler."

"Corey Yarwood." When their hands touched, Corey's fingers tingled. Sean's grip was firm and confident. He met Corey's eyes steadily.

The door of the bar suddenly slammed open, crashing against the wall. Sean startled, yanking his hand from Corey's and looking past him in alarm.

With a heavy sigh of annoyance, Corey pocketed his cell phone and rolled his eyes. He turned to face their attackers, not surprised to find all three drunks staggering their direction. Back inside the bar, Linda was coming through the lifted counter of the bar, cordless phone in hand.

"He ain't no Marine, he's a faggot, too," spat one of Carl's companions.

Corey's entire body tensed. It was a reaction ingrained in him over the years. He still wasn't used to living without Don't Ask, Don't Tell. Looking from one ruddy face to the other, he realized it didn't matter anyway. It was the easiest insult these fuckers could muster in their inebriated states. They probably didn't even really think Corey was gay.

"Get in your car and get out of here," he said to Sean over his shoulder.

Corey didn't wait for the drunks to say anything else, or to make the first move. He didn't want anyone hurt and he couldn't afford having to have his Gunnery Sergeant bail him out of jail.

He strode toward the men with purpose, hands clenched at his sides. Since they were cowards, there was a chance they'd scatter in the face of a genuine threat. Too full of liquid courage, the three stood their ground. Corey kicked out with his left leg, connecting with Carl's gut and knocking him to the ground. He hooked his left arm around the neck of the man in the center and jerked him forward, off balance. Spinning the guy around easily, Corey locked his elbow around the man's throat, restricting his breathing just enough to make him focus on survival instead of combat.

"Don't even think about it," Corey said angrily, pointing a

finger at the last man standing. He placed the guy in the choke hold between himself and Carl, knowing it would prevent Carl from launching a direct attack. If he could get to his feet, that was.

"You three don't make me call the Sheriff," Linda shouted from the doorway, holding up the cordless phone. "If I do, you three are gonna spend the night in Vista jail. Three drunks ganging up on a war hero isn't gonna play well with the deputies and you assholes know it!"

The one drunk who was still standing looked hesitant now, as he eyed Corey. The guy in his arms had stopped struggling. Carl slowly pulled himself to his feet, but didn't look like he was contemplating any aggression.

"Are you guys gonna play nice or does the lady have to make that phone call?" Corey asked calmly.

"You three get on down the road," Linda said, visibly shaking with anger.

Carl and his companion slowly began to walk along the outside of the building, heading toward the street. Corey shoved the third drunk away from himself, just enough to make him stumble and deny him any chance to turn and attack.

"Are they going to be okay walking home like that?" Corey asked Linda.

"They do it every night," she replied with disdain. "They all live in apartment complexes nearby, which is why they come here."

Again, Corey realized, with a sick feeling, that he was looking at his own future if he wasn't careful.

"Thank you for everything," Linda said suddenly. "I hope they don't put you off coming back in. They probably won't remember any of this in the morning."

Corey shrugged. "We'll see what happens this weekend." His desire to see Sean again would probably overpower any reluctance.

"Hope to see you then." Linda smiled and tugged the door closed.

Corey pulled out his cell phone again and turned, expecting to see an empty parking lot. He stopped short at the sight of Sean standing in front of his SUV, watching. He could just make out Aimee's riveted expression through the tinted passenger window.

He told himself that Sean was just making sure Corey didn't get hurt. There was no reason for Corey to be pleased Sean hadn't fled when he'd told him to.

"I thought I told you to take Aimee and go home," Corey called as he started across the parking lot again. He wanted more contact with Sean despite himself.

"I couldn't just leave you here to deal with that," Sean said mockingly. "I'm not a selfish asshole."

"I had it under control." Corey stopped several feet from Sean, not daring to get closer.

"Yeah, I saw that," Sean replied enthusiastically. "You could have seriously hurt those guys, but you didn't. Did you really learn that in the Marines?"

"Yeah," Corey answered. "And there was no need to hurt them. They surrendered."

"That's really impressive." Sean smiled wide, showing off perfectly straight, white teeth.

Corey stood staring at him stupidly. Shit. He hadn't been this tongue-tied by a man since Jonah Carver. "They were drunk. There was nothing to it."

"I'd have just thrown punches and ended up with a bruised face, which I can't afford to have happen," Sean replied hastily. "Where's your car?" he asked, glancing around the otherwise empty parking lot.

Corey held up his phone. "I'm just going to call a taxi."

"Let me give you a ride home," said Sean eagerly. "I can't leave you here to wait for a cab after you helped us."

Corey waved him off. "No, that's okay. I take cabs all the time."

"It's the least I can do. You can't live far." Sean's persistence was having an effect on Corey.

"I live on base," he told Sean, frighteningly close to caving in.

"That's fine." Sean walked around Corey to the passenger side of the SUV. He opened the door and reached for Aimee's seat belt. "Crawl into the back seat."

"Why me?" she demanded petulantly.

"Because you're just going to pass out anyway and you're two feet shorter than he is," he retorted, bundling her into the back seat.

"I don't want to be an inconvenience," Corey protested.

Sean rolled his eyes. "She really is going to pass out as soon as we start driving. This isn't the first time I've been through this. Get in."

Almost as soon as Sean pulled onto the street, Aimee's head lolled back and she was sound asleep.

"She lives closest so I'll drop her off first," Sean said quietly.

"I appreciate this." Corey really did like being this close to Sean rather than by himself in a taxi.

"It's the least I can do, for you putting your body between us and three violent drunks." Sean glanced at him with a small smile.

"I didn't know if you could handle it on your own or not, but I knew I could," was the only thing Corey could think to say.

"I probably could have gotten us out of there but not unscathed." Sean still spoke softly and it felt intimate.

They were silent until Sean pulled into Aimee's apartment complex. When Sean opened the car door and shook her awake, Aimee seemed groggy. She stumbled out of the SUV, falling up against Sean.

Corey unfastened his seatbelt and climbed out. Sean might need some help getting her safely into her apartment. With him on one side and Sean on the other, Aimee stumbled her way toward a set of metal steps.

As she slowly took one step at a time, Corey heard her say, "Sorry to have to make you do this, Sean."

"You called me because you knew I'd still be awake," he replied with the weariness of a frequently inconvenienced friend who had heard all the apologies before.

"I just don't know why I can't find a guy who loves me," Aimee whined sadly.

"They do love you. They just don't love you in the exact way you think they should so you're never satisfied." Sean sounded like they'd had this conversation several times before. Drunk *and* sober.

Corey's stomach lurched as Sean's words hit particularly close to home.

They reached the second floor and turned right. Aimee rummaged in her purse, probably for her keys. "You always say that to me," she mumbled.

Sean slid a key from his own ring into a deadbolt and opened the apartment door. "You expect men to behave in a certain, precise way and you reject them when they don't." He pushed the door open for Aimee to enter. "You have unrealistic expectations and no man is ever going to live up to them."

Corey immediately thought of Jonah, and how no man he'd met since seemed to measure up. He breathed through the sudden tightening in his chest.

Aimee leaned in and pressed a kiss to Sean's mouth. "You would."

"And I'm emotionally unavailable *to you*," he replied calmly, giving her a gentle shove to get her moving into the apartment. "Are you okay to get yourself into bed?"

"Yes, *dad*," Aimee answered, words heavily laced with sarcasm.

Sean secured the doorknob lock, closed the door and used the key to secure the deadbolt. He met Corey's eyes with a shake of his head and a heavy sigh. "Come on, let's get you back to base."

When they were back on the road, Corey's curiosity got the better of him. "Did I hear you tell Linda you were going to be in the bar this weekend with a guitar?"

"Yeah," Sean answered quickly. "I play there on weekends a lot. It supplements my income and gives me a chance to try out new material on a live audience."

Corey was intrigued. "New material? You write songs?"

"Among other things. I'm usually up until three or four a.m. writing, which is why Aimee calls me to come get her," Sean said ruefully.

Why Corey was glad to know Sean hadn't been awake with another man, he wasn't sure.

"What about you?" Sean asked suddenly. "Have you been a Marine long?"

"Since I was twenty-one," Corey answered. "So yeah, almost seven years."

"That means you've been deployed a couple of times, doesn't it?" Sean's tone was careful.

"Twice," Corey said tightly, swallowing against the lump in his throat.

"It's good you made it home safe both times," Sean said quietly, letting the topic drop.

Corey resisted the urge to tell him that he hadn't made it home safely either time. He'd just met this guy and confessing the kind of damage Corey had sustained; the nightly anguish he endured, would be crazy.

Not that Corey didn't sometimes suspect that he was.

A silence settled over them that wasn't entirely uncomfortable. Corey liked that Sean didn't feel the need for constant chatter.

"You know what impressed me the most tonight?" Sean asked after many long minutes. "That you didn't react at all when those guys called you a fag."

Corey had to admit that was the smoothest introduction of that topic he'd ever witnessed. "It wasn't personal." Corey shrugged. "They were just throwing out a general use, one size fits all insult."

"Still, I've seen guys lose their shit over that general use insult," Sean said dourly.

"Even if it wasn't true, those guys weren't worth my career." He waited to see what Sean would do with the information he'd just been given.

"Are you…" Sean hesitated, as if selecting his words carefully. "Did you come out after the repeal?"

"No, but not because I'm hiding it," Corey explained. "I'm just private by nature. Most of the guys I work with don't know anything about my personal life at all." Making friends just meant more chances that someone would uncover his demons.

They neared the main gate at Camp Pendleton and Sean slowed the vehicle. "You should come out this weekend, let me buy you a drink."

"The ride home is thanks enough," Corey said, forcing a smile. He was disappointed their time together was at an end. "You don't have to buy me a drink, too."

"I didn't say I wanted to buy you a drink to say thanks," Sean said levelly. He met Corey's eyes, expression inscrutable.

Corey wanted to. He wanted to see Sean again. He nodded. "Yeah, maybe I will."

Sean's smile lit up the dark interior of the vehicle as he pulled to a stop near the gate to let Corey out. "Good. See you this weekend."

Corey showed his I.D. to the kid now on duty and slipped back on base virtually unnoticed. He slid quietly into his room and retrieved his hidden bottle from the ceiling. He knew he shouldn't, but Corey swallowed down the last of the contents. Afterward, he stood alone in the center of his room, breathing heavy.

He stripped down to his skivvies and shut out the light. Crawling beneath the scratchy covers, Corey lay in the dark. He closed his eyes, feeling the room tumble around him slightly. He sighed in relief; probably no nightmare tonight.

Sean's face drifted across the back of his closed lids. Corey slid his hand beneath the waist band of his skivvy shorts as he remembered light brown hair, hazel eyes, and a brilliant smile. He squeezed his dick, stroked himself several times. No joy. He was too fucking drunk to get hard.

Corey threw his arm over his eyes and waited until the blackness overtook him.

CHAPTER TWO

Corey squinted against the bright morning sunlight, despite the Oakleys he wore. He was still one of the first instructors at the pool, despite his headache and queasy stomach. Those would pass. They always did.

Master Sergeant Whitfield was already there, dressed in full utilities and cover. He was an older Marine, combat hardened in the first Gulf War and Somalia. He was several inches shorter than Corey but still bulky with firm muscle.

Corey wore his black PT shorts and the black T-shirt that proclaimed him an instructor. Today, he and his fellow instructors would begin the three month task of turning men from Marines into Recon.

The rest of the instructors assembled quickly, some dressed in utilities, others in PT gear like Corey. It was easy to remember nearly six years earlier, when Corey had come to this same pool as a boot PFC, eager to become a Recon Marine.

"Staff Sergeant Yarwood," Master Sergeant Whitfield barked. "You'll stay on the deck today, since this is your first class. Keep an eye out for ones going under and haul them out."

"Yes, Master Sergeant," Yarwood answered sharply.

He listened as Whitfield handed out the rest of the assignments for the day. There were three Navy Corpsmen at the pool today, ready to treat the Marines who needed it. They would also have the final say on whether some of them continued on in training or washed out.

Sixty five Marines, officers and enlisted, humped into the pool area chanting the cadence called out by one of the sergeants in the class. The instructors lined up against the fence as the master sergeant ordered the Marines to attention in two lines.

Whitfield outlined what the Marines could expect to endure over the next twelve weeks. Corey knew that no explanation could ever come close to accurately describing the hell of the Basic Reconnaissance Course.

Next, the Master Sergeant introduced the course instructors. He saved Corey for last.

"Staff Sergeant Yarwood. He might be a brand new Staff Sergeant. He might be the newest instructor here. Do not make the mistake of thinking he is anything other than a battle-tested Recon Marine." Whitfield's words surprised Corey. "He's seen combat in Iraq and Afghanistan. He's received a Purple Heart and earned the Bronze Star in defense of this great country of ours. He has served with Recon Marines who are fucking legends. He's a goddamn hero."

Corey leaned tensely against the fence. He resisted the urge to run his fingers over the scar in his hair. It was his souvenir from the concussion he'd received when he'd been blown up and shot at while serving with Jonah Carver, trying to protect Kellan Reynolds. They were the legends the Master Sergeant had mentioned.

The students were ordered into the pool, still wearing full utilities and deuce gear. They'd been allowed to remove their boots but it was a small help. Corey paced back and forth along the edge of the pool in his go-fasters as he watched for Marines to give in or go under, as they tread water for 45 mikes.

Corey remembered his own time in the pool under these circumstances. This had been child's play for him. It wasn't until the 30 yard, under water swim that he'd begun to wonder if he was cut out for this.

Ten minutes in and one Marine was swimming to the side and pulling himself out of the water. Corey went over to make sure he was all right.

"I can't do it," the Marine gasped.

Around the pool, instructors began to jeer the Marine.

"Are you quitting all ready?" Corey shouted, still looking for signs of ill health and seeing none. "You've gotta be kidding me!"

The Marine stood. Corey saw bars on his collar. Shit. He reminded himself it didn't matter. He got in the Lieutenant's face. "Are you quitting?" he yelled.

"Yes, Staff Sergeant," the Lieutenant said, still out of breath.

"Say it again!" Corey shouted. "Say it so I can hear you, are you quitting?"

"Yes, Staff Sergeant." The Lieutenant's voice cracked as he tried to shout his reply.

"Get out of my pool!" Corey pointed toward the pool gate where a sergeant stood ready to record the names of the Marines who quit or were eliminated. "Get the hell out of my pool."

Corey went back to pacing the edge of the pool.

"Good job, Staff Sergeant," Master Sergeant Whitfield said quietly as he walked by, arms folded over his broad chest. "You didn't let the bars intimidate you."

"Thank you, Master Sergeant," Corey replied, proud that he'd gotten off to a good start with Whitfield.

Forty-five minutes later, Corey and his fellow instructors dropped several eight-pound simulated M16s into the water, letting them sink to the bottom. A few of the more experienced instructors stripped off their shoes and shirts before looping buoy ropes around their chests and going into the water with the class. Corey stayed at poolside.

The tired Marines were ordered, one at a time, to retrieve a rifle from the bottom of the pool. They then had to pass the rifle from Marine to Marine, while still treading water. There were some Marines who had no trouble retrieving and passing the rifles. Others struggled. The safety divers stayed close, ready to intervene if needed.

Corey kept his eye on a PFC treading several feet from where he stood. The Marine passed off the rifle too quickly, always going under briefly when he did. He surfaced gasping and coughing. Corey was going to have to toss him from the class, he was struggling too hard too early. That didn't mean the kid didn't have heart, though.

This time, when he handed off the rifle, the PFC came up choking on water and swimming for the edge of the pool. Corey met him there, helping the Marine to climb out of the water.

"On your side, Private," Corey said firmly, kneeling beside him. "Lie down and catch your breath."

One of the Corpsmen, HM2 Carville, came over to evaluate the Marine as he coughed and gasped.

"You gave it a good try, Private." Corey helped the PFC to sit up when the doc declared him winded but otherwise fine. "You're just not cut out for Recon." He helped the kid to stand and gave him a gentle shove toward the pool gate.

At the two hour mark, more safety swimmers went into the pool, some in wet suits and snorkel gear, as they gathered the nearly exhausted Marines in the shallow end of the pool. Corey kicked off his go-fasters, knowing a lot of water was going to splash up onto the deck and he might very likely have to go into the pool himself.

"Be ready, Yarwood," Whitfield said as he strode by the deep end of the pool. "A lot of them are gonna need to have their asses hauled out."

"I remember, Master Sergeant," Corey replied. "Shallow water black out."

"You made it on your first try, didn't you, Staff Sergeant?" Whitfield asked.

"I touched the wall on my first try, Master Sergeant," Corey answered. "But I don't remember surfacing."

"That's why you're here now, Staff Sergeant." Whitfield clapped him on the shoulder. "You give all you got and keep on pushing."

"Yes, Master Sergeant." Shame swamped Corey. Would he even have this job if anyone knew he had to drink himself to sleep every night?

The first two Marines who tried didn't make it across the

pool. They got sent back to the shallow end to try again. A third surfaced halfway across, held up his fingers in the 'okay' sign and recited his name.

"I'm okay, Staff Sergeant," the Marine called.

"What do you mean you're okay?" Corey shouted from the pool deck. "You only made it halfway. Get back there and do it again."

Corey stepped to the edge of the pool as a Marine drew close to the wall near where he stood. As the Marine's head broke the surface, Corey bent over to evaluate him. The corporal lifted his hand with a circled thumb and forefinger. Whatever he said to Corey was unintelligible.

"Slow down, say it again," Corey said, watching closely for any signs the Marine was going to black out and slip under the water.

"Lopez, Alberto, I'm okay, Staff Sergeant," the Corporal gasped.

"Very good, Corporal, out of the pool," Corey told him, moving to the right to monitor the next Marine nearing the wall.

When the Marine, a Sergeant, surfaced with a gasp, he didn't lift his hand or speak. Corey was aware of a safety swimmer, the corpsman, and another instructor coming toward them. He watched as the Marine slowly sank down into the water.

"Get him!" Corey cried, even as his own fingers closed around the collar of the sergeant's deuce gear. He stepped back and hauled the limp body from the pool, getting a little help from the safety swimmer and his fellow instructor.

The sergeant surfaced from the shallow water black out almost as soon as Corey had him on the deck. He was breathing and griping immediately. Helping the sergeant to sit for the doc to evaluate him, Corey went back to the pool edge. As long as the corpsman cleared the sergeant, he was still in the program.

"Staff Sergeant Yarwood," Master Sergeant Whitfield barked.

Corey turned and the Earth fell out from beneath his feet.

Standing with Whitfield was Jonah Carver, dressed in his full service uniform, mirrored aviator glasses beneath the low brim of his barracks cover.

"You have visitors, Staff Sergeant," Whitfield called. He turned back to Jonah and shook his hand. He also shook the hand of the man standing behind Jonah before he walked away.

Corey crossed the pool deck toward Jonah, his heart hammering in his chest. He felt under dressed and grungy, in his PT gear, with Jonah looking so tall and handsome in his olive green uniform and polished brass. Corey swallowed hard when he realized the man with Jonah was Kellan Reynolds.

Kellan wore a tailored suit that was nearly the same color as Jonah's uniform. He was just as handsome as Jonah. It was easy to see why Jonah had such strong feelings for Kellan. Corey wanted to hate him. He would hate him, if Kellan wasn't such a likeable son-of-a-bitch.

He came to a stop several feet in front of Jonah and saluted. It wasn't required but Jonah was a fucking First Sergeant now and Corey would always have a deep and abiding respect for him as a Marine and as a man.

Jonah returned the salute before his face split into a wide smile. "Knock off the formal shit, Yarwood," he said, extending his hand.

Corey shook Jonah's hand vigorously. "It's great to see you again, Top. I had no idea you were even on this coast."

Kellan stepped forward, his own hand extended. "Congratulations on the promotion, Staff Sergeant," he said as he and Corey shook.

"Thank you, Mr. Reynolds," Corey said genuinely. "I'm under no illusion that your letters to the Corps didn't weigh heavily in my favor every time I was up for promotion." Corey had received four increases in pay grade since he'd been on the periphery of Kellan's investigation in Iraq.

"Letters I wrote because you deserved them, Staff Sergeant," Kellan replied.

"Honored you feel that way, sir."

"Look at you now," Jonah said as he surveyed the Marines in the pool, "an instructor at BRC."

Corey shrugged. "I think they want me here just because I served with the two of you."

Jonah rounded on him sharply. "I call bullshit. I know what medals you've been awarded."

Corey shifted his weight uncomfortably. Some of those medals had been awarded after his last deployment to Afghanistan. "So what brings the two of you to California?" he asked. "Last I heard, Mr. Reynolds had a fancy new job with the Department of Defense and you were his Military Liaison."

"Oh, we've been *promoted*. I am now the Senior Enlisted Advisor for the Deputy Under Secretary of Defense for Strategy, Plans and Force Development," Jonah said with both formality and disdain. It was so very like Jonah.

Corey laughed. "Congratulations?"

"Unfortunately, this isn't a social visit for us," Kellan said, suddenly solemn.

"I didn't suspect it was, sir," replied Corey, anxiety knotting in his gut.

"The Ghazni City Council has filed a formal complaint with the Marine Corps over the events of the battle there." Kellan broke the line of his suit jacket by burying his hands in his trouser pockets.

"I'm aware of that, sir." Corey remembered the hours of questioning and the nights he'd gotten drunk to forget the memories those questions had dredged up. "I cooperated fully."

"The conclusion reached by the NCIS investigation is not being accepted. The Afghan government has gotten involved and they've provided additional evidence." Kellan spoke carefully, as if he wanted Corey to understand what he wasn't saying, as much as what he was.

Corey knew it would be easier to read Kellan if he weren't

wearing a pair of dark sunglasses. "Are you here to investigate that supposed evidence and determine if there's been a cover up?"

Kellan gave a sharp nod. "We are."

"You'll have my full cooperation, sir." Corey may not like the memories but he had nothing to hide.

"We've read your reports on the incident and the notes of your interviews during the previous investigation," Jonah said. "Is there anything at all you want to change? Anything you remember differently than you did before?"

"No, Top, there's not." Corey's chest tightened. He didn't like the implication of that question.

Kellan and Jonah exchanged a look. With a glance at Corey, Kellan said, "It's been a pleasure to see you again, Staff Sergeant." He turned and left the pool area.

With a tilt of his head, Jonah led Corey farther away from the other instructors. "There are gaps in your story," he said quietly. "Events you make no mention of, that are reported in detail by other Marines."

"I'm aware of that, Jonah." Corey folded his arms over his chest, even knowing it wouldn't protect him from Jonah's words.

"If you've remembered anything new since the event, or if you've remembered that you left something out of your initial report, let us know now." Jonah's voice was kind and soothing, it held no accusation. "Kellan can protect you if he knows going in that your reports need to be amended."

Corey stared tight-jawed at Jonah, wishing he could see pale blue eyes behind the mirrored glasses. "I haven't remembered anything new."

Jonah sighed explosively. "If Kellan finds the other reports to be accurate, it'll call into question your command of the detachment. You didn't participate, but it was your duty to know what your men were doing."

"I had men in two different locations." Corey repeated what

he'd been saying ever since that fucked up day. "I was with the group that had the greater need. I wasn't derelict."

Jonah nodded and said nothing. He glanced at the pool but Corey didn't think he really saw. "Are you drinking again, Corey?"

Fuck. It was trying to keep Jonah's respect that had convinced Corey to stop drinking the first time. "Can't sleep if I don't," he said, teeth clenched and voice raw.

"Get yourself to a counselor," Jonah said sharply. "You're still active duty and not in a combat zone. You don't have to buck command or a slow moving VA."

Corey fisted one hand on his hip and ran his fingers roughly over his cropped hair. "That wouldn't look good with Kellan starting an investigation into the events in Ghazni City."

Jonah shot Kellan an aggravated look. "Come on, Corey, this is Kellan we're talking about. He'll treat genuine memory loss and PTS with the compassion and consideration it requires, if that's what we're dealing with here."

Corey nodded vigorously. He knew this was true. He might envy Kellan his relationship with Jonah, but he still admired and respected him.

"At least go to a regular doc and get something to help you sleep," Jonah continued, his tone more mild now, "so you can quit the alcohol."

"Don't want to jeopardize my cushy new job," Corey said ruefully.

"You don't want to jeopardize a promising career." Jonah corrected him.

This conversation echoed some of the ones he'd had with Jonah the first time his drinking got out of hand. "When do you two start your investigation?" Corey changed the subject, not yet ready to admit Jonah was right again.

"Kellan starts digging into documents tomorrow." Jonah let the topic change without comment. "He probably won't be ready for interviews until next week."

"Copy that." Corey was relieved that Jonah didn't press the issue.

Jonah cuffed him on the arm. "I'll let you get back to work before the Master Sergeant throws you into the pool."

Corey chuckled. "It's good to see you again, Jonah."

"Always good to see you, Corey," Jonah said over his shoulder as he left out the pool gate.

Just as Corey reached the edge of the pool, a Marine surfaced several feet out. He gasped and tried to speak but made no sound.

"I got him!" Corey shouted, stepping down onto the lower metal rail of the pool. He grasped the collar of the limp Marine's uniform as a safety swimmer helped lift his weight from the water. Laying him out for Carville to examine, Corey glanced at his fellow instructors. "How many attempts did this guy make?"

"This was number four," Gunnery Sergeant Quiñones replied. "He's been half-assing it all day. If he'd put the same effort into his first try, he probably would have made it."

"Gentlemen," Master Sergeant Whitfield barked. He tilted his head to indicate the instructors should follow him. When they were out of earshot of the Marines scattered on the deck, Whitfield asked, "Anyone have a reason for *not* wanting to bounce this one?"

Corey and his two fellow instructors all indicated that they did not. Stepping past them, Whitfield asked the corpsman if the Marine was okay to be up and around. When Carville said he was, Whitfield told the Marine he was out of BRC.

When he'd gone through BRC, Corey had felt bad for the half of his class that dropped out or were disqualified. Now that he'd been through combat and knew how critical it was to have Marines at his back who would never give up, never only give a half measure, he didn't feel bad at all.

Master Sergeant Whitfield lined up all the Marines who had survived the first day. The first day was the easiest. It only got harder from here. Whitfield dismissed the Marines as the instructors secured their gear and the pool.

Thirty mikes later, the instructors were gathered in the Master Sergeant's office for the debrief of the day's training. The next day was going to be rough for instructors as well as students, since it would last about fifteen hours. Corey welcomed it. Exhaustion might make it easier to sleep and to stay asleep, without nightmares.

Whitfield dismissed them for the night. Corey changed into his utilities and headed for the chow hall. With his tray piled high, he looked for an empty table.

"Staff Sergeant Yarwood!"

Corey turned to find several members of his former platoon seated at a table. They made room for him. He took a seat next to Lance Corporal Tyler Howe. Tyler had the brightest blue eyes and fullest, pouty mouth. He'd also served in Corey's command so he pretended he didn't notice.

"Scuttlebutt says the platoon is under investigation again," Sergeant Michael Nygaard said angrily.

Corey narrowed his eyes at Nygaard and clenched his jaw. "It's not scuttlebutt. I know the investigator and I served under his aide in Iraq."

There was harsh swearing around the table. Corey focused on his food.

"We're not going to get court martialed are we, Corey?" Tyler asked.

"Did you do anything wrong or lie about what you know happened?" he asked quietly.

"No!" Tyler looked surprised and appalled, as if the thought of doing either had never occurred to him.

"Then you'll be fine." Corey turned back to his tray.

"We need to stick together, otherwise they'll pin something on us we didn't do just to appease the fucking Afghans," Nygaard said with venom.

Corey kept silent. He'd always suspected that people who tried to circle the wagons in a crisis were the ones with something to hide. He focused on his food, blocking out the conversation that swirled around him. He responded when Tyler addressed him directly, but otherwise, he just wanted to eat and get out. He bolted his food like he was back in boot camp, even though he didn't have to. He had shit to do and an entire night to get through without getting drunk.

Corey said goodbye to his former platoon members and set out on foot for the base exchange. At least he didn't have to drive off base to get what he needed for tonight.

He had a large bottle of Nyquil and a smaller one of Benadryl in his hand when he glanced up and saw Master Sergeant Whitfield coming down the aisle toward him. Corey felt caught out. He took a breath and swallowed hard, reminding himself he hadn't been caught with contraband. He knew his guilt stemmed from the reason he was making this purchase.

"Feeling under the weather, Yarwood?" Whitfield asking, seeming genuinely concerned.

"Something might be coming on, Master Sergeant," he replied. "I'm trying to head it off. Already got plenty of vitamin C and zinc."

"Good thinking, Staff Sergeant." Whitfield stepped past him with a smile. "See you in the morning."

Corey breathed a silent sigh of relief and went to pay for his purchases.

CHAPTER THREE

Getting out of bed was damn difficult for Corey. He was glad he'd set the alarm on his cell phone, as well as his regular alarm. The Nyquil had helped him fall asleep the night before, helped along by the stellar orgasm he'd rubbed out while thinking of Sean's upturned nose and pouty lips. Neither of those had stopped the nightmare, so he'd popped a Benadryl to get himself back to sleep. Now he was groggy and slightly disoriented.

Corey hit the chow hall, loaded his tray, and knocked back his entire cup of coffee. He got a refill to go on his way out the door. He didn't encounter anyone he knew on his route to the training grounds, thankfully, since he wasn't in a chatty mood.

Several instructors were already gathered around when Corey arrived. Most of them were dressed as he was; in his utility trousers, black instructor's T-shirt, and utility cover. Corey was one of the instructors who would actually teach a skill set today. It was going to be a day of long hours as they all began to teach the candidates the tasks they would complete once inserted in an AO; the area of operation.

"How'd you sleep, Staff Sergeant Yarwood?" Whitfield surprised Corey by asking first thing.

"Well enough, Master Sergeant," Corey answered quickly. "Still fighting something off but I'm squared away."

"Glad to hear it."

Corey relaxed as Whitfield moved on to greet the rest of the instructors.

Fifteen hours later, Corey was more than ready for the class to be over. He sent a silent apology to the Marines who had been his BRC instructors, just in case he'd been a pain in the ass. He didn't think he'd been a total fuck up, but now he wasn't so sure. At least he'd passed the course in the end.

Corey hit the gym that evening. The class had worn out his

mind, he wanted to wear out his body as well. He fell into his rack that night, hoping it was enough.

The next morning, he realized that it had worked to a point. Still, Jonah was right; Corey needed to get to a doctor and get something to help him sleep. Hopefully they could give him something that wouldn't make him feel hung over the next morning.

Today was Friday, though. He could get legitimately shit faced tonight and tomorrow night, and not have to worry about waking up, sweaty and shaking, wanting to lift his weapon and point it at…someone.

The class was only marginally less frustrating today. Broken into teams, the Marines practiced the skills Corey had taught them about in principle the day before. Many of them mastered the tasks quickly. Others took a little more explanation, a few more demonstrations, before they eventually caught on.

When they broke for chow, Corey realized he was keeping a mental list of the Marines he thought should be bounced. He'd give them the afternoon to get their shit together. But if they weren't showing signs of at least comprehending the basics by the end of class, they weren't Marines that Corey wanted watching his six on a mission.

He was on his way to resume class, comparing notes with some of the more experienced instructors, when Master Sergeant Whitfield intercepted them.

"Staff Sergeant Yarwood, nice job with the class the last couple of days," Whitfield said.

"Thank you, Master Sergeant," Corey said sharply, falling back on his Marine training to mask his discomfort with the compliment.

"You're going to have to make some cuts tonight," Whitfield continued. "Are you prepared?"

"Yes, Master Sergeant, we were just conferring about that very thing." He gestured toward his fellow instructors. "They have the afternoon to show they're worthy of continuing the class, otherwise I'm ready to bounce them out."

"Excellent," Whitfield said pleasantly. "Carry on."

By the end of class, a couple of the stragglers had managed to catch up to the rest of the class. For most of the Marines on Corey's mental list, today was their last in BRC. Master Sergeant Whitfield concurred with the recommendations of Corey and his fellow instructors, and the cuts were made.

Finally heading back to the BEQ, Corey allowed himself to think about the coming night and his plans. His pulse quickened when he thought of seeing Sean again. He had to get that reaction under control. Glancing at his watch, Corey decided it was late enough to start getting ready to go.

Corey showered thoroughly and headed back to his room with a towel around his hips. He splashed on aftershave and tugged on a pair of dark wash jeans. As he smoothed the tight fitting gothic graphic T-shirt over his chest, he realized he was dressing with too much care for a Friday night of quiet drinking.

He shouldn't go back to that bar tonight. He should wait until tomorrow. Corey might think Sean was the hottest guy he'd met in years, he might constantly think about what it would feel like to have those pouty lips around his cock, but it couldn't go anywhere.

Fuck it. Corey stuffed his wallet in his back pocket. He called for a taxi as he headed for the main gate. It was just beer and music on a Friday night. If Sean seemed like he wanted more, Corey would let him down gently.

It was nearly 2300 hours when he entered the bar. He'd expected music when he entered, but all that greeted Corey was the dull roar of a sizeable crowd. He froze just inside the door, wondering if this was such a good idea. It was too crowded for him to find a seat where he'd be comfortable. There were too many strangers moving around and the steadily rising volume had him fisting his hands at his sides.

Corey glanced around, trying not to appear as though he was looking for Sean. One of the three women standing in front of the bar shifted her weight to her other foot and he caught a glimpse of the man seated on the bar stool. Sean was gorgeous tonight. His dark T-shirt clung to him, straining at the biceps. His thick brown hair was styled, spiked with a casual negligence. Sean saw Corey at almost the same moment, his expression morphing from polite interest to enthused pleasure.

Corey's heart was already pounding but it still leapt a little when Sean smiled at him. He carefully pushed his way through the crowd, trying not to flinch when someone innocently bumped him. He took a deep breath when he reached Sean.

"Hey, you made it." Sean's eyes sparkled as he continued to smile up at Corey.

"Yeah, I made it." Corey buried his hands in his front pockets.

"Ladies, this is my good friend Corey," Sean introduced him to the three women. He quickly rattled off their names but Corey didn't catch any of them. "Hey, we'll talk again on my next break, okay?"

Sean was polite but it was clearly a dismissal. The three women all looked surprised and confused but they complied, returning to their drink-laden table right in front of the small stage.

"I didn't mean to interrupt," Corey said awkwardly.

"Oh, you didn't interrupt anything." Sean rolled his eyes. "Those three have been hanging on me all night. I have to be polite and humor them, but that doesn't mean I enjoy it." He turned to the bartender and gestured toward Corey. "My friend needs a drink."

Linda appeared beside the other bartender, smiling at Corey. "Jack with a beer back, right?"

"Yes, ma'am." Corey grinned at her, impressed she'd remembered.

"It's on me," Linda said. "As a thank you for earlier this week."

Sean polished off his beer and stood up. "Here, take my seat," he told Corey. "I gotta get back to work. I get another fifteen minute break at midnight."

Corey settled onto the barstool Sean had vacated and thanked Linda for his drinks. He watched Sean step up onto the stage, slide a guitar strap over his head and shoulder, and perch on the edge of a stool behind a microphone. When he strummed the strings, the bar filled with the sound and the crowd grew quiet. Corey was suddenly nervous. He wanted Sean to be good and he had no idea if he was or not.

He recognized the song just a few notes in. It was one he liked, written and recorded by a current band that used a lot of guitar and real drum kits. Sean's single acoustic guitar gave the song a different feel, but he played well and it sounded good. When Sean started to sing, Corey's eyes went wide and his breath caught in his chest. Sean's voice was smooth and clear, each note—each word—crisp and precise.

Sean had a mesmerizing stage presence. He glanced all around the room, making and holding eye contact. Corey wanted to think Sean looked at him more often, held his gaze a little longer, but it had to be wishful thinking.

With a flourish of fingers, Sean changed songs. This one was a harder song, somewhat angry and desperate. Sean's voice changed in pitch and tenor, taking on a rougher edge and gaining a touch of vibrato.

If Corey wasn't already frighteningly attracted to Sean, he would be now. Christ, how he loved a man who was good at something and performed that task with confidence.

Several songs later, Sean paused to talk to the audience. "If you guys would indulge me for a few minutes, I'd like to try out some new material on you." His laugh was self-deprecating. "Yes, I'm an aspiring song writer. Be honest with me. If something's good, let me know. If it sucks, don't spare my feelings." Sean's smile was blinding.

As Corey listened to Sean sing his own words, his heart broke. It was a breakup song. Lovers having a final argument inside of a car, pulling to the side of the road, slamming doors, and finally speaking the sad truth to each other. Corey's pulse pounded in his throat as he wondered how autobiographical the song was.

He wondered if Sean would care how closely it paralleled his own life.

Corey swallowed against the lump in his throat. He'd done his damnedest over the years not to think about Kathryn—Kathy— he sure as hell didn't want to start back now.

Sean changed keys and transitioned into a different song. This one was angry, demanding acceptance and respect, refusing to compromise. Corey wondered what kind of shit Sean had been through.

The third of Sean's songs was more upbeat and rhythmic. It was about two lovers who were invincible as long as they had each other. It held an optimism Corey didn't think he'd ever had, or ever would.

All three songs received enthusiastic reactions from the crowd. Corey was just buzzed enough to add his own claps, cheers and whistles to the cacophony. Sean's pleased smile tightened something in Corey's chest.

The next song was a cover of a popular song from a relatively new Irish rock band. Corey ordered another drink. He thought it might be his third. The buzz in his head told him it was likely his fourth.

"You come in a cab again, Devil Dog?" Linda asked as she handed over his whiskey.

"Yes, ma'am," Corey replied reflexively.

She gave him a wicked smile. "Sean is one lucky guy."

Corey's stomach did a slow roll. "How's that?"

"You conveniently need a ride home. Sean conveniently lives nearby." Linda winked and moved on to her next customer.

He glanced over his shoulder at Sean, wishing and wanting, but knowing he just couldn't have. Not right now.

On Sean's next break, he paused at tables to talk with the people who had obviously come to hear him sing. The three women from earlier tried to keep him from moving on, but Sean gracefully disentangled himself and headed for Corey.

"Switching to soda, Sean?" Linda asked.

"Yes, please." He graced her with a kind smile. "Gotta drive home later."

Sean leaned an elbow on the bar beside Corey. He smiled brightly, his hazel eyes sparkling. Corey wanted to run his thumb over Sean's lush lower lip. Who the fuck was he kidding? He wanted to lean in and run his tongue over Sean's lip, just before he nipped at it until it was swollen.

"Jesus," Sean whispered harshly. He turned and rested both elbows on the bar. He flushed through his tan. "The way you're looking at my mouth is making me hard."

Corey inhaled sharply, his chest tightening. "Sorry." He glanced around to see if anyone had noticed. Several of the women were watching the two of them but none looked angry or appalled. Some even looked predatory.

"I'm not," Sean replied, taking a sip of his drink. "Let's just be discreet while I'm working."

"I usually am more discreet," Corey told him.

"I can imagine." Turning to face him again, Sean asked, "So, what did you think?"

Corey was confused for a moment. "About your singing? You're fucking awesome." He wished he could say something more insightful.

Sean chuckled and looked pleased. "Thank you. What did you think of the original songs?"

Corey hesitated. Sharing his earlier thoughts with Sean would reveal too much about his own raw emotions. "I think they're better than some of the covers you did."

"Glad you liked them." Sean glanced around the room and waved at someone in the corner. He polished off his drink and stood tall. "You sticking around 'til my next break?"

"I'll be right here," Corey answered without thinking.

Sean gripped Corey's shoulder as he stepped away. To

onlookers, it probably looked like a casual touch between friends, but Sean's hand lingered before he skimmed it down Corey's arm.

His skin burned where Sean had touched him. Corey could still feel Sean's touch, even after Sean stepped onto the stage.

During this set, Sean performed a few songs that had been recorded by female pop singers. With his talented fingers on the guitar strings, and a few creative lyric changes, Sean made the songs uniquely his own.

The three original songs he performed this time carried the positive messages of self-acceptance and self-reliance. One song was an unapologetic celebration of life. Corey guessed that Sean had performed that song before when some people in the crowd sang along.

As he watched Sean perform, a woman stepped up to the bar beside him. Corey marked her movements and her distance from him, but didn't look at her. At least until she leaned down into his line of sight.

Corey stiffened as he focused on the woman. She was looking at him in confusion, her eyes narrowed and brow furrowed. It was Aimee. He relaxed slightly as he returned her gaze.

"Have we met?" she asked. It was obviously not a pick up line.

"Last Tuesday," Corey answered. "I helped Sean get you safely into your apartment."

Her expression cleared and her eyes filled with recognition. "Corey!"

"You remember?" He'd thought she'd been too drunk to catch his name.

"I vaguely remember someone else helping me up the stairs. But Sean's mentioned you several times since then." Aimee turned and quickly ordered a drink.

Corey glanced at Sean and found him watching from the stage. What had Sean told her about Corey? What did it mean that he'd been a topic of conversation more than once?

"I'm glad you came out tonight," Aimee said. "Sean was sure he'd never see you again."

Christ. Resisting his growing attraction to Sean was hard enough without knowing the attraction was mutual. "I'm glad I came out. He's really good."

"Yeah, he is," Aimee said emphatically. "He graduated from USC's drama program. Our boy's a musical theater major."

Corey couldn't mask his surprise. "No shit?"

She shook her head. "He does it all and he does it well."

Corey stared at Sean, seeing him differently now. He realized Sean wasn't playing around. This was seriously his career.

Aimee paid for her drink and turned to leave. She paused and said, "Sorry you had to see me like that. On Tuesday." She looked chagrined. "But thank you for helping me get home safely." She leaned in and kissed his cheek. "You and Sean have fun tonight."

Corey stared at her back as she walked away.

Not long after, Sean took his final break of the night. He moved through the room again, greeting those he'd missed previously. Corey slid a napkin over the top of his drink and went to the head.

He probably should have predicted it, but Corey was still surprised when Sean came in several minutes later. Corey quickly buttoned himself up and moved to the sink.

"I saw Aimee find you," Sean said.

"She didn't know who I was at first," Corey replied.

"Well, she was pretty tanked that night."

Corey dried his hands and knew he should get the fuck out of there. He didn't need the temptation Sean presented. His feet just wouldn't move. "How much longer do you have to play?"

"Half an hour." Sean stepped to the sink. "It won't take me long to pack up. I leave the amp here until tomorrow night." He dried his hands and stepped in close.

Corey could feel the heat of Sean's body. He could see dark

flecks in his hazel eyes. Sean's skin was so smooth and brown, Corey's hands itched to touch. He curled them into fists to stem that urge. Sean's eyes dropped to Corey's mouth and his expression was expectant.

"I could use a little help loading gear into my car, if you can stay 'til the end," Sean said, his voice low and rough.

Corey wet his dry lips and Sean's eyes narrowed.

"I don't have to work tomorrow. I can stay," Corey replied, knowing he was playing with fire.

"Good." One side of Sean's full mouth quirked upward. "I should get back."

Corey startled, suddenly remembering where they were and that Sean was working. He tugged the door open, feeling sluggish and clumsy. He let Sean precede him back into the bar and immediately realized his mistake. Sean's ass looked perfectly round and taut in the snug jeans he wore.

When he resumed his seat at the bar, Linda announced last call. Corey ordered a final drink.

Linda gave him a hard look. "You know I can get in trouble for serving someone who is already too intoxicated?"

Corey held her gaze steadily. "I just made it to the head and back without stumbling, running into anything, or getting into a fight. I'm good."

She relented and served Corey his drink. "Don't make me sorry. I kinda like you."

Sean made every minute of his short, final set count. He played simple, familiar songs with upbeat tempos and his audience loved it. By the time he took his final bow, the crowd was mostly on its feet, clapping thunderously.

Sean set his guitar on the stand and sat on the edge of the stage to talk to some of the patrons for awhile. The three women lingered at their table until Linda called out that it was closing time.

"I'd love to, but I have to take Corey back to base," Sean said, disentangling himself from one of the women.

"We want Corey to come, too," her friend said, smiling at him.

"I've got duty tomorrow," Corey said without thinking about it. "I've already stayed out too late."

That finally seemed to appease them, although they all made a show of pouting about it.

Sean leaned on the bar next to Corey. "You said earlier you don't have to work tomorrow. Did you just lie to those ladies?" he asked conspiratorially.

"Yeah," Corey replied in an equally covert tone.

"Well played." Sean waved as the women filed out the door into the night. When it was finally just the two of them and the bartenders, he slumped onto the stool next to Corey.

"Should we get you packed up so you can get home?" Corey asked.

Sean stared at him inscrutably for several moments before he stood. "Sure."

It didn't take long. Sean put his guitar in its case. That left packing up the microphones and cords. The amp would stay until the next night. Sean waved to the bartenders as the two of them left through the rear door, Corey lugging the plastic container of electronics.

Their shoulders bumped as they loaded everything into the back of Sean's SUV. Corey took several steps backward, as if the contact had scalded him. Sean closed the hatch and Corey fished his cell phone out of his pocket.

Sean chuffed a laugh and held up his keys. "Seriously, dude, I'll take you back to base. You don't have to call a cab."

Corey took another few steps backward. "You've been working all night, man, you don't need to make that extra drive."

"You stayed to help me with my gear, it's the least I can do," Sean replied.

Corey wanted to prolong his time with Sean but he knew if

he got in the car, he'd want to touch. If he started touching, he wouldn't want to stop.

"Actually, I thought we could stop somewhere and get breakfast," Sean continued when Corey was silent. "Maybe have a conversation not interrupted by a crowd."

Corey tensed. He wanted to say yes but if he did, it would fuck everything up. "Thanks, but no." He sounded more abrupt than he'd meant to.

Sean stiffened visibly. His smile faded and Corey could practically see a wall slam down behind his eyes. "Okay. Well, thanks for the help and get home safe." He turned on his heel and headed for the door of his SUV.

Fuck. Sean was a nice guy and Corey genuinely like him. He'd hurt Sean's feelings, possibly embarrassed him. "Sean," he called. When he didn't immediately appear at the rear the car, Corey called louder. "Sean, it's not what you think."

Sean reappeared and stood, feet braced apart and arms folded defensively over his chest. He didn't speak and his expression was tight.

Corey sighed explosively. He ran the back of one hand over his sweaty forehead. He couldn't look at Sean, which wasn't like him. "I want to go to breakfast with you," he said, voice strained. "But if I did, I'd be sober by the time I got back to base." Corey chanced a quick glance and could tell by Sean's expression he'd said the wrong thing.

"Don't let me keep you, then." Sean started to turn away.

Corey scrubbed a hand over his shorn hair in frustration. "I can't sleep," he blurted.

That got Sean to stop at least. He leaned his shoulder against the SUV and looked willing to listen.

Corey hunched his shoulders, fisted his hands in his front pockets and stared at his boots. "Since my last deployment…I don't like to sleep…when I do…" He took a deep breath and clenched his jaw. Corey glanced up at the night sky but didn't find anything there that made this easier. He swallowed hard and continued. "I have nightmares. Once I wake up, it's hard to get back to sleep. Drinking helps."

Swallowing down his nausea, Corey glanced at Sean. He still leaned against the SUV, but his expression had softened and he had uncrossed his arms and stuffed his hands in his front pockets. Pity had been the last thing he'd wanted to see in Sean's eyes when he looked at Corey.

"Well, you've deployed how many times? Twice?" Sean asked. At Corey's nod he continued. "I'd be surprised if you *didn't* have some sort of lingering issue from that."

Corey shrugged, lost for words in the face of Sean's acknowledgement of his weakness.

"I have no idea what you went through or what it's like to have nightmares," Sean continued, "but it seems like self-medicating with alcohol can cause as many problems as it solves."

"For now, it helps me fall asleep and not have nightmares." Corey glanced away. "Or at least not wake up and remember them."

"Have you talked to someone about the nightmares?" Sean asked quietly.

Corey snorted. "Someone else recently told me I need to get some sort of help." He sighed wearily. "I guess I should."

"Well, get in the car," Sean said suddenly. "I can get you back to base quicker than if you wait for a taxi."

Corey started to protest.

Sean held up a hand, palm out. "Just get in the car, Corey. It's too late to be arguing about this." He sounded as tired as Corey felt.

The ride back to Pendleton was silent save for the radio Sean had set to low volume. Corey hugged himself and actually began to feel drowsy.

When Sean pulled up to the main gate, Corey unfastened his seatbelt. "Thank you for the ride. Sorry to put you out."

"You're not an inconvenience, Corey, I wish you'd get that," Sean said with frustration. "I'd like it if you came out again tomorrow, but I understand if you can't. Or won't."

Corey was surprised. He'd been sure his confession had killed whatever attraction was brewing between them. "Maybe. I'll see how I feel tomorrow."

Sean looked resigned. "Sleep well, Corey."

Corey wanted nothing more than to lean across and kiss Sean, but he wasn't about to start something he knew he couldn't finish. "Thanks again." He climbed out of the SUV and headed for the gate.

It took all the strength Corey had not to look back.

Chapter Four

Corey slept late the next morning. His sleep had been restless, despite the alcohol. It was probably because of Sean.

Once he'd showered and grabbed chow, Corey carefully cleared his ceiling stash of empty Jack Daniels bottles. He wrapped them in a towel, put them in a rucksack, and placed them in the back of his Jeep. He'd dump them in a dumpster or something, next time he was off base.

Corey took his dirty clothes to the nearest base laundromat. He filled a single washer. He didn't have much in the way of civilian clothing. The load was mostly his skivvies. Next weekend he needed to take his uniforms to the dry cleaner.

He spent the day lying to himself that he wasn't thinking about Sean. No matter what he did or who he talked to, somewhere on the edges of his mind, Sean hovered.

Late in the afternoon, Corey flopped down in his rack and threw an arm over his eyes to block the light. He wondered if he could catch a nap. It didn't take long before his mind wandered back to Sean. Corey hadn't been this attracted to a man in at least five years.

He managed to doze for about an hour. When Corey woke, he realized he was going back to the bar tonight to see Sean. He ran his thumb and forefinger over his eyes. He had to do something, he couldn't go on like this. Sean seemed okay with Corey's issues. Maybe they could jerk each other off a couple of times and Corey could get Sean out of his fucking system.

He took his time showering, being more thorough than usual. Back in his room, he applied a little cologne, not enough to end up smelling like a back alley rentboy. Corey laughed at himself when he couldn't decide what to wear. He was acting like a nervous virgin getting ready for his first date.

Giving himself a mental kick in the ass, Corey admitted he

was going to show off what he had and hope Sean wanted to get a closer look. His jeans were faded to the perfect shade. They hugged his ass and rode low on his hips. The button front black shirt he selected had short sleeves that barely fit over his biceps, leaving the muscles of his arms on full display. Corey left several buttons open, revealing the skin of his chest and the edges of his dog tags.

Checking himself in the mirror, he saw the lower edge of his First Recon skull and crossbones tattoo on his right shoulder. The eagle, globe and anchor over his heart was partially visible, too. He hoped Sean liked tattoos.

Corey's taxi was waiting for him when he reached the main gate. He climbed in and gave the driver the name and address of the bar. He realized he was going to arrive pretty fucking early, Sean might not even be there, yet.

The taxi dropped him off just after 2000 hours. He knew Sean didn't go on until 2100. Corey decided he'd nurse one drink while he waited.

Stepping inside, he forced himself to take a deep breath. He swallowed hard and tried to force himself to relax. The crowd was already filling up the tables and Corey immediately felt the pressure of all those bodies. He told himself he could do this.

He had spotted his preferred stool, unoccupied, and was halfway there when he noticed Sean on the stage. At nearly the same moment, Sean looked up from the microphone he was working on and spotted Corey.

Sean's eyes widened and his mouth fell open slightly. He looked stunned for a brief moment. Corey stood tall and let him look, as Sean dragged his eyes the length of Corey's body. As he watched, a flush appeared high on Sean's sharp cheekbones and his eyes grew heated. When Sean's pink tongue darted out to wet his lower lip, Corey's cock twitched in his jeans.

He had Sean's full attention. Hopefully he'd get the chance to work Sean out of system sooner rather than later.

Finally, Sean moved. He stepped down off the small stage

and took a couple of steps toward Corey. "I didn't think you were going to show." He sounded out of breath.

"When I'd gotten some sleep and thought about it, I realized this was where I wanted to be," Corey answered.

Sean flashed a quick, self-conscious smile. "Good. I'm glad you're here."

"Need some help?" Corey inclined his head toward the stage.

"No, but thanks," Sean said hastily. "I just finished. Want to get a drink before I have to start catering to the crowd?"

"Definitely." Corey led the way to the corner stool he preferred for the view of the bar it gave him. Sean slid onto the stool next to him.

Linda came down to their end of the bar. "Well, if it isn't my handsome Devil Dog. How are you this evening, sweetheart?"

"Thirsty," Corey evaded.

She laughed. "The usual for you two gentlemen?"

Corey watched her make their drinks and learned that Sean drank rum and Coke. Captain Morgan's rum, no less. Corey paid for his own drink since Sean's was part of his arrangement for providing entertainment.

"You're a cheap date," he muttered before he could stop himself.

Sean snorted into his drink. "I'm easy, too."

"Not for me, you're not." Corey couldn't make himself look at Sean.

They were silent for several interminable moments before Sean leaned in and said quietly, "Do you even know how fucking hot you look, tonight? I'm getting hard just looking at you."

Corey grinned, heat pooling in his belly and his cock pushing steadily against his fly. Finally, he met Sean's eyes. "I clean up pretty good for a grunt, huh?"

"I knew last night you cleaned up well," Sean replied. "But this is something else." He traced a finger over the edge of the tattoo on Corey's arm. "I want to take that shirt off of you and get a good look at your ink. I probably couldn't stop, though, and I'd end up running my tongue over the one on your chest." Sean stared blatantly at Corey's chest where his shirt stood open to reveal part of the Marine Corps logo.

"Are you good with your tongue?" Corey asked, blatantly staring at Sean's pouty mouth. He wondered if they could skip the hand jobs and just have Sean wrap those sinful looking lips around his dick.

Sean gave a husky laugh, his eyes sparkling. "I really like this side of you."

Before Corey could escalate their banter, someone appeared on Sean's other side and threw an arm around his neck. For a fleeting moment, annoyance bordering on anger colored Sean's expression. By the time he turned to greet the newcomer, Sean's face had settled into a polite mask.

Corey let himself be introduced to the interloper. He even shook the guy's hand. He didn't care who the guy was, though. He knew he didn't have a right to his anger. Sean was working, and interacting with the crowd was part of that.

"Looks like the crowd is getting restless," Sean said, taking a long pull on his drink.

"You'd better get to work, then," Corey replied. As much as he'd like Sean to himself, the man had a job to do and Corey was going to get the hell out of the way and let him do it.

"Is going to breakfast after this still out of the question?" asked Sean.

Corey stared at Sean while he contemplated his options. His desire for alone time with Sean won out over his desire for a peaceful sleep. "No. I've reconsidered. Let's see how we both feel when the time comes."

Sean's smile showed off his perfect teeth. His eyes seemed lit by genuine happiness. "I gotta go, but I'll be back."

"I'm counting on it." Corey smirked as he watched Sean saunter over to a table filled with people.

Linda appeared across the bar from Corey. She rested her elbows on the counter, leaned in and smiled at him.

"What?" Corey asked, uncomfortable under her scrutiny.

"The two of you," she answered frankly. "It's just fun to watch."

Corey's stomach lurched. He glanced around the bar to see if anyone was paying Sean or him too much of the wrong kind of attention. "Are we obvious?"

"Not at all," Linda said dismissively. "I only notice because I know Sean. I don't think his fan base would have a problem with it, but it's good for his image to cultivate that air of availability. To the men *and* the women."

"How available is he?" Corey hated that he wanted to know.

"To them?" she inclined her head toward the rapidly filling bar. "Not at all. You're completely separate from all of this, though. I've always wondered what kind of taste he has in men. I have to say I'm a little disappointed you play for his team."

Corey flushed and hid behind his beer bottle.

Linda rested her chin on one palm. "Do you even know what you look like?" she asked, eyes narrowed.

Corey shrugged. He knew he had a well muscled body, but so did a lot of other Marines. It kind of went with the job, so Corey had never thought much about it.

"You have the sweetest face, the brightest blue eyes, and a bow-shaped mouth that some women would kill to have," Linda said. "And the way you fill out that shirt is illegal in some states."

Corey flushed hotter and pretended he wasn't embarrassed, taking another long drink of his beer.

"Linda, Corey is blushing," Sean said, appearing beside him and setting down his empty glass. "What did you say to him?"

She picked up Sean's glass. "I was telling him what it is you see in him. I don't think he knew." She held up his glass. "Another one?"

"Just water for now," Sean replied. "I gotta go on soon." He took the sweating bottle of water she handed over before he turned to Corey.

"Don't ask me to repeat what she said," Corey said emphatically. "Once was enough."

Sean laughed and briefly laid his hand on Corey's forearm. "At least I got to see you blush." He took two steps toward the stage. "See you in an hour?"

"I'll be right here."

Sean performed songs Corey hadn't heard the night before. He wondered if that was because he'd missed the first set last night, or if Sean routinely changed things up. This set was made up of hair-band songs from the late 80s, segueing into grunge rock from the early 90s. Corey had never heard these songs performed like Sean performed them and he liked it. There was heart and emotion in every note he played, every lyric he sang.

His selection of original songs intrigued Corey. One reminisced about what sounded like an abusive relationship and how it was overcome. One was about a broken heart and the mundane exchange of personal belongings in the wake of a breakup. The final song was filled with longing for someone to love who would love in return. Once again, Corey wondered how autobiographical these songs were.

On his first break, Sean made his way around the room, greeting people he hadn't gotten to earlier. It still wasn't long before he sat down next to Corey. Linda brought him a bottle of water and a fresh rum and Coke.

"Enjoying yourself?" Sean asked.

"I love the entertainment," replied Corey.

"Good, I'm glad to hear that." Sean's smile was almost shy as his cheeks colored slightly. "What do you think of the original songs?"

Corey wanted to ask just how personal the songs were that Sean wrote. He hesitated, wondering if that wasn't too personal a question to ask someone he'd really just met.

"That bad, huh?" Sean laughed uncomfortably and looked away. "Don't worry about it. I shouldn't have put you on the spot, like that."

"No!" Corey said hastily. "I like them. All of them. I was just wondering how much is really about you, or if you just, I don't know, write words that sound right with that music?"

"Oh." Sean look relieved. He looked back at Corey and smiled slightly. "They're all about me. I write about the things I've lived and learned. Not always literally, but always in some way."

"They all make me feel something when I hear them," Corey said, remembering the times his heart almost broke for Sean. "I think that's what you're going for, isn't it?"

"Yeah." Sean shrugged. "Well, that and to entertain."

"Oh, you're entertaining." Corey chuckled, running his eyes the length of Sean's form.

Sean stood up slowly, giving Corey a dark look. "Your smile is fucking lethal." With a shake of his head, he picked up his bottle of water and headed back to the stage.

During the next break, Corey made a quick trip to the head while Sean greeted friends and fans. He was on his way back to his seat when Sean intercepted him.

"It's hot in here. Come out back with me to get some air?"

Corey indicated Sean should lead the way. As they exited into the rear parking lot, they were greeted by the small group that had come outside for cigarettes. Sean shook a few hands, introduced Corey, then led them further out to avoid the smoke.

Outside, the temperature was cooler and the noise level dropped significantly. Corey took a deep breath, the muscles of his neck and shoulders releasing their tension suddenly. His phone vibrated in his pocket. Corey tugged it out, not bothering to hide the irritation that had his back tensing again.

He was aware of Sean watching him as he checked the phone's display. When Corey saw Michael Nygaard's name, he curled his lip in disgust. "Fuck him," he muttered, shoving the phone back into his pocket.

"Problem?" Sean asked, expression tense.

"Not if I don't answer the phone," Corey replied.

Sean nodded and folded his arms over his chest, feet planted. His expression was smooth but Corey saw the muscles in his jaw flex. His posture reminded Corey of the night before, in this very parking lot. His chest tightened as he realized something had gone wrong when he'd dropped his situational awareness.

"I'll go back inside so you can have some privacy." Sean turned stiffly and took two steps toward the door.

A chill ran through Corey when it occurred to him what Sean was assuming. "It's just some asshole I served with in Afghanistan. He only calls when he needs something and he can't get someone in his platoon to do it for him."

Sean turned back and stared hard at Corey for several long moments. Corey held his gaze steadily, assuming Sean was gauging whether or not to believe him.

"You didn't blow me off last night 'cause you had a boyfriend waiting back at base?" Sean abruptly demanded.

"No fucking way," Corey replied with an emphatic shake of his head.

Sean pressed his lips into a thin line like he was still deciding if he could believe Corey. He finally sighed explosively. "Okay," he said quietly, his tension easing slightly. "I should get back on stage."

Corey watched Sean's stiff back as they walked back into the bar. He resigned himself to the fact that he was going to have to actually tell Sean a few things about himself if this was ever going to get past flirtation.

Things were cooler between them after that and it bothered Corey. He started out telling himself it was because he wanted Sean. He needed to work Sean out of his system. By the time the night was over and Sean was putting his guitar into its case, Corey missed Sean's previously warm enthusiasm.

Corey climbed up on stage and began to tear down the microphones and the stand.

"You don't have to do this tonight," Sean said in a flat tone.

"If I help you'll be done faster and we can get breakfast that much sooner," he replied as if that had always been the definitive plan.

Sean's expression was still implacable but Corey thought he might see a spark of hope in his eyes.

"Okay," Sean said on a sigh.

Corey made a trip to Sean's SUV with the amplifier. They both wished Linda a good night as they carried the rest of the gear out the back door together.

"Any idea where you want to go?" Corey asked, closing the hatch of the SUV. His cell phone buzzed in his pocket. "Fuck." He tugged it out, intending to ignore the call. It wasn't a number he didn't recognize but was a 760 area code. "This might be the base."

Corey's stomach twisted when Sean folded his arms across his chest again. It was undoubtedly Sean's tell.

"Staff Sergeant Yarwood," he barked into the phone.

"Staff Sergeant Yarwood, this is Corrections Sergeant Manny Lopez at Vista Detention Facility," said an unfamiliar male voice.

Corey rolled his eyes in annoyance. He wondered which of his fuck-up friends had gotten his ass tossed into jail. "What can I do for you, Sergeant?" he asked, resigned. He was achingly aware of Sean watching him closely.

"We have a Sergeant Nygaard in custody for homicide and he asked us to contact you," Lopez answered.

Corey's eyes shot to Sean's and he froze. His heart slammed against his ribs as he asked, "I'm sorry, did you say homicide?"

Sean's eyes widened and he frowned, his mouth falling open slightly in surprise.

Lopez spoke again. "Sergeant Nygaard has confessed to beating his girlfriend to death."

"Fuck," Corey whispered. His mind raced and he began to walk slowly in a circle as he tried to sort this out. "I don't understand why you're calling me."

"When we arrest you active duty folks for something this serious, we're required to notify your command," Lopez replied. "Command usually takes care of notifying family so arrangements can be made for bail and attorneys."

Corey rubbed a hand up and down the bristles of hair on the back of his head as he continued to pace in a circle. "Nygaard and I don't share a billet any longer; we haven't since we returned from Afghanistan. Even back then, I was never his Platoon Sergeant."

"When we asked him for a contact number at the time the detectives booked him in, he gave us yours." When Corey didn't reply, Sergeant Lopez kept talking. "When he gave us the number he said you'd understand. You know what happened to him and why he is the way he is."

Corey pinched the bridge of his nose. His body was tense from head to boots and he was breathing like he'd just swum the length of the BRC pool underwater. He clenched his jaw against a sudden wave of nausea. "I have no idea what that means," Corey said through his teeth.

He jumped and gasped, curling his hand into a fist at the feel of a hand gripping his arm. Corey's eyes snapped open to identify his attacker and found Sean's hazel eyes watching his face closely. When Sean's concerned expression shifted to confusion and wariness, Corey took a deep breath and shook out his fisted hand.

"If you know of previous incidents of violence involving Sergeant Nygaard, the homicide detectives are going to want to talk to you," Lopez said. "Has he beat up his girlfriend before?"

"I didn't even know he had a girlfriend," Corey exclaimed. "Is it possible he's talking about a combat incident?" He didn't need an answer to that question, Corey already knew.

Sean was running his palm up and down Corey's arm soothingly. He stepped closer, until Corey could feel the heat of his body. It bolstered him, he drew strength from it. It was a new and unfamiliar sensation. Without thinking, he curled his fingers around the back of Sean's neck, cradled him, and stroked his thumb over Sean's sharp cheekbone.

"No one seems sure of anything other than the fact he beat a young woman to death with his bare hands," the sergeant answered. "You'd be allowed to see him briefly if you thought it would help to sort this out, but I still have to notify his command."

"I don't have access to a car," Corey bemoaned. Sean waved a hand to get Corey's attention. "Give me just a second, Sergeant."

"I'll drive you if you need to go," Sean said. "This sounds serious."

"That would be asking too much," Corey answered sharply.

"It'll give us a chance to talk," Sean whispered, his eyes almost pleading. "This has to do with that phone call earlier, doesn't it?"

That made Corey pause. Until this moment, he'd forgotten that Nygaard had tried to call him directly, earlier in the night. "Okay." Corey relented.

He told the Corrections Sergeant he'd be there in thirty mikes and disconnected the call.

"Let's go," Sean said, pulling his keys from his jeans pocket.

As they pulled onto the freeway onramp, Corey turned to Sean. "I'm sorry you have to do this."

"It's obviously not your fault," Sean replied evenly. "Now tell me who this guy is, what he supposedly did and why you're getting pulled into it."

"I have no fucking idea where to start," Corey said in frustration. "Nygaard was one of several sergeants in my platoon in Afghanistan." He rubbed his jaw, feeling the barest hint of stubble. The disgust he always felt of late, when he had to deal with Nygaard, curled through him. "He's a decent Marine but he gets belt-fed when he has to so much as take a shit."

"You're a staff sergeant so you outrank him, right?" Sean asked.

"I was promoted meritoriously when we returned from deployment." Corey shifted in his seat and his leg began to bounce violently. "In Afghanistan, we held the same rank but my job within the platoon meant I was higher up in the hierarchy. He was in charge of a team of five Marines when we went on missions."

"So, what did he do to make you hate him?" Sean sounded baffled.

Corey straightened his legs as much as he could. He fisted both hands where they rested on his thighs. "I didn't say I hated him."

Sean glanced repeatedly from the road to Corey's face. "You didn't see your face when you checked your phone the first time he called."

Clenching his jaw, Corey turned away from Sean to stare out his window. "He acts like he and I are friends. He talks like there are some big secrets only the two of us know. He pretends we've been through some sort of hellish battle that bonded us forever." He turned back to look at Sean. "It's fucking creepy and it pisses me off."

"Is it possible something you guys experienced affected him more than it did you?" Sean's question was frighteningly intuitive.

"Just before we came home, the platoon was hit by an IED and we lost a couple of Marines." Corey straightened his dog tags and his leg started to bounce again. "The LT ordered me to take part of the platoon and engage the hostiles inside a nearby house. We eliminated the threat. The Afghanis won't let it the fuck go."

"And now this guy has murdered his girlfriend?" Sean questioned. He continued without waiting for Corey to respond, "So many of you guys have come back with PTS. Is it possible that's this guy's problem?"

Corey remembered how Nygaard was always a little more enthusiastic about their kills, and at the same time he seemed to have zero empathy and compassion for the populace. "I might be wrong but I don't think PTS turns us evil. It might turn a wife-beating asshole into a killer but I don't think it turns good men into killers." Corey needed to believe that was true.

Sean was silent for a long while.

Dread settled, cold and heavy, in Corey's gut. He hastily blurted to Sean, "I haven't had any violent incidents since I've been back."

Sean looked at Corey in surprise. "That thought never occurred to me. Why would you think I thought you were dangerous?"

"I don't know." Cory shrugged in aggravation. "It just seemed like that's where that entire conversation ended up." He'd cut his own fucking hands off before he let himself harm Sean. "So…I just…I ignored that call earlier because I hate this guy and I thought he was calling 'cause he wanted to hang out, or was drunk somewhere and wanted a ride. He's not an ex."

"I get that now," Sean said quietly. "I just couldn't think of any other reason you would show that much hatred for someone who was calling you."

The pain in Corey's belly eased. He took a deep breath and managed to get his body to relax a little. Maybe he hadn't totally fucked things up with Sean. "I just don't know why he was calling *me* earlier. I have no idea if it was before or after he'd killed her." Corey hoped to hell ignoring that phone call hadn't cost a woman her life.

Corey snorted derisively when another thought occurred to him. "He probably wanted help hiding her body," he said with hostility, scrubbing both hands over his short hair.

"Jesus," Sean whispered.

They were silent as Sean pulled off the freeway and made the short drive to Vista Detention Facility. It was easy to find the public parking.

When Sean shut off the engine, the resulting quiet was jarring.

"Do you want to wait here?" Corey asked. "I don't know how long this is going to take. I'm not sure they'll let you come in, though."

Sean's answer was to open his door. "If they won't let me in, I'll wait in the car."

Corey's relief was acute and he hadn't been aware he'd wanted Sean to come with him. He hoped the deputies would let him inside.

At the after-hours public pedestrian door, Corey thumbed the button on the small call box.

"Can I help you?" A tinny voice barked.

Looking up into the camera above the door, Corey said in a loud voice, "Staff Sergeant Corey Yarwood, USMC, I'm looking for Sergeant Manny Lopez regarding Marine Sergeant Michael Nygaard."

"Just a minute, Staff Sergeant," the voice replied.

Corey walked in a small circle to hide his agitation and anxiety. He glanced up to see Sean standing a few feet away, hands buried in the front pockets of his jeans. He was watching Corey closely. At least he didn't have his arms folded over his chest again.

The door opened and a deputy sheriff emerged, dressed in the familiar uniform of khaki blouse and olive green trousers. His brass nameplate said his last name was Pierce. "Staff Sergeant Yarwood?"

Corey took a single step forward. "I'm Yarwood. I needed to catch a ride here." He indicated Sean. "Can my friend come in with me or does he need to wait in the car?"

"If he drove here, I assume he's got picture ID?" Pierce asked.

"Yes, sir," Sean answered quickly.

Pierce held the door open wide for them both to enter. "Let's get you two logged in as visitors and then I'll take you Sergeant Lopez's office." Stopping in front of a wall filled with medium sized lock boxes, the deputy said, "Put all your personal belongings, except your picture IDs, in a lockup. Wallets, cell phones, car keys, anything and everything."

It took just a few seconds for Corey and Sean to stash their gear in boxes and punch their codes into the electronic locking mechanisms. Next, Deputy Pierce led them down a short corridor toward a counter topped with bullet resistant plastic, much like he'd begun to see in banks.

VDF was much like every other jail Corey had been in. Luckily, he'd always been the one doing the bailing, never the one getting bailed out. It was cold and sterile, with concrete floors and smooth, off-white walls. The fluorescent lighting reflected off of the flat white of the walls, the glare nearly painful. Doors, sills and the counter ahead were all painted a pleasant shade of royal blue, but nothing could really make a jail a happy place. The scent of antiseptic never completely wiped away the musty jail smell. Beneath it all was the constant odor of unwashed bodies, excrement and vomit.

Corey glanced over his shoulder and was surprised to find Sean glancing around curiously. He was most likely cataloging the experience so he could reference it later on for a role he might someday play. Corey knew Sean was affected by the sterility of the jail when he ran up and down his own arm briskly, as if trying to build up any heat possible to ward off the undeniable chill. The slight wrinkle in his ski-jump nose spoke volumes on Sean's opinion of the smell.

Their footsteps echoed off the hard, bare walls. For safety and security, all the doors were locked. Since it was Saturday night, none of the civilian staff would be working. The Corrections Deputies were all inside the secure portion of the jail, watching over the prisoners. The chaotic ruckus of the population was nearly as loud as their footfalls. Corey was glad they wouldn't have to enter any further into the facility than prisoner intake.

When they reached the chest-height counter top, Sean handed over his California driver's license and Corey produced his military ID card. The deputy behind the secure plexi-glass wore a brass nameplate that said his name was Daniels. This deputy ran quick checks on each of them for wants, warrants, and criminal histories. He declared them clean and handed back their IDs.

As Pierce led them deeper into the jail, the lighting dimmed dramatically to a level that made Corey think of emergency lighting. He realized the brightest source was the ambient glare of multiple computer monitors.

They reached a blue door with a wide, inset window. Deputy Pierce signaled to someone on the other side and Corey heard the whirring and clicks of an electronic lock disengaging. He looked at Sean and found him watching the process with open interest. When he noticed Corey watching him, Sean gave him a small, encouraging smile.

Deputy Pierce held the door open and as they passed through into the sallyport, he said, "Mr. Chandler, we can't let you talk to the prisoner. You'll have to wait in Sergeant Lopez' office."

"That's fine," Sean said emphatically. "I don't even know the guy. I just gave a friend a ride."

Prisoner intake wasn't what Corey had expected. Movies, television, and past experience had prepared him for large holding cells of metal bars. Instead, he was surprised to find the walls lined with small cells made of ballistic plastic. Each cell had a single bench and a commode.

Corey spotted Nygaard immediately. He was in the nearest holding cell, seated on the bench and slouched back against the wall. Nygaard was wearing a white skivvy shirt and pale blue scrub pants. It looked like there were thin, white slippers on his feet.

"They took his clothes as evidence," Pierce said when he noticed Corey looking.

Nygaard spotted him right then, his expression changing to hopeful and pleading. He stood and pressed his palms to the clear containment wall. Corey gritted his teeth and looked away.

Sergeant Manny Lopez was a tall, paunchy man in his early 40s. His grip was firm when they shook hands and Corey introduced

Sean. He offered both Sean and Corey seats in his office.

"Can you tell me what happened?" Corey asked.

"I can tell you what the detectives told me and what the arrest reports say," Lopez answered. "The suspect was at home with his girlfriend of three months, Maritza Arroyo, and her younger sister, Luisa. He'd been drinking steadily since late morning. As tends to happen, the drunker he got, the more belligerent he became."

That was part of the reason Corey preferred to drink alone. He hadn't been an angry or hostile drunk before deployment but he wasn't quite as sure about things now as he used to be.

Sergeant Lopez continued, "The victim's sister says the suspect kept starting arguments with the two of them. He deliberately provoked them and reacted physically to their angry reactions. The suspect ended up in a bedroom, lying on a bed and continuing to drink directly from a bottle."

Jesus. How many times had Corey done that very thing? The difference was, he made sure he was alone. He swallowed hard and didn't dare look at Sean.

"The victim allegedly entered the bedroom to take away the alcohol and to try to convince the suspect to sober up, or at least go to sleep." Lopez referred to a large stack of papers on his desk. "The witness statement says the suspect exploded into a violent rage and began hitting the victim. Her sister tried to intervene, at which point the suspect physically picked her up and forcibly removed her from the apartment. He locked her out, so she began to shout loudly and pound on the door. Minutes later she heard her sister screaming for her life inside the apartment."

"Oh God," Sean whispered.

Corey's heart stopped when he looked over at Sean. Expression pained, Sean appeared to have tears in his eyes. The realization that Sean was a civilian slammed into Corey with hurricane force. He wasn't accustomed to blood and violence like Corey and Sergeant Lopez were.

It took all of Corey's Marine discipline not to reach out and touch Sean. He wanted to put an arm around him in comfort. He'd settle for just taking his hand but he didn't dare do it in the middle of a county jail.

Sergeant Lopez also noticed Sean's distress. He set aside the papers he'd been reading. "The victim's sister found a neighbor to call nine-one-one. The deputies arrived, made entry and found the suspect cradling the victim's lifeless body, both of them covered in her blood."

Sean made a pained sound and ran a hand over his forehead in agitation.

"What has he said about why he did it?" Corey asked, struggling to wrap his mind around the facts.

"He hasn't said much. He was hostile and combative with the deputies." The sergeant leaned back in his chair. "He claims he doesn't remember anything, which means he probably had a PTS flashback, caused by whatever it was happened to the two of you in Afghanistan. That could mean he can't be held legally responsible."

Corey's heart raced and he sucked a harsh breath in through his clenched teeth. He couldn't remember anything happening that would cause the kind of trauma that would make a good man beat a woman to death and not remember. His disgust for Nygaard made him nauseous.

"I don't know what he means," Corey said sharply. "Maybe if I talk to him he'll get specific."

Lopez' voice took on a conspiratorial tone. "Ordinarily, there'd be no chance, it would be too dangerous. In your case, Staff Sergeant, I have no doubt you can take care of yourself," he said with a knowing smirk.

Sergeant Lopez called out to the deputies staffing the security pod in Prisoner Intake. The raised platform sported video monitors, alarms, and electronic door controls. One of the deputies came down the short set of stairs and led Corey across the long expanse of concrete floor toward Nygaard's cell.

Corey glanced around at things he hadn't noticed before,

like the larger holding cell that held multiple prisoners, many of whom were asleep on benches and the hard floor.

The deputy ordered Nygaard to sit on the bench at the back of the small enclosure. When Nygaard had complied, the deputy signaled the pod to unlock the cell door.

"No physical contact," he said. "If either of you breaks that rule, if either of you raises your voice, we're opening the door and pulling you out."

"Copy that." Corey didn't take offense. He recognized the desire deep inside himself to put a fist into Nygaard's face.

Gears whirred and Corey heard a loud clack. The deputy slid the clear door open and gestured him inside.

"One more thing," said the deputy, "the cell is mic'd. There is no expectation of privacy. For either of you."

"None is needed," Corey replied in a low tone as he stepped into the cell.

As the door clanged shut loudly behind him, Corey braced his hands on his hips and looked down at Nygaard. He looked like shit. He looked like he'd been through a firefight. Nygaard had a black eye forming. There were scratches along both cheeks and on his throat. His hands were bloodied and bruised, his knuckles raw and swollen.

Corey's lip curled in disgust. These wounds had not been sustained in combat. They'd been sustained while beating an innocent woman to death. Michael Nygaard was a big, strong, lethally trained Marine and he'd used it all against a weaker opponent.

"What the fuck did you do?" Corey heard himself ask in a voice laden heavily with loathing.

"I don't know, man," Nygaard replied pathetically. "I don't know how it happened."

"I didn't come here to listen to your fucking excuses," he snapped, voice rising. "Why the fuck did you have them call me instead of your platoon sergeant?"

"You know what we went through." Nygaard's leg bounced in agitation. "You know what they did to us and what we had to do."

Corey's heart thundered. He breathed through his mouth as a buzzing started in his ears and he grew lightheaded. He squeezed his fingertips hard into his hipbones through his jeans. Nothing Corey had ever been through made him capable of using his hands on someone he cared about, in any way other than to bring him pleasure. "I don't know shit about what made you do something like this. You're a goddamn United States Marine, Nygaard. Stop making excuses for yourself and man the fuck up."

Nygaard's knuckles were white as he gripped the edge of the bench. "Come on, Corey, you know how the women get over there. They get up in our grills and screech at us like they're losing their minds."

"Staff Sergeant Yarwood," Corey corrected Nygaard. This was an official meeting. They weren't friends and Corey wasn't going to allow informality between them. "Christ," he spat with revulsion, "they're never a threat to us. We're fucking Marines. If you can't give me a real reason why you had them call me, I'm fucking out of here."

"You know what they did to us that day," Nygaard blurted angrily, his face ruddy and spittle landing on his lower lip. "You know what they made us do to them."

Corey swallowed against a suddenly tight throat. Nothing happened that day that could justify Nygaard's actions. He started pacing the very short length of the cell. Corey changed tactics, hoping to shut Nygaard down so he could take Sean and just get the fuck out of here. "How does anything that happened over there justify what you just did to an innocent civilian?"

"I didn't know who she was." Nygaard's eyes were wild. "I didn't know where I was. I woke up with her in my arms, covered in blood, and all I could think about was that poor man we put on the hood of the Humvee."

Corey came to an abrupt halt, heart in his throat. A chill swept through him. "What the fuck are you talking about?" Anyone they transported in that manner wasn't deserving of a Marine's pity.

"She was so bloody. I couldn't recognize her." Nygaard stared at his own trembling hands as if he was seeing them for the first time. "The only thing I could think about was that day."

"You're so full of shit." Corey knew his voice was raised. "I'm fucking out of here."

"This is your fucking fault!" Nygaard shouted, coming up off the bench. "I was following *your* orders!"

Corey turned back, arms tense at his side and he prepared to take on the threat. There was movement outside of the cell and Corey assumed it was the deputies preparing to intervene.

"I didn't order you to murder your girlfriend with your bare hands!" Corey yelled, pointing a single finger at Nygaard for emphasis.

"You ordered me into that house. You ordered me to handle it!" Nygaard stepped forward and wrapped his fist in Corey's shirt.

Corey dealt with the threat in front of him. He twisted Nygaard's wrist and freed his shirt. Cory wrapped his free hand around Nygaard's throat and used it to pin him to the clear wall of the cell.

The cell door slid open and there were many sets of hands on him. They pulled and tugged at his arms and shoulders. Corey released Nygaard and allowed himself to be dragged from the cell.

Several deputies led him back to Sergeant Lopez' office. Lopez came out and looked him over. "You okay, Staff Sergeant?"

Behind him, Sean watched Corey with a mixture of concern and wariness. Corey's heart sank. He'd forgotten Sean was here. He hadn't wanted him to witness this ugly side of Corey.

"I'm fine," Corey replied contritely. "I'm sorry about that. I know I wasn't supposed to touch him." It was like he'd been in combat. His heart raced and he couldn't get enough air in his lungs. Everything was brighter, clearer, and louder. Corey clenched and unclenched his hands, trying to ease the feeling they were being stabbed by a thousand pins and needles.

Lopez shook his head. "Nothing to be sorry for. A murder suspect physically assaulted you and you defended yourself until we could extract you."

Corey snorted at the collusion. "I don't think I was any help. He's not making any sense. If he says PTS made him do it, I suppose it could be true. I think I know what event he's talking about, but nothing happened that comes close to justifying what he did."

"At least you tried," the Sergeant replied. "I'll have someone escort you out." He shook both of their hands as Deputy Pierce led Corey and Sean to the exit.

They crossed the parking lot to Sean's SUV. Corey wanted to kick his own ass. What had he been thinking, taking Sean into a jail? Sean was too fresh and clean to become sullied by this kind of reality.

Sean stopped walking abruptly and stepped into Corey's path. "Did you get hurt, or anything?" He asked quietly, opening Corey's shirt and peering at his chest.

Corey's skin tingled and he resisted the temptation to lean in to Sean's touch. "I'm fine. He didn't do any damage."

"Well, he tore up your shirt a little," Sean said.

Corey tried to straighten his stretched shirt. He'd lost a couple of buttons so it hung open down past his sternum. "I'm sorry about that." He muttered apologetically. "I should have had you wait in the car."

"What am I, a fucking child?" Sean demanded angrily. "I know what kind of shit goes on in the world. Now let's get you home. You look tired."

Corey nodded his agreement, suddenly overwhelmed with

exhaustion.

As Sean drove, Corey slumped in his seat and rested his temple against the window. It was blessedly silent for an extended period before Sean's soft voice gently broke into Corey's raging thoughts.

"You know I could hear your conversation in there, right?" he asked, barely loud enough for Corey to hear him. "The sergeant was monitoring you for your safety so we listened in."

Corey closed his eyes against the pain, knowing what Sean must think of him. "Yeah?"

"Whatever it was he was talking about might not have caused him to do what he did to that woman, but *something* uglier than usual happened to you." Sean paused as if weighing his words. "Is whatever happened there the reason for your nightmares?"

He remembered Sean's expression when they'd learned what Nygaard had done to his girlfriend. Corey didn't want to do that to Sean again. "A lot happened over there. It was just one of many things."

"But is that the incident that causes most of your nightmares?" Sean was relentless.

Corey signed in resignation. "Yeah." He exhaled heavily.

"What made this incident so much worse than all the other bad shit you went through?" asked Sean gently.

"Nothing," Corey answered by rote. "My honor is clean."

Sean glanced at him sharply, trying to look at Corey and the road at the same time. His head turned back and forth several times before he spoke again. "Your honor is clean. Why did you say that?"

"What?" Corey didn't follow.

"You said your honor is clean," Sean parroted his own words back to him. "Most people would say their conscience is clean."

Corey looked away with a shrug, something heavy settling in his gut. He wrapped his arms tighter around himself. "Marines have to do a lot of things in combat we wouldn't ordinarily choose to do."

"I get that," Sean said firmly. "It's war."

Corey gave a single abrupt nod, relieved by Sean's understanding and acceptance. "Everything I have ever done has been necessary to keep my Marines and myself alive, while executing the lawfully given orders of my command."

From the corner of his eye, Corey saw Sean nod. "I have no doubt. But can this guy…Nygaard? Say the same?"

Corey wanted to say yes. He started to say yes. He drew breath to pronounce the word but it stuck in his throat. He had the word on his tongue, ready to say it. He just couldn't do it. "I don't know," he finally managed. "Maybe that's what the investigation is trying to answer," Corey mused.

"Investigation?" Sean's eyebrows lifted in surprise. "You're under investigation?"

Fuck. He hadn't meant to say that. He didn't need Sean thinking he was the type of Marine whose behavior needed to be scrutinized. "No, the incident, not me. The Afghanis say things happened but I wasn't a part of any of that. My part of the mission isn't under scrutiny."

"But Nygaard's is." It wasn't a question. "Is this why you hate him?"

A good question. Corey didn't know for sure, but he was beginning to guess. "I think it might be part of the reason why I don't like to be around him, yeah."

Sean fell silent and Corey was too exhausted to try to decipher how he was feeling about this FUBAR goat-roping. He glanced at his watch and saw that it was more morning than it was night. He dug his phone out of his pocket.

"It's too late for you to drive me back to base," he said, finding the number for the taxi company. "Just drop me back at the bar so I can meet my cab."

"I am not dropping you off at the bar," Sean said heatedly.

"This has been one majorly fucked up night and I am not making you drive all that way to Pendleton and then back home alone." Corey was actually angry at Sean for his stubbornness. "If you just drop me at the bar, it's a short drive home for you. It won't matter if I fall asleep in the back of the cab."

Sean didn't argue immediately. "I'm almost always still up at this hour, I'm not going to fall asleep," he replied. "But if you're really worried about it, I can take you to my place and you can have the cab pick you up there."

Besides the fact that Corey was afraid to be alone with Sean someplace private like his home, he could see no flaw in that plan. "I suppose I could also help you unload your car if we did that."

"Unloading is easy," Sean said with a grin. "Everything gets stored in the garage. Only my guitar goes inside."

"How many mikes out are we?" Corey asked, calculating when to tell the taxi to meet him.

"Excuse me?" Sean looked puzzled. "Mikes?"

Corey chuckled and ran a hand over his face. "Sorry, I must be more tired than I realized. It's military jargon. Minutes. How many *minutes* will it take to get to your place."

"Oh." His expression cleared and he seemed nonplussed. "ETA just about five mikes." Sean remained straight faced as he drove.

Snorting a laugh, not quite sure if Sean was teasing or adapting, he dialed the taxi company. Sean rattled off his address and the dispatcher told Corey it would be at least fifteen minutes before they could get a driver to that particular part of town.

Sean backed into the attached garage of his townhouse and cut the engine. He opened the rear hatch of the SUV and showed Corey where to store the plastic storage bins and the amplifier. Leading the way into a corridor, Sean carried only his guitar case.

"You can keep an eye out there for your cab," he said, gesturing toward a heavy looking door with a small, square window set high up. Which meant it was face level for Corey. "And I'll just run up and put this inside."

Corey watched Sean take the flight of stairs two at a time and disappear down the hallway to the left. There were sounds of a key in a lock and some other quiet rustling. Corey leaned against the door so he could peer out the window. A very short time later, Sean came bounding down the stairs.

The corridor was dim, lit only by the single bulb on the upper landing. Sean leaned against the door, on the other side of the small window, mirroring Corey. Moonlight streamed in, cutting through some of the darkness, and bathing Sean's prominent features in silver and shadow.

Corey's chest tightened painfully and he stopped breathing. Sean was so fucking beautiful. The moonlight caught the highlights in his light brown hair. His eyelashes looked longer and darker in the dimness and they swept softly against his cheeks as he looked down at his own feet. His sharp cheekbones cast dark shadows and his hazel eyes were so pale they were luminous. Sean's damned upturned nose that drove Corey fucking mad, was even more pronounced in the soft light. Corey's eyes locked on Sean's full, shapely mouth. The bow shape of his upper lip and the poutiness of his lower lip were enticing. They looked so soft and warm and Corey ached to just lean in and kiss Sean.

"So, I realized that I don't even have your number," Sean said, just above a whisper. He held his cell phone in his hand, thumb hovering.

Corey thought about it and realized Sean was right. Because he'd known where to find Sean this weekend, it hadn't occurred to Corey to get his number.

"Unless you don't want to exchange numbers?" Sean spoke softly but Corey could hear his disappointment like a forty-mike-mike.

"No! I mean, yes. Shit." Corey hastily pulled his phone from his pocket. "I was just trying to figure out how that had happened at all," he muttered. "I'd have been really pissed when I got home."

Sean chuckled as he keyed in the numbers Corey rattled off. Corey thumbed in Sean's number and paused when he went to type his name. "How do you spell Sean?" Realizing what he'd asked, Corey added hastily, "I mean, I *know* how to spell Sean but how do *you* spell it?"

When Sean laughed, his eyes crinkled and his wide smile made Corey feel like he'd been punched in the gut. His laughter was low and husky, both delighted and mischievous. Sean gave the traditional spelling of his name, the one Corey had always liked because it was simple and uncomplicated.

"C-o-r-e-y?" Sean asked.

"Yep. Simple and no frills," Corey replied.

"To the point, with no extraneous bullshit," said Sean.

Corey couldn't help but smile.

They stood, shoulders against the door, staring at one another in silence. Sean's eyes grew wide and his expression serious. He took one slow step forward until he was right in front of Corey.

Corey stood frozen, his eyes roaming over Sean's handsome face, taking in his smooth, tan skin and the heat just beginning to smolder in his eyes. He caught the scent of Sean's cologne and had to bite back a moan, it smelled so good.

Slowly, Sean lifted both hands, palms out. He stood, letting Corey understand his intentions. Corey shifted to lean back against the door, silently consenting for Sean to touch him. Sean stepped close enough that Corey could feel the heat of his body all along the length of his own. Gently, he placed his palms on Corey's chest. He stood patiently, as if awaiting Corey's reaction.

With his back to the door, Corey stood unmoving, feeling scalded by the heat of Sean's hands through his shirt. He was trapped by Sean's eyes, staring directly into his, unblinking. He was sharply aware of Sean's hands running slowly down his chest and over his stomach. Sean's lips parted as he held Corey's gaze steadily.

Corey's own lips parted as he breathed heavily, wondering where Sean's hands were going to wander to next. His heart was pounding and he knew Sean had to be able to feel it as he slid his palms over Corey's chest again. A quiet sound escaped Corey as Sean's hands curled up over his shoulders and skimmed down his arms. He hadn't been touched like this in so long.

One of Sean's hands dropped down to Corey's hip and panic flared in his chest. As much as he wanted to press himself against Sean's firm, muscular body, he knew Sean would feel his lack of reaction and take it the wrong way. To Corey's relief, Sean didn't bring them in closer. He slid his other hand behind Corey's neck and cradled his head.

Corey glanced down at Sean's wet, red lips. He felt the urge to push forward and taste Sean's mouth, but he held back. Sean was driving this between them so Corey waited to see where he would take them.

When he finally did lean in, Sean didn't press their mouths together. Instead, he rested his forehead against Corey's. Sean's hazel eyes held so much heat they nearly glowed. He seemed able to look right into Corey and see all the secrets he tried to keep hidden. Corey had never experienced anything like this.

Uncurling his fists from his side, Corey brought one hand up to rest against the side of Sean's waist. The other he used to run over the defined muscles in Sean's arm. Something brushed, feather-light, across Corey's lower lip. He licked at it gently, tasting the dry saltiness of Sean's thumb. As Sean skimmed the pad of this thumb over Corey's lip, Corey kissed it, lapped at it with his tongue, considered drawing it into his mouth to suckle at it.

Sean's breathing was ragged. Corey wanted to look down at Sean's mouth, lean in and kiss him. He was trapped by Sean's eyes though, they wouldn't allow him to look away. Finally, with agonizing slowness, Sean tilted his face. He left their foreheads pressed together, even as his mouth settled over Corey's, soft and warm and gentle.

Corey closed his eyes and tightened his fingers on Sean's arm and waist, ready for him to deepen the kiss. It didn't happen. Sean pressed soft kisses to Corey's mouth. They were gentle, nipping kisses that made Corey's lips tingle. He returned Sean's kisses, biting at him playfully. Their lips grew moister and Corey thought Sean made a low sound of pleasure, but he might just have felt it through his hands, he wasn't sure.

Sean cradled Corey's head and pressed firmer kisses to his mouth. At the soft, warm feel of Sean's tongue gliding across his lower lip, Corey gasped quietly. Sean flicked his tongue teasingly over Corey's mouth, lapping at him but never pushing inward or seeking entrance. It was fucking maddening. Corey licked at Sean's tongue, trying to urge him to push in, take things further, but Sean only flicked the tip of his tongue against Corey's before he darted away.

Sean's fingers tightened slightly on Corey's head and he changed the angle once more. Corey sighed when Sean's mouth pressed hard against his, tongue finally seeking entrance past his lips. Corey opened eagerly, licking at Sean's mouth and finally getting his first, heady taste.

His blood was fire in his veins. Corey fisted his hand in Sean's shirt and gripped his arm tight enough he thought he'd leave bruises. He let Sean hold him steady as their tongues tasted and tested one another. Corey dragged harsh breaths in through his nose and heard Sean do the same. He wanted to pull Sean into his arms and flush against his body.

Except he couldn't ignore the fact that his dick wasn't getting hard. He had the most beautiful man he'd ever known kissing him stupid and Corey's cock wasn't showing the least signs of stirring. He wanted Sean, badly, so it had to be the alcohol. That, and he was tired and drained. Corey hoped Sean didn't step in closer because he'd get the wrong idea.

He was vaguely aware of the sound of an engine behind him. Sean pulled back from the kiss with a soft, wet sound. Corey opened his eyes slowly to find Sean watching him closely, pupils blown wide and lids heavy.

"Your taxi is here," Sean said just above a whisper, inclining his head toward the window.

"Guess that means I have to go," Corey replied, reluctantly untangling himself from Sean.

"If you have trouble sleeping this week, or wake up from a nightmare, call me," said Sean as he covered Corey's hand on the door handle. "Let's see if a friendly voice to talk to might work better than a lot of alcohol."

Corey doubted it, but he'd known after his talk with Jonah that he had to get his drinking back under control. "I'll give it a try, as long as you're sure."

Again, Sean lifted a hand to cradle the back of Corey's neck. He skimmed his thumb along Corey's lower lip. "I am."

Corey kissed the pad of Sean's thumb, pushed the door open and crossed the street to the waiting taxi.

CHAPTER FIVE

Corey slept fitfully and finally gave up all together around noon. He showered, dressed, got in his Jeep and left base.

As he drove, he called Tyler Howe.

"Hey, man, what's up?" Tyler answered.

"Has the platoon been notified yet that Nygaard was arrested last night?" Corey asked without preamble.

"No shit?" Tyler laughed. "He get drunk and punch somebody?"

"He beat his girlfriend to death," Corey said angrily. "Did you guys even know he had a girlfriend since we've been back?"

Tyler instantly sobered. "Fuck. Yeah, the guys have been giving him shit for moving in with her a couple of months ago. He pretty much just met her, so we've been calling him pussy whipped. He killed her?"

"That's what the cops say," replied Corey. "What are you doing right now?"

"Nothing important, why?"

"Meet me at the one-oh-one Diner," Corey said firmly, making it clear Tyler didn't really have a choice.

"Give me thirty mikes."

Corey finally let his mind wander to where it had wanted to go since he woke up; Sean. He ran his fingers over his lower lip as he remembered how it'd tingled at the feel of Sean's mouth sliding over his. Corey wanted to feel that again. He wanted to pull Sean against him and not have to stop and leave.

The 101 Diner was a greasy spoon on the south end of Encinitas, right on the 101 where it passed through the city. It wasn't much to look at but they made a spectacular roast beef sandwich with green chilies on it.

Corporal Tyler Howe walked in looking like a blue-eyed surfer kid, dressed in board shorts and a tank top. His buzzed haircut was the only thing that gave him away as a Marine.

"So how the fuck did you find out about Nygaard before command did?" Tyler said, sliding into the booth opposite Corey.

"I'm sure command knows about it now," Corey replied. "I just wondered if the scuttlebutt had reached troop level, yet."

"Not a fucking peep," Tyler said. "How the fuck did you find out?"

"He asked them to call me when they booked him." Corey glanced around to make sure no one was paying them any attention. He caught sight of the waitress heading their way so he held on to what he had to say next.

They each ordered the roast beef and green chili sandwich and a soda. After the waitress had brought their drinks, Corey continued.

"He wanted to talk to me 'cause, as he put it, I knew what happened to him and I knew why he is the way he is." Corey shrugged. "I went to see him as a friend and told them to call your command."

Tyler stared at him, wide-eyed. In so many ways he was still a sweet kid from Texas, not yet completely hardened by combat and the Corps. "What the fuck did he mean by all that?" Corey watched as Tyler paled. "He's not talking about Ghazni, is he?"

"It started to sound like it." Corey rubbed at the tension in his neck. "He never really said anything completely lucid. He said things like I knew what we were ordered to do. I knew what the women are like over there, as if that justified his beating his civilian girlfriend to death stateside."

"Jesus. With his bare hands?" Tyler asked incredulously. "That shit ain't right."

"He looked like he'd been in a firefight, but it was a Marine against one civilian woman." Corey shook his head in disgust. "I don't think I want to know what she looked like."

"I still don't understand why he had them call you, man. You've made it obvious you hate his guts since we've been back." Tyler was playing with the condensation on his glass.

This surprised Corey. "I have? I didn't mean to. I tried to hide it. I don't want to hang out with him like this but that shouldn't affect how we function as Marines."

"I always knew you didn't like him a whole lot when we were in Afghanistan, but you put up with him." Tyler sat back in the booth and leveled his gaze at Corey. "But after that day, after we got home, there've been times I thought you were gonna pull your Ka-Bar on him. The best thing that ever happened was your promotion and transfer to BRC."

Corey stared at Tyler in stunned silence. He hadn't realized his dislike of Nygaard had escalated after the events in Ghazni. He said nothing when the waitress brought their food and refilled their glasses.

When they were alone again, he said quietly, "Nygaard said I ordered him to do it. Do you remember what I ordered him to do except secure the perimeter of the house?"

"Nope," Tyler answered around his food. "That's all you told him to do."

"Did anything happen with the transporting of bodies that was out of the ordinary?" Corey's stomach finally eased enough he thought he could eat.

"We ran out of body bags again." Tyler shoved a French fry into his mouth with a shrug.

"That I remember," sighed Corey.

"Did he say anything else?"

"Not really. He laid hands on me and they dragged me out of the cell."

Tyler snorted. "Nygaard never was very bright. It sure sucks to be you, right now. First this investigation hanging over your head, now Nygaard is trying to suck you into his bullshit drama."

Corey shook his head emphatically. "He's on his own with

that shit. If he can get a doctor to say he was out of his mind with PTS, fine, but I'm not gonna say it."

"Are you *sure* we don't have anything to worry about with this investigation?" Tyler again seemed like the young kid he really still was.

"We didn't do anything wrong and unless you lied in your after action reports about stuff you knew was happening, we have nothing to worry about." Corey started to wonder if something very bad had happened that he was unaware of. It sure seemed like some people thought he knew all about it, though.

As they left the diner, Corey said to Tyler, "Keep your mouth shut about all of this shit. Keep your ears open and let me know what the scuttlebutt says about everything."

"You want me to do recon on my own platoon?" Tyler seemed dubious.

"It's starting to look like something happened that day that got covered up," replied Corey. "Do you really want to be on the wrong side of that when Kellan Reynolds gets to the bottom of it?"

Tyler's expression darkened. "Jesus, Corey, you're talking about Marines we served with. Don't they have any honor?" He glanced around, as if he was trying to come to terms with his shifting reality. "Right. Ears open, mouth shut. Got it."

They embraced briefly, loud backslaps making it brotherly, before they climbed into their vehicles and left.

For the rest of the day, Corey resisted the urge to stop and buy several bottles of Jack. He was going to try this thing with calling Sean, even if it was just an excuse to talk to him. The very first classroom day Master Sergeant Whitfield scheduled, Corey was taking himself to the on-base clinic to get something appropriate to help him sleep.

He could feel the shit storm coming and he couldn't afford to be caught out as a drunk. Besides, it was affecting his dick's ability to get hard and that was a no-go.

Corey took a second shower, as warm as was comfortable to try to relax his tense muscles. He set his alarm and cell phone to wake him, and crawled into his rack. He wondered how long he should lay there not sleeping before he gave up and called Sean.

Thoughts of Sean triggered memories of that kiss. Corey still couldn't get over how fucking arousing it had been. He never thought a soft, slow kiss could be so intimate. He was used to hot mouths, wet tongues and muffled noises in dark corners. Corey wanted more of the slow kisses, but this time without any interruptions.

Remembering the kiss made his dick stir in his skivvies. He was sober so maybe he could get hard. Coming would certainly help him get to sleep. He slid his hand inside his drawers and gave his cock a few experimental strokes. He kept his eyes closed and remembered Sean pressing their foreheads together, looking into his eyes and stroking his thumb over Corey's lip.

Corey's erection grew in his hand. It hardened beneath his fingers. He stroked himself harder and faster, deciding he might be able to come this time. He knew what it felt like to have Sean's mouth on his and Sean's tongue against his own. Now, Corey imagined what it would be like to feel that tongue on his cock.

The mental image of Sean's hazel eyes staring up at him from between Corey's legs was all it took. Corey's back arched and his balls tightened as he came. His cock twitched in his fist and he felt warm spunk land on his skivvy shirt. Fuck, it felt good. His body just hadn't been very cooperative since he'd been back.

Taking off his shirt, Corey chucked it across the room, glad he'd just done laundry and had plenty. As he settled back down against his pillow, Corey's body relaxed. He was warm and languorous. Sleep crept over him slowly at first, before abruptly dragging him all the way under.

A part of him knew he was safe in his bed, but even that didn't help.

The gunfire erupted around them and Corey fell out of the Humvee, scrambling for cover. All around him, Marines shouted and swore. In the distance, Lieutenant Adams shouted orders. Desperate screams nearby told Corey Marines were wounded. The smell of explosives was heavy in the air. AK47 rounds bounced all around and slammed into the sides of the Humvees.

Lieutenant Adams was beside him. He ordered Corey to punch out toward the house sitting on the low rise. Once there, he was to neutralize the threats he found inside.

Corey quickly made his way to the house. He took cover along the way behind shattered walls and blown out vehicles. When the small arms fire from inside the house slackened, Corey darted for the front door of the house. He kicked in the front door, lifted his weapon to his shoulder, and made entry.

Silence fell around him and Corey smelled blood. He smelled a lot of blood. Corey glanced around him in horror. The room was filled with bodies. Dead bodies. Their blank eyes stared up at him accusingly. Blood ran thick on the floor; it covered the bodies of the dead, splattered up the sides of the walls.

He was surrounded by the bodies of slaughtered women and children.

Corey sat straight up in his rack, a shout dying in his throat. He was drenched in sweat and breathing raggedly. His heart was beating out of his chest. Corey raised his hands to wipe the sweat from his face and realized they were trembling.

All he could remember was an endless sea of eyes staring at him with accusation.

He sat up and pushed the sheet away, swinging his feet to the floor. A glance at the clock told him it was two a.m.

Corey snatched his cell phone from the bedside table and called Sean. It was answered after a single ring.

"Are you okay?" Sean's deep, smooth voice drifted across the connection.

Immediately, Corey felt soothed, the tension in his muscles easing slightly. "Bad dream," he replied, resting his elbows on his knees and closing his eyes to just listen.

"But you're awake now and nothing can harm you." Sean's voice was soft and reassuring. "I'm here with you now. Tell me about the dream."

Corey sucked in a harsh breath. He didn't want to remember. He didn't want to say the words. He wanted Sean to distract him until the memories faded. "I don't want to talk about it. I just want to forget it."

"That's fine," Sean agreed easily, "maybe next time. Talking about it might help you identify what it was that caused all this. Writing it down, changing how the dream ends."

The soft strains of guitar music drifted over the connection. "Is that you playing?" Corey asked, hoping for a distraction.

"Yep. I'm talking to you with my Bluetooth so I can be 'hands-free'," Sean replied.

Corey sat up, shifting his feet restlessly. "I didn't mean to interrupt anything. I'll let you go."

"You're not interrupting anything," Sean said quickly. "Lie down, make sure you're relaxed and comfortable, and let's talk."

Corey gave a surprised laugh. "I didn't call for phone sex, but if you insist." He lay back in his rack and focused on slowing his breathing.

Sean's laugh was husky and heat spread through Corey's chest, even as his lower belly tightened with desire. He vividly remembered successfully getting himself off to a fantasy of Sean.

"Mutual orgasms weren't on my agenda but I'm willing to consider it as a last resort. So, tell me about your day," Sean said, the strumming of the guitar continuing in the background. Corey bit back a groan at Sean's words.

"How did you sleep? Any news on Sergeant Nygaard's situation?"

"No nightmare last night," he sighed, letting his eyes drift closed. "I still didn't sleep well, but it's been worse. I had lunch with my corporal from my old platoon. They hadn't been notified about Nygaard yet, so nothing new to report."

"So you don't hate everyone from your old platoon, if you had lunch with a corporal." There was a pregnant pause. "You called him *your* corporal; do the two of you have history?"

Corey *knew* Sean's casual tone was feigned. "No, I was a Team Leader in Afghanistan, and he was literally my corporal and Humvee driver. Strictly a military designation. He's a good kid. A good Marine. He had my back during the FUBAR event that's under investigation so I want to make sure to I have his now."

The music paused. "Good. Glad to hear it." Sean sounded distracted. The music started up again.

"What did you do today?" Corey asked, aching to feel Sean's voice flow over him.

"I put together some audition pieces and started practicing a few of them." Sean played the same series of notes over and over, as if trying to master the sequence. Corey thought he detected a slight change toward the end. "Yes, that's it," Sean said, just above a whisper. The music stopped.

"What are you auditioning for?" Corey was genuinely interested in the answer. He realized he was going to find out what of Sean's previous work he'd be able to get his hands on to watch. He was certainly going to check out his future work, too.

The music began again. Corey liked the melody he could hear, even though he didn't recognize it.

"Let's see," Sean said slowly. "I have an audition for a play at the Old Globe. I have a callback for a musical at the La Jolla Playhouse. I've got several readings for TV shows, but those will come down to whether or not I have the right look for them. And, an audition for a recurring part in an existing series."

"Wow." Corey didn't know what else to say. "Aimee told me you graduated from USC. You're good at this, aren't you?"

"Pretty good, yep. Getting better with each job I do." The song Sean was playing seemed to increase in intensity.

"Good enough to audition for a part in your own TV show?"

Corey asked.

Sean laughed and the sound made Corey smile.

"Not my own show, no. Just guest roles on other people's shows. Most of the new starring roles get cast during the first part of the year and are filmed during pilot season in March." Sean sounded distracted again. The music paused briefly before starting up again.

"You sound busy," Corey said. "Should I let you go?"

"No, you should not," Sean said firmly. "I have an audition with HBO in a few weeks. I might get lucky and get picked up for one of their new off season series. One of the good ones that only has a thirteen episode season and the writers worry about quality instead of advertising."

"That would be cool," Corey said around a yawn. He tugged his blanket up around his chest. "I could tell everyone I knew you before you were rich and famous."

"Fuck that," Sean said hotly. The music stopped all together. "You'll visit me on set and wait for me in my trailer so you can cater to my every, egomaniacal whim."

Corey laughed, a nearly forgotten sense of joy welling up inside of him. "I'll retire from the Corps and become your personal bodyguard."

The now-familiar notes of music began again. Corey thought he could actually make out the structure of a song.

"Now that is a spectacular plan," Sean said with a laugh.

Corey lapsed into silence as he lay listening to Sean's fingers move expertly over the strings. It occurred to him that Sean might have been writing this song as they talked. He'd have to ask.

"Are you still with me?" Sean's voice was like a caress.

Corey gasped, realizing he'd lost time. "I think I might have drifted off for a minute."

"Good." Sean's voice was quiet, but in the deep of the night, it felt like he was right there with Corey. "That's what I wanted.

Think you can sleep through the night now?"

Corey burrowed deeper into his rack, tucking the covers around his shoulders. He had his cell on his pillow and his ear resting on it. He took a deep breath and let it out slowly, his eyelids too heavy to stay open. "Yeah, I think I can," he muttered.

"Good. Call me again tomorrow if you need to." There was a long pause. "Hang up your phone, Corey."

"'Kay. Thanks," he snuffled against his pillow. "G'night."

"Good night."

Corey managed to end the call and slide his phone to the bed beside him. The next thing he knew, his bedside alarm clock was jolting him awake.

CHAPTER SIX

Corey stepped into the BRC offices early Monday morning, feeling more rested and refreshed than he had in longer than he could remember. They had classroom sessions this week and he was going to take advantage of the schedule and get himself to the doctor.

"Good morning, Master Sergeant," he greeted.

Whitfield looked up and his expression darkened when he saw Corey. "Staff Sergeant Yarwood, you were supposed to be my easy Marine," he said.

Corey's stomach plummeted. "Master Sergeant?"

Picking up several stacks of papers, Whitfield began to read, "Today at fifteen hundred hours, you're to report and be interviewed in conjunction with a DOD investigation into the events surrounding an incident during your last deployment." Whitfield tossed aside one of the sheaves of papers. "The District Attorney needs to interview you regarding statements made last night by Sergeant Michael Nygaard." Another group of papers fell to the desk. "The defense attorney for Sergeant Michael Nygaard is demanding an interview as well."

Corey drew himself to attention and stared at a spot on the wall just beyond Master Sergeant Whitfield. His blood rushed in his ears at the realization that his life was spiraling out of his control. Christ. When had Corey ever really had control?

"At ease, Staff Sergeant," Whitfield said with a dismissive wave of his hand. "All indications are that you haven't done a damn thing wrong."

Corey was weak with relief as he stood at ease. "I have done nothing to shame myself or the Corps, Master Sergeant," Corey replied.

Whitfield picked up the summons for Kellan's investigation. He shook his head slowly. "What the fuck happened in Ghazni,

Yarwood?"

"Beg your pardon?" Corey swallowed hard, hoping the question was rhetorical.

"Everything seems to stem from whatever it was that happened in Ghazni," Whitfield said. "Whatever it is that's being covered up has to do with what Nygaard allegedly did the other night. Now he wants to claim that what happened there was so traumatic he wasn't responsible for his own actions."

"Honestly, Master Sergeant, I don't know what happened in Ghazni." Corey sighed heavily. "At least I don't know what it is they're covering up. I don't even know who's doing the covering up."

"Reynolds sure has his work cut out for him," Whitfield muttered. "How did you get sucked into this shit with this Nygaard?"

"Completely against my will," Corey said through clenched teeth. "He asked for me to be called at the time he was booked into Vista jail. I responded as a *friend*, Master Sergeant. I may hate his guts but he's a fellow Marine."

"Understood, Staff Sergeant," Whitfield replied. "I expect you to continue to provide honest and honorable assistance in this matter."

"Should I speak with a JAG officer?" Corey asked.

Whitfield's head snapped up and his eyes narrowed. "What the fuck for, if you haven't done anything wrong?"

"This thing with Nygaard goes outside of the Corps," replied Corey. "I don't want to unknowingly say or do anything to embarrass or damage the Corps."

Whitfield regarded Corey intently for several long moments. "If you have concerns in that regard, by all means make contact."

"Yes, Master Sergeant. Thank you." Corey added that to his growing list of things he needed to do this week.

"As for today, you will report to Division HQ at fifteen hundred hours for your interview with the DOD investigation."

Whitfield handed Corey the written order to appear.

"Yes, Master Sergeant." Corey hesitated. "We're scheduled for classroom instruction time later this week, correct?"

"Affirmative." Whitfield looked at him questioningly.

"I need to schedule a medical appointment, if time allows." Corey worded his request carefully.

"Is the cold not clearing up?" Whitfield asked.

"It's fine," Corey assured him quickly. "Nothing wrong that will affect my job performance, I promise."

"I'm not worried about your job performance, Staff Sergeant." Whitfield watched Corey shrewdly. "You do what you have to do to take care of yourself."

Corey gave a sharp nod, acknowledging the Master Sergeant's accurate assumption. "I'll coordinate with the schedule and advise you of the appointment time."

At 1430 hours, Corey notified Whitfield he was stepping off to report to Division HQ. He also told the Master Sergeant the date and time of his medical appointment he'd scheduled for later that week. Corey climbed into his Jeep and drove the several miles from the Basic Recon training facility to the building that housed 1st Marine Division's headquarters.

Unlike most of the facilities on Camp Pendleton, Division HQ wasn't dull and utilitarian. It was an attractive structure with painted walls, thick Berber carpet, and sturdy wooden office furniture.

Entering the quiet building with its rarified air, Corey removed his cover and folded it into a leg pocket on his trousers. His orders had specified utilities were appropriate but Corey felt like he should be in his olive green service uniform.

Approaching the civilian Admin seated behind a low desk, Corey said, "Staff Sergeant Corey Yarwood, reporting as ordered, ma'am."

"They're waiting for you, Staff Sergeant," she replied levelly. "Follow me, please." She rose and led Corey to a heavy door of dark wood.

When she reached for the handle, Corey leapt forward. He also reached for the handle, careful not to make contact with the woman. "Let me get that for you, ma'am."

"Thank you, Staff Sergeant." She stepped back and waited for him to open the door and hold it for her. She had the calm air of someone who was used to this ritual.

Corey followed her down a short hallway, their footsteps muted by the thick carpet. She paused outside of an open doorway and indicated he was to enter.

"Thank you, ma'am," Corey said, giving a slight bow as he passed her.

"You're welcome, Staff Sergeant." She closed the door behind him.

Corey found himself in a small conference room. Directly ahead was a long table of dark wood. On Corey's side of the table was a single, well padded chair. It was a hell of a lot nicer than the conference room chairs in the training facility.

Seated behind the table were two men and a woman. Corey froze. Neither Kellan nor Jonah were anywhere in sight. The Earth seemed to tilt beneath his feet. He took a deep breath and fisted his hands at his sides.

"Have a seat Staff Sergeant," said the man seated in the center. He wore the olive green of the Marine Corps' service uniform.

Corey briskly crossed the room. The man on the left was civilian. Up close, Corey identified the other two as Marine Corps captains.

Standing behind the single chair, Corey snapped to attention and saluted. When his salute was returned, Corey sat down. His feet were flat on the floor, spine straight, palms resting on his thighs.

"Relax, Staff Sergeant," the officer in the center said. "We're just asking questions today. Nothing you haven't answered before."

"Yes, sir." Corey didn't relax his posture.

The captain picked up a small black device. He pointed it at the end of the table. Corey saw a video camera pointed right at him. The red light came on and the officer set down the small remote.

"Staff Sergeant Yarwood, to my right is NCIS Special Agent Chris Hoffman."

"Sir." Corey greeted. The agent gave Corey a quick, easy smile.

"To my left is the Marine Corps representative to these proceedings, Captain Madeline Evans."

"Ma'am." Corey inclined his head respectfully in her direction.

"Staff Sergeant," Captain Evans replied, her expression open and pleasant.

"And I am Captain Mirai Hirata with the Marine Corps Judge Advocate Services." The lawyer's dark eyes held Corey's steadily. His eyebrows lifted quizzically as he made sure Corey understood who all the players were.

Corey's gut twisted painfully. "Sir? May I ask why NCIS and the J.A.S. are involved?"

Captain Hirata now looked puzzled. "This is a criminal investigation, Staff Sergeant. But don't be concerned, you're a witness, not a subject of the investigation."

That didn't comfort Corey as much as it was probably intended to. "It's just that I was told Kellan Reynolds was conducting the investigation, sir."

"He is. He's heading up the investigation. We're gathering information on his behalf and under his direction," Hirata replied.

Corey gave himself a mental kick in the ass. He should have known this wasn't going to be as easy as a casual chat with Kellan and Jonah. "Yes, sir. Understood, sir."

The questions began where they always did. Corey was asked to recall the date and time of the incident in Ghazni, Afghanistan.

He recalled the IED blast that claimed the lives of three Marines. Corey was then ordered by his Lieutenant to take half of the platoon and make entry into a nearby house where they were being fired upon. Corey had taken his men into the house. Once the house was secure and the enemy neutralized, Corey had ordered Sergeant Nygaard to take a team of five Marines and secure the perimeter of the house.

Corey and his men gathered up the corpses of the men they had killed and returned to the Humvees. He found his platoon commander, Lieutenant Dominic Adams, had led an assault on an enemy vehicle that had approached their position.

With everything secured and their casualties loaded into the Humvees, the platoon was RTB—return to base—he elaborated, not sure if his audience had seen combat to know the radio jargon. Corey completed and submitted his after action. As far as he had been concerned, the incident was behind them all.

Until they had returned home and Corey had begun to hear the scuttlebutt. He'd cooperated with the Marine Corps' investigation and, once again, had thought it was all in the past.

Corey completed his story and expected to be dismissed, as he always had been in the past. He watched the three people in front of him consult reports and other documents. They shared the notes they had each written as Corey had told his story.

"We have some questions for you now, Staff Sergeant," Captain Evans said.

"Yes, ma'am." Corey replied. His leg bounced violently. He swallowed hard, his mouth dry as a bone. If he was a witness, this shouldn't be adversarial. Corey cleared his throat. "Excuse me, Captains. Is it possible to get some water?"

"Of course." The reply came from Special Agent Hoffman. Corey watched him retrieve a bottle of chilled water from a small table across the room. As he handed Corey the bottle, he asked, "Is there anything else you need? This is pretty grueling."

The cool water was soothing on Corey's dry mouth and throat. He downed half of the bottle before answering. "Not as grueling as the incident itself, sir."

"No, of course not," Hoffman said gravely. His expression darkened, his eyes held shadows Corey recognized in those who had seen violence and death.

"All due respect, I'll be happy when this is finally resolved and I don't have to keep reliving it." Corey shocked himself with his confession.

"Is there any one thing that bothers you to think about, more than anything else?" inquired Captain Evans.

Corey's mind went blank. The loud crunching of the bottle in his hand startled him. He looked down, surprised to see his own hand crushing the plastic. "No, ma'am," he choked in response.

"All right then," she said carefully, making notes on her legal pad. "When Lieutenant Adams ordered you to take half of the platoon and make entry into the nearby structure, did he specify what course of action you were to take in order to execute your mission?"

No one had asked that question before. Corey thought back to that day, replaying in his mind the words the LT has used and what his responses had been. "No ma'am. His orders were to enter the structure and neutralize the enemy firing on our position."

"What was your understanding of how you were to execute your orders?" Evans pressed. "As a Recon Marine, you're used to functioning with minimal instruction and supervision."

"That's correct ma'am." Corey was heartened by the fact that Captain Evans didn't seem disdainful of Recon, despite their reputations for being arrogant. "I executed my mission according to Marine Corps regs and training, and under the current ROE."

Evans made a notation on her pad. "And when you made contact inside the house, what did you find?"

Corey paused, picturing the scene as he and Tyler had pushed through the door, weapons raised and firing. He identified a room full of hostiles, all armed. Corey squeezed off two rounds.

Tyler's M16 chattered beside him, doing the same. More Marines entered from a different doorway to their left. Across the room, several more combatants fell to the floor.

The noise level dropped slightly. Corey sighted at a man directly ahead pointing an AK47 in their direction. Two quick and light squeezes of his trigger and Corey watched the man fall. Two more loud cracks sounded beside him as Tyler fired. The last man standing dropped to the floor, leaving only U.S. Marines on their feet.

In his mind's eye, Corey quickly counted seven neutralized enemy combatants. Once the firefight was over, he and Tyler had moved around to ensure they were all dead and that all weapons were accounted for.

"My men and I successfully neutralized seven hostiles with a minimal amount of gunfire exchanged. I then secured ten AK47s, several cases of ammo and a crate of grenades." Corey's answer was perfunctory.

"Did the detachment remain together throughout the action?" Evans asked.

It was a leading question. Corey was on the record as having sent Sergeant Nygaard with a team to secure the perimeter of the house and check for additional, hidden threats.

"Once we had neutralized the threats inside of the house, I ordered Sergeant Michael Nygaard to take a team of five men and secure the perimeter," Corey replied.

"Did you order Sergeant Nygaard to take any specific action beyond the securing of the perimeter?"

"No, ma'am," Corey answered almost before the captain had stopped speaking. He'd been ready for that particular question. "The order I gave specified a single task for him to execute, and was to be carried out according to our training and the standing ROE."

All three of them made notes on their legal pads.

"Who reported to you that Sergeant Nygaard had successfully

completed his mission?" Captain Hirata asked, surprising Corey.

Things had happened so quickly, his memories of these particular events were hazy. Corey struggled to recall who had reported to him. He twisted his hands around the water bottle. Corey's knee bounced violently as he couldn't locate the memory. His chest heaved with every breath, Corey almost couldn't hear over the sound of his heart thundering in his ears.

"I...I sought out Nygaard and his men." Corey vaguely remembered exiting the house through the rear entrance. He was sweating in all of his gear, adrenaline flooding his system like it always did in combat. The cold air of Ghazni felt good on his flushed and sweaty face.

"And when you located him?" Hirata pressed.

The room spun. Corey swallowed back nausea. "I ordered him to collapse the perimeter and return with us to the Humvees," Corey answered through clenched teeth.

His answer met with silence.

"Where on the perimeter did you locate Sergeant Nygaard?" Hirata asked in a level voice, his expression implacable.

"I don't recall the exact location." Corey shook his head, trying to clear it. "At least not now. I don't remember what my after action reports might contain. Events were more clear at that time."

"Staff Sergeant Yarwood, relax and take a couple of deep breaths," Captain Evans ordered. She wore a concerned expression that confused Corey.

Taking another drink of water, Corey realized his hands were trembling. He took several deep, cleansing breaths. He flexed his fingers, working the stiffness out of knuckles. Corey rolled his tense shoulders and stretched the tightness in his lower back.

"That's better," Evans said, giving him an encouraging smile. "Now, when you located Sergeant Nygaard, what did he say to you?"

"That he had successfully completed his mission," Corey

replied. He gasped as a memory flashed through his mind. Nygaard, staring up at him, eyes wild and hate filled. He'd said something and Corey had very nearly lifted his weapon and pointed it at a fellow Marine.

Why the fuck had he felt that way?

"What action did you take next?" Evans asked.

"I ordered him to collapse the perimeter," Corey answered readily. "We gathered up the bodies of the hostiles we had neutralized, to document our adherence to the ROE and ensure they were returned to appropriate family members. I ordered the platoon to return to the Humvees, where I reported a successful completion of my mission to Lieutenant Adams."

Corey could tell by their faces that he had provided more information than they had asked for. He hadn't intended to control the interview but the officers hadn't missed his sudden, uncharacteristic verbosity.

"When you rejoined the rest of your platoon, did you see evidence of further combat?" Hirata asked.

"There was a small, white vehicle that had been disabled by gunfire, sir," Corey answered. "The dead bodies of four Arab males lay beside the vehicle. The LT informed me that the vehicle had engaged them with hostile intent and they had neutralized the threat."

"Did you have occasion to examine the bodies, Staff Sergeant?" Special Agent Hoffman asked.

"Examine, sir?" Corey confirmed curiously. "No. During the execution of my duties, I observed wounds consistent with two-two-three rounds."

"And what duties were you executing?" questioned Hoffman.

"Securing the bodies for transport so they could be documented and returned to family," replied Corey.

Hoffman continued his line of questioning. "Did you assist with any of the documentation?"

"Only with the hostiles from inside the house." Corey was

sure these details were in all of his reports, so he wondered what the agent was trying to confirm.

Hoffman scanned the papers in front of him. "Who handled the documentation of the combatants from the hostile vehicle?" His pen was poised, ready to make a notation.

"The Lieutenant oversaw that, sir." Corey wished he could see what all of their notes said.

"Were some of the bodies transported back to base on the hoods of Humvees, Staff Sergeant?" Captain Evans asked abruptly.

"Yes, ma'am," Corey replied, switching his attention to her. "As unfortunate as that was, it couldn't be helped."

"Why was that?" she asked, as if she already knew the answer.

"We didn't have enough body bags for the number of bodies we had to transport, ma'am." Corey paused until she nodded for him to continue. "In an effort to prevent incidents of PTS in Marines, we do not transport un-bagged bodies *inside* of the Humvees with U.S. personnel."

Captain Evans glanced at Captain Hirata. It was Hirata who asked, "To your knowledge, were any of the bodies shown any disrespect or subjected to any desecration?"

Corey's blood turned to ice. He stared at Captain Hirata, unable to formulate a reply. It wasn't a question he'd been asked before and it finally gave Corey a clue as to what might be driving this investigation. "No, sir, I did not. I neither gave, nor received any orders for my Marines to behave without honor. Had I observed any such inappropriate behavior, it would have included it in my after action reports."

"Who did you submit your completed reports to, Staff Sergeant?" Hoffman asked quickly.

"My platoon commander, sir." Another question Corey was sure they knew the answer to. "Lieutenant Dominic Adams."

"Have you read any of your reports *after* they were submitted to and approved by Lieutenant Adams?"

Corey very nearly answered yes. "I have not had access to my reports since submitting them. I only have my original drafts, which I read through before interviews such as this one."

"Is that a no, Staff Sergeant?" Hoffman lifted a single eyebrow.

"It's a no, sir."

Hoffman's nod told Corey he'd anticipated that answer.

"Have you been approached by anyone regarding how to answer our questions here today?" asked Hirata.

Corey should have been surprised by that question. "Early last week, I encountered members of my former platoon in a public area here on base. When Corporal Tyler Howe inquired as to whether we should be concerned about this investigation, I informed him that because we did nothing wrong, we had no need to worry. Sergeant Michael Nygaard attempted to recruit those of us there into coordinating stories."

The three interviewers conferred quietly with one another. Corey finished the last of the water in the bottle.

"That's all we have for you now, Staff Sergeant," Captain Hirata said. "You're subject to recall as we progress, though."

"Understood, sir." Corey stood at attention. "Captain Hirata, is it possible to have a moment of your time?"

The three interviewers looked at him in surprise.

"Is it regarding this investigation?" Hirata asked.

"Indirectly, sir," Corey answered. "I'm going to have to answer questions regarding the incident Saturday night involving Sergeant Nygaard."

Hirata nodded his understanding. "Give us five minutes?" he asked his companions. When they were alone, the captain told Corey he could resume his seat. He carried his own chair around the table and closer to Corey's.

"Relax, Staff Sergeant," Hirata said with a smile. "This is an informal conversation."

"Thank you, sir." Corey took a deep breath. "When I saw

Nygaard in jail on Saturday, he made reference to something I think might be this incident. He said I ordered him to do things, but he wasn't specific."

"What do the events in Ghazni have to do with his murdering his girlfriend?" the captain asked.

Corey sighed explosively and ran a hand over his the bristles of his hair. "I don't know, a PTS defense, maybe? I want to cooperate but not at the expense of the Marine Corps."

"Let's do what we can to prevent that," Hirata replied. "Have both the prosecution and defense requested interviews?"

Corey nodded, relieved at the attorney's reaction.

"Have the Master Sergeant forward copies of the requests to me. We'll make sure you don't have to run the gauntlet alone." Hirata's smile was warm and reassuring.

"Thank you, sir. I appreciate that." Corey wanted to ask if his suspicions about the motivation for this investigation were accurate. He decided against it.

Captain Hirata seemed to notice Corey's hesitation. "Is there anything else I can help you with?"

"No, sir, but thank you." He just wanted to get out of this room. He needed to be alone to think.

Captain Hirata dismissed him. Corey fled the conference room once he had his salute returned.

Climbing into his Jeep, Corey slammed the door. He retrieved his cell phone from its hiding spot beneath the seat. He pulled up Tyler's number and called it, closing his eyes and willing Howe to be able to answer.

"Hey, man. How'd it go?" Tyler sounded calm and friendly.

"Fine, I guess," Corey replied. "I got asked questions nobody's asked before, though."

"Yeah? Like what?" A note of concern laced Tyler's voice.

"Did you see anybody fuck with the bodies we took back to base?" he asked.

"Hell no!" There was a long pause. "Jesus Christ, did somebody really do that kind of shit?"

Corey's leg was bouncing in agitation again. "I don't know. Is anybody in the platoon talking about anything like that?"

"No, but what I am hearing is shit about those guys in the car not being armed."

"Fuck," Corey spat. "Did the LT know?"

"Guys that were there say the Lieutenant gave the order."

"This is so FUBAR." Corey stared blindly out the windscreen.

There were noises in the background of the call. Corey heard muffled voices.

"Dude, I gotta get back to work," Tyler said hastily.

"Call me later," Corey replied and ended the call. He closed his eyes and leaned his head back against the seat. He should get back to work, there were still a couple hours of training left to conduct. He just needed a moment.

He replayed the events of Ghazni in his head. He remembered ordering Corporal Howe to keep the house secure while he went out after Nygaard. Why? And why didn't he remember what happened after he left the house?

Corey had trouble catching his breath. His heart raced. Opening his eyes, he located Sean's phone number and called it.

"Hey, did you sleep okay the rest of the night?" Sean's smooth voice was warm and comforting.

"Yeah, thanks," Corey replied, out of breath. Why was he out of breath?

"Corey, what's wrong?" Sean's voice was calm but now it held a note of worry.

"Nothing. I don't know," he gasped. He couldn't get enough air and his heart beat so fast it hurt.

"Where are you?" Sean asked sharply.

"In my car," he answered and tried to take a deep breath.

"Jesus Christ, you're not driving are you?" Sean sounded panicked.

Fuck. Corey didn't mean to scare Sean. What the hell was wrong with him? He couldn't get a damn thing right. "No. I'm parked."

"Are you on the base?"

"Yeah," Corey gasped.

"Give me a second to pull over," Sean muttered. "Did something happen?"

"No," he answered weakly.

Why the fuck couldn't he remember leaving the house in Ghazni? Why couldn't he breathe? Why was his heart pounding? Corey tugged at the neck of his skivvy shirt. It was too tight and was cutting off his air. His hand shook. He wrapped it around the steering wheel, hoping that would steady him. He gripped his cell phone so tight his fingers ached.

"Corey, tell me what's wrong." Sean's voice was quiet but firm.

"Can't catch my breath," he replied between gasps. "Fucking heart's coming out of my chest." The accusatory eyes of the dead women and children from his nightmare were suddenly very vivid in his mind. Corey jammed his feet into the foot well, as if he could push the images away.

"Listen to me, Corey," Sean said in a low voice. Corey envied his calm. "Put your phone on speaker and set it down close by."

Corey wanted to ask why but he didn't have enough breath to form the words. Stiffly, he lowered the phone so he could see the display. It took several moments for Corey to get his hand to cooperate and relax its hold on the phone.

"Are you still there?" Sean's soothing voice filled the inside of the Jeep.

"Yeah," Corey whispered.

"Rest both hands on top of your thighs. Just let them rest there, don't make fists."

Corey stared at the white knuckles of his hand that held the steering wheel in a death grip. He concentrated hard until his fingers peeled away. He let his hands fall into his lap.

"Corey?"

"Yeah. Okay," he answered, voice hoarse.

"Close your eyes and let your head rest against the back of the seat."

Corey complied. His mouth was open wide as he struggled to get enough air into his lungs.

"Are you still with me, Corey?"

"Yeah," he gasped his reply.

"Take slow, deep breaths. Breathe in through your nose and out through your mouth. Make sure you can count to eight with each breath."

Corey's chest heaved. He couldn't understand what Sean meant.

"Inhale through your nose, Corey," Sean repeated. "One. Two. Three. Four. Five. Six. Seven. Eight."

Corey tried but he couldn't slow his breathing that much.

"Exhale through your mouth now." Sean counted to eight. "Come on, do it again."

Corey focused on the sound of Sean's voice. He matched each breath to Sean's counting. He found a rhythm. Corey matched the rhythm of his breathing to the gentle sound of Sean's voice.

"Okay, you sound better now." Sean sounded less anxious. "If your hands are fisted, unclench them," he encouraged. "Stretch your neck and roll your shoulders to get them to relax. Just make sure to keep breathing slow and steady."

Corey obeyed as if Sean was an officer issuing orders. He didn't question and he didn't hesitate.

"Relax the muscles in your lower back and your legs."

Corey's feet were still jammed hard into the floor of the Jeep.

His legs and his hips screamed at him. He relaxed his legs and breathed through the sudden burn of the release of tension. When the discomfort passed, the relief was acute.

"Corey, how are you doing?" Concern was back in Sean's voice.

"Better," Corey replied quickly, wanting to reassure Sean he was okay. His breathing was steady and his heart wasn't slamming violently against his ribs anymore. Corey shook out his hands and rolled his neck. The pain in his chest eased and it was that much easier to breath. "I'm better now," he said, voice stronger.

"Good." Sean sighed explosively. "That was a full-blown anxiety attack. What brought that on?"

Corey had no fucking idea. "I just got out of my first interview for this investigation they're doing into the shit that went down in Afghanistan. But it wasn't a big deal. I just had to tell what I saw and did. Whatever went wrong didn't involve me."

"Okay, maybe it was just the stress of the interview itself on top of the shit that went down Saturday night," Sean suggested.

Corey gave a wry chuckle. He picked up his phone, took it off speaker and pressed it to his ear. "None of this is nearly as stressful as combat."

"Well, that's sort of the core problem itself, isn't it?" asked Sean.

Corey sobered. He knew Marines who had been through worse than he had and they hadn't lost their minds. He was at least as strong as they were. "I think I just got pissed at myself 'cause my memory of this one thing is hazy."

"Your memory is hazy?" Sean asked carefully.

"Yeah, it's just pissing me off. And then when I was trying to remember something that happened, for some reason that nightmare I had flashed through my mind."

"Corey, is there a professional you can talk to about your nightmares?" Sean sounded challenging, as if he expected Corey to argue.

Running a hand over the back of his still tense neck, Corey replied, "You sound just like Jonah." Immediately he regretted his words.

The sound of a car engine hummed in the background. Corey guessed Sean was driving once again. Guilt ate at him that he'd completely interrupted whatever Sean was in the middle of.

"I don't know who Jonah is, but if he thinks you should get some counseling I agree." Sean sounded distracted. "Does he know about the drinking?"

Corey sucked in a harsh breath in surprise. "He just assumed. Jonah encouraged me to get help for it a few years back." Hell. He just made himself sound like a fucked up mess.

"Maybe if you gave him a call he could help you again," Sean suggested stiffly.

Too much shit had changed. Corey had to get himself squared away this time. "We don't serve together anymore. I'm not his responsibility."

"Jonah's a fellow Marine?" Sean asked, sounding surprised.

"Yeah, he was my sergeant back in Iraq." Corey glanced at his watch. "Shit, I gotta get back to work. I'm sorry I even bothered you with this crap. You have things you need to do."

"Corey," Sean said loudly, breaking into Corey's rant. "Let's have dinner together tonight."

Jesus, that idea excited him. It was scary how much he wanted to see Sean again. "Class runs kinda late tonight," he hedged. "We average sixteen hour days."

"When have late nights ever been a problem for me?" Sean asked dryly.

There were plenty of enlisted cantinas, civilian restaurants, and fast food places on base, but Corey was getting damn sick of eating alone. He'd done a suck-ass job of staying in touch with friends since he'd been back. "Where do you want to go?"

"Just come to my place," answered Sean. "We won't have to worry about the time. I'll just have everything ready for when you can get there."

Corey hesitated. He still hadn't forgotten how his dick had refused to cooperate on Saturday night.

"Just dinner, Corey," Sean said, as if reading his mind. "I have to drive to L.A. tomorrow so no overnight guests."

"What's in L.A.?" he asked, before he could stop himself. It wasn't his business.

"Auditions, what else?" Sean replied.

"You can tell me about them tonight." Corey reached for the ignition, ready to head back to work.

"Call me when you leave the base so I know you're on your way. See you tonight, Corey."

CHAPTER SEVEN

Corey stood in front of the door to Sean's apartment. He tugged at the hem of his T-shirt and wiped his palms on the thighs of his jeans. Taking a deep breath, Corey gathered his courage and pressed the doorbell.

The door was opened quickly and Corey stopped breathing when he was face to face with Sean. "Hi," he greeted lamely.

"Hi," Sean replied simply. He wore an old, faded pair of jeans that hung low on his narrow hips. His T-shirt was as soft and faded as Corey's own.

At Sean's welcoming gesture, Corey stepped over the threshold. It looked like Sean was trying to suppress a smile and failing miserably at it. With Corey inside, Sean closed and locked the door.

Turning back to Sean, Corey struggled for something witty to say. His mind was wiped clean when Sean stepped in and slid his arms around Corey's chest. Reflexively, Corey wrapped his own arms around Sean and held him close.

"How are you feeling?" Sean asked, his lips moving lightly against the side of Corey's neck. "I was worried about you earlier."

Corey breathed deep and discovered Sean had showered recently. He smelled of spicy soap and musky shampoo. Corey detected a hint of cologne and to his joy and amazement, his cock shifted in his jeans. He ran his palms over Sean's muscular back, taking pleasure in the feel of his firm body pressed against his own.

"I'm fine now," Corey murmured against the warm skin below Sean's ear. "I'm sorry about earlier."

Sean pulled back out of his arms and Corey felt chilled in the sudden absence of his heat.

"Don't be sorry. You should always call me if you need my help," Sean replied. He skimmed his hands over Corey's chest.

"Thank you," Corey said, looking anywhere but at Sean.

"Are you hungry?" Sean asked, turning to walk down the short hall.

"Starving," Corey confessed, following him. "And something smells really good." He hoped the sounds his stomach was suddenly making weren't as loud as they seemed.

At the end of the hall, Sean turned right into the kitchen. Corey caught sight of the floor to ceiling windows that made up the entire far side of the great room. They were only on the second floor but the view was stunning.

"Wow," Corey blurted.

"That view is one of the main reasons I bought this place," Sean said from the kitchen. It was separated from the rest of the apartment by only a breakfast bar.

"You own this place? You're not renting?" Corey asked incredulously, crossing to look out at the canyon below.

Sean chuckled. "That always surprises people. I guess they assume I'm a starving artist. I get work pretty steadily so I make a damn good living."

Corey admired the mottled colors of the oak trees, chaparral, and Manzanita. "I'm actually not surprised, but I am impressed," he said.

"I don't know how impressive it is, but thanks," Sean replied with a hint of embarrassment. "Ordinarily, I'd open a bottle of wine with this, but tonight, all you get is soda."

Corey crossed to the kitchen. "You're right, that's probably best," he conceded. When he saw the plates, heavily laden with food, his eyes widened. "You didn't cook, did you?"

Sean snorted. "No. I *can* cook but I was too damn tired. This came from a great little restaurant down the street. They make great calzones and antipasto."

They ended up on the sofa, eating at the low table in front of them. Sean turned on the television but it ended up just being background noise.

"How did your auditions go?" Corey asked.

"Really well," Sean answered enthusiastically. "I've got a shot at the part of Benedick in 'Much Ado About Nothing' at the Old Globe. I think they want me for the production of 'Guys and Dolls' at the La Jolla Playhouse but I'd rather do Shakespeare."

"Why is that?" Corey would have thought he'd want to work at the theater that was closer to home.

"I've done a lot of musical theater," Sean replied. "I've even done 'Guys and Dolls' before. Shakespeare would be more of a challenge."

Corey could relate to that logic. He appreciated a good challenge. "Did you say you're going to L.A. tomorrow?"

Sean nodded, mouth full of food. "I've got two days of auditions and readings," he answered when he'd swallowed. "So I'm staying up there tomorrow night."

"That makes sense."

"You still call me if you need me, though," Sean insisted. "Speaking of which, tell me about that interview today."

Corey hesitated. He didn't want memories intruding on what was shaping up to be a nice evening. He didn't want to see the same expression of pain on Sean's face that he'd seen Saturday night.

"You need to talk about this stuff, Corey," Sean said into Corey's silence. "Keeping it bottled up makes what you're going through worse."

"You don't need to hear about the ugly shit I've had to do." Corey picked at his food, not looking at Sean.

"Don't give me that crap," Sean retorted. "I'm a big boy, I can deal. It's not like I don't know what it is you do."

"Yeah, well, there's knowing and then there's *knowing*." Corey pretended to watch the television.

"If you're not going to talk to a professional about what's going on, you need to talk to me," Sean insisted.

"I'm seeing a doctor Thursday," Corey said quickly, going back to pushing his food around the plate. "I made the appointment when I hung up with you today."

"Good!" Sean declared. He actually looked relieved.

Why Corey wanted so much to please Sean, he had no idea. "It's just with my regular doctor, to get something to help me sleep. I'll talk to him about the other stuff while I'm there."

"That's awesome. It's a start." Sean was nearly vibrating with pleasure. He abruptly sobered. "Your boss, or your commanding officer, or whatever you have, won't give you a hard time about getting this kind of help, will they?"

Corey remembered Whitfield's easy accommodation of the medical appointment. At the time, he'd been surprised by the Master Sergeant alluding to Corey getting whatever help he needed. Now he was just grateful.

"Actually, I think he suspects something is up." Corey sighed. "He told me today to make sure I take care of myself."

"You don't really have an excuse then, do you?" Sean said with a smile.

"It's still not easy," Corey said quietly.

There was a long silence before Sean stunned Corey. "So tell me about Jonah."

Corey didn't immediately reply. He stared down at his hands as he rubbed his palms together nervously. He had nothing to be embarrassed about. Jonah hadn't rejected him. It wasn't like Corey hadn't been good enough. It was just that Jonah had only ever loved Kellan.

"So, that's how it is," Sean said quietly, standing abruptly and collecting their plates. "Never mind, I didn't mean to pry."

"No, that's not how it is," Corey said as he gathered up the last of their dishes and followed Sean to the kitchen. He didn't like the suddenly blank expression Sean was wearing. "We served together in Iraq and that's all there ever was. He's never loved anyone other than Kellan Reynolds."

"You have feelings for him, though," Sean said, back still to Corey.

"He was the first *man* I ever had a crush on," Corey confessed, his face warming. "If you ever saw Jonah you'd understand. He's six-foot-three inches of California surfer boy, sex on legs." Corey gave a self-conscious laugh as he ran a palm over his still heated forehead. "I thought I loved him but what the hell did I know back then?"

"Did he at least let you down easy?" Sean glanced at Corey with sympathy.

"I don't know if he even knew." Corey shrugged. He stood next to Sean at the sink and dried the dishes as he washed. "If he knew then yes, he let me down very easy."

"He cared enough to help you stop the drinking the first time." Sean handed over the last plate and turned to wipe down the breakfast bar.

"I learned how to take care of the men under my command from Jonah," Corey replied. "It's not just about giving orders. You gotta help them be better men and better Marines."

"How long did you serve with him?" Sean asked.

Corey shut off the water and turned around. He leaned back against the sink and faced Sean who mirrored him across the small kitchen. "We were in the same company for about six months. I got transferred to his custom assembled team for a special mission that lasted about three days. After that, he got sent stateside and I spent some time in a Navy hospital."

Sean's eyes widened. "You were wounded?"

"Our convoy of SUVs got hit by RPGs. Rocket propelled grenades." Corey gestured for Sean's hand. He placed Sean's fingertips over the slightly raised scar barely hidden by his pale hair. "I had a concussion and my scalp was lacerated clear to the bone."

Sean's expression shifted from wariness, to curiosity, to sympathy. His touch was light but Corey felt it all the way down his spine. Even his cock shifted slightly.

Suddenly, Sean gave Corey a wide, mischievous smile. Corey's heart kicked up in pace as Sean's hazel eyes warmed. "Does this mean you have a Purple Heart?"

Corey snorted and returned Sean's smile. "Among other things, yes."

"You'll have to show it to me sometime." Sean trailed his fingers down Corey's cheek.

Corey hadn't looked at any of his medals since they'd been awarded to him. He wouldn't even wear the ribbons on his uniforms if he wasn't required to do so. "If I show you my medals will you sleep with me?" As soon as the words were out of his mouth, Corey was horrified. *Why the fuck had he said that?*

Sean's expression grew heated. He lifted a single eyebrow as he replied, "If you show me your medals I'll sleep with you *sooner*."

Blood flowed into Corey's cock so fast it ached. His face turned hot and he swallowed against a suddenly dry throat as Sean's words truly registered. Corey opened his mouth to reply but nothing came out.

Sean smiled brilliantly again. "For such a big, dangerous guy, you sure are cute when you're flustered." He leaned in and placed a soft, sweet kiss on Corey's lips.

Corey moaned against Sean's mouth. Regaining his senses, he pulled back on a gasp. "I didn't mean that."

Sean gave him a confused look. "What? You don't want to show me your medals? Or you don't want to sleep with me?"

"No! I mean yes! I…fuck." Corey ran both hands over his face, struggling for composure.

Sean laughed. "Go sit down and relax. You are just too easy to wind up."

Corey fled to the sofa and collapsed down onto it. He was pretty fucking sure the only other man who had ever left him this tongue-tied was Jonah Carver.

Sean handed Corey a fresh soda and dropped down onto the sofa next to him. "I'm curious about one thing," he said. "If you were the one with a head wound, why was Jonah the one who was shipped home?"

"He and Kellan had to testify in front of Congress," Corey replied with a laugh. "A fate I was able to escape." He still enjoyed using that against Jonah.

"What the fuck did you guys get yourselves into?" Sean demanded, returning Corey's smile.

"Remember about four years ago, when all the private defense contractors got indicted?" Corey asked. "They were rigging the contracts system and colluding to cause the deaths of U.S. service personnel?"

"Yeah, that was fucked up," Sean replied. "Didn't they have some investigators kidnapped and killed, making it look like terrorists had done it?" Corey watched as Sean's mind raced through memories and made the necessary connections. "No way! That was you?"

"No, that was Kellan and Jonah," said Corey. "I was just collateral damage."

"No, seriously," Sean persisted, "you were part of that investigation?"

"All I did was work as part of the security detail that protected Kellan and four FBI agents while *they* conducted an investigation." Corey had hardly gotten to fire his weapon. "It was Jonah who sprinted through the streets of Diyala to rescue a kidnapped Kellan."

"How many times have you used that story to get laid?" Sean asked as he laughed.

Corey loved the way Sean's eyes crinkled when he laughed. His smile was so wide and genuine. He was fucking gorgeous and Corey wondered how the fuck he'd managed to end up here with Sean. "I've never told anyone before."

Sean continued to smile at him. "What other fascinating

secrets are you hiding?" he asked playfully.

Corey didn't dare answer. He had a lot of secrets and he didn't think very many of them were interesting.

A news broadcast flashed across the television screen, surprising Corey. He glanced at his watch and confirmed it was 2300 hours. "Shit, I gotta go."

Sean rose from the sofa with him. "I suppose it is late, for those of you who have to get up early."

"Early mornings and long days," Corey replied mournfully.

When they reached the door, Sean unlocked it but didn't open it. Instead, he leaned back against the wall. "If you have trouble falling asleep, call me."

Corey waved his hand dismissively. "It sounds like you have a busy day tomorrow, you don't need to hold my hand tonight."

Sean reached out and laced his fingers with Corey's. "But I want to hold your hand," he said with a playful smile. "And if you have a nightmare, call me. I don't have to be on the road until mid-morning, so don't worry."

Corey sighed heavily, realizing he was beaten. Keeping their fingers twined, he stepped into Sean's space, just shy of touching. He could feel the heat of Sean's body all along his own. He caught Sean's clean scent again and heat built low in his belly. A flush rose on Sean's cheeks. His eyes were dark and his nostrils flared slightly, as if he was breathing in Corey's scent.

Linking the fingers of his other hand with Sean's free hand, Corey lifted Sean's arms over his head. He pressed Sean's arms to the wall, pinning him gentle but firm. Sean gave no resistance. In fact, he seemed to melt into the wall behind him. Shifting his grip, Corey clasped both of Sean's wrists with one hand. He used the fingers of his newly freed hand to skim down Sean's cheek.

Sean's eyes widened at the touch and Corey heard him draw a harsh breath through his parted lips. Corey watched Sean's lush, generous mouth closely, forcing himself to be patient. He slid his fingers along Sean's jaw, feeling little stubble. He must have shaved when he'd showered earlier. Corey smiled slightly at the thought that Sean had gotten cleaned up just for him.

"What?" Sean asked, his flush darkening.

Corey smiled wider and shook his head. "You. Just you." He skimmed the pad of his thumb lightly over Sean's lower lip, just as Sean had done to Corey the night they'd shared their first kiss.

Sean pressed a kiss to Corey's thumb. Corey watched, fascinated, as Sean's tongue slid out to lick lightly at him. His cock pulsed slightly at the soft, warm, wet feel of Sean's tongue on his skin.

Corey slid the tips of his fingers over Sean's lips, down his chin, and along the line of his throat. Sean tilted his face up slightly, his eyes sliding nearly shut as he moaned softly. Corey lifted his hand, cupped Sean's face, and leaned in.

He wanted to be gentle and go slow, like Sean had the other night. But once Corey felt the touch of Sean's lips on his own, he needed a deeper taste. Holding Sean's jaw lightly, Corey tilted his head and parted his own lips. He urged Sean to open to him. He didn't have to work very hard.

When Corey felt Sean's lips part beneath his own, he pressed his tongue in and licked deep into Sean's mouth. Aggressively, Corey rubbed his tongue against Sean's eager one. Unlike the soft kisses of that first night, this one was hard and hungry. Sean made a needy sound low in his throat and Corey's cock throbbed in response. Pulling back to adjust his angle, Corey dove back into the kiss. He didn't quite seal their mouths and Sean's harsh breaths ghosted over Corey's lips.

When Corey flicked his tongue across the backs of Sean's teeth, he received a soft moan in response. Corey pushed deep into Sean's mouth, chasing his tongue. Sean made a sound high in his throat that sounded desperate. Pulling back slightly, Corey gently bit Sean's lower lip. Sean made a high pitched, needy sound.

Corey's cock was semi-hard. He was so relieved his body was finally responding in a familiar way. The kiss was wet now, their mouths gliding slickly against one another. Corey took a chance and closed the remaining distance between their bodies. With his chest and his hips, Corey pressed Sean firmly into the wall.

Groaning into Corey's mouth, Sean pushed back against him. He ground their hips together and Corey could feel that Sean was hard. Corey's cock was nearly as hard and he rubbed himself against the length of Sean's firmly muscled body.

Sean made soft sounds, almost like whimpers, and it was the hottest thing Corey might have ever heard. He broke the kiss, running his palm down Sean's chest. He felt the firm muscles beneath Sean's shirt, as well as the way his chest heaved with each harsh breath and hungry sound. Corey kissed his way the length of Sean's jaw. He pressed wet, open mouthed kisses to Sean's throat, flicking his tongue over the hot skin. His lips brushed over a pulse point and Corey felt how hard Sean's heart was pounding. He sank his teeth into the tender skin.

It was like Sean had been struck by lightning. He arched off of the wall, crying out. He tried to tear his wrists from Corey's grip, but Corey held him fast.

"Jesus Christ, Corey," Sean said in a raw voice. "What the fuck are you doing to me?"

Corey pulled back to look at Sean. His face was flushed and it bled down his throat to disappear beneath his shirt. The hazel of his eyes had been consumed by the pupils. He breathed through swollen lips like he'd just sprinted a mile.

"It was just a kiss," Corey said, more out of breath than he'd realized.

Sean's laugh had a hysterical edge. "You need to let me go now or I won't want you to leave at all."

Corey released Sean's wrists even as he pressed their foreheads together. He didn't want to leave. Yeah, Corey had wanted to fuck Sean, to work him out of his system, but this was more than that. He wanted to stay the night with Sean and all that usually entailed.

Which meant it couldn't be tonight.

With one last kiss to Sean's swollen mouth, Corey stepped back. "We'll pick this up later. When neither of us has anywhere to be the next morning."

"Oh, absolutely," Sean said, still out of breath.

Sean looked so wrecked, Corey knew he had to leave that moment, or he wouldn't leave at all. "Thanks for dinner and ... everything." He jerked open the front door.

"You're welcome," Sean called after him as Corey charged down the stairs as if pursued by the devil himself.

CHAPTER EIGHT

Corey walked around the BRC candidates who were his to instruct today. They were all seated on the ground, sketchbooks in their laps and fingertips covered in pencil lead. Some had already grasped the concept and were just struggling with the execution. Others didn't seem to be grasping the fundamentals.

He stood behind them for several minutes, allowing them to struggle just a while longer before he provided guidance. Corey closed his eyes and lifted his face to the sun. His Oakleys did a good job of shading his eyes and the warmth felt soothing on his skin. He remembered he actually enjoyed being in the sun when he wasn't hung over and hurting.

Corey had climbed into his rack last night, jacked off remembering Sean's kiss, and fallen right to sleep. He hadn't awakened until his alarm had sounded that morning. He was vaguely disappointed. It meant no nightmare, but it also meant Corey hadn't talked to Sean since they'd parted the night before.

Stepping forward, Corey crouched down beside one of the Marines curled around his sketchbook as he slowly recreated the mock village in the distance. The Marine had the basics of the sketch right, but he was struggling to calculate size and distance.

"What do you see out there that you know the size or the distance of?" Corey asked quietly.

The Marine sergeant stared at the village in the distance for several long moments. "The oil drum," he finally answered.

"Good," Corey encourage. "Now use what you know about the oil drum to figure out the things around it. That's how you get perspective. If something you know is smaller looks larger than the drum, you know it's closer to you than it might appear to be."

The sergeant peered through his scope again and made some notations on his drawing about the size of the oil drum.

Corey watched him work through some calculations until he determined the size and relative distance of the earthen baking oven. He knew the moment the Marine remembered what the average height of doorways was in Afghanistan and Iraq, because he jotted down the accurate dimensions of the first structure.

Corey stood and moved on to the next student, confident the sergeant was grasping the concepts of triangulation. He wondered briefly if Sean was on the road to L.A. yet. He dropped down next to a lieutenant who could probably calculate distances pretty well, if he could figure out how to draw a passable sketch.

"Draw what you see," Corey said softly.

"I'm trying," the lieutenant said, his frustration obvious.

"Tell me what it is you see." Corey kept his voice low and friendly.

"A village," replied the lieutenant, giving the expected and obvious answer.

"A village is made up of millions of smaller parts," explained Corey. "Structures, the oven, the scrub surrounding the village, the occupants. The structures themselves are earth and wood and glass and metal." He lifted his hands to frame a small segment of the village. "Break it down into its smaller, basic elements, and tell me what you see."

"The corner of a building and a shadow," replied the lieutenant with much less frustration.

"So, straight lines and squares, right?"

"Right," the lieutenant answered thoughtfully.

"Now, draw what you see," Corey instructed. "And when that's done, draw what you see is connected to it."

Next, Corey dropped down next to a lance corporal who seemed to grasp the concepts, but his calculations weren't giving him the right dimensions. Corey had the young Marine review the process he was using. Dropping down to sit in the dirt next to him, Corey corrected his assumptions and his equations. The kid struggled with the math a little, but not so much that Corey thought he wouldn't master it eventually.

"Good. Keep working on it," he said as he climbed to his feet.

"I can't do it," came a strident voice from somewhere in the group of students.

One of Corey's fellow instructors stood. "Can't is not in a Marine's vocabulary," he barked down at the man sitting on the ground. "I don't want to hear 'can't' come out of your mouth. Get it done, Marine."

"Yes, Gunnery Sergeant, sir," the Marine replied mournfully.

Corey was pretty sure that one would be among the next ones to wash out when the training got physical again. He'd most likely find himself targeted by the instructors, even as they tried to determine what the man was made of.

"Staff Sergeant Yarwood."

Corey turned toward the sound of the Master Sergeant's voice. He saw him standing with Captain Hirata. Corey's stomach did a slow roll. He approached the two men and saluted the Captain.

"I hope everything is okay with my instructor, Captain sir," Whitfield surprised Corey by saying.

"Your instructor is as inconvenienced by all of this as the rest of us, Master Sergeant," Hirata answered. "I'm going to try to keep the disruptions to a minimum."

"We'll deal with the disruptions, sir," Whitfield said. He turned to leave, giving Corey's shoulder a brief squeeze. "Just concerned about a good Marine. Have a good day, Captain."

"I really am going to try to limit access to you in an official capacity, Staff Sergeant," Captain Hirata said. "But both the prosecutor and the defense in Nygaard's case want to use you to their own benefit."

"I don't see how I can be a benefit to the defense, sir," Corey confessed his bafflement.

"They're claiming the incident in Ghazni, coupled with Nygaard's previously undiagnosed Traumatic Brain Injury, caused him to kill his girlfriend," Hirata explained.

"So they want me to tell how fucked up things were in Ghazni?" Corey asked.

"That's the way it looks right now," Hirata confirmed. "And the prosecution wants you to address Nygaard's history of inappropriately aggressive behavior and to tell how things at Ghazni weren't fucked up enough to make Nygaard do what he did."

"Shouldn't Lieutenant Adams be addressing any alleged discipline problems?" The implementation of discipline was the job of the officers, even when Corey had been the one to oversee it.

"The Lieutenant's testimony is germane to an ongoing Marine Corps investigation and for reasons of national security, the civilian legal system will not be allowed access to him." Hirata's reply was stiff and formal and the hair on Corey's arms stood up as a chill raced down his spine.

"I've discussed this with Mr. Reynolds," Hirata continued, "and he concurs that you are not to have contact with either the prosecution or the defense without me being present."

"Yes, sir," Corey agreed. He wished Kellan hadn't been told about this fucked up mess he'd found himself in the middle of.

"Not only do we not want you unwittingly giving away details of the investigation, but Mr. Reynolds is adamant that you're to be protected from any attempts to shift the blame."

Corey wanted to know what blame could possibly be shifted to him. He believed Kellan's sense of integrity wouldn't let that happen, though. "I appreciate that, Captain."

"I think it goes without saying, Staff Sergeant, but I'm saying it anyway; you're not to speak to the press," Hirata said.

Confusion and alarm rocketed through Corey's system. "I have no intention of talking to any reporters, sir. Why would they have any interest in talking to me, anyway?"

"Nygaard's attorney is talking to them," Hirata answered.

"He's saying your testimony will mitigate Nygaard's actions."

Corey heaved a disgusted sigh. "At least I live on base. It'll make it harder to get to me."

The Captain chuckled. "If one of them manages to ambush you, don't say a word, just execute a strategic retreat. They'll find a way to manipulate the most innocent of statements."

"Solid copy, sir."

As the Captain left, Corey turned back to the class. He found them gathered in the shade eating lunch. The younger Marines had made the mistake of complaining about the quality of the portable meal. Corey could hear the veterans schooling the infants about this gourmet meal, when compared to the quality of the average MRE.

Taking advantage of the official break, Corey pulled his cell phone from his pocket and turned it on. He tried not to be hopeful. He told himself it was ridiculous to hope. Still, when he saw the voicemail from Sean, he was stupidly euphoric.

Corey walked in a circle as he listened to the recording of Sean's voice. He didn't need his fellow Marines to see him grinning like an idiot.

"Hey, I didn't hear from you last night. I hope that means you didn't have trouble sleeping, and there was no nightmare. 'Cause if you didn't call 'cause you thought you'd be bothering me, I'm going to be pissed." The humor in Sean's voice was easy to hear. "It's ten o'clock and I'm heading out for L.A. The drive will take a couple of hours so call if you get a chance. After that I have a lot of meetings, auditions, and readings so I'll be busy until kind of late. I'll call you when I get to my hotel." There was a long pause. "I hope you'll answer." Corey grinned. It mattered to Sean if Corey answered his call or not. "Anyway, I just wanted to say 'hi' and make sure you're okay...call me if you have a chance... hope you're having a good day...um...I guess that's it...so... hope to talk to you soon. Bye."

Sean was always so supremely confident; Corey found it charming that he got a little insecure. Especially over Corey.

Checking his watch, he saw it was well past noon. Sean was probably busy, but Corey tried to call him anyway. He'd at least leave Sean a voicemail.

"Hey, it's me." No shit, Corey. "I got your voicemail. Sorry I couldn't take your call. I didn't call last night because I was asleep. That's good, I guess." Now it was Corey's turn to make an awkward pause. "So, call me when you get a chance. If I don't hear from you, I might try to call back…oh, good luck with all those meetings and shit today." Really, Corey? "I hope it works out the way you want it to…um…have a good day…and…I guess…I'll talk to you later. Bye."

Corey disconnected the call, giving himself a mental ass kicking. He couldn't have been any less smooth if he'd tried. So much for the badass killer Marine. He jumped slightly when his phone vibrated. His heart leapt, thinking it might be Sean returning his call. Disappointment swamped him like a cold ocean wave when he saw it was Tyler.

"Hey, dude," he greeted, forcing joviality he didn't feel.

"Hey, man, I gotta make it quick, but I wanted to tell you some of the guys in the platoon are pissed as all fuck at Nygaard." Tyler sounded out of breath. His voice was low, like he was trying not to be overheard.

"They oughtta be," Corey replied. "*I'm* fucking pissed at Nygaard."

"This is something else. It's bad enough what he did to that girl, but he's talking about what happened in Ghazni. You remember what he said when we heard about this new investigation. He was going around to everybody telling us we had to stick together and if we just all told the same story they couldn't do anything to us. Now that he's fucked up and is looking at going to prison for life, he's selling out the whole fucking platoon." Tyler sounded angry and worried.

"Where the fuck did you hear this?" Corey demanded.

"He's been on the fucking news, Yarwood!" Tyler hissed viciously. "He started out going around trying to get us all to keep whatever secret he's been hiding, and as soon as it's his ass in the sling, he starts blaming the Corps, the platoon, and his fellow Marines."

Corey laughed mirthlessly. He really shouldn't have expected anything else from Nygaard. "What an asshole," he growled. "What pisses me off even more is it looks like there's actually something to hide. He did something out there and now he wants to blame the rest of us 'cause he's a fucked up prick."

"What happened after you left us in the house, Corey?" Tyler asked quietly.

The question felt like a kick to his gut. Corey dropped to a crouch and struggled to slow his breathing. "What are you talking about?"

"Whatever the fuck it is they're hiding, it happened when Nygaard took his team and went to secure the perimeter," Tyler replied adamantly. "You went looking for them, Yarwood. What did you find?"

"Nothing. We collapsed the perimeter and pulled back to the Humvees." Corey's voice sounded robotic to his own ears. He'd been giving that same answer for so long now, but even he didn't believe it anymore.

"Yeah. Okay. What-the-fuck-ever," Tyler snapped. "Since you're not watching the news, you don't know that he's saying we all desecrated the bodies we had to transport back to base, do you?"

Corey stood and began to pace. "Have you been interviewed by the investigation panel, yet?"

"No, I'm up tomorrow. Why?"

"They're going to ask you about that."

"Jesus Christ, Corey," Tyler exclaimed. "We didn't do anything wrong!"

"I know we didn't," he said firmly. "Tell them the truth when they ask. You have *nothing* to hide."

"Know what's really fucked up?" Tyler asked rhetorically. "The

LT is nowhere to be found. The platoon is under investigation, one of our sergeants is accused of murdering his girlfriend and is blaming the rest of us, and our platoon commander is MIA. Gunny's been leading our training."

Corey wondered if Lieutenant Adams knew what it was Corey couldn't seem to remember. "Just stay out of trouble and tell the truth when you're interviewed tomorrow. That's all you can do."

"Shit. Gotta go. Thanks, man. Talk to you later." Tyler ended the call before Corey could answer.

Shutting off his phone and pocketing it, Corey rejoined the class. He had to get himself squared away or he'd be shit for the rest of the day.

He wondered what Sean was doing at that moment.

§ § §

Corey showered after the gym. He drove across base to his favorite restaurant for a to-go order. As he passed the enlisted cantina, he thought about stopping in. He didn't really like to be around people much anymore, but it will wasn't much fun to eat alone. Corey nearly stopped, until he remembered how loud the cantina could get and kept on driving.

He watched a DVD on his laptop, and wondered when it might be okay to call Sean. Corey remembered that he'd left the last voicemail; it was Sean's turn to call him. If Sean wanted to talk to him, he'd call.

Corey thought back to the message he'd left. He'd told Sean he'd try to call later so maybe it was his turn to call.

Fuck it.

Picking up his phone, Corey called Sean. He closed his eyes as he listened to the rings, hoping he didn't seem like a needy pussy.

He knew he was about to get voicemail again. Corey pulled the phone from his ear to hit 'end' when he heard something on the line.

"Hello…shit…hang on…hello? Corey?"

"Yeah," he replied carefully, listening to the sounds of shuffling and rustling in the background of the call.

"I took a shower and didn't have my phone in the bathroom with me." Sean sounded out of breath. "I didn't hear it ring at first. When I did, I knew it would be you calling and I scrambled to answer it."

Knowing Sean was eager to take his call warmed Corey. He settled back against his pillow, getting relaxed and ready to talk for awhile. "How did your day go?"

"Busy," Sean sighed. There were more sounds of shuffling. Sean grunted.

"Did I call at a bad time?" Corey asked, afraid he didn't have Sean's complete attention.

"No!" Sean exclaimed. "I was going to call you in a few minutes anyway. I'm just getting comfortable and getting my guitar out of the case. So how was *your* day?"

Corey sighed heavily. "It was fine. The class went well. I just found out some stuff that pissed me off."

"Let me guess," Sean said darkly. Soft guitar music drifted across the connection. "It's got something to do with this Nygaard guy."

"I guess his lawyer has been going on the news and making bullshit accusations." Corey closed his eyes and listened to Sean strum the guitar. "I got a call from Tyler, the corporal I told you about. Nygaard is throwing other Marines under the bus, after he'd gone around pressuring all of them to stonewall the investigative panel."

"That's pretty shitty."

"That's just not the kind of shit Marines do to each other," Corey explained. They were supposed to be brothers. You were supposed to know your brothers had your back.

"You've got Tyler's back, though, right?" Sean asked.

Corey paused, not sure where this was going. "Yeah. Of course."

"So he's not all alone in this. That's good."

"Tyler's a good Marine and didn't do anything wrong," Corey affirmed.

"Then it's good he has you to look to as an example, and not just Nygaard."

Corey had no idea how to reply to *that*. "Yeah, I guess so. So how did your auditions go?"

"Fine, I think. I won't know for a while. I'll probably have to go through some callbacks."

They both fell silent as Sean played his guitar. The song made Corey feel melancholy. He didn't recognize it.

"Is that something you wrote?" he asked quietly.

"I'm I the middle of writing it," Sean replied.

"Wow. I like it. It's kind of sad, though."

"You haven't heard the words yet," Sean said ruefully. "It gets worse."

"Is it too early for you to sing it for me?"

"Not as long as you remember it's a work in progress," answered Sean. "The first and third verses are more or less done but I'm still struggling with the second one. Hang on, I'm gonna put you on speaker."

The melody made something in Corey's chest ache. Sean's smooth voice blended perfectly with the musical notes. He sang the first verse about a woman upset by another failed relationship and angry with those around her who judge her. Something about it made Corey think of Aimee.

Sean hummed through most of the second verse. He sang a few lines about a man with sad eyes and a beautiful smile. The man was always alone, even when he sat in a crowded room. Corey's heart broke for the faceless young man.

The chorus of the song was angry. It expressed frustration with people living in the past or paralyzed by fear. Corey could relate to that. It had taken him years, and some angry words from

Jonah, to stop living in the past.

The third verse stole Corey's breath. He knew Sean was singing about the agony of writing his music. He sang about how the songs fought their way out of him and letting them out was the only way to ease his pain. Agony gave way to irony when Sean sang of how the songs were taken from him and when they were misunderstood, the agony returned.

As the final notes of the song faded away, Corey swallowed past a lump in his throat.

Sean's voice was suddenly right in Corey's ear. "Oh shit. You're not saying anything. You hate it, don't you?"

"No!" Corey blurted. "Fuck no. It…it made me *feel* a lot of emotions." He didn't know the words that would say what it was he was feeling. He wasn't even sure what it was he felt. "I'm just not smart enough to say it right."

"Don't *even* go there!" Sean said angrily. "You and I both know that's bullshit."

"I seriously don't know how to tell you what I liked about that song or how it made me feel," Corey protested. "It's not bullshit."

"Fine," Sean said tightly, and Corey knew they were far from done discussing this. "So name one emotion you felt while you were listening."

"Sadness," Corey replied without thinking.

"Which part?"

"The second verse."

"Even though it's not finished?" Sean sounded surprised.

"I guess." Corey shrugged even though Sean couldn't see. "What made him so sad in the first place?"

"I don't know. Which is why the verse isn't finished." There was something different, something odd, in Sean's voice now. "You know what I've been wondering? Why you joined the Marines. I asked you how long ago you joined, but I never asked why."

Corey's head spun with the change in topic. "Um…I needed to make a change."

"What were you doing before you enlisted?"

Having this discussion with Sean was worse than when he'd had it with Jonah. "Going to school."

"So you dropped out of college to become a Marine?" To Corey's surprise, Sean's voice held no judgment.

"Yeah." He didn't want to have this conversation. He wanted to keep secrets from Sean even less. When Sean remained silent, Corey heaved a resigned sigh. "My girlfriend of four years dumped me and moved out."

There was a long, tense silence.

"Girlfriend?" Sean didn't mask his surprise.

"I had to get dumped and join the Marines to figure out what she already knew," replied Corey. To his surprise, that confession hurt less than it used to.

"How long did it take you to sort it out?"

"I caught on pretty quick. Accepting it took a few years longer."

"Is that why you used to drink?"

Sean's intuition was astounding. "I used to tell myself it was because my heart was broken, but yeah, it was easier to avoid myself if I was drunk. I used to hide out in my room on base and get drunk at night so I didn't have to think about it. That's how I spent my twenty-first birthday."

"That's so sad," Sean said quietly. "I feel bad for you but I know you don't want pity. Still, that's a hard way to grow up and find yourself."

Corey was distracted from answering by the sound of Sean once again playing the guitar.

"So, question from the list of things to ask when getting to know someone," Sean suddenly asked, the music stopping abruptly. "Are you out to your family?"

The shift was so unexpected, Corey wasn't sure he heard correctly. "Uh…my ex-girlfriend outed me when she left."

Sean started to strum the guitar again as he said, "That's just brutal. How did they handle it?"

Corey shifted uncomfortably on his rack. "They didn't really react. I think they thought it was just a phase." He snorted self-deprecatingly. "They were more upset that I joined the Marines."

"Worried about you getting hurt?" Sean asked.

"That and they always pictured me going to college and getting a nine-to-five job, buying a house nearby so they could visit their grandchildren." Corey sighed. "You know. The usual."

"Are you an only child?" Sean was playing the same few bars of music over and over.

"I have three younger sisters," answered Corey. "I was *the son*. Even now, they're baffled as to why I'm still a Marine. I think they thought I'd do four years, realize I was really straight, and come home to finish school and get married."

It sounded like Sean hit a few wrong cords on the guitar. "Do you ever think about doing that?"

"I've been away from home too long now," Corey said with a sigh. "Getting married, having kids, and getting their needs met secretly might be how gay men hide it in the mid-west, but it's not for me."

Sean laughed. "There are a lot of gay men in Hollywood who live that way, too. It isn't just the mid-west."

Corey joined in with Sean's laughter. "You'll have to tell me some names, sometime."

"You can guess a few of them," Sean said conspiratorially.

"So, what about you?" Corey asked. "Are you out to your family?"

Sean laughed heartily. It was a deep, rich sound that filled Corey with warmth. He couldn't help but smile in response.

"My family says they knew when I was a toddler that I was gay. *And* an actor," Sean said around bursts of laughter.

"Were you *fabulous* as a kid?" Corey asked.

"There are pictures of me playing dress up in my mother's clothes and putting on musicals," Sean replied. "I've got an older brother and sister and I used to recruit them as supporting cast."

"You, my friend, are a cliché," Corey said between gasping laughter.

"Well, I was until I hit junior high. Then I realized I liked sports as much as drama club."

"And now you're a sexy mix of butch and fabulous." Corey squeezed his eyes shut and bit back a mortified groan.

"Is it a mix you like?" Sean asked quietly.

Corey wanted to make a clever comment. He wished he could think of something witty to say. "Yeah, it is."

The silence dragged on and Corey had no idea how to break it. He'd put himself out there and now Sean wasn't making any comment.

"Since you're obviously not going to ask, I think you're a sexy mix of strong and gentle." Sean managed to sound both fond and annoyed.

Corey cleared his throat. "That's good. Now can we talk about something else?"

Sean laughed softly. "And you call *me* a cliché."

At Corey's urging, Sean told him about his brother and sister. Afterward, he told Corey about the big audition he had the next day. The third time he yawned, Corey couldn't quite keep it silent.

"You need to get some sleep," Sean declared.

"I'm fine," Corey insisted. "I can function on very little sleep."

"There's no reason for you to just function," Sean argued. "You should be getting enough rest right now."

"Yes, *Dad*," Corey whined in jest.

Sean laughed and Corey wondered why he couldn't always be this funny.

"Call me tomorrow night," said Sean. "I might still be driving home so you can keep me occupied. And if you have a bad dream tonight, call me. I'll be awake for a while."

"Good luck tomorrow. You'll impress the hell out of them." Corey's chest tightened with an unfamiliar sense of pride and admiration.

"I'm glad you think so."

After Corey ended the call, he stripped down to skivvies and climbed back into his rack. He was already relaxed, his eyes heavy and refusing to stay open. He was pretty sure he'd sleep through the night again.

§ § §

Corey broke cover and charged across open ground. He fingers ached as they gripped his M16. His breathing roared in his own ears but he wasn't winded. Something else made him breathe hard. All around him, small plumes of dust marked AK47 rounds hitting the ground. Corey kept running.

He spotted a burned out truck and ran toward it. Corey took cover, slamming his back against the flattened, oversized tire. He aimed his weapon around the side of the tire, seeking a target.

Corey wondered what an Iraqi village was doing in Afghanistan.

"You're with me, Yarwood!"

Corey ducked back behind the tire. He glanced over and saw Sergeant Carver crouched behind the front fender. It didn't make sense but Corey would follow Sergeant Carver anywhere.

"Three…two…one," Jonah shouted over the deafening gunfire.

Corey burst from behind the truck. His heart hammered as he and Jonah sprinted toward the front door of a dwelling. His legs burned, even though it was a short distance. Corey could hump twenty miles in full pack. He shouldn't be fatigued.

He slammed his back against the wall beside the wooden door. Jonah was on the other side.

"Make entry, Staff Sergeant," Jonah ordered. His blue eyes were hard and intense.

Corey did not want to enter the house.

"You have to enter the house, Yarwood," yelled Jonah.

"Due respect, Sergeant, I'd rather not." Corey had never refused an order in his entire career. There hadn't been many he'd felt the need to question, either.

"Get inside that room and face what's in there, Staff Sergeant," Jonah insisted. His expression was compelling.

Corey's chest heaved with each breath. He could barely hear over the sound of it. He felt every beat of his heart in his throat. He gripped his M16 with sweaty palms. Corey swallowed down his nausea and stepped away from the wall. He gave a mighty kick and planted his boot right beside the lock mechanism.

The door swung open, hitting the inside wall with a thunderous crash. The ensuing silence was deafening.

Corey stood frozen in the doorway. His Oakleys were effective against the outside sun but left him blind against the darkness spilling menacingly from inside the structure. Corey wanted to turn and run. He wanted to wake up so he didn't have to cross the threshold.

His breathing was out of control. With each gasping inhalation, Corey smelled the sickeningly sweet scent of fresh blood. His heart slammed against his ribs and his pulse hammered in his throat, his temples, and his hands as they gripped his weapon.

Corey's legs were leaden as he took one hesitant step forward. Darkness enveloped him and he blinked as his eyes adjusted. The heat was oppressive and sweat rolled from beneath his Kevlar and down his face and neck.

He took another step. His boot made a wet sucking sound as he pulled it from the floor. He stood in something sticky. Corey had to tug his foot free with every step. The tacky, wet sounds drowned out his gasping breaths and thundering heartbeat. Breathing through his mouth did nothing to mitigate the nauseating smell of fresh blood and evacuated bowels. These were the smells of fresh death.

Corey tried to swallow but his mouth was dry. He blinked again and saw movement across the room. He swung the muzzle of his weapon in that direction.

Sergeant Nygaard stood across the room. A small group of women and children knelt huddled at his feet. Nygaard held his M16 pointed at the back of one woman's head.

"I need your help, Corey," Nygaard pleaded. "You have to help me."

"Help you with what?" Corey demanded.

"You gotta have my back, that's what Marines do," Nygaard continued as if Corey hadn't spoken.

"Have your back with what?" Corey shouted, not lifting his cheek from the stock of his M16.

"You ordered me to," said Nygaard, his eyes were wide open and wild.

"I didn't order you to do *this*!" Corey cried out angrily.

"You have to help me keep the secret." Nygaard's expression was crazed.

Corey's finger twitched on the trigger. "You did this shit all on your own. I don't have to help you with any fucking thing."

"You have to make them be quiet."

"Make who be quiet?" Corey was afraid he already knew.

Nygaard gestured toward the women and children at his feet. "Make them be quiet."

Corey sighted down the barrel of his rifle. He chose one of the kneeling women as a target. Her eyes met his and they were filled with anger and accusation. Slowly, he squeezed the trigger of his M16. The weapon roared as the firing pin struck the base of the casing. The rifle recoiled hard into Corey's shoulder.

He sat up in his rack, the shouted word "No!" dying on his lips. Corey wiped sweat from his face with both shaking hands. He couldn't catch his breath. His heart beat so fast, for several seconds he thought he was dying.

Shoving off the bedclothes, he swung his legs over the side of his rack and fumbled to turn on the bedside lamp. The dim light did little to push back the threatening shadows. With barely a thought, Corey picked up his cell phone and located Sean's number.

To Corey's relief, his call was answered on the first ring.

"Are you okay?" Sean's question was softly spoken.

Corey couldn't answer. He couldn't form the words. He sat with his forehead in the palm of his hand and tried to slow his breathing.

"Corey, remember to breathe in for a count of eight. Breathe out for a count of eight." Sean spoke slowly, his voice quiet, but Corey could hear the concern. "That's it, slow it down," he encouraged.

Finally, Corey felt in control of his body again. "I'm sorry," he murmured.

"What for?" Sean sounded exasperated.

"Half the time when I call you I'm freaked out," he replied. "You must think I'm a fucked up mess."

"I think you're doing pretty damn good considering you've been through something I can't even conceive of. Tell me what you remember."

Corey released a shaky breath. He fisted his free hand and pressed it hard to his mouth. Not everything was clear, but he remembered more this time than he ever had before. The Iraqi village in the middle of Afghanistan; Jonah encouraging Corey to do what he had to do, standing at his back as he did; dead women and children; Michael Nygaard responsible for the slaughter; Corey's culpability. Even awake, when he closed his eyes, Corey could see the haunted, accusing eyes of the innocents staring at him.

"Corey, if you don't want to tell me about it, at least write it down and go talk to a professional about it," Sean pleaded.

"I was in combat," Corey blurted. "But the location didn't make sense. Jonah was there but he shouldn't have been. He ordered me to make entry into a structure. That asshole Nygaard was there." He inhaled deeply, struggling for words.

"But none of it was real," Sean said calmly. "It didn't really happen and nothing can hurt you."

The sound of quiet guitar music reached Corey. It was a quiet song and Sean strummed lightly. Corey rolled his head to ease the muscles in his neck and back. He took a deep breath and it came easier than it had just moments before.

"The room was full of dead Afghani women and children," Corey said. "And I think Nygaard killed them. He tried to get me to help him, like implicating me would keep me silent."

The music stopped for several seconds before it resumed. "But you aren't going to keep silent, are you? You're going to tell the truth about what you know, right?"

"Right." It was the one thing Corey was sure of.

Neither of them spoke for a long while. Corey lay back down on his rack. He sighed heavily, feeling his body relax finally.

"I finished the verse to the song," Sean said after awhile.

"Good. I knew you'd get it figured out." Corey tugged the covers up to his chin. "Can I hear it?"

Sean played the song from the beginning. Corey listened to the second verse closely. Sean sang about a soldier, all alone on his birthday and getting drunk. The verse saddened Corey slightly, as Sean sang about how beautiful the soldier was when his smile chased away the sadness in his eyes.

"What do you think?" Sean asked when he was done.

"That's amazing. You're a fucking poet." Corey's eyes were too heavy to open and his tongue was thick in his mouth, making it difficult to speak.

"I don't know about that," Sean said dubiously. "But I do know that you need to go back to sleep."

Corey realized he was nodding off, even as they talked. "Okay. Call me tomorrow?"

"Absolutely. Good night, Corey."

"'Night."

Corey ended the call and set his phone aside. Just as he drifted off to sleep, he realized the new verse of Sean's song was about things Corey had confessed to him about why he'd left home.

Corey was astounded; Sean had written the verse about him.

Chapter Nine

Corey concluded his segment of the classroom instruction they were conducting. He kicked the students loose for a short break. His work was done for the afternoon, thanks to Master Sergeant Whitfield.

He was ten minutes early for his appointment with the doctor. There were a few other enlisted Marines in the waiting room, but no one Corey knew. He settled uncomfortably into a chair that let him see the entrance door and the door to the back office. He tried to read the outdated magazine but he couldn't concentrate. He sat instead, fingers laced, his leg bouncing violently.

Luckily, they didn't make Corey wait too long. A nurse appeared and called his name. He did his best to keep up the small talk he knew was expected. She was fast and efficient at getting his vitals before leaving him alone in the chilly exam room.

Corey had always hated exam rooms. He hated the way the paper crinkled every time he moved, it always seemed so loud in the empty rooms. The charts and posters that were hung on the back of the door and on the walls were enough to make him paranoid about every small ache, pain and freckle.

A knock at the door gave Corey a warning just before the doctor entered. A tall, dark haired man, wearing a blue dress shirt and matching tie, entered the room. He was smiling. "I'm Doctor Goldman." He held out his hand and Corey shook it, impressed with the strength of his grip. "You must be Staff Sergeant Yarwood."

The doctor sat on the low, rolling stool and reviewed Corey's thin chart. He asked a few questions for clarification, before setting the folder side. "So, what is it I can do for you, today, Corey?" His expression was expectant, as if he already had an idea of what Corey's complaint might be.

"I've been having trouble sleeping," Corey said, tugging at the cuffs of his uniform blouse. "It's starting to affect more than just how tired I am during the day."

"Understandable. Sleep deprivation has an impact on your overall health." Goldman took a deep breath. "How long have you been back from deployment?"

"Nine months," Corey replied. "I kept waiting for it to get better as I adjusted to being back."

"That sometimes happens," the doctor said easily. "But nine months is an awfully long time for it to keep going on. Is it just trouble getting to sleep or do you have trouble staying asleep, too?"

Corey sucked in a sharp breath. He ran one palm along his thigh while he gripped the side of the exam table with the other. "Sometimes…I wake up from a nightmare and can't get back to sleep."

Doctor Goldman nodded knowingly. "Are you having flashbacks or anxiety attacks too?"

Corey started to answer in the negative, before he remembered that day he'd sat in his Jeep and desperately called Sean. "I hadn't until recently. No flashbacks, but I had a panic attack a couple of days ago. At least that's what I think it was." He described what had happened, what he'd felt. When he told about calling Sean, Corey simply called him a friend.

Goldman stood up and pulled his stethoscope from around his neck. He listened to Corey's heart and his breathing. He took his pulse, palpated his glands and examined his eyes and ears. "You guys are all in such good shape and good health, but that's no excuse for me to get lazy in my due diligence."

"I appreciate that, sir," Corey responded automatically. He always appreciated it when someone insisted on doing a good job, at all times.

The doctor resumed his seat on the stool and took out his prescription pads. "I'm going to give you a prescription for a common sleep aid," he said as he wrote. "But I'm also referring you to the Warrior Clinic for counseling."

Corey sighed and ran both palms along his thighs. "Yeah, I sort of expected that."

Goldman looked up at him in surprise. "I usually get more of an argument. You guys usually think you're too tough to need help."

"Well, a couple guys I really respect told me recently that it was time to talk to someone about some of this stuff." Corey ran a hand over his mouth and down his chin.

"Good for them." The doctor tore two sheets from his pad. "Get this filled at any pharmacy. Come back in a month and we'll see how you're doing." He handed Corey the second sheet. "Take this down the hall to the clinic and have them schedule you an appointment. No reason not to get that taken care of since you're here."

Corey chuffed a laugh at Goldman's too bright smile. "No, you're right."

As they both stood to leave, Doctor Goldman turned toward Corey. "You're going to be fine, Corey. You're getting help before anything gets out of control. You really will be okay."

"Thanks." Corey's face warmed at the sincerity and concern in the doctor's expression.

It was a short walk down a deserted hallway to the counseling clinic. The discreetly labeled door opened into a warm and inviting reception area. To Corey's relief, there was no one there except the receptionist. She greeted him as soon as he entered.

Corey crossed to the desk where she sat. He guessed she was about his age. "How can I help you, Staff Sergeant?" she asked, openly eyeing his insignias.

Handing over the paper Goldman had given him, Corey replied, "I guess I need to make an appointment, ma'am."

She never lost her smile as she read Goldman's scrawl. She handed over a clipboard with a sheet already attached and a pen held on by a string. "Why don't you fill this out while I pull up the schedule and see what works best for you." She paused, making her next words almost sound like an afterthought. "Be really, really honest with your answers. No one cares how you've been coping and nothing leaves this office. But it's easier to figure out just what kind of help you need if we have all the accurate information."

Corey nodded his understanding and took a deep breath. As he answered the questions, Corey understood the reason for her request. He shifted his weight from foot to foot, resisting the urge to lie or at the very least downplay. He was truthful about the level of his alcohol use. He was relieved he could honestly answer 'no' to all the questions about his level of off-duty violence. He described his issues with sleep, answered no to flashbacks but yes to anxiety attacks.

The question about erectile dysfunction brought him to a full stop. He ran the back of his hand over his forehead. Fuck. Reluctantly, he answered yes.

He handed the clipboard back to the receptionist. "My current billet is BRC. I regularly put in sixteen-hour days. I'm not sure I can make it back in here in less than a week, when we have night training."

"Doctor Ingram keeps Saturday hours specifically for Marines like you," she said brightly. "Eleven a.m. this Saturday?"

Corey stood dumbfounded for several seconds. He should have known they would have a solution to any excuse he could muster to avoid getting help. "I have night training Friday. Anything in early afternoon?"

Her smile widened. "One p.m. is open."

"That'll do," he replied.

She jotted the appointment down on a little card and bid him a good day.

Prescription filled and back in his Jeep, Corey tried to call Sean. He was pleased when the call was answered.

"I was just wondering when I was going to hear from you," Sean greeted him.

"I just saw the doctor and I'm on my way back to work so I thought I'd call."

"How did it go with the doctor?"

Corey filled him in on the events of the last hour. "So, we'll see if the meds help and then I get to find out just how fucked up in the head I am."

"You're not fucked up. You're completely treatable. So, I was thinking," Sean hesitated, "maybe we could go to dinner or something, Friday night."

"We're conducting night training Friday night," Corey told him. "It'll be one or two a.m. before we're done. I know you're always awake that late but I'm going to be wiped. And I have that appointment Saturday."

"Okay, it was just a thought," Sean said tightly. "But you have stuff to do, and that's cool. I should let you go now, you probably have to get back to work."

Corey was stunned by Sean's rapid change in demeanor. His tone of voice was strained. Corey knew that tone, he'd used a few times when he realized he was being blown off. "Are you working this weekend or something?" he asked quickly.

"No, not really," Sean answered quietly.

"Then what's wrong with Saturday night? My appointment is in the early afternoon, after that, I'm free." He kept his own voice enthusiastic so Sean would know he wanted this.

"Saturday is great." The pleasure was back in Sean's tone and Corey silently breathed a sigh of relief.

"I gotta get back to work but I'll call you tonight."

"I'll answer."

§ § §

When Corey arrived at the counselor's office on Saturday, the outer office was empty. Not even the receptionist was there. An inner door stood open. A tall, middle aged woman appeared.

She smiled. "You must be Corey."

"Yes, ma'am," he replied, rooted to his spot.

"I'm Doctor Ingram. Come on back." She stepped aside and let Corey step past her into the back office.

He shouldn't have been surprised the doctor was a woman. He buried that thought. Glancing around, Corey realized the inner office was more like an inviting living room. There was comfortable looking furniture arranged in a loose circle. The desk in the corner was the only indication this was a place of business.

"Sit where you'd like," Doctor Ingram said. "Make yourself comfortable."

Dropping down onto a loveseat, Corey discovered it was as comfortable as it appeared. He picked up a nearby throw pillow and placed it in his lap, idly plucking at a loose thread.

Ingram set a bottle of water on the table in front of him, along with a box of tissues. That made Corey nervous. It was bad enough he had to talk about this shit, he didn't want to become a blubbering idiot.

"Thank you, ma'am," he said, never letting his manners lapse.

The doctor settled into a large, square, well-stuffed chair. She curled her legs beneath her. Corey recognized the form he'd filled out the other day, set on top of a legal pad. "Now, Corey, don't worry about what I write down. I'm not making a diagnosis. I'm not speculating. I take notes on things I want to remember to ask you so I don't have to interrupt you while you're speaking. I'll also have things I'll want to revisit during future appointments. Okay?"

"Yes, ma'am," Corey replied. It sounded reasonable.

"There are a couple of things I want to go over so I've got a clear idea of what we need to work on."

Corey nodded.

"I'm guessing it's the nightmares and insomnia that are causing you the most trouble?"

"Yes, ma'am. Doctor Goldman gave me a prescription for

that. It's only been a couple days but so far, things seem better."

"Good. That's really good. You've reported only one anxiety attack. By taking care of the sleep issues and coming here, you've probably headed off more frequent and more severe episodes, so that's also good."

Doctor Ingram paused and Corey wiped his sweaty palms on the thighs of his jeans.

"You've reported no flashbacks and no hyper-vigilance, but I'm willing to bet you have very mild symptoms and just don't recognize them." The doctor canted her head as she regarded Corey closely. "Do some of your memories seem more vivid that others? Do you lose time? Several minutes where you don't know what you were just doing? Are you uncomfortable in crowds? Do you feel aggressive if you don't have a wall at your back and all exits in view?"

Corey sat in stunned silence for several moments, mouth hanging slack as he stared at Doctor Ingram. "I don't lose track of time," he managed through his tightened throat. "But all the rest? Yeah." He ran the tips of his fingers over his forehead. "So, I'm more fucked up than I realized," Corey said, gripping the throw pillow tightly.

"Not at all," Ingram said emphatically. "You're reacting very reasonably, considering what you've most likely been through. Now, how about your personal relationships? Has your relationship with your family changed since you've been back?"

"No. We haven't been close since I joined the Marines," Corey answered.

"How about your friends? Fellow Marines?"

Corey thought about it. He used to spend weekends with other Marines from his platoon. He frequently spent evenings in the various enlisted cantinas. He realized he hadn't attended a Single Marines event since he'd returned from deployment. "I guess I've been keeping to myself a lot. I mean, I go out sometimes, but that's usually to get drunk."

"I did see you've been self-medicating with alcohol," Ingram said, referring to Corey's completed form.

"I'm trying to stop that. It was mostly to help me sleep so…" Corey shrugged.

Doctor Ingram made some quick notes. "Next time, we'll talk about how that's going. Are you doing any socializing?"

"I hang out with a corporal from my old platoon sometimes." Tyler was easy going and didn't try to make Corey talk about the things they'd done during their deployment.

"Have you made any friends among the Marines at your new assignment?" the doctor asked.

Until she asked, Corey hadn't thought that was strange. "No ma'am. I guess I haven't."

"Emotional distancing and isolation is a symptom, too. I'm not too worried, though. I think it will fix itself as we make progress in other areas." She paused and consulted Corey's questionnaire. "Now, I know this is going to feel invasive and overly personal," Ingram said slowly, "but we need to discuss it. You've reported erectile dysfunction."

Corey's face flamed. He blew out a tense breath and looked down at the pillow in his lap. "Yes, ma'am."

"What types of issues are you having? Are you able to get an erection? Or do you just have trouble maintaining it once you have one?" Her question was professional and clinical but Corey was still embarrassed.

"I have trouble getting hard, yeah." He forced himself to meet her eyes. "Sometimes even when I do I can't co…orgasm. One time I damn near rubbed myself raw and it still wouldn't work."

"Corey, have you had sex since you've been back from Afghanistan?" Ingram asked gently.

Sighing, Corey confessed, "No, ma'am."

"Were you in a relationship before your deployment?"

"No, ma'am."

"So, this issue hasn't adversely affected an emotional

relationship, correct?"

Corey hesitated.

"Or has it?" the doctor persisted.

"I met someone, recently," Corey said hesitantly.

"Good! That's very good, Corey." Doctor Ingram smiled brightly. "Can I ask this person's name so we can discuss it?"

He rubbed a hand over his suddenly dry mouth. "His name is Sean."

"Sean. Okay. Have you discussed with Sean any of what's going on?" Neither the doctor's voice nor expression gave any sign of surprise or disapproval.

"Actually, yeah," Corey replied. "He's been trying to help me with the nightmares so I can cut back on the drinking."

"I'm really glad to hear that. That's tremendous. But, no sex, yet, correct?"

"No, ma'am." Corey couldn't help his smile, despite his discomfort over discussing something so personal. "I really want to, though."

Ingram nodded knowingly. "So your drive is intact? That's good. You have the desire. Your body just doesn't want to cooperate right now, it seems. Have you had any physical contact with Sean? Kissing? Petting? Frottage?"

Corey's face flamed, even as his groin tightened pleasantly at the memories. "Yes. All of that."

"Have you avoided sex because you couldn't get an erection?" Ingram asked gently. "Or are you avoiding it out of anxiety?"

Corey sat up straighter, pleasure sweeping through him at thoughts of Sean. "Neither. It's just been timing. The first time we kissed, I wanted to drag him into his apartment and...sorry." Christ, but he was suddenly talkative.

"Don't be sorry. You wanted to have sex with Sean," Doctor Ingram encouraged.

What the hell. He was here to get help for these problems.

"Yeah, there wasn't time, but that was okay 'cause I couldn't get ha…an erection. The second time, though, no problem. I'm just afraid I won't be able to orgasm." Instead of feeling ashamed, Corey felt like a weight had been lifted.

"Okay, you definitely have some anxiety issues," Ingram said as she wrote notes on her legal pad. "I'm going to give you a prescription for something you can take when you have an actual episode, rather than something you take every day. I think that, and getting you sleeping regularly, will solve quite a few problems. The rest we can talk about until you come to terms with them." She took out a prescription pad and began to scribble. "Would you like a prescription for a little blue pill? Physically, you're fine. But they might give you a boost that will calm your anxiety and keep you from worrying yourself *into* dysfunction."

Corey had never considered taking that type of medication. Now, though, he didn't want to take a chance at ruining things with Sean tonight.

"Ma'am, that would be so great," he replied, not bothering to hide his smile.

CHAPTER TEN

Corey exited the pharmacy, prescriptions in hand. He threw away the packaging in a nearby trashcan. Inside his Jeep, Corey retrieved the canvass bag from the back seat that he used to store things he frequently used. Tossing the prescription bottles into the bag, he threw it back into the rear seat and reached for his cell phone.

He hoped Sean was available for an early dinner. Corey was ready to get their date started. His patience was at an end.

"Hey, I was just thinking about you," Sean said when he answered. "How did your appointment go?"

"It sucked but it was okay," Corey replied. "I'm glad it's over."

"You're going back, though, right?" asked Sean.

"Yeah, Wednesday night." Corey didn't want to talk about himself anymore. "So, any thoughts on what we're gonna do tonight?"

"I know it's cliché, but I was thinking dinner and a movie." Sean's answer was hesitant. "We haven't had a lot of uninterrupted time to just sit and talk to each other."

Yeah, Corey really liked that idea. Good food to focus on and an evening to themselves to get to know each other. "I like that idea a lot. Is there someplace in particular you'd like to go?" He took a chance and started toward Sean's apartment.

"I can think of a couple of places but they're all down here. What's up by you?" Sean asked.

"It doesn't matter what's up by me because I'm on my way to you," Corey replied. "Unless now is a bad time?"

"No! Shit. Yes. No." Sean was obviously moving quickly. "Where are you now? I need time to shower."

Christ. Corey's cock started to harden at the thought of Sean, naked and wet. He knew just how fresh and clean Sean would smell when Corey arrived. "If now is a bad time, I can wait until later," he said reluctantly.

"You don't have to come here," replied Sean. "I can come get you."

"You've played chauffeur for me enough already. I'm not drinking so I can do the driving tonight."

"Okay, okay." Sean capitulated. "Have you left the base yet?"

"I'm pulling out of the main gate now." Traffic was clear and Corey pulled out onto Vandergrift Boulevard and headed for the Five-South.

Sean made a nervous sound. "I might need more time to dress after you get here, but I can be mostly ready by then. Do you remember how to get here?"

"I've got advanced training in navigation," Corey answered with a laugh. "I can find your condo again."

As he'd anticipated, Corey had no trouble finding his way back to Sean's. He pressed the doorbell with his thumb and heard chimes in the distance.

Sean seemed harried when he opened the door. "Hi," he greeted warmly, standing aside for Corey to enter. "I just need to get dressed and we can go." Sean led Corey down the short hallway into the great room.

Corey swallowed against his suddenly dry throat. Sean wore nothing but a pair of track pants that hung low on his hips. He struggled not to stare at Sean's tan skin and defined muscles. "Typical civilian; taking your time to get ready to go anywhere," he joked, trying to distract himself from the dimples just above the swell of Sean's ass.

Sean laughed, obviously not offended. "It's the hair."

Corey didn't give a shit. He liked Sean's hair. He had highlights added to his dark blond locks but it wasn't ridiculous or feminine. It looked good. Sean wore it long on top and had mastered that artfully disheveled appearance Corey secretly admired. Short, soft strands framed Sean's handsome, sharp featured face. He wondered what it would feel like to run his fingers through the strands of Sean's hair.

"The end result makes it worth it," Corey said, glancing nervously around Sean's living room to hide the warmth in his face.

"Did you change clothes after your appointment?" Sean asked from his bedroom doorway.

"No. Why?" Corey looked down at himself, suddenly worried he looked like shit.

"You met with your counselor dressed like that?" Sean asked incredulously.

"What's wrong with it?" Corey cataloged his un-scuffed lace up boots, clean dark wash jeans, and dark blue short-sleeved Henley.

"Absolutely nothing." Sean's heated gaze traveled Corey's length, a mischievous smile teasing around his mouth. "If your counselor is gay, he probably had a hard time keeping his mind on his work."

Corey barked a surprise laugh. He glanced down at himself again, realizing his shirt clung to him, revealing the muscles of his chest and abs. Christ, his thighs looked huge in these jeans. "My counselor is a woman so I think you probably wish she *was* gay."

Sean blew out an exaggerated breath and with a shake of his head, disappeared into his bedroom.

Corey smiled to himself, pleasantly surprised that someone like Sean found him so attractive. He was glad he'd planned ahead and picked up lube and condoms at a pharmacy off base.

Sean emerged wearing a snug pair of distressed jeans and a white, crew neck cotton shirt so thin, Corey thought he could see skin through the fabric. It was going to be a long dinner.

When they were settled in the Jeep, Sean directed Corey to a nearby steakhouse. He said the food was good, the booths semi-private, and the staff didn't mind if you lingered awhile.

Corey's cell buzzed so he checked the display, ready to ignore the call. He paused when he saw it was Tyler Howe. The corporal might just be checking in to see if Corey needed someone to hang out with tonight.

Corey answered, putting his phone on speaker. "Hey, man, how's it goin'?" he greeted.

"Dude, it's pretty fucked," Tyler answered in a strained voice.

Alarm raced through Corey's system. "What's wrong?" From the corner of his eye, he saw Sean look over in concern.

"Fuckin' Nygaard keeps calling me. Even when I don't answer, he leaves me messages." Tyler sighed heavily. "He wants to see me. He wants to explain why he killed that woman. He says he wasn't in control of himself and he needs me to know why."

"Tell him to go fuck himself," Corey responded hotly. "Don't let him suck you into his shit." His hands clenched tightly around the steering wheel, his knuckles whitening.

"Dude, he put his dad on the phone with me." Tyler's tone was mournful. "He swears Nygaard has that brain trauma thing and doesn't deserve to be punished for anything."

Anger burned in Corey's chest. "That's a load of crap. He's always been a loose cannon and an asshole. Now he's got himself in a shit-load of trouble and he wants to make it everyone else's fault."

Tyler's frustrated sigh was loud. "If I just go let him say what he wants to say, maybe he'll leave me the fuck alone. If I keep dodging him, I think he's gonna keep calling me."

Corey shrugged his tense shoulders even though Tyler couldn't see. "It sounds like you made up your mind. Why the fuck are you calling me?" he snapped.

"He wants to talk to you, too," Tyler replied. "If we go together we can show we're on the same side about this."

Corey rolled his eyes and sighed explosively. It was hard to take another breath. "How do you know he wants to talk to me?"

"His old man told me. The lawyer told them they can't contact you about your testimony without going through the J.A.S. lawyer." Tyler made a scoffing sound. "I guess the guy told them it's fine to have you over and just tell Nygaard's side of the story."

After Hirata had talked with Nygaard's defense lawyer, he'd warned Corey he might have to have contact with Nygaard, at least until the Corps discharged him. He'd admonished Corey to keep his mouth shut and his ears open, if that happened.

Shifting in his seat, Corey twisted his whitened knuckles on the wheel. His heart was pounding its way out of his chest, his left leg bounced violently. "I don't give a shit what his excuses are, and you shouldn't either. Tell him and his old man to fuck off."

"Jesus Christ, Corey," Tyler snapped. "Don't you want to see if he'll admit what the fuck it is he's been hiding about what went down in Ghazni?"

That was about the last thing Corey wanted. He struggled to drag a harsh breath into his lungs. "When do they want to talk?" he asked in a strangled voice.

"Right now," Tyler said derisively. "They're fucking barbequing like Nygaard's just having a couple buddies over to visit."

"Fuck that!" Corey barked. "I'm on a fucking date, Tyler. I *am not* interrupting my plans for this fuck-stick."

"Oh, shit!" Tyler gasped, sounding mortified. "Dude, I didn't think…I mean, I didn't know…you don't usually…you haven't… fuck. I'm sorry, man. I'll let you go."

A gentle hand on his arm made Corey glance at Sean. "Hang on a sec, Tyler."

"Do you need to go talk to this guy?" Sean asked in a low voice. "Will it help you to confront him and maybe get some answers?"

"No, don't worry about it," Corey said with an impatient shake of his head.

"Corey," Sean said heatedly. "It's still early. We can get dinner afterward. You need to deal with some of this shit."

Jesus. He'd gone from thinking he was going to get laid tonight to fighting back panic at the thought of confronting Michael Nygaard.

"You don't have to take me home," Sean said into Corey's silence. "I'll go with you and when you're done, we can pick up where we left off."

The last thing Corey wanted was to expose Sean to Nygaard's toxic personality again. He had no idea what the fuck was going to come out of Nygaard's mouth that might change the way Sean viewed him. "Fine. Let's go and get this over with." Corey decided to let the shit hit the fan now, early enough the pain would be minimal if Sean started to see him as a monster. Or if he even started to see himself that way.

Tyler told Corey where to pick him up so they could arrive as a united front. When he disconnected, Corey threw the phone to the floorboard between his feet. It struck with a loud thud and bounced a time or two before settling with a plastic clatter. He couldn't catch his breath and the only thing he could hear was the thundering of his own heart.

Sean's hand was suddenly covering one of his own on the steering wheel. Sean said something but Corey couldn't hear him.

"Corey, slow down and pull over," Sean said firmly, raising his voice almost to a shout. His hand patted Corey's before gripping his fingers again.

He tried to focus on why Sean wanted him to pull over. Corey didn't understand. Sean repeated his demand. Corey glanced down at Sean's hand covering his and caught sight of the speedometer.

"Fuck," he gasped, pulling his foot off the gas pedal. The street ahead looked tunneled, buildings and landscaping rolling by in a blur. He'd had no idea he'd been going that fast.

"It's okay," Sean said from beside him. "Just slow down and carefully pull to the side of the road."

Wrapping himself around a telephone pole or slamming into the rear of semi by himself was one thing, but he had Sean with him. "I can't fucking breathe," Corey gasped.

"I know." Sean rubbed the back of Corey's hand. "Once you pull over we can fix that."

Finally, Corey found a safe section of shoulder. He braked harder than he meant to, bringing them to a jarring halt. He slammed the gearshift into park and leaned his head back against the seat. He clutched at the front of his shirt, wishing it would let him breathe and his chest would stop hurting.

"Where are your prescriptions?" Sean asked.

Corey didn't understand what Sean was asking.

"You said the counselor gave you prescriptions. Did you fill them?" Sean's tense voice broke into Corey's silence.

Finally, his brain engaged. Corey turned to look for the bag in the backseat.

"I'll get them," Sean said, unfastening his seat belt. "What am I looking for?"

Corey gasped out a description. Sean reappeared with the bag, already tugging at the zipper. Corey started to reach for the contents but Sean pushed his hand away. "I've got it. Xanax. That's got to be it."

Sean deftly took Corey's nearest hand and poured a single, small tablet into his palm. He unscrewed the lid of the water bottle sitting in the center console. Corey tossed the pill into his mouth and took the water bottle from Sean with a violently trembling hand. When he'd swallowed the pill, he handed the bottle back and clutched at his shirt front again, wondering how long the medication would take to work.

"Just lean your head back and close your eyes," Sean said softly. "Breathe slowly in through your nose and out through your mouth."

Corey complied. He closed his eyes and let Sean's warm, smooth voice drift over him as he counted to eight over and over again.

In a single instant, Corey's shoulders relaxed, the pain in his chest eased, and he took a long, deep breath, filling his lungs. He lifted his head and opened his eyes slowly, wondering if there was ever going to be a time when Sean didn't have to always see him at his worst.

Sitting up, Corey ran both hands over his face. There was a light sheen of sweat on his skin and his shirt was sticking to him in places. Fucking great.

A plastic rattle sounded beside him and Corey glanced over. Sean still held Corey's canvas bag open in his lap. He sat shaking one of the prescription bottles, smirking at Corey.

"Good to know you and I are on the same page about some things," Sean said, still smirking.

Corey focused on the bottle he held and realized it was the Viagra. The bottle of lubricant and large roll of condoms were obvious inside the bag, as well.

"Jesus," Corey moaned, reaching for the bag. Sean must really think he was fucked up.

To Corey's surprise, Sean slapped his hands away again. "I got it. Just sit there and relax."

"It's not what you think," Corey protested.

"Jesus, I hope it is!" Sean exclaimed with a laugh.

"No, the Viagra is because—" Corey stopped short. He was fucked either way. Sean would think he was a perv, popping Viagra to have marathon sex. Or, Sean would know the truth; that Corey's dick didn't work three-quarters of the time.

"The Viagra is because you're battling anxiety, and anxiety makes us all go limp every once in a while." Sean shrugged and put everything back into the bag, zipping it closed. "I'm flattered that it matters enough for you to plan ahead."

Corey sighed. "It is way too fucking early in this…whatever it is…for this much drama."

"If this is as bad as it gets, I can deal with this easily. Do you need me to drive?" Sean's expression was placid.

Corey chuffed a laugh. "No, I'm fine now." He put the Jeep in drive and carefully pulled back into traffic.

They found Tyler parked where he said he'd be, at the end of the block where Nygaard lived.

"You brought your date?" Tyler asked as he climbed into the back of the Jeep.

"He wanted to come," Corey replied blandly. "I'm beginning to think he's just fucking nuts."

"Well, then, he's perfectly equipped to deal with you," Tyler quipped as Corey rounded the corner.

Sean laughed.

They sobered as Corey pulled to the curb across the street from Nygaard's house. The garage door was open but Corey didn't see anyone moving around. Sean and Tyler climbed out of the Jeep. Corey sat frozen, his hands gripping the steering wheel again. He swallowed hard. Why the fuck had he agreed to do this?

Corey jumped when his door opened. Sean stood there, watching him closely. "The fact that just agreeing to do this gave you a panic attack, means there is something here you need to confront. If you're not ready, you're not ready. But you're going to so much effort to make things better for yourself, why stop short?"

Sean extended his hand to Corey, encouraging and offering support at the same time. Reluctantly, Corey took it and slowly climbed out of the Jeep.

Stepping in close, Sean spoke so only Corey could hear. "You might think that all of this makes you look weak. The fact that you're facing this entire thing head-on means you're strong."

Corey sighed and nodded. He clenched his jaw, unable to look Sean in the eye. He took a deep breath, and steeled himself for the coming confrontation. If Sean thought he was strong, Corey was damn well going to *be* strong.

Together they crossed to Nygaard's house. As they reached

the driveway, an older man who strongly resembled Nygaard came out of the garage.

"Thank you gentlemen for coming." He extended his hand. "I'm Jim Nygaard, Michael's father."

They each shook his hand as they introduced themselves.

"Sean isn't a Marine, he's a friend of mine," Corey said sharply. "Nygaard needs to make this quick, 'cause I'm not making my friend sit through our dirty laundry all night. Understood?"

"Of course, of course," Jim said, leading them all through the garage. "It means a lot to Michael that you'd come hear him out, so it means a lot to our family."

Corey looked closer and saw the haggard appearance Jim Nygaard tried to mask with a smile. There was a tightness around his eyes and mouth, a tension about him that belied the façade of the gracious host. Corey dialed back his resentment toward the man. However inconvenienced Corey was, Nygaard's father was dealing with what probably felt like a world gone mad.

Jim Nygaard led them all into a spacious backyard with a raised wooden deck. Michael Nygaard sat at a table on the deck. Another man, who looked like he was also related to Nygaard, stood in front of a barbeque grill.

"Hey guys! You made it." Nygaard jumped to his feet. He shook each of their hands. Corey introduced Sean stiffly and reluctantly. "You guys want a beer? Dad, get the guys some beers."

"No." All movement stopped at Corey's loudly spoken word. "This is not a social call. We are not here for a fucking barbeque. Say what you have to say so we can get on with our lives."

The tension was palpable and Corey felt bad for Nygaard's father. But they were not friends. Nygaard's actions were inexcusable, and Corey was not going to be charmed or manipulated into acting like they were all friends.

"At least sit down and make yourselves comfortable," Jim Nygaard said into the awkward silence.

Nygaard was putting his family through enough already,

Corey didn't want to make it any worse, so he dropped down into a chair directly across the table from Nygaard. The third man approached, carrying a platter laden with grilled meat.

"Guys, this is my older brother John," Nygaard said.

Corey stood and shook John's hand politely. Tyler and Sean followed his lead, both gracious as they introduced themselves to John. Corey resumed his seat, crossed his arms over his chest and said to Nygaard, "You wanted to talk, so talk."

"First, Corey, I want you to know how much it means to me that you came to the jail last Saturday," Nygaard said solemnly. "We're not in the same command anymore, so you didn't have to come, but I appreciate that you did."

Corey stared at Nygaard, not responding to any of his words. He wasn't in the mood for trite niceties. He wanted Nygaard to say something worth listening to.

"Anyway, I need you guys to know that what happened wasn't my fault," Nygaard said, twirling a half-full beer bottle in his fingers.

"Then whose fucking fault was it?" Corey demanded angrily. "You kicked her sister out of the house. You were alone in there with your girlfriend when she was beaten to death. You were covered in her blood when they found you. Who the fuck else's fault is it?"

"No, I did it, or at least I guess I did. I don't remember," Nygaard said hastily.

Corey threw up his hands in anger. "Why don't you just be a man and accept responsibility for your actions instead of always making excuses?"

"I have Traumatic Brain Injury, compounded by PTS." Nygaard sounded coached and Corey clenched his jaw. "I've seen a doctor and had some tests. One of the IED blasts must have caused the physical damage. But, Corey, you know what caused the PTS."

Silence settled over the group and a chill swept through

Corey. He held Nygaard's gaze without blinking, determined to give nothing away.

"No, man, no one knows what the fuck turned you into a coward and a woman beater," Tyler said with vehemence, abruptly breaking the strained silence. "You keep fucking up, you expect everyone to cover your ass and lie for you, and when you finally go too fucking far, you throw your fellow Marines under the bus."

Corey glanced at Tyler in surprise and saw he wore an angry expression. Corey couldn't remember a time he'd seen the calm and steady Tyler this angry. He wondered if Nygaard realized just how bad he'd fucked up to have pushed someone like Tyler to such rage.

"So you've got a boo-boo on your brain and you went through some scary shit over there," Corey sneered. "We all went through some shit, but most of us deal with it like men; like Marines. You're a bully and a chicken-shit, and you always have been. Now that you don't have anyone to bully into covering up for you, you blame the Marine Corps and the same Marines you used to bully."

"You *know* I was fucked up before what happened with Maritza, Corey," Nygaard pleaded. "You saw it, you know it."

Alarm flooded Corey's body with adrenaline sending it spiking through his system. He leapt to his feet, knocking his chair backward. "I didn't see shit!" he yelled.

"You ordered me!" Nygaard shouted, also jumping to his feet.

"I ordered you to secure a perimeter." Corey clenched his hands, taking a step around the table toward Nygaard. "The rest is on you." Only Corey had no idea what 'the rest' was.

"You ordered me! You sent me out there alone when I needed you." Nygaard pointed an accusing finger. Tyler placed a restraining hand on Corey's arm at the same time Jim Nygaard tried to calm his son. "You know you did or you wouldn't have covered it up."

Corey pushed past Tyler, only vaguely aware of the shouts

around him. He advanced on Nygaard, intending to shove his words back down his throat. "I didn't cover up a fucking thing. Especially not for a fuck-up like you!"

"What we saw ain't in the reports," Nygaard shouted, trying to get past his father and brother to reach Corey. "It ain't in the reports just like what we did to those dead insurgents ain't in the reports. You covered it up and it fucked me up. This is your fucking fault!"

Corey lunged, vision going red in his rage. He barely felt Tyler's and Sean's hands on him as he tore loose and nearly got his hands around Nygaard's lying throat.

"Corey, don't let him get to you!" Sean was suddenly in front of Corey, pushing at his chest. "If you do, he wins. Don't let him win."

Corey stepped back several paces. Sean followed him. Tyler stepped between Corey and Nygaard, face red with rage.

"We're outta here," Tyler said with disdain. "You don't want to explain. You just want to blame someone else."

"I needed help back then and I couldn't get it 'cause no one told the truth in the reports," Nygaard shouted as Corey allowed himself to be led away by Sean.

His rage cleared abruptly and he had one startling clear thought. Corey stopped walking, jolting Sean to a stop beside him. He slowly turned back toward Nygaard in time to see him shake off his father and brother. "You forget," Corey said with quiet menace, "I signed off on your after-action, Nygaard. It said the same thing that everyone else's reports said. You had your chance to tell *your* truth and you didn't take it. You don't get to re-write history now, because you don't like the consequences of your own actions."

Corey turned on his heel and strode out of the yard, Tyler and Sean tight on his six.

As they crossed the street to the Jeep, Sean held out a hand, palm up. "Keys," he demanded.

"What for?" Corey frowned.

"You're too upset to drive," replied Sean. "Whatever this guy did was bad, if it can get you this aggressive on a dose of Xanax."

Corey looked down at his trembling hands. He fished his keys out of his pocket and handed them to Sean.

When they stopped at the end of the block to let Tyler out at his car, Tyler leaned forward and put his hand on Corey's arm lightly.

"Sorry to drag you into this shit, dude," he said, his expression sheepish. "I shoulda known better. I'm sorry I fucked up your night, but thanks for coming with me."

Corey couldn't blame Tyler for any of this shit. "You know I got your back."

With a quick pat to Corey's arm, Tyler turned to Sean and shook his hand. "It was good to meet you, man," he said. "Sorry you had to see all that ugly shit."

"It's okay," Sean said with a small smile. "I think it actually might have done Corey some good."

Tyler opened the door and started to climb out. "Take care of him. He's earned it."

"That is the current plan," Sean replied.

They drove in silence for a short time. Corey stared out the window, focusing on his breathing and struggling to calm down. He had an idea of what Nygaard was talking about, but he certainly didn't order the asshole to do what he had done. He certainly never covered anything up. But he couldn't remember everything that had happened so could he really be sure?

"Are you still up for dinner?" Sean asked quietly, breaking the silence.

Corey cleared his throat. "Yeah. Let's go. Let's just pretend none of this ever happened."

"I think we'd better just stop thinking about it for now," Sean replied. "But it sounded like there are some things you need to deal with. Just, maybe not tonight."

Corey wasn't going to argue. He just wanted to forget, at least for a time. He wanted normal. He wanted to focus on Sean and see if maybe there was still a chance Sean wanted to focus on him.

"You know, you don't have to humor me," Corey said suddenly, surprising himself. "If this is all too fucked-up for you and you just want to go home and never see me again, I understand. It doesn't make you an asshole or anything."

Sean heaved a deep sigh. "At some point, you'll have to tell me who the fuck, besides Jonah, left you with a broken heart, so you keep expecting everyone to walk away and leave you."

Corey's heart clenched. He swallowed past the lump in his throat. "I'd rather talk about happier things," he said in a rough voice.

"Yeah, you've probably earned that today," Sean said quietly.

Corey let himself be led into the restaurant and seated in a dark, corner booth. He complied docilely when Sean ordered them both iced tea.

"Do you have any preferences?" Sean asked when Corey still hadn't opened the menu. "If you're not fussy, I can order for us both."

"Yeah, sure," Corey said, trying to rally enthusiasm.

Sean made it easy. He ordered them both antipasto salad, lasagna with meat sauce, and crunchy sourdough garlic bread. When the waitress asked if they wanted a bottle of wine with their meal, Sean quickly declined in favor of iced tea with lemon. Very calm and matter-of-fact, he began to talk.

At first, Corey had to force himself to focus on Sean's words and ask polite questions, but it didn't last long. Sean had gotten his break with a supporting role in the touring cast of a popular Broadway musical. Corey had heard of it, but never seen it. That role had led to lead roles off-Broadway, until he'd finally landed two back-to-back lead roles in Broadway productions. He'd spent three years in New York, longing for home.

"There is absolutely nothing wrong with New York, but it's just not California," Sean explained. "I missed the weather and the laid back attitude. I was happy when I finally came home."

"I've never been there," Corey said.

"I'm auditioning for a role on Broadway in a couple of weeks," replied Sean, forking cold cuts along with his salad greens. "If I get the part, you'll have to come visit me."

Corey's heart sank. The thought of Sean leaving for New York left him more devastated than he thought possible. *Christ, when had he gotten so fucking needy?*

Sean smoothly transitioned to talk of the television shows he'd had guest roles on. Corey was surprised at the quality of the shows. He didn't watch much television, so he'd never seen any of Sean's episodes, but he thought he might try renting some DVDs pretty soon.

"Have you ever done anything besides acting?" Corey asked with genuine curiosity.

Sean hesitated. "Early on I did some modeling. My portfolio is pretty interesting," Sean said with a smirk. "I don't do as much print work as I used to. What I do now is usually in Europe. My early stuff is damn near pornographic, though."

"Are you fucking serious?" Corey asked in surprise, his mouth full of food.

"Damn near, but not quite," Sean was still smirking.

"Were you naked?" Just the thought had Corey's cock stirring.

"Yeah, but none of the photos were full-frontal." Sean shrugged. "Well, a lot of them would have been if it hadn't been for the strategic placement of props."

"Can I see this portfolio?" Corey asked hesitantly.

Sean chuckled. "Sure."

He listed the commercials he'd performed voiceover for, and Corey paused. Now that he thought about it, the voice in those commercials really did sound familiar. The greatest surprise came when Sean told him he'd provided the character voice for a series of animated movies. Corey couldn't go anywhere without seeing posters, toys, or some other thing associated with those movies. Sean told him that the production company was making noise about requiring him to attend the San Diego ComiCon the following summer for a panel and autograph signings.

"You have a geek fan base," Corey said with a laugh.

"Yes, I do, and they are some of the most exuberant fans of all." Sean was beaming with pride.

When their plates were cleared away, Corey sighed and sat back in his chair. He ran his hand over the back of his neck, realizing there was no tension there. Corey was surprised to find he was relaxed and happy.

"You look better," Sean said, studying Corey. "You seem like you're feeling better."

"I am." Corey agreed. "You managed to salvage the night." He was grateful and wondered how he could show it.

"It was easy. You're good company," Sean replied.

"I don't know about that." Corey snatched the check from the waitress when she approached. "It's the least I can do for what you've had to put up with, tonight," he said, to forestall Sean's objection.

"I haven't quite figured out yet, why you think spending time with you is such a burden," Sean mused.

Outside of the restaurant, Corey unlocked the Jeep. He was fine to drive now. He held the passenger door open for Sean.

With an arched eyebrow, Sean said, "So I get to be the girl in this relationship?"

"No." Corey frowned. "I'm just being a gentleman. If you get to a door first, I expect you to hold it open for me." That wasn't exactly true. Holding doors was a habit he'd developed with Kathryn and never seemed to have broken.

"You're on." Sean smiled as he slid into the Jeep.

Corey parked in front of Sean's condo as he was directed. He was climbing out when Sean reached back and retrieved the canvas bag. He unzipped it and withdrew what Corey knew was the bottle of Viagra.

Corey's stomach plummeted when he considered what Sean must think of him. "I don't need those," he protested when Sean tried to hand them to him.

"Just come on," Sean said, exiting the vehicle.

When Corey joined him for the walk to the door, Sean said, "If you're afraid I'll think you're trying to come off as an extra hard, super-hung stud with the stamina of Zeus, I already don't think that."

"And the alternative is so much better," Corey growled.

"Stress gets to us all, at one time or another," Sean replied with a smile, holding the outer door open for Corey to enter first. "You're under more stress than usual so it's a reasonable symptom for you to have."

Inside the condo, Sean took a bottle of water from the fridge and set it on the counter in front of Corey. He poured a blue, diamond shaped pill into Corey's palm. Reluctantly, Corey took the pill. He wondered if being freaked over Sean knowing about this would override the pill's ability to do its job. "It's supposed to take twenty to thirty minutes."

"Relax, Corey," Sean said quietly, stepping close and running a hand up his arm. "You don't have to be *ready to perform* on cue. Let's take our time and just enjoy each other, yeah?" Sean narrowed his eyes and cocked his head. "You don't feel pressured, do you? I don't want you to feel you have to do something you're not really interested in—"

Corey didn't let him finish. He wrapped a hand around the nape of Sean's neck and brought him in for a kiss. He didn't want Sean thinking Corey wasn't very, very interested in being with him.

He nipped at Sean's lush mouth, licking lightly against his tongue before darting away to change the angle and push in again. Sean mouthed at Corey's lips and licked back at him, following Corey's lead and giving him unquestioned access.

"Okay, then," Sean sighed, pulling back with a satisfied smirk. "That answers that. Just relax, make yourself comfortable. I'm not going to drag you into the bedroom and demand you start performing."

Corey almost made a joke about that actually sounding like fun. He stopped himself, though. He really was a little afraid he wouldn't be able to *perform* when Sean was ready for him to.

Sean walked past him and Corey turned toward the expansive windows looking out over the city. He walked to stand in front of them. Lights glittered on buildings and cars. The full moon still hung low in the sky and appeared huge. Corey thought the ocean might be visible during the day and when he paused to orient himself, he realized the windows faced the correct direction for it to be possible.

A sound caught his attention and Corey turned to see Sean in the doorway to his bedroom, leaning against the door sill. He was bathed in moonlight, the light and shadow making his features ethereal. He watched Corey closely, expression guarded.

"You're absolutely gorgeous standing there," Sean said breathlessly. "The moonlight makes your hair look golden. Your eyes are such a pale blue they're nearly white."

Corey wanted to return the compliment but nothing he could think to say was as eloquent as Sean's words.

"Whatever happens tonight, stay with me." Sean continued, catching Corey off guard. "Just don't leave me alone."

"Okay," Corey replied, voice rough. He took a step in Sean's direction, heart thumping against his breastbone.

"I don't know what this is. I have no idea where we're gonna go." Sean's throat worked as he swallowed. "I just know that I couldn't want you any more than I do right now."

Corey froze, halfway across the room. He couldn't catch his breath, only this time it was pleasant.

"I only need one thing from you." Sean still leaned against the doorsill but now Corey could see his calm was feigned. "Stop trying to run away from me."

Corey's stomach knotted. "I don't want to," he said hastily. Sean's expression told him he'd said that wrong. "I mean, I don't want to leave. I also don't want to hear you tell me to go."

Sean nodded slowly, as if he was piecing together a puzzle and the image was finally taking shape. "It'll get difficult. I just need to know you'll fight until there's nothing left to fight for, instead of calling a retreat."

"I used to know how to do that," he replied. "Fight, I mean."

"Why did you stop?" Sean asked quietly.

Corey swallowed hard. He buried his fists in his front pockets, his shoulders rising up tensely. "Kathryn was gone long before she moved out. We'd moved in together to go to college. Two years later she came home and said it wasn't working. She moved into the second bedroom we used for storage while she looked for a place of her own. I begged and pleaded for weeks. When she left, she left behind all the photos of us together from over the years. She didn't take anything I'd ever given her."

"What did she say when you pleaded with her?" Sean asked.

Corey sighed explosively. "That I could never make her happy because I didn't really want to. Because I really wanted to be with a man, and not a woman."

"It must be hard to try to…care again, when the only time you ever have in the past, that person walked away." Corey nodded, at Sean's words. His throat was too tight to speak. "This time, though, I'm not going to be the one to let you go."

Corey stared helplessly at Sean. He wasn't simply asking Corey not to walk away if things got a little rocky, he was vowing to do the same. Corey closed the final distance between them, standing close enough to feel the heat of Sean's body.

"You don't know what it's like to be involved with an active duty Marine," he said hesitantly, resisting the urge to touch Sean.

"You don't know what it's like to be involved with a working actor," Sean retorted.

Corey couldn't help his chuckle. "Fair enough. So, where do we go from here?"

Sean stood straight. "Kiss me," he whispered. "Slowly. I like it when you're slow and gentle."

Corey leaned in even as Sean pressed closer. He settled his mouth over Sean's lips, placing soft kisses along the seam. He wrapped his arms around Sean and pulled their bodies tight together. Sean's scent drifted to him, pleasant and spicy. Corey had grown very fond of that scent. He flicked his tongue lightly and Sean opened for him. Corey rubbed their tongues together gently, not pushing deep, not demanding more. Sean's fingers clutched at Corey's shoulders and his breath quickened along Corey's cheek.

Pulling back, Corey pressed their foreheads together and let his rushed breathing blend with Sean's. "I really want to be with you," he whispered.

Sean's smile was brilliant. He walked backward into his bedroom, pulling Corey along.

Corey ached to feel skin. He wanted Sean's heat against him with no barriers. He grabbed the hem of Sean's white shirt and tugged it up over his head, throwing it aside. Corey swiftly pulled his own Henley up and off, making his dog tags clink against each other. They reached the foot of Sean's bed and Corey wrapped one arm around Sean's waist, using it to pull him closer. He slid his other arm around Sean's shoulders and held him in place.

They were pressed together at their chests and stomachs. Sean's skin was smooth and warm against Corey's. He felt firm muscle beneath that smooth skin. Corey looked at Sean's face and found him staring at Corey's dog tags. Sean lifted his hands and slid his fingers along the stainless steel chain at Corey's neck and chest. Corey watched as Sean pressed his lips to the chain where it lay against his collarbone. He sighed in pleasure as Sean tongued the chain, moving downward until he reached Corey's tags.

Corey cradled Sean's head as he watched him lick the skin around and beneath Corey's tags. Sean nipped at the chain, his teeth clacking softly in the quiet room. Corey moaned softly as Sean placed open-mouthed kisses along his chest. He gasped when Sean took each of Corey's budded nipples into his mouth in turn, suckling them, dragging his teeth over them gently.

Sean grasped Corey's ribcage and gracefully dropped to his knees. He skimmed his palms down Corey's stomach and reached for the fly of his jeans. Corey watched Sean's focused expression as he parted Corey's jeans and lowered the waist of his briefs. Corey's cock was hard and easily sprang forward and into Sean's palm. Corey exhaled shakily.

Sean gripped Corey's hips and swallowed his erection down. Corey hissed and clenched the muscles of his stomach as Sean's mouth wrapped around him. Wet heat enveloped the head and slid down his length. Sean's tongue pressed to the underside of Corey's cock and he sucked hard when he pulled back.

Corey moaned. He looked down at Sean's sharp features, his lashes fanned over his cheeks and his red lips full, as they stretched around the width of this dick. He pushed his fingers through Sean's soft hair and cradled his head gently. Corey clenched the muscles of his arms to keep himself from pulling Sean forward. He struggled to keep his hips still so he didn't shove himself deep into Sean's throat.

"That's all you," he whispered. "The pill hasn't kicked in yet. That's all you, doing that to me."

Sean moaned around Corey's cock and sucked hard, just before flicking his tongue over the head. His eyes flicked up and Corey saw the hazel was nearly obscured by his widened pupils. He ran his thumbs over Sean's cheekbones affectionately.

Corey's chest heaved as he watched Sean slide up and down the length of his dick. He breathed heavily through his mouth as the first cluster of sparks raced the length of this spine. A slight pressure built in his temples and in his chest. A fresh surge of blood pulsed into his cock and Corey knew the Viagra was kicking in.

It became more difficult to keep his hips still. Corey pushed his fingers through Sean's hair again, loving the feel of the strands running along his skin. Heat swirled through his belly and settled low, his pelvis tingling.

"Sean," Corey whispered harshly. "Fuck, that's good."

Another surge of blood flooded his erection. Corey's balls tightened and lifted slightly. The pressure in his chest and temples increased and he was sure his dick doubled in size. His orgasm was approaching quickly. It had been too fucking long since he'd been with someone this way and he didn't want to blow without Sean pressed against him, until he could look into Sean's eyes.

"Christ, Sean, I'm close," he said through clenched teeth.

Sean pulled off with a loud, wet slurp. He worked his fist over Corey's aching cock, running the head over his lips as he spoke. "Do you want to come this way? Take the edge off?"

"No," Corey answered sharply. "Your mouth feels so good but I don't want it like this the first time."

"Okay," Sean said, giving the reddened head of Corey's dick a final kiss. "Let's get your shoes off." Still on his knees, Sean unlaced Corey's boots.

As Sean stood, Corey kicked off his boots and shoved his jeans down over his hips. Sean unlaced his own shoes and quickly stripped out of his clothes. Corey watched the moonlight play over the muscles rippling beneath Sean's tanned skin. He reached out and ran his palms down Sean's back and over his firm ass.

Sean stood and leaned into Corey's hands, arching and moaning in pleasure. He turned Sean in his arms and their erections nudged each other, Sean's leaving a wet smear on Corey's hip. Corey followed as Sean knelt on the bed and tugged Corey after him. When Sean turned and crawled up toward the headboard, Corey's cock twitched and ached at the sight. Sean's perfect ass was on display, his balls hanging low between his legs. Corey stroked his hand over his own erection as he followed up the length of the bed. He hadn't given it much thought before, but now, Corey wanted to bury himself in Sean's ass.

Rooting around in a drawer, Sean produced a bottle of lubricant and a condom. He handed them over to Corey with a smile. "You strike me as a toppy kinda guy."

"I can go either way," Corey replied, "but tonight, I want to be inside of you."

Sean leaned forward and kissed Corey, pushing his tongue in deep. He pulled back abruptly but kept their lips pressed together. "Do you want to prep me, or should I take care of it?"

Corey wrapped his free arm around Sean's waist and tugged him close. He pressed their hard cocks against each other and slid the sweat-slick skin of his chest over Sean's. "Are you fucking kidding me? What kind of man would leave you to do that yourself?"

"An impatient one?" Sean answered breathlessly.

"Haven't known any Recon Marines, have you?" Corey abruptly turned Sean to face the headboard, pushing gently at his shoulder. Who the fuck would be stupid enough to want to rush this with Sean?

Sean went eagerly, kneeling with his knees spread, dropping his head and keeping his ass on display for Corey. His mouth watered at the sight. He knew Sean's scent and smell would be strong in that intimate place.

Corey gripped Sean's rounded ass. He pressed an open-mouthed kiss to the base of his spine and licked along to the top of his cleft. Sean's skin was salty from sweat. He moaned softly when Corey licked him.

Spreading Sean wide, Corey tongued lightly at the clenching fissure he found there. Sean moaned and Corey flattened his tongue, dragging it from the base of Sean's balls to the tip of his spine. Sean sighed and shifted slightly. He breathed deeply and Sean's musky scent reached him, as strong and spicy as he'd thought it would be. Corey moaned against Sean, circling his hole with the point of his tongue. Sean pushed back into him with a groan.

Interesting, that.

Pressing his thumbs next to Sean's opening, Corey spread him wider, stretching the fissure slightly. He licked around the opening, dipping in slightly. Sean pushed backward rhythmically, making low, animalistic sounds. Corey pressed his face to Sean's cleft and inhaled, the scent sending a jolt through his cock and making it bounce between this legs.

He pressed his mouth to Sean's hole, kissing it lightly before flicking his tongue over and inside the clenching rim. He felt it give slightly. Corey circled Sean's opening and it relaxed and opened for him.

Reaching for the lube, Corey covered a finger and pushed it into Sean's hole. Heat surrounded him immediately. Corey slid his finger into the last knuckle and twisted to spread the lube. Sean gave a filthy moan, rocking backward into Corey's hand.

Quickly adding lube to two fingers, Corey pushed them inward. Sean's hiss made Corey think he'd gone too fast and too hard. He froze. "Okay?" he asked, mouth pressed against one of Sean's tense ass cheeks.

"Fuck, yeah," Sean said without hesitation.

Corey slid his fingers in and out more carefully, gently smoothing the lubricant along the tight walls of Sean's ass. "I didn't mean to hurt you."

"You didn't," Sean assured him. "I like the stretch. I like feeling full."

Corey added more lube and slid his fingers in once more. He steadied Sean with a hand on his hip. Each time he withdrew them, he gave a small tug to Sean's rim, adding a little more stretch.

"Yeah, just like that," Sean whispered hoarsely, rocking back against Corey.

This time, he firmly pushed three lubed fingers into Sean's ass. He twisted and tugged, slicking Sean's body, giving him the stretch he liked.

"Ready?" Corey reached for the condom.

"Hell, yes," Sean replied emphatically.

Corey squeezed lube onto the bare head of his cock before rolling the snug latex down his shaft. He added slick to his sheathed erection and aligned himself with Sean's opening. Gripping Sean's hips firmly, Corey breached him slowly. He carefully slid inward, watching Sean's ass open up around him, letting Corey's dick slide in smoothly. He focused on the sight of himself disappearing inside of Sean.

"Fuck!" Corey hissed when Sean abruptly pushed back into him, taking Corey's cock all the way to the hilt. The sudden tight heat shocked Corey. His fingers tightened reflexively on Sean's hips. Corey couldn't remember ever being with anyone as enthusiastic as Sean.

He held on tight as he rocked his hips back and forth, sliding himself in and out of Sean. He watched the play of muscle in Sean's broad back as he pushed against the bed and slammed himself down Corey cock. The firm muscles of his ass flexed with his motions.

Sweat beaded on Sean's skin. The short hairs on the back of his neck were damp. As if it had a mind of its own, one of Corey's hands reached out and buried itself in the hair at the back of his head. Sean lifted his head at the first touch of Corey's hand.

Gently at first, Corey tugged the handful of hair. Sean groaned and arched his neck. Corey tightened his grip and pulled harder. Sean gave a soft cry. Corey released Sean's hip and used the grip in his hair to tug him backward as he snapped his hips forward.

"Corey!" Sean gave a desperate cry.

Corey sped his hips and pulled Sean's hair roughly. His cock swelled at the sound of Sean's keening cries. Corey fisted his hand in Sean's hair and gave a forceful tug. Sean obeyed easily, lifting his shoulders off the bed and coming to his knees.

"Oh fuck," Sean groaned, settling in Corey's lap. He rested his head on Corey's shoulder.

Corey left his hand in Sean's hair, holding him in place. His free arm, he wrapped around Sean's waist. Corey pressed his face to Sean's sweaty throat and inhaled. Sean's spicy scent and his cologne now mixed with the aroma of his sweat. Corey's cock throbbed in Sean's ass.

"Jesus, this feels good," Corey murmured against Sean's shoulder. "*You* feel good." He bit the tendon that joined Sean's neck and shoulder, rubbing soothing circles into Sean's taut and tense stomach.

"Oh God, Corey," Sean gasped, one hand reaching back to grip Corey's hip, the other coming up to grasp the back of his head. Sean ground down on Corey's lap, as if trying to get Corey's cock deeper inside. "Fuck," he whispered.

Corey dragged his tongue up the length of Sean's arched and bared throat. Sean's mouth hung open and he gasped for each breath, chest heaving. Color was high on his cheeks. He was fucking gorgeous. It was unbelievable that he was here in Corey's arms, looking like he was in ecstasy.

"Can you move like this?" he asked, biting along Sean's jaw.

"Yeah," Sean groaned. He lifted his head languorously, eyes open but unseeing. He tilted forward in Corey's lap, but his hands never lost their grip. He rose up slightly and pushed himself back down. Sean moaned as Corey's cock slipped back up inside of him. "Don't let go," he whispered, eyes falling shut again.

"I won't," Corey answered in a rough voice as he kissed down Sean's neck. He didn't think Sean even knew he'd spoken. "I've got you." As Sean rose up, the heat of his body receded from Corey's cock. As his ass settled against Corey's thighs, his heat engulfed Corey's cock once again. His walls were slick and tight, each movement had his muscles clenching tight around Corey.

Sean found a rhythm. He rode Corey's cock at a steady pace, grunting and sighing with each thrust of his hips. His lips were red and swollen where he'd bitten them to hold back his cries. Corey kept his hand pressed to Sean's stomach, feeling the firm muscles shift and flex beneath his slick skin.

"Fuck, Corey," Sean muttered in a low, rough voice. "Jesus Christ…harder…please…fuck."

Corey moved in counterpoint to Sean's body. He shoved his hips upward as Sean pressed down. He pulled back quickly, leaving just the head of his cock inside Sean's ass and stretching his rim. Their skin slapped loudly as Sean's ass met Corey's hips.

Pressing his face to the damp hair at the base of Sean's neck, Corey grunted with his exertions. Sean was hot and tight around him, their sweat-slick skin had them sliding against each other.

Sean's groans became strident cries and Corey slammed into him. Each inhale was a desperate gasp. He shouted with nearly each of Corey's thrusts.

"Fuckfuckfuckfuck, God yes," Sean chanted through clenched teeth. "Fuck, Corey, like that, just like that."

Corey used the hand still clenching Sean's hair to turn his head. He roughly forced Sean to face him so he could fuse their mouths together. Sean whimpered into Corey's mouth, rubbing their tongues together desperately and licking deep. His breath was harsh against Corey's cheek. Corey swallowed down each of Sean's cries, keeping their lips sealed, even as the kiss became hot, wet and sloppy.

He gave a hard thrust of his hips and Sean broke the kiss on a shout. "Oh, you fucker," he growled, pressing his face to Corey's and rubbing against him like a big cat. "Fuck, that feels good." Corey felt Sean shift slightly in his lap, adjusting the angle Corey's dick made entry. "Right there," Sean gasped. "Oh, fuck, Corey, right there, right there, right there."

Corey let his mouth hover just above Sean's feeling the heat of his breath with each pant. Slowly, Corey slid his palm down the defined ridges of Sean's belly. He felt the base of Sean's bouncing erection against the edge of his finger. Corey wrapped his hand around the long, hard shaft and gave a firm stroke toward the head.

Sean acted like he'd been struck by lightning, his body arching and straining in Corey's arms. "Motherfucker," he shouted. "Kiss me, Corey. Kiss me again," he begged.

Corey pressed their mouths together hard enough to clack teeth. He licked at Sean's tongue, breathing too hard to seal their lips. They panted heavily against each other, rubbing their tongues together, licking each other's lips. Corey jacked Sean's dick, quick and hard. He slid his palm over the long, thick veined shaft, squeezing the firm head and giving his wrist a twist. Sean's cock was thick, flaring into a gorgeous mushroom head. Corey wanted to taste it. He wanted to feel it slide up inside of him. For now, Corey wanted to feel it shoot Sean's load while he held Sean's hard body in his arms.

"Are you close?" Corey asked against Sean's lips. "You gonna come?"

"Fuck yes, you bastard," Sean gasped. His fingers tightened on Corey's hip and the back of his head. "You're gonna make me come."

Corey kept up the punishing combination of fucking into Sean's body and rapidly stroking his cock. He knew the tight arch of Sean's spine meant Corey was nailing his gland. The erratic flex of Sean's hips told Corey he was stroking Sean's cock just right. "I wanna feel you come. I want your ass to clamp down on my cock. I want you to shoot your load on my hand. Would you do that for me?"

"Don't stop," Sean whispered. "Don't let go."

Corey held on to Sean and continued to stroke his dick. He fucked up into him, slamming their bodies together. He watched Sean's expressive face. Every emotion he was feeling drifted over his features. Sean was in the throes of ecstasy. He looked focused on chasing down is impending orgasm. He looked eager and desperate.

He was beautiful.

With a gasp, Sean froze. He bit down on his lower lip and

stopped breathing. His cock swelled in Corey's fist, blood rushing into it. Sean shuddered violently, his tremors rolling through him and into Corey. His cock pulsed several times before a flood of jizz coursed out the tip. "Oh, fuck, I'm coming," Sean cried out. "Jesus, Corey, please, please, please. Oh, God, Corey."

The sound of his name on Sean's lips was intoxicating. Corey's cock twitched each time Sean called out his name as he rode out the waves of his climax.

"Yeah, just like that," Corey murmured, smiling. "Fuck, that's hot. Come for me, Sean. Come for me, just like that."

Sean vibrated against Corey. His hot spunk coated Corey's hand and slid down his fingers. The muscles of his ass clamped down hard on Corey's erection. He could feel every tremor as it ran through Sean's body. He swallowed down each of Sean's gasping breaths.

It felt like forever before Sean collapsed against him and still it was over too soon to suit Corey.

Sean's fingers loosened their grip on him. Corey eased his arms around Sean's chest, keeping their heated bodies pressed together as they kissed. Sean glowed. He kissed Corey, slow and languorous, his eyes closed. Corey could feel the rapid beat of his heart, his breath still coming in rapid gasps.

"Okay?" Corey asked, holding Sean pressed against him.

"Fuck yeah," Sean replied with a quiet laugh. His eyes opened slowly and he smiled drunkenly at Corey. "That was insanely hot."

"Yeah it was," Corey chuckled.

Still smiling, Sean twisted in Corey's arms. He leaned forward, wrapping his hands around the top rail of the headboard. He arched his back and glanced backward over his shoulder. "Your turn," he said suggestively.

Corey was helpless. He gripped Sean's hips, lowered his forehead to the middle of Sean's back, and began to move his hips.

Sean's ass was slick and hot. His muscles gripped Corey's cock tightly. As Corey thrust up into him, Sean pushed downward. Their bodies slammed together with a loud slap, Corey's hips tingling at the contact. Sean's muscles bunched and flexed with his efforts. Corey rested against Sean's back, breathing in his scent and just feeling him move.

"Come for me," Sean whispered. Corey only just heard him. "Come on, come inside me. I wanna feel you. Need to feel you."

Sean's pleading was like a punch to Corey's gut. His body locked up then quivered. His cock twitched repeatedly inside of Sean's ass. Reflexively, Corey's fingers tightened on Sean's hips. He knew he was bruising that flawlessly tanned skin. He didn't give a fuck.

Corey's orgasm slammed into him with the force of a storm driven wave. He gave a guttural moan before he shouted against the slick skin of Sean's back. Corey's balls rose up, tight against his body. His come pumped from the end of his dick and into the tip of the condom. His thighs burned and his back ached as his muscles stayed locked and his orgasm rolled through him. "Oh, fuck, Sean," he breathed against Sean's spine. "Jesus Christ. Fuck me, I'm coming," he muttered, his lips moving against Sean's skin.

"That's it, that's it," Sean chanted. "Just like that."

When Corey's climax released him, he grabbed onto the headboard next to where Sean held it in a death grip. He struggled to stay upright so he didn't collapse on top of Sean. His cock wasn't softening as quickly as it usually did and Corey knew that was the Viagra.

"So, ready to go again?" he asked Sean jokingly.

"And if I said yes?" Sean teased.

"I'd make you prove it." Corey emphasized his point by stroking Sean's limp, spent cock.

"Sleep first?"

"Good plan."

Corey carefully slid his still semi-hard cock from Sean's hole. As gentle as he was, Sean still gave a quiet hiss. Corey stumbled to the head and disposed of the rubber. He wet a washcloth and grabbed a dry hand towel.

Back in the bedroom, Sean was struggling to clean himself with a crumpled baby wipe and a trembling hand.

"Let me do that," Corey admonished gently. "I used those things when there was no other choice. You don't have to settle for that."

Sean collapsed backward against the stack of pillows, managing to avoid the wet spot he'd created. Corey knelt between his upraised knees. Slowly, with gentle strokes, he cleaned all of Sean he could reach with the wet cloth. Corey bent over Sean's supine form as he worked, nipping at his jaw and placing soft kisses on his swollen lips. He smiled at the sounds of contentment Sean made, arching into Corey's hands as they skimmed over his cooling skin.

Corey used the hand towel to clean up as much of Sean's drying come from the comforter as he could. It was a losing battle, but he made the effort.

Impatiently, Sean took the cloth from Corey's hands and threw it blindly across the room. "Enough. Lay down."

Corey chuckled. "Do you get cranky when you're tired?" he asked playfully, sliding beneath the bedclothes Sean pulled aside for him.

"I get cranky when I'm ready to snuggle and you're being obsessively fussy," Sean replied, sliding closer to Corey until their sides were pressed tightly together.

Corey expected Sean to turn and settle in his arms. Instead, he rested his head on the pillow beside Corey's, touching at all points along their sides. Corey was disappointed. "I'm done being obsessively fastidious," he said.

"Mm. Good." Sean sighed deeply. "The sunrise through this window is spectacular. It's the wrong angle to see the actual rising sun but the sky over the Pacific is gorgeous."

"I've seen the sun rise in so many places around the world," Corey mused. "They're always beautiful. Especially the ones you didn't think you were going to live to see." Now why had he said that? Sean didn't need that kind of dark talk after such spectacular sex.

"I'm really glad you lived to see them all," Sean murmured. "I'll have to get up and close the blinds when it gets too bright, but maybe we'll wake up early enough to catch the sunrise."

"I thought you were a snuggler." Corey hadn't meant to say that.

"I am." Sean seemed to rouse himself to answer. "I don't want you to feel smothered or …I don't know, trapped maybe. I don't know if lying all on top of you will cause nightmares or a panic attack." Sean's laugh was tinged with hysteria. "I'm giving you space."

Corey turned onto his side. He buried his face in Sean's neck, wrapped an arm around his waist and draped a leg across both of Sean's. Both of Sean's arms came around Corey's shoulders and one large palm ran soothingly up and down his spine.

"This good?" Corey asked, voice muffled against Sean's skin.

"Yeah, it's great," Sean whispered.

Beneath him, Sean relaxed completely and Corey knew it was safe to sleep.

§ § §

The first thing Corey thought when he awoke was that Sean was right about the sunrise. It was a gorgeous mix of reds, oranges and pinks. The gray pre-dawn gave way to the early morning blue and everything looked fresh and new.

The second thing Corey thought when he awoke was that Sean's morning wood felt good pressed against his ass.

Sean must have realized Corey was awake. His hands were warm as they ran up Corey's thigh, his ass cheek, and his back. He sighed at the feel of Sean's lips on the back of his neck, the top of his spine.

"You're right," Corey whispered. "The sunrise is nice."

"Just lay there and enjoy it." Sean flicked his tongue over Corey's earlobe before nipping at it lightly.

Corey's erection pulsed against his stomach and he moaned softly. He pushed back against Sean's cock, nestled in the crack of his ass. Corey arched his neck to give Sean better access. He shivered as Sean placed open-mouthed kisses and swipes of his tongue along the length of Corey's throat.

He wanted Sean's mouth on his. Corey started to turn so he could face Sean and press their lips together. Sean halted him with a firm hand on his hip. Corey made a sound of protest low in his throat.

"Shhhh." Sean soothed Corey by circling his palm against Corey's belly.

Behind him, Sean shifted slightly. Corey heard the soft snick of a bottle lid opening, followed by the click of it closing. He took a deep breath and relaxed his body, expecting Sean to push fingers up inside of him. Instead, he heard the wet glide of lube being stroked along the length of a cock.

Before he could ask, Corey felt the blunt head of Sean's dick nudge at the backs of his thighs. With a push of his hips, Sean slid his erection between Corey's legs, along the length of his taint. Sean sighed against the back of Corey's neck, his breath hot on the sensitive skin.

"You don't have to do that," Corey said, voice rough from disuse. He started to adjust his position so he could turn toward Sean. "I'll suck you off or you can fuck me."

Sean pressed the length of his body to Corey's to hold him in place. "What makes you think I don't like it this way?" he said against the shell of Corey's ear. The firm tip of his tongue teased Corey's ear, raising gooseflesh. "If you blow me or I fuck you, that's you getting me off. *This* is me getting you off." Sean emphasized his point by taking Corey's hard-on in his lubricated hand.

Corey jerked like he'd been shocked at the touch of Sean's

hand on his dick. He sucked a harsh breath in through clenched teeth and his hips bucked involuntarily into Sean's fist. Corey lifted his hand and reached blindly behind himself. He found Sean's soft hair and wove his fingers through it, drawing his face down close.

Sean cooperated, nuzzling the sensitive spot behind Corey's ear. His hand moved quickly on Corey's cock, squeezing firmly. Corey moved his legs restlessly and Sean secured him by hooking his own leg over Corey's. It felt so fucking good, Corey's orgasm had already begun to build up inside of him.

"I'm not going to last," he groaned, chest heaving as he breathed heavily through parted lips. "*Christ*, you're gonna make me come quick."

"Good," Sean replied, sounding pleased with himself. He kissed his way down Corey's neck. "Don't try to hold back."

Corey flexed the muscles in his thighs and Sean groaned against his shoulder, even as the thrusts of his hips became stronger and faster. Sean's hard-on slid easily between Corey's legs, gliding against his taint. The thick head bumped Corey's balls, making them tingle and dragging his climax up faster.

Sean shifted again and Corey was forced to release the back of his head. He turned to watch Sean lick the point of his shoulder before dragging the flat of his tongue down Corey's bicep. When he reached Corey's tattoo, Sean firmed the tip of his tongue and used it to trace the edges of the ink.

He watched in fascination as Sean worshiped his tattoo while stroking his dick. Corey pushed his hips into Sean's tight grip. His balls tightened. Heat spooled out from the base of his spine and flooded his pelvis. He was so fucking close.

"I love your tats," Sean said against Corey's ink, his soft lips and hot breath sending a shiver through Corey's body. "What does this one stand for?"

Corey struggled to focus. He knew he needed to answer Sean but all he wanted to do was fuck Sean's hand and come his brains out. "It's the 1st Recon logo," he gasped.

"You're proud of being Recon, aren't you?" Sean traced the skull in Corey's tattoo. "It's a big deal, isn't it?" At least Sean sounded breathless now, too, as he slid his cock between Corey's clenched thighs.

"Yeah," he gasped, just before his lower belly tightened and his dick pulsed in a few times. "Oh fuck, I'm gonna come."

"Good, I wanna feel you," Sean replied, panting through parted, red lips.

Corey stared at Sean's mouth. He wanted those lips pressed to his own. It felt like Sean was miles away, as he mouthed at Corey's arm. He wanted Sean closer. Corey tried to tell him. He wanted to ask Sean to kiss him. Hell, he'd fucking beg for it, if he could just form the words.

Sean's shrewd hazel eyes flicked up to Corey's and he must have seen something. He slid up Corey's body, slightly, his brows furrowing slightly. "What, Corey, what do you need?"

"Kiss me." Corey's voice was much more desperate than he'd planned. He'd be embarrassed later. "Please kiss me."

Sean didn't hesitate. He slid up Corey's body and pressed their mouths together. The rhythm of his hips and his hand were erratic. Corey wasn't any better. He licked at Sean's tongue as they rocked and thrust against each other, breathing harshly through their noses.

Corey's orgasm slammed into him and come abruptly shot from the end of his dick. He tore his mouth away from Sean's with a shout as he keened, high in his throat. His muscles clenched as wave after wave of ecstasy rolled over him. Sean buried his face against Corey's throat and swore harshly. Hot come coated the insides of Corey's thighs and splashed across the back of his ball sac. Sean's body vibrated against Corey's, even as Corey shuddered his way through the end of his climax.

"Oh, fuck," Corey panted as he fell back against the pillows, totally spent. He knew he should clean up but he couldn't even get his eyes to open.

Beside him, Sean moved sluggishly, jostling the bed as he

climbed out. He was back moments later, warm cloth in hand. Corey did his best to cooperate, giving Sean access to all the places come had begun to dry.

Corey drifted in and out of sleep, only just aware when Sean closed the blinds on the large window. The room was plunged into semi-darkness. When Sean's warmth settled against him again, Corey snuggled back against him.

"Now we can sleep without bright sunlight in our eyes," Sean said drowsily.

Corey meant to thank him, but he didn't stay awake long enough.

Chapter Eleven

On Monday, during his first break of the morning, Corey called the J.A.S. offices on base. The Marine who answered the phone put him right through to Captain Hirata. Corey was surprised. He'd expected the attorney to be elsewhere, conducting interviews for Kellan's investigation.

"How can I help you, Staff Sergeant?" Hirata sounded friendly.

Corey was again surprised at that friendly tone. He kept expecting anger and accusation. "Captain, sir, I might have done something stupid on Saturday night." He and Sean had discussed the events of the previous evening over Sunday brunch. They'd agreed that Corey probably hadn't done anything wrong, but was treading enough of a fine line he should get ahead of any possible repercussions.

"Is this in regard to either the investigation into Ghazni or Sergeant Nygaard's arrest?" the captain asked.

"Yes, sir." Corey walked in a circle, hoping it would ease some of his agitation. He buried his free hand in the pocket of his trouser pocket and clutched the bottle of Xanax. "I think Nygaard might be trying to blame what happened in Ghazni for the murder of his girlfriend." Corey told himself he didn't need the Xanax, but it was reassuring to know they were within easy reach.

Captain Hirata had Corey tell the entire story, starting with Tyler Howe's phone call and ending with their stormy exit from the Nygaard home. He left out the details of his anxiety attack, but owned up to his own angry, physical reactions to Nygaard's words.

"I think you might be right, Staff Sergeant," Hirata said as if considering the different implications. "He's going to try to throw everyone involved in Ghazni under the bus and then claim those events caused him to commit murder."

"That's how it seems, sir," Corey said, sighing inwardly in relief.

"Did Sergeant Nygaard, or any of his family members attempt to garner your sympathy or pity?" Hirata asked.

Corey snorted. "Begging your pardon, Captain," he said sheepishly, "that was the whole point of having us over to talk."

"Understood," Hirata said indulgently. "But did you get the impression that you or Corporal Howe were being recruited as actual character witnesses for Sergeant Nygaard?"

Corey stopped walking as an icy wave of realization and dread washed over him. "I was thinking he was trying to get one or both of us to let something slip." Corey replied. "Then he could tell his lawyer and they'd use it against us." His mind raced. "But now that you mention it, sir, it would be in his favor if either one of us would be willing to blame the Corps."

"I'll have a talk with Nygaard's attorney," Hirata said with anger. "It's treading a very fine line but it smacks of witness tampering." The captain sighed heavily. "I didn't want to have to do this but I have to protect the integrity of Mr. Reynolds' investigation. As a witness in that investigation, Staff Sergeant, I'm instructing you to have no further contact with Sergeant Nygaard."

"Yes, sir," Corey answered briskly. Now he had the perfect excuse to never talk to Nygaard again.

"I'll notify Corporal Howe of the same thing," Hirata continued. "I don't want any of our witnesses tampered with while we're still getting to the bottom of this."

Corey rolled his shoulders to ease the accumulated tension. Thankfully he still held witness status. "Yes, sir. And I apologize for any trouble we caused."

"It's understandable that you and the corporal need to understand why Nygaard did what he did," replied Hirata. "We just can't allow our search for the truth to become a casualty."

"I agree, sir. Thank you, sir." Corey disconnected the call and gripped the prescription bottle in his hand. He rolled his head to stretch his neck. It was easy to take a deep breath. His heart was still beating a little fast but his chest didn't hurt.

Corey left the bottle in his pocket and returned to work.

§ § §

Corey darted across the clearing, sliding to a stop behind the bombed out truck. He slammed his back against the over-sized rear tire. The radio chattered in his ear but Corey couldn't make out the words.

Mortars landed nearby and Corey startled. Gunfire raged all around him, AK47 rounds kicked up small plumes of dirt. The heat was sweltering. Sweat rolled down Corey's face and the back of his neck, pooling in his uniform.

Corey struggled to get enough air into his lungs, but he couldn't catch his breath. The air around him reeked of garbage, burning oil, fresh blood, and singed flesh. When Corey could finally drag a harsh breath into his lungs, he gagged.

Tyler Howe appeared out of nowhere and slammed into the tire next to Corey. "Where the fuck is Nygaard?" Tyler shouted over the raging sounds of battle.

"No fucking idea," Corey shouted back, struggling to breathe through his open mouth.

"You gotta go after him, Sergeant." Tyler darted glances all around them.

"I can't." Corey's heart slammed in his chest.

"You gotta figure out what he's up to, Corey," Tyler pleaded.

Before Corey could argue, a brusque order rang out. "Sergeant Yarwood, you need to make entry into that structure!"

Corey whipped his head around at the sound of Jonah Carver's voice. It vaguely registered with him that he'd never served with Tyler and Jonah at the same time. Corey looked around. This was Afghanistan. Jonah didn't belong here.

"Sergeant Yarwood, make entry into the structure," Jonah

ordered. "We'll cover your six."

"We gotta know what he's doing in there, Corey," Tyler said.

Corey startled again as a mortar landed just a few feet away. The truck behind him shuddered as it was peppered with bullets. He waited for the gunfire to ease up. Corey darted a glance around the tire, at the single family dwelling just a few meters away. He was driven back behind cover by AK rounds striking nearby.

Squeezing his eyes shut, Corey banged the back of his head against the truck tire, over and over. His Kevlar protected him, but the sound was deafening and his teeth rattled in his skull.

"Sergeant Yarwood," Jonah barked, "man up and make entry into that structure!" His words were sharp and stern, but when Corey looked over, Jonah's expression was encouraging.

Corey gathered his feet beneath him, sitting back on his haunches. His legs shook, his knees were weak. Leaning his head against the truck again, Corey looked up at the sky, unseeing. Sean would be pissed with him for not facing this shit and dealing with it.

Ignoring the constriction and pain in his chest, Corey sucked in a harsh breath. With a last glance around the tire to confirm his route was clear, Corey broke cover.

Hands wrapped tightly around his M16, he ran the short distance. Reaching the structure, Corey slammed his back against the wall beside the wooden door. Seconds later, Jonah was beside him. On the other side of the door, Tyler took up position.

Corey panted desperately, suddenly lightheaded. His legs trembled, hands aching from his crippling grip on his weapon.

"On three, Corey," Jonah ordered, shouting over the raging battle.

Corey looked over. Jonah's expression was implacable. He tilted his head toward the dwelling. The casual gesture was incongruous with the chaos around them.

Corey gathered his courage. He stepped in front of the flimsy wooden door. He took a deep breath, lifted his leg and slammed his heavy boot into the lock mechanism. Wood splintered. The door swung inward, slamming against the wall.

It was pitch dark inside. The unmistakable smell of death wafted toward him. Corey retched.

"You gotta go find out what he did," Tyler said.

Corey lifted his weapon to his shoulder and cautiously stepped across the threshold. Bile rose in his throat, so he swallowed rapidly several times. He clenched his jaw as the odors of piss and shit assaulted him. These were the smells of evacuated bowels and recent death.

"Shit, shit, shit, shit," Corey chanted through his teeth. He peered through his rifle site, searching for a threat; a target.

The room flooded with light, blinding Corey. He blinked several times then squinted, struggling to make anything out.

"Right on your six, Corey." Jonah was directly behind him. Corey knew his words were meant to be reassuring.

Corey released a shaky breath. Jonah had his six and wouldn't let anything bad happen. Corey shook his head sharply, blinking to clear his vision. The light dimmed and he could make out shapes and figures.

It didn't make sense. Several dozen bodies were laid out in rows. They took up nearly all the floor space. Sergeant Nygaard and several Marines loomed over the bodies, weapons trained on them. But they were dead, there was no need to cover them. There was no threat.

"What did you do, Nygaard?" Corey asked, voice quavering.

"They were a threat," Nygaard responded in a flat tone. "I eliminated the threat."

Corey looked around the room again. He saw no weapons.

"What did you do?" he demanded angrily.

"They were threatening us. They lied. They were hiding weapons," Nygaard's response was mechanical.

"Where did they hide the weapons?" Corey's question was

met with silence.

He looked around again. Horror overwhelmed him. The bodies were civilian. They were women and children. All of them. And they were unarmed.

Corey sat up straight in his rack. Someone was shouting and it had awakened him. He took a deep breath. His throat hurt, but at least the screaming had stopped.

Sweat rolled down Corey's spine and pooled in the waist of his skivvy shorts. Fuck. The scream had been his.

The blanket was wrapped around his legs. Corey kicked it off. He swung his legs to the floor. He rested his elbows on his knees and cradled his head in his hands. Corey cleared his throat. He knew he'd shouted loud enough to be heard in other rooms. No one would check on him, though. Nightmares in the BEQ were common these days.

Corey's hands trembled as he cradled his head. He struggled to catch his breath. Blood roared in his ears and his heart beat so fast, his chest hurt.

The image of dead women and children was burned into the backs of Corey's eyelids. He couldn't escape the memory of that scene. He ran a hand over his sweaty face. It was a dream, Corey told himself. It was only a dream. It couldn't be a memory of anything that had happened in Ghazni. It couldn't.

He swallowed against his dry throat and reached for his cell phone. He always slept better after he talked to Sean. There was no point in denying it any longer.

"Hey, you okay?" Sean asked the moment he answered.

Corey tried to swallow but his mouth was as dust-dry as his throat. "No," he croaked, reaching for the water bottle on his nightstand.

"Corey, what's wrong?" Sean's worry carried clearly over the call. "It's another nightmare, isn't it?"

"Yeah," Corey replied, voice raw from his shouts. "This one felt real. I can't get it out of my head."

"Tell me about it." Sean's urging was gentle but unrelenting.

"No." Corey was emphatic. He didn't want Sean exposed to this shit. He didn't need to know about the ugliness in Corey's world, or the heinous things Corey was capable of. "You don't need to hear about this shit."

"You need to talk it out. You need to confront it and deal with it."

"I will, I'll talk to my counselor on Saturday." Corey dug into his fighting hole.

"Jesus Christ, Corey," Sean said with frustration, "I'm not a fucking child. I know what goes on in the world. You can tell me about your nightmare."

"I don't want you tainted with this kind of ugly shit." Corey's anger flared.

"Tainted?" Sean was incredulous. "Telling me about your nightmare won't harm me, it won't damage me."

Corey sighed explosively. "I'm afraid of what you'll think of me." His gut knotted painfully.

Sean was silent for so long, Corey checked his phone to make sure the call was still active.

"Wow, okay," Sean laughed mirthlessly and a chill ran down Corey's spine. "You know, just because I'm an actor doesn't mean I'm shallow and insensitive."

Sean's anger was like a physical slap. "I know," Corey answered hastily, confused as hell. "I don't think you're shallow *or* insensitive."

"Then why the fuck do you think my opinion of you could drop so easily?"

"I don't know," Corey muttered. "Christ, you really shouldn't be wasting your time with someone as fucked up as me."

Silence again.

"Do you even remember a fucking word I said Saturday night?" Sean's question was laced with icy rage.

The room spun and Corey gripped the edge of his rack with his free hand. It didn't help. How had he managed to fuck this up so bad, so fast? "That's not what I meant." He couldn't hide the defeat in his voice and was too exhausted to try. "I can't do this. I keep fucking this up. My shit keeps fucking this up and I can't deal with both, right now. You don't need me calling you in the middle of the night to unload my shit and fuck up everything I try to say."

"Corey, stop and take a breath," Sean said sharply.

Corey gasped, finally refilling his lungs with precious oxygen. "Sorry."

"You're running, Corey," Sean said. "You're trying to make it sound like you're doing me a favor, but you're running. You promised me, Corey. Now stop it."

Corey couldn't remember anyone ever throwing the bullshit flag on him like this. "You're right. Okay. You said you didn't know what this thing was or where it was going. But do you really want *this*? Is this the direction you really want to go in?"

"Yes," Sean answered without hesitation.

"I guess I don't understand why." Corey's confession twisted his gut. He couldn't figure out why Sean would even put up with this shit, but he was grateful Sean seemed to want to stick around.

"I can't believe you just said that," Sean muttered, his annoyance palpable. "Corey, tell me about your goddamn nightmare, and don't clean the story up thinking you're protecting me. I want the unvarnished truth."

Corey gave an exaggerated growl. "I'm gonna be so pissed off if this keeps me from getting laid again."

Sean huffed a quiet laugh. "Stubbornness is what's going to keep you from getting laid," he said quietly.

Corey actually chuckled at that. He paused to take several swallows of water before relating the events of the dream to Sean.

The soft strains of guitar music drifted through the

connection. Corey let the notes settle over him and soothe him. It made telling the story easier, at least until he reached the end. Reliving the memory of the slaughtered women and children brought back the pain in his chest.

"Fuck, I want a drink so bad right now," he admitted quietly, running a hand over the bristles of his hair. He realized he needed it cut.

He heard Sean's sharp intake of breath. "No," Sean said gently.

Corey chuckled darkly. "Don't worry. There's nothing here. I tossed it out a while ago."

"Good. I'm proud of you." The affection in Sean's voice warmed Corey. "So, what's the worst thing that can happen to you when you talk about your nightmare?" he surprised Corey by asking.

"Nothing," he answered. Remembering the images that scared the shit out of him.

"Exactly."

The word hung between them as the only sound was Sean strumming his guitar.

Taking a deep breath, Corey asked, "You don't think what I do is ugly and violent?"

"Of course I do," Sean replied quickly. "But I don't think *you're* ugly and violent."

Corey was struck dumb. After a moment he asked, "Even if I said I don't think it's just a dream?"

"I'm sure there are pieces of real memory mixed in," Sean said softly. "But if you mean what I think you mean, you should call your counselor."

Corey sighed, not ready to agree yet. "Well, thanks for listening," he said, stifling a yawn.

"It's my pleasure, and you know that." Sean took a deep breath. "So, about tomorrow night..."

Corey braced himself.

"I was offered a part in a television show at the last minute. I have a nighttime call tomorrow."

"Oh." Corey was glad Sean couldn't see the way his face flamed in shame. He reminded himself that everything wasn't always about him. "That's great." Sean's words sank in fully. "That's fucking fantastic! Good for you. Is this one of those things you auditioned for?"

"No, actually. My agent just submitted me for the part and the director of this episode has worked with me before, so he just hired me." Sean sounded pleased and proud. "It's actually a three-episode arc and I get to play the villain."

"That's okay, I like bad boys," Corey said playfully, grateful for something pleasant to focus on.

Sean laughed in response. "So, I'll be working tomorrow night. If you need to call and I don't answer, leave a message. There is a lot of down time and standing around on these things, so I'll be able to call you back."

"You don't need me interrupting your work." Maybe not, but Corey hoped Sean *wanted* him to interrupt.

"Did you hear what I just said?" Sean asked, his annoyance rising once again.

Corey laughed at his own obstinacy. "All right. If I need you, I'll call."

"You can call me if you just want me." Sean's voice was low and suggestive.

"We'd never get off the phone." Fuck it. Why keep fighting it?

"Some night we'll have to get off *on* the phone," Sean quickly replied with a naughty laugh.

When they finally ended the call and Corey settled down to try to sleep again, he realized he was more than just relieved and relaxed. Corey couldn't remember when it had happened, but somewhere along the way, he'd become happy.

CHAPTER TWELVE

Corey stood behind the five Marines who were his responsibility today. They were holding sniper training and in addition to instructing, Corey was serving as Assistant Range Master. He had to monitor readiness and safety on the firing line, and notify the Master Sergeant when everyone was ready to commence fire.

Some of these Marines had already attended Sniper School and today was remedial for them. As a Recon Marine, even those who weren't qualified as Snipers might someday have to act as a sharp shooter. Today, Corey and his fellow instructors were ensuring these Marines would be able to do that.

"Ready on the right?" Whitfield shouted.

Corey watched as the instructors on the right hand side of the range each lifted a fist into the air and replied, "Ready on the right."

One last time, Corey looked over his five Marines to make sure all weapons were unloaded and muzzles were aimed down range.

"Ready on the left?" came the next shout.

Corey lifted his fist and replied, "Ready on the left!"

"All ready on the firing line," Whitfield called. "Shooters, load your weapons."

There was a loud cacophony of magazines being inserted and bolts sliding forward.

"The firing line is hot." Whitfield shouted the next command. "All ready on the right? All ready on the left?" Corey still held his fist in the air. He would drop it only if he saw a safety violation or when firing began. "Commence fire," Whitfield ordered.

Dozens of rifles fired simultaneously and Corey nearly jumped out of his skin. He'd been on the range more times than he could count. He'd expected the loud gunfire. He had no reason to startle.

Corey focused on his five Marine charges. He glassed the targets downrange with the optics around his neck. He had one Marine dropping points left and right. He'd wait and see if the Marine could dial it in on his own.

He paced the firing line, sweat rolling down his back and chest, despite the coolness of the morning. Corey breathed in and out, counting to eight like Sean always encouraged him. It was hard to do with a racing heart.

His palms were sweaty as he lifted his optics again and glassed the targets. The lieutenant was still missing the center ring on nearly every shot. Corey watched him make adjustments to his windage and elevation. His next round was high and right. Sighing, Corey carefully approached the officer's position from the rear. At this level, the LT should know better than to jerk the trigger.

Corey knelt beside the lieutenant's right hip. "Ceasefire, Marine," he ordered quietly, not wanting to disrupt anyone else on the firing line.

The lieutenant removed his finger from the trigger and rested it against the guard.

"Take a couple of deep breaths and relax," Corey instructed. "Now line up your shot. Take a breath and let it out. You should be dead center through the sight. Are you there?"

"Yes, Staff Sergeant." The officer's response was muffled by his cheek pressed to the rifle stock.

"Good." Corey struggled to block out the sound of the gunfire that surrounded him. "Now this time, when you take your shot, squeeze the trigger slowly. Don't jerk it. Relax your hand around the grip so that only your trigger finger moves and draw it backward, slow and steady."

Corey jumped, adrenaline flooding his body when the lieutenant's rifle roared to life. Standing abruptly, Corey glassed the target. The officer's shot had just winged the ten-ring.

"Nice job, Marine," Corey said encouragingly. "Now adjust your sights as needed, just remember to squeeze instead of jerk."

The lieutenant resumed firing and Corey quickly backed away from the line. He forced himself to look at the Marines in his charge to make sure all was well. He kept backing away, glancing around the range, looking for threats.

Corey's heartbeat was nearly as loud as the gunfire. His chest heaved and he couldn't slow it. He ran the back of a hand over his forehead, wiping away a film of sweat. He needed to take cover. Corey was out in the open in a kill zone and he had to take cover.

"Yarwood, man, you don't look good." Sergeant Spencer appeared at his side and Corey had to pull his punch. "What the fuck?"

"It's too loud," Corey said as he looked around for a place to take cover.

"You need to square yourself away, Staff Sergeant," Spencer said, grabbing Corey's bicep.

Yanking his arm free, Corey started toward one of the sheds behind them.

"Yarwood, come on, chill the fuck out." Staff Sergeant Norris was suddenly beside him. "If the Master Sergeant sees you away from your post he'll bust you down."

Corey pressed his hands over his ears. It didn't block the sounds of the battle that raged around him.

"Get back up to the line," one of the other instructors said. "Come on, man, you need to get your shit together."

"Yarwood, hey." Someone waved a hand in front of his face and Corey was able to focus on it. "Come on, Corey, knock this shit off."

They nudged Corey toward the firing line. "Just ignore everything else. Block it out. Just worry about what's important."

Corey stepped back in place behind his Marines. His fingers and toes tingled but his brain was numb. Spencer and Norris quickly resumed their own positions along the firing line.

"Cease fire! Cease fire! Cease all fire on the firing line!" Whitfield shouted.

Immediately, all gunfire stopped.

"The firing line is cold," the Master Sergeant called. "Make and show safe."

The Marines all removed their magazines, ejected chambered rounds and stepped back from the firing line, leaving their weapons in place.

Staff Sergeant Norris was back at Corey's side. "Pull it together, Yarwood," he said harshly.

Corey nodded. Now that the gunfire had stopped he could breathe. The need to take cover was easing.

"You're a Marine, man, you're fucking Recon," Norris continued. "We've all been through some shit, but we don't go losing it in the middle of a training class. You're better than that. If the Master Sergeant finds out, you'll be riding a desk."

Corey nodded his understanding. If Norris would just go the fuck away, Corey could slip a Xanax and get himself squared away.

It was surprisingly easy to hide behind a Humvee with a bottle of water and swallow the tiny pill. It was like none of his fellow instructors *wanted* to know what he was up to. Corey almost pulled out his cell phone to call the counseling office. He couldn't be losing his shit in the middle of training.

Norris' words echoed in his head. Corey pocketed his phone. He was a fucking Recon Marine. He had to be strong enough to deal with this shit on his own.

Thank God the fucking Xanax worked fast. During the second relay, Corey was still jumpy and his palms were sweaty, but this time he kept his shit together. It was a long motherfucking day.

Corey was grateful when instruction ended and testing began. Master Sergeant Whitfield ran a single relay of ten Marines, one he could manage himself, the rest of instructors lending a hand as needed. Corey stood well back from the firing line, hoping to minimize his exposure to the loud sounds that part of his brain obviously still associated with combat situations. Mostly, he just tried to keep Whitfield from noticing he was slowly falling apart.

Despite Corey's best efforts, the lieutenant who kept shooting high and right failed the sniper test by a full five points. It put him in danger of failing out of BRC. Corey gnawed on a hangnail, consumed with guilt. If he weren't so fucked up, he might have been able to help the LT better than he had.

As he tossed his ruck into the Humvee for the drive back to BRC HQ, the Marines who rode with him began to climb into the victor. Spencer was suddenly at his side.

"Dude, a bunch of us are going to the SMP thing over at Margarita tonight. You should come with."

Corey used to do a lot of shit with the Single Marine Program. Not just the meal and movie events, but he used to go on the excursions and camping trips. Hell, he'd even volunteered at the base animal shelter. Since he'd been back, he hadn't done shit.

"Nah. Thanks, man." Corey wondered if it was too early to try calling Sean.

"Seriously, man. Norris says you're fucking belt fed today." Spencer glanced around, gauging who might overhear. "They're serving beer. You need to loosen the fuck up, Corey."

Rage spiked through Corey and he turned on Spencer menacingly. "I don't need to loosen the fuck up. I need you, and Norris, and fucking *Nygaard* to quit telling me how the fuck *you* think I should be acting. I got Nygaard telling me I gotta lie for him so he doesn't have to man up about beating a woman to death with his bare hands. I got the fucking DOD telling me I gotta tell the truth about the bad shit a bunch of Marines are lying about doing. I got you telling me I gotta get drunk to stop being a tight ass, and I got better men than you telling me I gotta stay sober. How 'bout I make my own goddamn decisions about what I gotta do?"

Corey clenched his jaw, breathing harshly through his nose.

His fists clenched at his sides. Spencer looked stunned, his face flushing. Corey didn't know if it was embarrassment or anger and he didn't give a fuck.

"Okay, so things are fucked up for you," Spencer retorted angrily. "Maybe having a few beers and getting it off your chest will keep you from taking it out on your fellow instructors. You know, this Nygaard asshole is talking shit about the whole Corps. You might find sympathy easy to come by if you bothered to talk about it."

He watched Spencer's stiff back retreat. Corey climbed into the Humvee and slammed the door closed. None of the other Marines said a word, even though he knew they'd heard the entire exchange. At least they were smart.

As Corey reached for the ignition button, a voice spoke quietly from the seat behind him. "You NCOs are the backbone of the Corps. Stick with the good ones and don't let the bad ones have the last word."

Corey was surprised to hear words of encouragement from the lieutenant he'd tried to help earlier. His throat tightened, making words impossible, so Corey simply nodded to say he'd heard.

When he'd secured the Humvee for the night, Corey started to leave. He stopped at the sound of Whitfield's voice.

"Staff Sergeant Yarwood. My office."

Fuck. He knew he was about to be reamed for losing his shit on the range.

Corey stepped into the Master Sergeant's office and closed the door as ordered. He stood at attention, eyes locked on a picture behind Whitfield's shoulder. "You needed to see me, Master Sergeant?"

"At ease, Corey," Whitfield said, voice absent of all censure. He sounded almost friendly. "J.A.S. needs you to report again tomorrow morning."

"Yes, Master Sergeant." Corey took the written order from

Whitfield. It gave no indication what he was needed for this time. "Understood."

"You don't have to report for class until eighteen hundred hours, so I don't anticipate that you'll be late, since they're having you report to them at ten hundred hours." Whitfield read through his copy of Corey's orders to appear for questioning. "But that also means you'll have to wear your service uniform this time. Sorry about that."

Corey was taken aback by the Master Sergeant's smile. "Not a problem. It's still in the same bag I picked it up from the dry cleaners."

"You're all squared away, then." Whitfield met Corey's eyes directly. "If something comes up in this interview and you need to report to class late, advise me as early as possible."

"Yes, Master Sergeant," Corey answered by rote. He had no idea what Whitfield might be alluding to.

"There's going to be simulated combat in tomorrow's training, you remember that?" Whitfield asked.

Corey's stomach did a slow, queasy roll. "Affirmative, Master Sergeant."

Whitfield went back to sorting through papers on his desk. "Now that you know what's likely to happen, see what there is you can do to be ready to deal with it." His tone was matter-of-fact.

The silence between them was interminable. "Yes, Master Sergeant," Corey stirred himself enough to respond.

"Dismissed, Staff Sergeant."

Corey fled the office like he'd lit it on fire. He climbed into his Jeep and took out his cell phone.

"Good timing," Sean said when he answered. "I don't have to be on set for another thirty minutes."

Corey sighed. At the first sound of Sean's voice, all the tension fled his body. He leaned his head back, closed his eyes and smiled. "I was hoping you weren't in the middle of anything."

"Just got done with hair and make-up," replied Sean. "It's all hurry up and wait."

Chuckling, Corey said, "Sounds like the Marine Corps."

"Then we relate to one another's professions. Excellent."

"How long is this shoot for?" asked Corey. This week was shaping up to be pretty fucked up and he wanted something to look forward to.

"This is my only night shoot, but I work tomorrow and Thursday and I have Friday off. What are you thinking?"

Corey stared down at the tail of his uniform blouse. He tugged nervously at a frayed thread. "I want to see you again."

"I want to see you, again, too," Sean quickly replied.

This time, the knots in Corey's stomach and the tightness in his chest were pleasant. "I have night time training the next two days. But Friday night is open."

"How about the rest of the weekend?" Sean sounded hopeful.

Corey smiled to himself. "Yeah. The weekend is wide open," he answered quietly.

"Okay, then."

"Okay, then." Corey's smile grew idiotically wider.

"So what are your plans for this evening, while I'm slaving away under hot Tungsten lights?"

Corey hesitated. He knew if he told Sean what had happened earlier, he'd encourage Corey to attend the SMP event. Corey wasn't sure he wanted to be around people.

"Hey, what's wrong?" Sean asked, sounding concerned.

"Nothing's wrong," Corey hedged. "Some guys want me to meet them for an SMP dinner and a movie thing tonight and I don't know if I want to go."

"SMP?"

"Single Marine Program."

Sean was silent long enough for Corey to grow anxious.

"What, like a Marine Corps dating service?"

"No!" Corey gave himself a mental kick. Of course Sean wouldn't automatically understand. "It's to keep Marines without families from feeling isolated and lonely. It's not about dating. Some guys leave their parents' homes and get shipped across the country and they don't know anyone."

Sean laughed. "Oh, okay. Cause I was picturing Devil Dog speed dating."

It was Corey's turn to laugh. "Not even close. Did you really think I'd arrange a date with you and then go cruising?" He'd meant the question to be a joke but decided he wanted a real answer.

"I didn't want to think so, but then again we've only fucked the one time." Sean's tone sounded casual but Corey felt the weight behind the words.

"Yeah, well, that was my first time with *anyone* since I got back from deployment." Corey had no idea why he objected to Sean's use of the word *fuck*.

"Oh." Sean's pause was interminable. "That should not make me as happy as it does," he finally said with a chuckle.

Something heavy lifted off of Corey's shoulders. Before he could respond, Sean had a brief conversation with someone on his end.

"Shit, they're calling me to the set," Sean said hastily. "I'll call you later."

Corey barely said goodbye before Sean ended the connection. He smiled down at the dark phone in his hand. He decided he'd meet up with the other NCO instructors tonight. At least until Sean called.

CHAPTER THIRTEEN

Corey removed his barracks cover as he stepped inside. The receptionist seemed to recognize him as she greeted him with a smile and immediately escorted him back to the same conference room.

The receptionist closed the door as she left and Corey stood at attention. Immediately, Captain Evans said he should be as he was. He slowly approached the chair he'd occupied during his first interview.

"Good morning, ma'am," Corey greeted with a nod, turning his cover around and around. "Captain. Sir," he said to Hirata and Special Agent Hoffman.

"Good to see you again, Staff Sergeant," Hoffman said, handing Corey a bottle of water.

"Thank you." Corey nearly refused the water, until he remembered the previous interview.

"This is going to take a little while. Feel free to make yourself comfortable," Captain Evans said. She shed her olive green uniform coat and folded it, carefully laying it over the back of a chair.

Captain Hirata was already in his khaki uniform sleeves. Hoffman was less careful with his suit jacket, and as a civilian, was free to roll his shirt sleeves above his elbows.

Corey unfastened the belt of his coat, pushed the buttons through their holes and shrugged out of his coat. He folded the olive green material with as much care as had Captain Evans. Draping the garment over the chair to the left, Corey made sure the heavy set of ribbons and medals didn't crease the fabric.

"Good. Now I'm much less intimidated," Captain Evans said, smiling as they both took their seats.

Captain Hirata chuckled as he came around the end of the table and, to Corey's surprise, took the chair to his right.

"Ma'am?" Corey asked in confusion, fearing he'd offended an officer.

"You're a heavily decorated NCO, Staff Sergeant," Evans replied, still smiling. "That chest full of ribbons makes those of us who've never seen combat jealous."

Corey sat frozen, unsure how to answer. He was required to wear his medals and ribbons, he wasn't flaunting his combat experience.

"Relax, Corey. It's a compliment," Hirata said, opening a thick manila file folder.

"If you say so, sir," Corey answered carefully.

"Would you two leave the kid alone?" Hoffman cried in mock outrage. "This is stressful enough for him."

"Let's get started then," Hirata said, spreading papers out in front of him. They appeared to be after-action reports. "The quicker we get through this, the quicker the Staff Sergeant can flee our company."

Realizing they were all trying to set him at ease, Corey allowed himself a small smile. "I appreciate that, sir. I have an appointment to have needles inserted beneath my fingernails."

The room filled with laughter.

"And a sense of humor, too," Captain Evans mused.

"Unfortunately, what we need to talk about today is very unpleasant," Agent Hoffman said, looking regretful.

"We need you to be honest, precise, and candid," added Evans.

"Understood, ma'am."

Agent Hoffman used a remote control to activate the video camera.

Captain Hirata began to read from a neatly typed sheet of paper. "Okay, Staff Sergeant, to recap: your platoon was on patrol in Ghazni when one of the Humvees was struck by an IED, resulting in the deaths of three enlisted Marines. In the ensuing chaos, it was determined that occupants of a nearby dwelling were firing on your position. Your platoon commander ordered you to take a detachment of half the platoon and neutralize the threat. Is that accurate?" Hirata looked up from the notes and waited for Corey to confirm.

"Affirmative, sir."

The captain looked back down at his notes. "You followed proper Marine Corps procedure and training, in conjunction with the ROE at that time, to secure the structure and neutralize the threat, all while sustaining zero additional casualties. Is this also accurate?"

"It is, sir." Corey's leg began to bounce.

"At this point, you ordered Sergeant Michael Nygaard to take five Marines, exit out the rear of the dwelling and ensure the perimeter was secure and that there were no additional threats nearby." Hirata set his notes aside. "Are these the facts as you remember them, Staff Sergeant?"

Corey smoothed his tie down his chest. "They are, sir."

Captain Hirata handed Corey several sheets of printed paper. "Do you recognize this document, Staff Sergeant Yarwood?"

Corey skimmed over the document with a nod. "It appears to be my after-action report on the incident, sir."

"Please read the entire document *carefully*," Hirata said. "Verify for us that this is the report that you wrote and submitted to your platoon commander."

Corey read the report, easily recalling the facts, recognizing his own writing style and word usage. The facts were exactly as he remembered them, and as he remembered writing them.

Until he reached the section where he had ordered Nygaard to secure the perimeter.

With a brisk shake of his head, Corey tapped the offending paragraph. "I didn't write this," he said, looking up at the others in disbelief.

No one looked surprised.

"That is not the report you wrote and submitted?" Captain Evans asked.

"It is, up until this paragraph." Corey emphasized his point by tapping his finger on the paper. "This isn't what happened, and it's not what I wrote."

Hirata handed him a pen. "Note anything that you yourself did not write."

Corey kept reading and marking. The remainder of the report was filled with complete falsehoods. When he was finished, he handed the report to Captain Hirata.

"Who changed my report, Captain?" Corey asked angrily.

"That's something we still need to determine," Hirata replied.

"Is your original report still accessible?" Captain Evans asked.

"It's saved on the hard drive of my battalion issued laptop, ma'am," Corey answered.

Evans frowned. "That's convenient, but unusual," he said. "You weren't required to return the laptop when you changed billets?"

"I was told there was no need since I would be instructing at Basic Recon," replied Corey. "I'm still considered a part of the Recon community."

"Someone's going to regret that oversight before this is all over," Evans said, glancing at Hirata briefly. "We'll need you to provide that report to us, ASAP, Staff Sergeant."

"Yes, ma'am. I'll email it after class this evening." Corey took a long drink of water. He tugged at one leg of his uniform trousers.

"I have some questions for you, Staff Sergeant," Agent Hoffman said, "regarding the events as they have been presented in the various reports submitted by your platoon."

Corey's gut felt like it was knotted around a lead weight. He was thankful he'd heeded his counselor's advice and taken a dose of Xanax. "Was mine the only one that was modified?"

There was a long moment of silence. "We're not sure, yet," Hoffman answered. Before Corey could question further, he pressed on. "At any time during the incident, did you receive orders, or issues orders, to engage hostiles at any location other than the site of the IED blast or the structure you made entry into?"

"No, sir," Corey answered. He knew what the Special Agent was trying to establish.

"Did you engage any hostiles, or order anyone else to engage hostiles, anywhere other than inside the structure you entered?" Hoffman asked.

Corey's leg bounced. He shifted in his chair. "No sir. The only hostiles we encountered were inside the structure and were neutralized as soon as we made entry." He ran both hands down his tie to smooth it.

"And all of those hostiles were young, adult males, correct?"

Corey paused, scenes from his recent nightmares flashing through his mind. "Correct, sir." He reached for his bottle of water.

"When you located Sergeant Nygaard and his team, had they secured weapons and or explosives?" Hoffman spoke slowly, watching Corey intently.

Gesturing toward the report he'd handed back to Hirata, Corey answered. "That's one of the things that was altered in my report. The only weapons my team secured and inventoried were the ones from the dwelling we entered." He took another drink of water. His mouth kept going dry.

Hoffman handed Corey a stack of color photographs. "Have you ever seen these before?"

Scanning the photos, Corey recognized them immediately. "These are the photographs I took to document the identities and conditions of the men we killed inside the dwelling. I used the digital camera issued to me by the Marine Corps and downloaded them to the laptop, also issued to me by the Corps."

"Do any of those photos misrepresent how the bodies were handled?" Hoffman rested his chin on his steepled fingers.

Corey frowned. He looked back through the pictures. They weren't pretty, but they were, after all, pictures of corpses killed during war. "No, sir. They are accurate representations."

Hoffman tilted his head to one side and narrowed his eyes. "Does the after-action report you just read correctly detail how the bodies were handled during transport back to base?"

"Yes, it does, sir." Corey tried to clear his dry throat. "That's one of the paragraphs that was not altered."

"At any time, were the bodies used to taunt civilian residents?" The special agent shrugged, as though he wasn't quite sure what question to ask. "Were the bodies desecrated in any way that could be found offensive by the Muslim faith? Are you aware of any Marine mutilating any of the corpses post-mortem?"

Corey was too horrified to wonder what game Hoffman was playing. "No, sir. Absolutely not. Had I witnessed anything of that nature I would have put a stop to it. *Immediately*. My Marines conducted themselves with honor, sir." In his peripheral vision, Corey saw Captains Evans and Hirata exchange a significant look. He glanced back and forth between the two.

"He's so earnest and genuine," Evans said quietly.

"His credibility is nearly unimpeachable," replied Hirata.

"Makes our job easier," Evans murmured as she went back to writing on her legal pad.

Corey frowned, not happy about being talked about as he sat right there, listening. He held his tongue, though. He was in the company of officers.

Hoffman collected the photographs from Corey and handed him another stack. "Do you recognize these photos, Corey?"

"No sir, I've never seen them before." He knew what they depicted, though.

"Do you recognize the bodies in the photos?" Hoffman clarified his question.

"They appear to be of the hostiles that attacked the platoon while the detachment and I were securing the structure," replied Corey.

"Did you examine those corpses at the time of the incident?" The special agent made the question sound off-the-cuff.

Corey wasn't buying Hoffman's act, but he wasn't sure where this line of questioning was leading. "No, sir. I had other duties and this was overseen by Lieutenant Adams."

"Staff Sergeant, please examine those photos and tell me," Hoffman nodded toward the stack of pictures in front of Corey, "if you had come across those bodies while on patrol, how you would have believed they'd been killed."

Corey looked closely at the pictures, analyzing the positions of the bodies, the wounds that were and were not visible, and the pattern of the pooled blood.

Adrenaline flooded Corey's body. He gasped, shoving away the photos. He hastily snatched the bottle of water beside him, washing down the bile rising in his throat.

"Are you all right, Corey?" Evans asked, watching him with concern.

"I need a minute, ma'am," he replied, voice shaky and hands trembling.

"Did you see something, Staff Sergeant?" Hoffman asked, gathering up the photos.

"It's what I didn't see," replied Corey.

"And that was?" Hoffman pressed.

"Gunshot wounds to the bodies." Corey took a deep breath. "If those men had been killed during a gun battle they instigated, there would be bloody gunshot wounds to their bodies, as well as their heads. Those bodies have no visible wounds. The blood has pooled beneath their heads, but there are no wounds visible on their faces. Those men were not killed in a gun battle. They were executed." Realization struck Corey like concussive blast. "I need to talk to a lawyer," he said, starting to rise from his chair.

"What about?" Captain Hirata asked.

Corey fumbled into his uniform coat, his fingers struggling to fasten the buttons. "As the senior NCO, I'm going to take the fall for what Nygaard and the lieutenant did." His mind raced over what he knew had happened and what he'd begun to suspect as well.

"No one's taking the fall for anything, Staff Sergeant," Captain Evans replied.

All three of them had risen from their chairs. Hirata crossed to a credenza and lifted a telephone handset to his ear.

"I need to be dismissed." Corey struggled with his belt, slowly edging his way toward the door. "Permission to be dismissed?" He didn't know who the ranking officer was, Hirata or Evans.

"You're not in trouble for anything that's gone on, Corey," Hirata said, setting down the phone. "Just try to calm down for a moment."

The door to the conference room opened slowly. Corey whirled to assess the incoming threat.

"Hey, Corey, I heard you were coming in for another interview today." Kellan Reynolds was smartly dressed in a suit. His expression was open and his greeting friendly. He opened the door all the way and stepped into the room, leaving Corey's path to the egress clear.

Until Jonah Carver appeared in the doorway. He was also dressed in his olive green service uniform and he stood, tall and menacing, scowling between Kellan and Corey.

"Staff Sergeant Yarwood seems to have gotten the impression that he's a suspect in our inquiry." Hirata said quietly from behind Corey. "We were just trying to explain that he's been of immeasurable assistance to us by providing independent verification of facts we've already established."

Corey needed to get out of the room but Jonah still stood in the doorway, expression dark. Kellan glanced at Jonah over his shoulder.

"Again with the *punim*," Kellan hissed. "Get out of the doorway so he doesn't feel trapped."

Jonah's expression smoothed and he slowly stepped into the room, standing to the side of the open door.

Corey took a deep breath and focused his attention on Kellan. "Officers don't like to discipline other officers," Corey said the only thing he could think of. "It was my after-action that was altered. This is going to fall on me."

"No, Corey," Kellan said fiercely, "not on my watch."

Corey wanted to believe him.

"Staff Sergeant," Hirata waited until Corey turned to look at him before he continued, "your report was altered without your knowledge. You did *not* submit a falsified report. None of this is on you."

"I promise you, Corey," Kellan said, "no enlisted Marine will be held responsible for something he did not do. If I so much as tried to do that, do you think Jonah would let me get away with it?"

Corey darted a glance at Jonah, standing silently by the door. At Corey's look, he gave a single, sharp, shake of his head.

Taking another deep breath, Corey shook out his fisted hands and rolled his shoulders to ease the accumulated tension. He looked down at the high shine on his black shoes without really seeing. He trusted Jonah, which meant he should trust Kellan. Corey just couldn't shake the sense that all fingers were pointing at him.

"Corey, do you understand that you and Corporal Tyler Howe are our allies in this inquiry?" Kellan asked, breaking the line of his suit jacket to shove his hands into his trouser pockets. "Without knowing anything about what's going on, the two of you are verifying the claims of the Afghanis. The cover-up doesn't stop with Lieutenant Adams, but it also doesn't *include* you."

"Yes, sir," Corey said, voice rough. He cleared his throat awkwardly, shifting his weight from foot to foot and wondering how quickly he could make it out the door if he needed to.

"Captain Hirata is your lawyer, Corey, as much as he's one of my investigators," Kellan continued. "He's your shield against Nygaard's crap and anything your former lieutenant eventually tries to pull."

That was news to Corey. How had he missed that? "Understood, sir," he replied. "I apologize for overreacting."

"I don't believe it was an overreaction, Staff Sergeant," Hirata interjected. "It's possible that in our zealousness to ensure an untainted inquiry, we haven't been as forthcoming with you as perhaps we should be."

"Chris, do you require the Staff Sergeant for anything more today?" Captain Evans asked Agent Hoffman.

"Today, no." Hoffman began to gather up photos and paperwork. "I'll need to dig into details as we progress, but it doesn't have to be today."

"Great," Kellan said, smiling once again. "Let's kick Staff Sergeant Yarwood loose for today. We can resume when he's not feeling like we're quite so adversarial."

As Kellan exchanged a silent look with him, Jonah stepped forward. "Come on, I'll walk you out."

Corey followed Jonah, aware that neither of the officers had dismissed him. He supposed Kellan really did outrank them all.

"What time do you report?" Jonah asked as they slowly strolled down quiet corridors, their highly polished dress shoes making no sound on the plush carpet.

"Eighteen hundred."

"What are you going to do in the meantime?"

Corey glanced at his watch. "I have an appointment with my counselor in two hours. I called yesterday and told her what was going on today and she freed up an hour for me."

"What are your plans until then?" Jonah's question sounded casual, but Corey knew better.

"Change into my utilities. Get some lunch." Corey paused to consider his options. At some point he knew he was going to make a phone call. "Avoid thinking about all this shit until I get to my counselor's office."

"Does she have you on meds?" Jonah's question was free of judgment.

Corey laughed mirthlessly. "I took a Xanax before the interview and I still lost my shit."

"You're showing signs of hyper-vigilance and you perceived yourself to be under threat," Jonah replied. "It was a pretty reasonable response as far as I'm concerned."

They passed through reception and Jonah held the outer door open for Corey.

"This is some pretty fucked up shit, Jonah," Corey said darkly when they stepped out into the sunshine.

"The understatement inherent in that assessment is so extreme as to be nearly immeasurable," Jonah declared dramatically. Neither of them spoke again until they reached Corey's Jeep. "If you find yourself wanting to drink before you get to your counselor's, you call me."

"It's been more than a week since I've taken a drink," Corey said quietly, looking off into the distance. "You were a solid copy, Jonah. And you weren't the only one who noticed a problem."

Jonah watched Corey with narrowed eyes for several interminable moments. His gaze was shrewd and assessing. "Are you seeing someone, Corey? Do you have anyone watching your six?"

Corey glanced down at his shoes for a moment, considering how to answer. "Yeah. For a couple of weeks now."

"The other person who noticed your drinking?" asked Jonah.

Corey nodded.

Jonah lifted a single eyebrow. "Does he get it?"

Corey didn't have to ask what 'it' was. "He's a civilian so he'll never understand completely. But he gets *me*. He understands being a Marine is important to me. He's got his own life so sometimes *he's* the one traveling and working fucked up hours."

"Good. Cause I'd rather not have to kick his ass." Jonah was a master of deadpan.

Corey laughed. "Like Kellan would let you."

One side of Jonah's mouth lifted in a smile that used to make Corey's knees weak; the way Sean's smile did now. "So, I imagine you'll be calling him if you get into trouble in the next couple of hours," Jonah said, already heading back inside the building. "But if he's unavailable, call me."

"Yes, Top. On my honor as a Recon Marine." Still smiling, Corey climbed into his Jeep. Jonah's concern was comforting. Not that he'd ever admit that to Top.

After he grabbed lunch and changed into his utilities, Corey still had some time to kill before his appointment. He took another Xanax, just to be safe. He sat on his rack and contemplated calling Sean. He was still reeling from the earlier revelations, but he didn't feel the need for a drink. Corey simply wanted to call Sean just to talk to him.

He acknowledged his disappointment when he reached Sean's voicemail. "Hey, it's me. Just wanted to say hi. The interview was pretty fucked up. My counselor is squeezing me in this afternoon so I'll be fine. Call me when you get a chance, just to talk." He didn't want Sean worrying about something he couldn't do anything about.

Even though he was early for his counseling appointment, Doctor Ingram had the inner office door open and was waiting for him. "How are you, Corey?" she asked as soon as he stepped inside.

"Two doses of Xanax and a near mutiny, but I'm fine," he answered dryly, closing the inner door.

"Is any of that an exaggeration?" Ingram queried, watching him intently.

Corey flopped down on the love seat and immediately reached for his usual throw pillow. "I guess the part about mutiny is an exaggeration. It was a very inconvenient panic attack, I guess."

He told her about the earlier events, the things he'd learned and his final, overwhelmed reaction. As Corey talked, his anger welled up, spilling over into rage. Ingram asked him over and over how these events made him *feel*. His anger was only part of it. Corey felt used, misled, and betrayed. Finally, he relaxed into the sofa, feeling almost unbearably sad.

"This is normal, Corey," Doctor Ingram reassured. "You're supposed to feel these things. You need to feel them, acknowledge them, accept them, talk about them, and eventually move past them."

"I don't get why I freaked out the way I did," he replied. "I way overreacted."

"You've spent a long time having to react to threats in an extreme manner, or you'd lose your life," she explained. "Neither your brain nor your body fully understands that it's time to stand down; that it's okay to stand down. You perceive a threat of any kind and your default setting has been maximum response."

"Will it ever stop?" Corey desperately wanted to know.

"Oh yes," she said with a smile. "We'll teach you how to react and deal with things a little more rationally. I'm more concerned about this anxiety attack you mentioned when you called yesterday."

Corey told her about the panic he felt at the sound of gunfire. "That can't keep happening. I gotta be able to do my job."

"That doesn't sound like anxiety, Corey." Doctor Ingram frowned in concern. "That sounds like a flashback."

There's no way that was better. "I still gotta figure out how to stop it," he replied.

"And we will, just like we'll conquer the anxiety." Her expression smoothed. "And please don't let your fellow Marines talk you out of continuing to seek help. They mean well, but too many of you are coming back suicidal, with severe cases of PTS, for you to maintain this façade of tough guys not needing help with their emotions."

"I'm here aren't I?" Corey tried to smile. He'd realized after his talk with Sean that he cared more for what Sean thought about him, than he did his fellow Marines. So, he'd called Doctor Ingram.

"I want to talk about a couple of things we touched on previously." He watched the doctor consult her notes. "You've already said that the Xanax mitigates your anxiety somewhat. Do you think it's enough?"

Corey shrugged. "What do you think?"

"I think you're the only one who knows how you've been feeling," she responded evasively. "I can give you something stronger."

Corey considered this. He did always feel better after he took a Xanax. "I think I'm fine with what I've got."

Ingram scribbled another note. "Good. Okay. How are you sleeping?"

"Better. Fewer nightmares." He supposed he could at least be thankful for that.

"Fewer? But you're still having them?" she asked.

Corey sighed. He hated writing in that damn journal but it *had* helped him identify that little quirk. "I seem to have one after stressful days."

"It's good that you recognize that. It's a positive sign you've identified a causal relationship." She made more notes on her pad. "How have you been dealing with it when you awake from a nightmare?"

For some reason, Corey hesitated. "I've been calling my friend. Sean. I've been calling Sean." He tugged at the fringe of the pillow and swallowed hard.

"Something tells me that's been helping." Ingram's smile was kind. "And that brings me to your third prescription. Any opportunities to try out the little blue pills?"

Corey was suddenly fascinated by the tangled pillow fringe. "I took one just in case, but I had a reaction even before it kicked in."

"I'm glad to hear that." The doctor paused as if expecting Corey to continue. Finally she said, "Things went well, I take it?"

"Yeah. We're going to see each other again on Friday." As he glanced at Doctor Ingram, Corey couldn't hold back his smile.

She returned his smile. "It's good that you're being social, Corey." Ingram cocked her head, as if trying to determine what Corey needed to hear. "I was concerned about your emotional distancing of yourself."

"I went to an SMP event last night." Corey rushed through his confession. "I didn't stay long. I went home early to talk to Sean. But I went."

"Those are great social events," Ingram said with enthusiasm. Her expression indicated a thought had just occurred to her. "Do they still have the volunteer program at the base animal shelter?"

"Yeah, I think so. I used to do that, before I deployed last time." Corey really liked dogs. His lifestyle didn't allow him to have pets, but he always thought that someday he'd be able to manage it. In the meantime, working at the shelter had been fun.

"I want you to start doing that again," Ingram said, scribbling yet more notes. "Studies are showing fantastic results using dogs to treat extreme anxiety in veterans with severe PTS. I want you to go, handle the animals, let the oxytocin flood your system."

Corey couldn't help but chuckle. "You're giving me a prescription to pet animals?"

"In a way, yes," the doctor replied with a grin.

As she walked Corey to the door after his appointment, Doctor Ingram said, "Enjoy your date on Friday."

It seemed like she was teasing him. "Oh, I'm sure I will," he replied, letting the door close behind him.

CHAPTER FOURTEEN

Corey rang the doorbell at Sean's condo, adjusting the strap of his ruck on his shoulder. When they'd talked earlier, Sean had told him to pack for the weekend. It was time to admit that it was what they both wanted, so why play games?

Sean opened the door, wide smile already in place. "Hey." He stepped aside to let Corey enter and closed the door.

"Hey," Corey replied. Before he could say more, Sean leaned in and gave him a quick kiss.

"Put your bag in the bedroom and I'll finish dinner," Sean said, after pressing a second kiss to Corey's lips.

Corey dropped his bag on the floor at the foot of Sean's bed. When he stepped into the kitchen, Sean had his back to him as he cooked. Corey admired the breadth of his shoulders as the cotton of his T-shirt clung to him. His well-worn jeans fit his firm, rounded ass perfectly. Sean was barefoot, as he always seemed to be when he was at home. Corey envied how even Sean's feet were attractive. Corey had only just gotten rid of the last of the boot rot from his last deployment.

Sean glanced over his shoulder, probably sensing Corey's presence. He smiled and Corey's head spun.

"It's nothing fancy," Sean said as he checked the boiling pasta. "The sauce is from a jar but I added real ground beef." He bent to examine garlic bread in the broiler.

Corey's mouth fell open at the sight of Sean's ass as he bent at the waist. He crossed the kitchen and was behind Sean when he straightened. Corey wrapped his arms around Sean's chest and pulled him back. Sean made a soft sound of surprise, but readily leaned back into Corey's body.

Sean was warm and firm. Corey buried his face in the crook of Sean's neck and breathed deeply. Again, Sean was freshly showered. He smelled clean but with a hint of his usual cologne that Corey very much liked. Corey kept his arms around Sean's chest and didn't move. Sean crossed his arms over Corey's hands and seemed content to just stay leaning into Corey.

"Is everything okay?" Sean asked softly, after several long moments.

Corey had already told Sean about everything that had happened that week. Sometimes he wondered if he wasn't starting to sound like a whiny brat.

"Yeah, everything's as fine as it can be," he murmured against Sean's warm skin.

In a moment of harsh clarity, Corey abruptly pulled back and released Sean. He was becoming clingy as well as whiny.

Before Corey could retreat completely, Sean grasped his hand and pulled him close again. "I like it when you touch me," he said quietly, before releasing Corey's hand.

Corey's heart swelled to bursting. He didn't trust himself to speak so he leaned down and pressed a kiss to the back of Sean's neck.

They ate this time at Sean's small dining table. Corey asked question after question about Sean's recent job. He listened in fascination as Sean talked about the quirks of a world so foreign to Corey. There was more to it than he'd realized.

Corey felt so fucking guilty.

"You must get tired of listening to me bitch about my problems," Corey said, sitting back in his chair with a heavy sigh. "I didn't ask you about any of this when we talked on the phone."

"You had a lot going on this week," Sean replied, brows furrowed. "It was pretty much a normal week for me."

"I'm a selfish dick," said Corey with a shameful shake of his head.

"If you were a selfish dick, you wouldn't have just sat through an hour of me rambling about myself and my screwy job." Sean gripped Corey's knee beneath the table.

Corey was surprised. "I learned as much about *you* as I did about your job," he blurted. "There's so much more to you than standing around, looking pretty, and reciting a bunch of lines from memory. It's fun to hear about your work, but I like discovering things you like, learning about your past and your opinions. Shit like that."

"Yeah, I know what you mean," Sean said, smiling wide.

Corey felt like he was missing a joke. "What?" he asked with an awkward laugh.

"Well, for you to tell me about what's been going on with you, you have to explain everything to me," Sean said, still gripping Corey's knee. "I've learned a lot about the Marine Corps, about being a Marine, about what you guys go through in combat. But mostly I've learned about how much you love being a Marine, how quick and analytical your mind is, that you're focused and disciplined, and that you're very, very loyal."

Corey looked down at the napkin he was shredding. "You've been doing recon on me."

"Uh huh. And I like what I'm learning." Corey felt Sean lean toward him and he turned his face in time to accept Sean's soft, warm kiss.

"Good," Corey said when they parted.

"Let's clean up and watch a movie?" Sean asked.

Together, they cleared the table and filled the dishwasher. As Corey carried fresh bottles of soda to the living room, he watched Sean move the coffee table and shove a huge ottoman up against the sofa. It created a chaise lounge large enough for two grown men.

"Do you want to change your clothes?" Sean looked at him questioningly. "Did you bring something more comfortable?"

"Is there anything more comfortable than jeans and a T-shirt?" Corey was baffled at the question.

"Some people like to watch TV in sweats," Sean replied with a laugh. "I like my jeans, just fine. You can take your shoes off, though, act like you're staying awhile."

"Make myself at home?" Corey asked teasingly, hoping to keep Sean smiling.

Sean obviously wanted Corey to be comfortable in his home. He wanted Corey to like being here. Corey was just afraid to reveal too many of his bad habits too soon.

Inside Sean's bedroom, Corey removed his boots and tucked his socks inside. He slid them out of view, beneath the bed. When he reentered the living room, Sean had the BluRay player ready to go.

Corey dropped down onto the sofa and propped his feet on the ottoman. He laughed at his own ridiculousness. "You could have just told me not to put my shoes on the furniture."

Sean looked at him for several seconds with a blank expression, before Corey's meaning registered. He looked abashed. "No, I really didn't mean it that way." He laughed in embarrassment. "I do want you to relax and be comfortable. Screw the furniture."

"I'd rather screw you *on* the furniture," Corey said before he could police himself. He ran a palm over his heated face. "Christ, I must sound like a fucking pig a lot of the time."

"I don't know why you think that. You say what I'm thinking most of the time," Sean replied, still smiling openly. He dimmed the lights in the condo. "Do we need anything else while I'm up?"

The sight of Sean's sharp cheekbones catching the dim light jogged Corey's memory. "Yeah. I still want to see all those modeling pictures you say you have. Do you have a book of them somewhere?"

Sean looked surprised. "Yeah. Are you serious?"

"It's part of your work, isn't it?" Corey asked.

Sean retrieved a zippered portfolio from beside his single bookcase. "Yeah, but showing them off when it doesn't have to do with a potential job makes me feel vain."

Corey snorted. "You are *not* vain. That much I'm sure of." Corey knew that Sean was aware of how attractive he was but it didn't affect anything about him, or his behavior. When he really thought about it, it was strange that Corey didn't feel ugly next to Sean.

Taking the portfolio, Corey unzipped it. He motioned for Sean to sit right next to him while he viewed the photographs. Sean seemed reluctant, but he eventually complied.

Corey gasped at the first photo. Sean was beautiful. Whether color or black and white, Sean's eyes seemed luminescent in picture after picture. The older images were obviously of a very young, sometimes androgynous Sean. The more recent ones showed his well sculpted body and generous endowments. Fully clothed or wearing only a pair of briefs, Sean always looked poised, handsome and classy.

"You're about to reach the more *artistic* ones," Sean said, air quotes implied.

Corey was stunned when he turned the page and saw a black and white photo of Sean, face down on a rumpled bed, bare ass slightly lifted. His expression was enticing and Corey's cock twitched at the sight. He paged through photo after photo of Sean naked, or nearly naked. The frontal shots always obscured him with a towel, a piece of clothing, or sometimes Sean's own carefully positioned leg.

Corey's dick pressed painfully against his zipper. Sean was smoldering and sexy. He could look hungry, dominant, or as if he was begging to be fucked. Corey very nearly tossed the book aside and pushed Sean down onto the couch.

The first picture of Sean naked, posed with another man, took Corey by surprise. They were all beautiful, Sean twined around other well-built men. In each one, Sean's face was somewhat obscured, and Corey missed seeing Sean's eyes.

He knew the photos were staged and no sex had taken place. Still, with each page he turned, Corey became more and more jealous of the nameless men who held Sean's gorgeous, naked body in their arms.

Corey turned the page to reveal a photograph that made his

cock throb, at the same time it triggered a powerful possessiveness he'd never experienced before. Sean was naked, legs spread as he sat between the open thighs of an equally naked man. The framing of the photo left Sean's gifts to the imagination, but Corey knew what wasn't revealed. The other man tipped Sean's head back with a hand on his forehead, effectively leaving Sean's identity masked. Corey could still see that Sean's mouth hung open, as if he was crying out in ecstasy. The second model held Sean firmly back against him, arm around his waist, hand splayed possessively on Sean's taut abs. While Sean's eyes were unseen, the second model stared directly at the camera over Sean's bare shoulder. His expression was arrogant and knowing.

Jealousy flooded Corey, strong enough to taste. He slammed the book closed, causing Sean to jump.

"They're all staged," Sean said hastily, reaching for the portfolio. "I didn't have sex with any of them."

Corey held the book out of Sean's reach. "I know. And I wouldn't care if you'd done porn to pay your bills. Hell, I'm the one who kills people for a living," Corey growled darkly. "It's just...seeing you with other men...it fucking turns me on and pisses me off at the same time. That's pretty fucked up."

Sean stopped trying to grab the portfolio away from Corey. "I don't do those kinds of shoots anymore."

Corey dismissed Sean's words with a wave of his hand. "I know you have to do what you have to do. It's your job. As hot as it is to see you with another hot guy, I don't like the idea of anyone else touching you."

Sean sat beside Corey, tense and silent.

Corey gave a self-deprecating laugh. "Christ, you hear that all the time, don't you?"

"Hear what?" Sean looked surprised.

"That you're fucking gorgeous." Corey finally handed over the portfolio. What the fuck was he even doing there? What could Sean possibly see in him? "I must make you feel like you're slumming."

"What?" Sean demanded, incredulous. "Why would you say that? You can make better looking men than me come in their pants with just a look."

Corey laughed helplessly at the absurdity of the idea. He stared at his feet that had so recently been gray and scaly, sloughing skin in sickening chunks. "Yeah. Well. I like your pictures. I know my opinion doesn't matter, but I really like them."

He watched curiously as Sean paged through the portfolio and scrounged in one of the plastic sheets. He handed Corey a small copy of one of his fashion photos. He was clothed, but his dress shirt hung open, giving a mouth-watering view of his muscled chest and defined abs. "Your opinion matters to me. A lot."

"You get told all the time how good looking you are," Corey said, cupping the precious photo in one of his oversized, roughly calloused hands.

"Not by you, I don't." Sean's tone was shy and unsure.

Corey's head snapped up. "I didn't think you needed to hear it from me."

Sean shrugged. "One of the things I really like about you is that you treat me like any other guy. You're not fixated on my looks. You don't insist we always go out so people can see us together. You tell me about yourself. And not just the pretty things."

Corey didn't know what to say. He was just being himself with Sean. He didn't think he'd done anything all that special. Corey pulled his wallet from his back pocket and inserted the small photo.

Clearing his throat, he said, "Shall we start the movie?" He looked over at Sean as he set his wallet on the table beside him.

"Sure," Sean replied, retrieving the remote. He looked like he was trying to suppress a grin.

To Corey, Sean never looked sexier than when he was playful and flirty. Before he could think about it, Corey reached over and took Sean's face between both of his hands. Corey plunged his tongue into Sean's mouth. He licked at Sean for several moments, hearing his breathing speed up and feeling him slowly relax against Corey's body.

Pulling back with a wet sound, Corey was pleased with himself for putting that bemused, aroused expression on Sean's face.

He stopped trying to follow the movie. Corey wasn't even sure what they were supposed to be watching. The heat of Sean's body burned against the side of his own. He caught Sean's clean, musky scent with nearly every breath. Corey gave in to his urge. He draped his arm around Sean's shoulders and tugged. Sean eagerly lay back against Corey's chest, resting his head against Corey's shoulder.

Corey slowly ran his hands up and down Sean's arms. He nuzzled Sean's temple and ear, breathing in the scents of his skin and his hair. Sean twined their legs together, running a foot repeatedly along Corey's calf. He lazily skimmed one palm distractedly over Corey's inner thigh.

Sean's breathing was rapid and shallow. Corey took Sean's earlobe into his mouth and suckled it, dragging his teeth lightly along the soft flesh. Sean moaned softly. Corey ran his hands over Sean's chest and shoulders, skimming them over the quivering muscles of Sean's belly.

Corey pressed a line of open-mouthed kisses down the length of Sean's neck. Sean's hand on his thigh stopped moving, gripping him tightly instead. Corey slid his legs against Sean's restless ones. He nipped lightly at Sean's throat and neck. He soothed the same skin with swipes of his tongue. Sean arched against Corey, as if trying to give him more access to all the best parts of Sean's body.

The movie ended and Sean roused himself enough to lean forward to retrieve the remote. Corey dragged his own T-shirt up over his head and set it aside. Before Sean could lean back against him, Corey tugged his shirt up and off.

"I wanna feel skin," he murmured, pulling Sean's naked back up against his own bare chest.

Sean rubbed against Corey, releasing a noise from low in his throat that damn near sounded like a purr. Corey ran the tip of his tongue along the shell of Sean's ear. Sean shuddered against him. He moaned and Corey felt the vibration of it through Sean's back.

Corey ran his palms over Sean's shoulders and down his chest. He pressed his hands, fanning his fingers, against Sean's firm stomach. The muscles quivered at his touch. Corey slid his hands upward and palmed each of Sean's nipples. He took them between his fingers and tugged, making them swell and harden. Sean arched slightly, pushing his chest forward into Corey's hands.

The front of Sean's jeans tented, his arousal obvious. Corey sucked at Sean's neck, careful not to leave bruises, but wringing more moans from him. He was so focused on Sean's pleasure, Corey startled when Sean's hand settled on his groin and gripped his still flaccid cock through his jeans.

Corey gasped and almost shoved Sean's hand away. Relief swept through him when he remembered that Sean knew and understood. Corey didn't have to worry that Sean would misunderstand the cause. Because it certainly wasn't a case of Corey not wanting Sean.

"Did you bring your prescription?" Sean asked in a harsh whisper, as if reading Corey's mind.

"In my bag," he said against Sean's temple. "I'll take one when I'm done here."

Sean continued to rub Corey through his jeans. It felt good but his body still wasn't responding. Corey refused to worry about it. He'd jump start things in a minute. He lowered his hands and opened the front of Sean's jeans, revealing a huge bulge in the front of brightly colored briefs.

Corey eased Sean's erection out of his clothes and stroked it firmly. Sean lifted his hips, pushing into Corey's hand with each stroke.

"Do you wanna go into the bedroom?" Sean asked on a gasp.

Corey lifted his free hand to cup Sean's cheek. He turned

Sean's face toward his own, looking down at his puffy lips, feeling his hot breath as it ghosted over Corey's own mouth. "When I'm done with you," he answered in a rough whisper, staring into Sean's lust-darkened eyes.

He lowered his head and pressed their mouths together. Corey pushed his tongue past Sean's lips. He didn't seal their mouths, instead licking at Sean and encouraging him teasingly to do the same.

Sean gasped repeatedly into and against Corey's mouth. His hips moved rhythmically in time with Corey's hand. Corey kept his grip firm and his pace quick. He wanted to make Sean come. Corey wanted to hear Sean's cries. He wanted to see the hot spunk spill from the reddened tip of Sean's dick. Corey wanted to feel Sean's body shudder and shake against his own, as he rode out the waves of his climax.

He didn't have long to wait. Sean's hand released Corey's cock and came up to cradle the back of his head. His other hand covered Corey's on his cock, twining their fingers and taking up Corey's rhythm.

"Nuh," Sean grunted against Corey's lips, "you're gonna make me come," he growled.

"Good," Corey replied, smiling against Sean's swollen mouth.

At the feel of Sean's cock swelling in his palm, Core looked down. Their joined hands worked rapidly over Sean's generous erection. The dusky red head repeatedly disappeared in their hands, reappearing moments later. It glistened with the moisture of Sean's pre-come.

Corey tightened his grip when Sean's cock pulsed. He felt an extra rush of blood just beneath the skin. Sean's breath hitched and his body tightened.

"Watch it," Corey ordered in a low voice. "Watch yourself come in our hands."

Sean turned obediently to watch as the first pearly drops of come spilled from the slit of his dick. "Fuuuck," he hissed, his body vibrating and quaking violently. "Oh God, I'm coming."

Corey wrapped his free arm around Sean's chest and held him steady. Together, they watched Sean's cock pump stream after stream of come over his belly. Corey held him steady as Sean painted his tanned skin with sticky ropes of come. Some of the warm spunk coated their joined fingers, but most streaked Sean's body.

"That's so fucking gorgeous," Corey murmured to Sean as he held onto him. "You're so hot when you come." He held Sean's body tightly to his own as he quaked, trapped by his brutal climax.

"Shit," Sean sighed harshly when his orgasm finally released him. He collapsed against Corey, chest heaving as he greedily sucked in deep breaths.

Corey pressed his face to the join of Sean's neck and shoulder. He breathed deeply, enjoying the addition of sweat to Sean's heady scent. He couldn't believe his own cock was still soft after all that. He knew he had to get up and take one of his blue pills. Corey wanted to fuck Sean badly and he wasn't going to let his fucking emotional bullshit get in the way.

He hooked his heel on the edge of the ottoman and gave it a shove. It slid easily across the carpet. Corey manhandled Sean to a standing position, holding him steady as he didn't seem to have control of his body again.

Corey pushed himself to his feet. He wrapped his arms around Sean's chest and guided him to the ottoman. "I'm going to gather up some things," he whispered against the moist, warm skin behind Sean's ear. "Sit here and wait for me." Corey helped Sean to sit down on the edge of the ottoman.

Returning to the bedroom, Corey reached into the side pocket of his ruck. He retrieved the tall bottle of lubricant, a strip of condoms, and the amber prescription bottle. Corey poured a Viagra into his palm and returned the bottle to his bag.

Corey tried to be discreet when he returned to the living room and used the last of his soda to wash down the pill.

"So I've got about twenty, thirty minutes to get you turned on?" Sean asked from his seat on the ottoman, running his palms up and down his thighs.

Corey's heated blood chilled at Sean's words. That's what he'd been afraid of. He stepped in front of Sean again. Corey knelt on the ottoman, straddling Sean's hips. He pressed his stomach to Sean's warm chest. Sean looked up at him, pupils still blown wide with desire. Corey cradled his head with both hands and looked down into his beautiful eyes.

"I'm already turned on. I've been turned on since I got here. I can't get any more turned on," he said slowly and carefully, making sure Sean understood. "My head is fucked up and sometimes it fucks up my body, too. That pill just lets my dick catch up to what my brain already knows."

Sean frowned as Corey spoke, until understanding smoothed his features. He lifted his arms and wrapped them around Corey's hips, pressing his face to Corey's belly. "No, I know that. I'm sorry, I said that all wrong." Sean placed warm kisses along Corey's stomach, nipping at his hip bones. "I meant that I have some time to lick and suck you, before you get close to coming."

Corey slid his hands down Sean's chest until he gripped his rib cage. Sean's hands slid down to grasp Corey's ass. Sean turned his face upward again, he looked at Corey with a hungry expression. Corey leaned over and lowered his head. He dragged his tongue over Sean's lower lip, teasing Sean into responding in kind.

Corey licked at Sean, rubbed their tongues together and enjoyed Sean's taste. Sean strained upward into and against Corey's body. He breathed heavily, trying to push their mouths together and eagerly licking his tongue against Corey's.

Sean pulled back hastily, his hands coming around to open Corey's jeans. Reaching into his briefs, Sean gently pulled Corey's soft cock out into the cooler air. Corey slid off the ottoman and rose to his feet. He gasped when Sean's warm, wet mouth slid all the way down his length. He carded his fingers through Sean's soft hair, finally curling his hands into fists.

He watched Sean suck hard on him, drawing back and stretching Corey's cock as he did. Sean tongued him, flicking the tip into Corey's slit and circling around just the head. Sean easily buried his face in the sparse, pale hairs at the base of Corey's dick and he stayed there, breathing deeply with no effort at all.

It felt so fucking good. It wasn't like Corey had expected. It felt like it did when he had a hard-on, but without the same urgency. He enjoyed the feel of himself inside the tight heat of Sean's mouth, but Corey didn't have the same overwhelming desire to push his hips forward.

Sean pulled off and Corey's flaccid cock hung downward, nestling against the coarse hair. Gently, Sean eased Corey's ball sac out of his briefs and cradled them. He glanced briefly at Corey's face, his expression momentarily unguarded.

Corey didn't like the pain in Sean's eyes, knowing he was the reason Sean believed he had failed. Corey used his hands in Sean's hair to pull his head back. Sean groaned, his neck arching, his eyelids heavy. When Sean's mouth fell open on his groan, Corey almost forgot what he meant to say. He wanted to press Sean into the ottoman and devour his mouth.

"That feels so fucking good," Corey said, keeping his voice low and suggestive. "You have the best mouth, and I love having it on me."

Sean's fingers curled tightly into Corey's hips. Relief colored his expression, but only because Corey was looking for it. "Is there anything you need me to do to help?"

Corey gave in to his urge and leaned down to give Sean a deep, hard kiss. Their lips slid together wetly and Corey pushed his tongue in and licked at Sean's. Sean moaned into Corey's mouth, his fingers tightening on Corey's hips.

Breaking the kiss with a wet smack, Corey pushed Sean backward onto the ottoman, climbing on top of him and straddling his hips. Corey took one of Sean's hands and pressed his palm flat to Corey's chest, beneath his dog tags. "Feel that?" he asked breathlessly. "Feel how you make my heart race?"

Sean nodded silently.

"Ignore the way my dick is being stubborn," Corey continued.

He dropped down over Sean's body, his tags falling across Sean's chest, and fused their mouths. He held Sean's palm against him, both hands wrapped around Sean's wrist.

Corey took hold of both of Sean's wrists and pinned them up above his head. He mouthed along Sean's jaw, kissed his way down his throat. Corey released Sean and slid down his body, biting gently at his collarbones and the firm muscles of his chest. Sean's hands found the back of Corey's head and his fingers caressed Corey's scalp.

When Corey took Sean's nipples between his lips, Sean arched up off the ottoman with a gasp. Corey's tags trailed down Sean's skin and pooled on his belly as Corey sucked and nipped at each of Sean's nipples. Sean seemed to really like the feel of Corey's teeth, so Corey bit sharply at one of the hardened buds. Sean cried out and a shudder ran through his frame.

Reluctantly, Corey slid from the ottoman. He gripped Sean's jeans and worked them over his hips. Sean helped, moving awkwardly, his hands getting in the way as he also shoved the denim down his legs.

Free of his clothing, Sean planted his feet flat on the ottoman and let his thighs fall open enticingly. Corey smiled at him, fully aware of what Sean was doing. He knelt on the floor, reaching between Sean's legs and gripping his waist firmly. Sean wrapped his hands around Corey's wrists.

When he leaned over to lick at each of Sean's hip bones, Corey's tags fell between Sean's thighs and lay against his semi-hard cock. Corey gripped them and flicked them over his shoulder so they rested against his own back.

"That's okay, but don't you fucking dare take those things off," Sean gasped fiercely, his hips pushing upward into Corey.

Corey looked up at Sean in surprise. He was used to being asked to remove them because they were always in the way. Sean's adamant demand that Corey leave his tags on made his chest tighten. He'd thought he'd never find such easy acceptance from anyone except another Marine.

Smiling at Sean, Corey lowered his head and nuzzled at the musk-scented hair at the base of Sean's cock. He felt it twitch against his cheek, filling just a little more with blood. Corey fumbled around, searching for the bottle of lube. His fingers closed around it and he opened the lid with a soft click. He slicked a single finger of one hand.

Corey's heartbeat picked up slightly and there was a slight pressure in his temples. He thought he could feel his own pulse in his throat. His pelvis was warm and a tingling began at the base of his cock. Corey smiled against the inside of Sean's bare thigh.

He placed a palm on Sean's belly and felt the muscles quiver at his touch. Dipping down, Corey took Sean's mostly-soft cock in his mouth suckled it, slowly moving up and down the length. When Sean's hips lifted slightly, Corey pushed his lubed finger slowly into Sean's hole.

Sean cried out in surprise. His fingers spasmed and the muscles of his ass tightened around Corey's finger. Corey sucked hard at his dick and pressed his finger gently, but steadily inward.

"Oh, fuck," Sean groaned, his head rolling side to side, his thighs trembling.

Pulling off of Sean's nearly-hard cock, Corey asked, "You okay?"

"Yeah," Sean gasped, "you just surprised me."

Corey watched Sean's flushed face as he slid his finger in and out of his ass. He spread the lube, getting Sean slick and ready to be full and stretched.

Slicking two fingers, Corey pushed them inward, mindful of the slight resistance. Sean's mouth fell open in a silent cry of pleasure. Corey spread the lube along Sean's inner walls, tugging slightly to stretch his clenching rim whenever he slid his fingers outward.

Adding more lube to his fingers, Corey again swallowed down Sean's dick when he slid into his hole this time. Sean's hips pulsed rhythmically, his fingers clenched tight at Corey's head. A drop of pre-come on the tip of Sean's cock exploded with sweet flavor when Corey licked it up. Sean rocked firmly against him, his ass clenching tightly at Corey's hand.

Corey's pulse hammered in his temples, his throat and his chest. His groin flooded with warmth and his cock ached and tingled. Taking his free hand from Sean's clenched belly, Corey stroked his own cock several times. He was jubilant that he was hard now, and getting harder by the second.

Corey lubed three fingers and pushed them into Sean's body, twisting and sliding them to ensure Sean was well prepped. Releasing himself, he wrapped his second hand around Sean's erection, feeling the throbbing pulse of blood inside of it. Sean's cock was gorgeous. He was generous in length but much more impressive in girth. The mushroom-shaped head was flushed dark red, the thick shaft was heavily ridged and veined. Corey knew those features would feel fantastic inside of him.

Searching carefully with a lubed finger, Corey located the spongy gland deep inside of Sean's body. With a tight stroke of Sean's cock, Corey crooked his middle finger into that special spot inside of Sean.

"Oh, fuck, Corey," Sean cried gutturally, his upper body lifting off of the ottoman. His fingers dug painfully into Corey's shoulders. "Jesus…I…fuck," Sean chanted senselessly.

In Corey's fist, Sean's cock pulsed and twitched. He felt blood rushing into the already engorged shaft. Sean's ass clamped down on Corey's fingers, as if his body didn't want to let Corey go.

Corey rubbed mercilessly at Sean's gland, watching the sex flush on his face, throat and chest darken. The defined muscles in Sean's stomach tensed and fluttered. His chest heaved with his harsh breathing.

"Is that good?" Corey asked, voice rough with his desire. "Do I make you feel good?" He'd never needed to hear it before. He always tried to be a giving lover, but he usually didn't care beyond making sure to get his lover off.

"Fuck, yes." Sean's answer was breathless and desperate. "Fuck, yes, you do."

Carefully sliding his fingers from Sean's body, Corey climbed sluggishly to his feet and pushed his jeans down off of his legs. He grabbed up the lube and a couple of condoms. He knelt on the ottoman, between Sean's open thighs. Corey took one of Sean's hands, twined their fingers, and wrapped them around his own erection.

"Feel that?" he asked, smiling wickedly down at Sean. "That's for you. All for you."

Sean gave Corey his own wicked grin. He propped himself on an elbow. "How do you want me? I can kneel on the floor and bend over the ottoman."

Corey put a hand to Sean's chest and pushed him back down. "You're perfect like you are." He doused the head of his cock with lube, tore open a condom and rolled it down his shaft. Propping himself with an arm beside Sean's head, Corey lined himself up with Sean's tight opening.

As he steadily pushed his hips forward, Corey lowered himself onto his elbows. His dog tags slid forward, coming to rest in the hollow of Sean's throat, the chain pooling on top. The head of his dick breached the rim of Sean's clenching hole, Corey's breath caught in his throat. Sean frowned, his eyes grew heavy lidded, and his mouth fell open with his cry. Corey paused, making sure Sean could adjust to the intrusion. When Sean's arms slid around him and his hands clung to the muscles in his back, Corey knew he was free to move.

He moved vigorously, the chain of his tags swaying rapidly between them. Corey worked his hips, sliding himself rapidly in and out of Sean's body. The grip of Sean's muscles on his cock was exquisite. Corey missed the heat when he pulled out and groaned when it enveloped him with each inward pulse of his hips.

Sean grunted and moaned rhythmically as Corey fucked him. He watched Corey closely through slit eyelids. His lush mouth was red and swollen, shiny wet from Sean's own tongue. He gripped Corey tightly and lifted his hips in time with Corey's strong, rough thrusts.

Corey slid his hands up to bury his fingers in Sean's hair. He pressed their chests together, his dog tags sliding to hang above Sean's shoulder. Corey slanted his mouth over Sean's, licking eagerly at his tongue. Sean's arms wrapped around him tightly, his legs locked around Corey's hips.

Sean's breath was hot against Corey's lips as he moaned softly in time with each of Corey's thrusts. The feel of Sean's body against and around him, the scent of his skin and his sweat, the sight of Sean in utter ecstasy, made Corey's gut tighten. Sparks tumbled down the length of his spine and scattered in his pelvis. Something in his chest clenched, heat spilling through him. Corey's balls tightened, lifting slightly toward his body. He was close. He wanted to share this with Sean.

Corey shifted and pulled back, reaching between their bodies and taking Sean's hard cock in his hand. Sean gasped into his mouth as Corey stroked him several times, trying to coordinate the rhythm of his hand with his hips.

"Are you close?" Corey asked in a harsh whisper against Sean's mouth.

"Yeah," Sean gasped. Sean squeezed his eyes shut, bit down on his lower lip, and turned his head to the side.

"Fuck, I'm close." Corey buried his face in the sweaty hair behind Sean's ear. He stroked Sean's dick and felt him shudder and quake beneath him. "I wanna feel you come against me," he murmured into Sean's ear.

Sean's body arched and tightened against Corey, arms and legs wrapping more firmly around him. Sean vibrated, his breath catching in his throat. Corey felt Sean's cock swell just before the first wet splash of fluid landed on his fingers.

"Oh, fuck, I'm coming," Sean gasped. "Fuckfuckfuckfuck," he chanted.

"Just like that." Corey smiled against Sean's ear, still stroking his cock. Hot, sticky come coated both of their chests and bellies. "Come on, come for me."

Just as Sean's fingers loosened in the muscles of Corey's back,

Corey felt the first wave of his orgasm roll over him. His hips faltered in their rhythm as his balls lifted, giving a strong pulse and sending come shooting out and into the tip of the condom.

Corey convulsed against Sean, burying his face in Sean's sweaty neck. He clenched his jaw to keep from shouting his pleasure. Corey's back and hips ached as he pressed against Sean, his climax taking violent hold. He rode it out, his cock and balls pulsing with each jet of come they spilled out into the condom.

With a shocking suddenness, Corey's orgasm released him. He buried both elbows into the ottoman, struggling to keep from collapsing onto Sean. Beneath him, Sean began to shake.

Lifting his head, Corey saw that Sean was laughing silently. Rubbing his cheek against Corey's, he gasped, "Holy shit!"

Corey laughed in response. "Is that good?"

"Yeah it is," Sean sighed, his body giving one last shudder.

On shaky arms, Corey lifted himself off of Sean. "We should get cleaned up."

"Do you just want to clean up or take a shower?" Sean asked.

Corey grinned. "If you're going to wake me up at dawn and make me come all over myself again, I'll wait to shower."

"You make it sound like a bad thing." Sean's laugh was giddy.

"Not a bad thing at all."

"Well, I guess you're going to wait to shower, then."

§ § §

"Corey? Can we get your help in the exam rooms?" Megan called.

Corey turned from the bags of dog food he was stacking in the store room. One of the vet techs, Megan, stood in the doorway wearing an imploring expression.

"Sure," Corey answered, wiping the sweat from his forehead on the shoulder of his T-shirt.

Most of the work Corey did during his volunteer time at the

base animal shelter was in the kennels. He took care of the heavy lifting and major repair work. He did anything the full-time staff didn't have time to do, as well as the tasks that required strong hands and a strong back. Corey spent time with the animals when they were in their kennels or cages, he wasn't called to help in the medical clinic unless an animal required a little more muscle.

Corey followed Megan into an exam room. Inside were a second vet tech and the veterinarian, Doctor Damien Fedorov. On the exam table was a very large, male German Shepherd, already wearing a muzzle.

"Thanks for helping out, Corey," greeted Damien. He was young, dark complexioned and handsome. "He's not aggressive, but he's stressed and defensive and we're going to have to hurt him some before we're done."

"Happy to help, Doc." Corey returned the vet's brilliant smile. He'd have to be dead not to find the doctor attractive, but that was as far as it went. "Hey, handsome," he crooned softly, running gentle hands over the large dog's tense body. "Yeah, it's a scary place, isn't it? All these strange people poking at you."

As carefully as he could, Corey wrapped one hand around the already bound muzzle, his other arm around the dog's large chest. He held the animal tightly to his chest, ensuring the staff could do the work they needed to do, and that the dog couldn't hurt himself or anyone else. The Shepherd was a large, muscular dog and it would take more strength than the vet techs had to hold him still.

"Where did this gorgeous, big boy come from?" Corey asked quietly, trying not to stress the dog further.

"Running around the base," Damien answered distractedly as he drew blood from the Shepherd's paw. "No tags, no chip, might be a stray from off base."

"He's somebody's pet," Megan said quietly from where she was assisting Damien. "He's had at least basic obedience training."

"Good. He'll adopt quick," Corey declared with feigned authority. "Does he have a name, yet?"

"Not yet," Megan answered.

"Why don't you do the honors, Corey?" Damien said, flashing a quick, knee-weakening smile.

"Gunner," Corey announced. "Nice, strong, German name."

"Gunner it is," Damien said with a nod. Megan made a notation on the dog's chart.

Damien was quick, and in just a few minutes, announced Corey could release the Shepherd. The dog shook himself roughly before sitting tensely on his haunches. Corey removed the muzzle and immediately, Gunner relaxed.

"If you're not busy, we could use your help in the medical kennels," Megan said, when Corey started to leave.

He followed Megan into the large, noisy room where the surgical patients were caged, along with puppies and kittens removed from their mothers too young. Megan went straight to a small kennel that held what looked like a Labrador puppy. The yellow pup yowled constantly and dread slowly curled through Corey's system.

His anxiety must have shown on his face. Megan cradled the puppy to her chest as she crossed to him, wearing a reassuring expression. "This little boy doesn't do well isolated in a cage. If you could just hold him for awhile, it'll lower his stress level and make him easier to manage. Plus it's better for his health."

"If you say so." Reluctantly, Corey took the small, surprisingly heavy puppy from her. The yellow ball of fur had quieted down when Megan had picked him up. Corey let the puppy stretch out along his forearm, head at his elbow, hind end cradled in his palm. He felt the pup heave a heavy sigh and almost immediately drift to sleep.

Megan gestured toward a rocking chair in the corner of the room. "Have a seat, relax, just rock him for a little while and let him sleep."

Awkwardly, Corey settled into the chair, keeping the slumbering puppy carefully pressed to his chest. Miguel, another vet tech, entered the room and gave Corey a double take.

Smiling broadly at Corey, Miguel said, "Papi, you're a natural."

Corey snorted self-consciously. What did it say about the kind of man he was that he was more comfortable with an M16 in his hands, than he was a puppy?

The clinic staff came and went, paying Corey little attention, beyond polite courtesy, as they worked. He sat quietly, rocking the pup, gently stroking its back as it slept. He found himself smiling slightly, at the small, fuzzy yellow body. Corey ran a finger over the tiny toes on all four paws. He poked at the floppy ears just to watch them twitch as the puppy slumbered on.

Corey's chest tightened with an unfamiliar affection. Maybe he wasn't as lame at this as he thought he'd be. "Does this little guy have a name?" he asked as Miguel walked by.

"Folco," Miguel replied with enthusiasm.

"Folco," Corey repeated. "Why does that sound familiar?" Realization struck him like a blow. "No fucking way! You named him for a cartoon character?"

Miguel grinned eagerly. "You watch Thresden Squadron?"

"No, but a friend of mine does the voice for Folco," Corey replied, already laughing at the idea of telling Sean he'd rocked his namesake to sleep today.

"Shut the front door," Miguel said, looking stunned. "You're not yanking my chain, are you? 'Cause that would just be cruel."

Corey chuckled. "No, the only reason I even know that show exists is 'cause he told me he did the voice for it."

The puppy squirmed and gave an annoyed whimper. Corey shifted Folco so he could grasp him behind his front legs. The pup looked at him with sleep-heavy eyes, hanging calmly between Corey's hands. He couldn't help the warmth that pooled in his stomach, a sense of well-being spreading through his body.

"That's right. You just go back to sleep." Corey amazed himself that he was actually using baby talk. He brought Folco to rest against his shoulder, cradling the pup's rump in the crook of his elbow.

"So, is this friend of yours hot?" Miguel asked, one hip leaning against the counter.

Corey chuffed a self-conscious laugh and hoped he didn't blush. "I guess you could say that."

"Ah, dawg, I knew it! It would absolutely suck if the voice of a kick-ass character like Folco was just a geek like me!" Miguel laughed as he left the room, arms full of medical charts.

Corey's phone vibrated in his pocket. He fished it out clumsily, trying not to wake Folco. He realized he was fucked if he was thinking of the dog by name. His phone displayed Sean's name and Corey laughed to himself.

"You have perfect timing," he greeted. "Folco is currently sleeping on my chest."

There was a long silence before Sean laughed. "You're doing *what?*"

"One of the vet techs here at the shelter named a puppy Folco, and the pup is currently asleep on my chest," Corey explained, not bothering to keep the humor from his voice.

"I'm not sure what's more fascinating," Sean said through his laughter, "the thought that someone named a dog after my animated character, or that you have a puppy sleeping on your chest. No, scratch that, the name thing happens all the time. Please, please, *please* have someone take a picture of you and the puppy!"

"When Miguel comes back I'll have him take one," Corey replied. "I think he'd do anything you asked."

"My fans are legion," Sean quipped. "So, I take it the volunteering is going well?"

"I don't know that I'm accomplishing much, but Folco seems happy," He scratched the puppy's neck just behind his ears and was rewarded with a soft groan of pleasure. "So you made it to New York safely?"

"Landed and checked into my hotel," Sean declared. "You

should see the size of this bed, I really wish you were here."

"What a coincidence, 'cause I wish I was there, too."

"I'll be back by the middle of the week." Sean sounded as though he was trying to be reassuring.

"Unless you get the part," Corey reminded him.

"I still have to come back and make arrangements to live in New York for a year." Sean made it sound so simple.

Corey had no reply.

"You still there?" asked Sean, hesitantly.

"Yeah."

"What's wrong?"

"Do you want this role?" Corey asked suddenly.

"It's a great role," Sean replied. "It would be my first lead role that isn't part of an ensemble. But, the movie role I'm up for out there pays better and would give me greater exposure."

"So, what does that all mean?" Corey was afraid to hope.

"I'd much rather take four months of work in California than a year's worth of work in New York," he answered succinctly. "But if I take this part, are you going to come visit me?"

When Sean had asked him that same question once before, Corey had been afraid to answer. He'd been afraid Sean hadn't really meant it. "Yes, whenever I can get leave, I'd visit. But it still wouldn't be that often."

"I can take some time off once in a while. Give my understudy a chance to step up."

This was the first time they had discussed the future at all. Corey's chest loosened as Sean talked about a future that involved the both of them. Together. He was so fucked.

"I would like it better if you stayed local." Sean had put himself out there. Only fair for Corey to do the same. "But if it's best for your career to take the job in New York, then that's the job I hope you get."

Sean's sigh sounded relieved. "We'll work it out."

Movement across the room caught Corey's eye. He glanced up to find both Megan and Miguel watching him from the doorway, and both were smirking.

"What?" he asked.

"Oh, mijo, you have it bad," Miguel replied with a shake of his head.

Megan sighed. "It's always the good ones."

"I gotta go," Corey hastily said to Sean, his face flaming. "I'll call you when I'm done here."

"Have someone take a picture of you holding Folco!" Sean demanded before they ended the call.

Miguel was happy to oblige. Anything for the voice of Folco.

CHAPTER FIFTEEN

Corey stepped out of the dark colored sedan Captain Hirata had driven to the law firm office. He tugged the coat of his service uniform straight and placed his barracks cover on his head, brim low over his eyes. He slid his Oakleys on as Hirata also exited the vehicle, donning his own cover.

"Ready, Staff Sergeant?" the Captain asked.

"Ready, sir." Corey wanted nothing more than to climb into the victor and head back to base.

"You'll do fine," Hirata said, leading Corey toward the office tower. "Remember, keep your answers as brief as possible and don't volunteer information. Force them to drag clarification out of you. Don't get defensive. It's my job to keep them on track and to deny them access to sensitive information."

"Yes, sir." Corey swallowed hard. There were still critical details he didn't remember. It also pissed him off that Nygaard was dragging them all through this. The fucking pussy couldn't just man up and accept responsibility for his actions.

"They're going to try to make you into the bad guy, or at the very least, an accessory to the cover-up," the captain continued. "Remember, he's the bad guy. You did nothing wrong."

"Except when I say I can't remember what happened and I sound like I'm hiding something," replied Corey in frustration.

"Can you remember leaving the first structure?" Hirata asked.

"No, sir." Stepping inside the building lobby, they both removed their covers and tucked them beneath their left arms.

"Then you're not hiding anything. And it's my job to control that aspect of the deposition." Hirata punched the elevator button with a sense of finality.

They exited the elevator and Hirata walked directly to the tall reception desk. "We're here for the Nygaard deposition," he told the very young woman seated there.

After the receptionist held a brief telephone conversation, a legal secretary appeared and escorted them to a large conference room. Corey glanced around at the office as they passed through. It was everything he'd expected: rich wood, polished brass, plush carpeting that muted all sound. The conference table was long and made of dark, gleaming wood. One entire wall of the room was windows.

Captain Hirata had briefed Corey to treat this meeting like combat. Thinking strategically, Corey searched for the high ground and an easily defensible position with good cover. He moved to the head of the conference table nearest the wall of windows and set down his cover.

Hirata requested bottled water for each of them. Corey looked around the room as the captain selected the chair to Corey's immediate right. This way, they both faced the only entrance to the room. Opposing counsel would have to look into bright sunlight to see either of them. The head of the table automatically conferred authority on Corey. He was satisfied with their strategic advantage.

Two men in expensive suits entered the room, with them was Michael Nygaard and a well-dressed woman of about thirty. She walked to the opposite end of the table from Corey and sat down at an open laptop. All three men arrayed themselves on Corey's left.

"Captain Hirata?" the first man asked, glancing between the captain and Corey.

"I'm Captain Mirai Hirata, Marine Corps J.A.S. attorney." He nodded in Corey's direction. "This is Staff Sergeant Corey Yarwood, subpoenaed to be deposed regarding Sergeant Michael Nygaard's defense against murder charges."

"I am Jerry O'Brien," the first man indicated the second. "My colleague, Martin Colvin. And you both know Sergeant Nygaard."

Corey shook hands with both attorneys but dismissed

Nygaard without a glance.

"Let's get this started, gentlemen," Hirata said, taking his seat and removing several items from his soft-sided briefcase. He set a legal pad and pen in front of himself and a small notepad and pen in front of Corey. "It's going to take some time as it is, let's dispense with the niceties."

Hirata was all aggressive Marine. Corey hadn't seen this side of him previously, and he was impressed.

The court reporter stood and adjusted a video camera so that it was aimed at Corey, then she turned it on. From the camera's original angle, the lawyers had intended for Corey to sit in the center of the table, facing the door. He was darkly pleased to have upset their plans.

As O'Brien stated the date, time, persons present and the reason for the deposition, Corey saw that he had to squint any time he looked up from his papers. It was yet another small victory that added to Corey's own combat advantage.

O'Brien read Corey's service record, including his training and dates of his promotions. "Now, your previous billet was with first rec—"

"Excuse me, Mr. O'Brien," Captain Hirata interrupted, "your summation of Staff Sergeant Yarwood's credentials is incomplete." He removed a file folder from his briefcase. Opening the folder, Hirata began to read additional details of Corey's record. "His promotion to Lance Corporal was meritorious, as opposed to all of Nygaard's administrative promotions. The Staff Sergeant was decorated for his participation in the investigation that led to the prosecution of those involved in the contractor scandal five years prior."

Corey sat tensely in his chair, staring down at the pad of paper in front of him. He listened uncomfortably as Hirata listed Corey's medals, commendations, and decorations. He knew it was necessary, though. Nygaard's lawyers would emphasize similarities. Hirata was going to emphasize Corey's integrity and spotless service record.

When Hirata was satisfied, O'Brien returned to his original line of questioning. He established that Corey and Nygaard were a part of a Recon platoon attached to the First Reconnaissance Battalion and deployed to Ghazni Province in Afghanistan.

Corey forced himself to make steady eye contact with O'Brien as the narrative and line of questioning drew closer to that critical time he still couldn't remember.

"At this time, you had secured the structure, as ordered by Lieutenant Adams?" O'Brien asked.

"Yes, sir," Corey answered.

"With the structure secured, you ordered Sergeant Nygaard to seek out hostiles on the perimeter?"

"No, sir." Corey was ready to clarify when he remembered Hirata's order not to volunteer information.

"You did *not* issue an order to Sergeant Nygaard?" O'Brien sounded eager and incredulous.

Corey gripped the arms of his chair. "Yes, sir, I issued an order to Sergeant Nygaard."

"Staff Sergeant, you need to make up your mind," O'Brien said waspishly. "Either you issued an order or you didn't."

Corey managed to suppress a sneer as he said, "My mind has not changed, nor has the nature of the order I issued to Sergeant Nygaard. I did *not* order the Sergeant to seek out hostiles on the perimeter."

O'Brien's eyes narrowed at Corey, and it was gratifying to know he'd surprised the over-educated POG. "What *was* the nature of the order you issued to Sergeant Nygaard?" he asked tightly.

"I ordered Nygaard to take five Marines and secure the perimeter of the structure. He was to hold that perimeter until I ordered him to collapse it." Corey deliberately dropped the rank from his answer.

O'Brien looked annoyed. "That's splitting hairs, Staff Sergeant."

"No, in fact it is not." Corey glanced at Hirata who nodded for him to continue. "Securing the perimeter of the structure is a defensive posture, meant to ensure no hostiles are inbound to pose a threat. Combat is engaged only if attacked. Seeking out hostiles is an act of aggression and requires movement to contact. I issued no such order." If the lawyers were relying on Nygaard to explain the nature of their duties, Corey wasn't surprised to realize that Nygaard himself wouldn't know the difference between those two concepts.

O'Brien drew breath and Hirata interrupted. "Asked and answered, Counselor. Move on."

"Did Sergeant Nygaard successfully execute this order?" asked O'Brien, sighing in frustration.

"He took five Marines and exited the secured structure. Beyond that, I do not know if Nygaard successfully carried out the order." Corey's fingers tightened on the arm of his chair.

"And why not, Staff Sergeant? Isn't it your job to know?" O'Brien's question was predatory.

"Yes it is. However, I have trauma-induced memory loss. I recall nothing after exiting the structure to go in search of Nygaard." Corey met the lawyer's gaze unwaveringly. Hirata had told him the crux of Nygaard's defense was his PTS, his lawyers couldn't impeach Corey without nullifying their own defense strategy.

O'Brien rifled through papers until he found one he read from. "Your own after-action report details your actions with regard to Sergeant Nygaard. Did you lie when you filed this report, or are you lying now?"

"Neither one, sir," Corey said sharply. He stilled his bouncing leg and eased his grip on the arms of his chair.

"That's argumentative," Hirata intervened. "Phrase your question in a less provocative manner."

O'Brien paused for several heartbeats. Then, "Your after-action report states you exited the secure structure, located Sergeant Nygaard, and ordered everyone to return to your

Humvees. Is that accurate?"

"I have no memory of those events," Corey replied. "My report reflects what I believed had happened at the time." Saying the words left a bitter taste in Corey's mouth.

"You no longer believe this is what happened?" O'Brien's brows lifted.

"I have no memory of what happened until my Marines and I rejoined the platoon at the Humvees." Corey was careful to make his answer precise.

"But do you believe—"

Hirata interrupted again. "The Staff Sergeant has no memory of that period of time. What he may or may not believe is of no relevance."

O'Brien turned to look at Hirata. "If the Staff Sergeant believes the events differ from his original report—"

Hirata cut him off sharply. "His beliefs of the events are based on what he has been informed of during the course of a Department of Defense investigation and are therefore a matter of national security. Move on, Counselor."

Corey straightened his spine in response to Captain Hirata's tone. For a moment, the mild-mannered lawyer was gone. In his place was a commanding Marine Corps officer.

O'Brien looked frustrated, bordering on angry. "When you rejoined the platoon, did you report to Lieutenant Adams?"

"Yes, sir." Corey took a deep breath and shifted his hands to his lap, trying to ease his growing tension.

"Did the Lieutenant issue you further orders?"

"Yes, sir."

"And what were those orders?"

Corey had been asked this question so many times, he didn't have to think about the answer anymore. "To recover the bodies of the dead enemy combatants from the dwelling, document the nature of their wounds, and prepare them for transport back to base."

He'd barely finished his answer when O'Brien barked his next question. "Did you execute those orders?"

"I delegated those orders to Corporal Tyler Howe," Corey shot back.

"What did you do while Corporal Howe was doing your job for you?"

Corey very nearly rose to the bait. A subtle hand gesture from Captain Hirata stilled his tongue. "You'll have to specify which of my many actions you wish to discuss. Sir."

"Were the bodies Corporal Howe recovered the only ones you were required to deal with that day?" O'Brien spoke slowly, as if to a child.

"No, sir." Corey fisted his hands in his lap.

The lawyer leaned over the conference table, looking almost predatory. "What were the other bodies that required your attention?"

"The three Marines killed in the initial IED blast," replied Corey, concentrating on keeping his voice steady, "as well as the five enemy combatants killed when they engaged the platoon from their vehicle."

"Did you witness that engagement?"

Corey tensed, raising his guard even higher. The answer was well established. "I did not, sir."

"Then you have only Lieutenant Adams' word for the fact that the occupants of the vehicle fired first?" O'Brien sat back in his chair but still gave the impression of waiting to pounce.

Sensing a trap, Corey paused to consider how to answer.

Hirata intervened. "The Staff Sergeant has already established he was elsewhere at the time of that engagement and therefore has no firsthand knowledge of events. Move on."

Corey bit back a relieved sigh.

O'Brien didn't seem deterred. "What is standard procedure

for the transporting of dead combatants back to your base?" His demeanor was deceptively casual.

Corey wasn't prepared for that question. He started to shift in his chair but caught himself. He had no idea what this line of questioning meant. "We photograph the bodies to verify identity, to document injuries and cause of death. The bodies are placed in body bags and transported back to base to await disposition, or to be claimed by the family."

"Where are the bodies placed for transport?" O'Brien's hostility was only thinly veiled .

"Inside the Humvees, or wherever room is available," answered Corey

"So it is *not* standard procedure for you to strap enemy combatants to the hoods of your Humvees?" O'Brien's question gave away his strategy.

"Standard procedure? No, sir," Corey replied. "However, on the rare occasions we do not have sufficient number of body bags, we secure the bodies to the hoods of the Humvees for transport."

"Rather disrespectful, don't you think, Staff Sergeant?" O'Brien's tone bordered on snide.

"Disrespect is not intended." Corey refused to get defensive. This was a military-wide practice, not his own judgment call.

"Strapping dead bodies to the hoods of your vehicles isn't intended to be disrespectful?" O'Brien's eyebrows rose to his hairline. "How about intimidating? Threatening?"

Corey wasn't sure how to respond.

"You're being argumentative," Hirata said sharply. "Ask a specific question pertinent to your client's defense."

"Did your platoon strap dead bodies to the hoods of your vehicles and drive though the village of Ghazni?" O'Brien asked with thinly veiled hostility.

"Yes, sir," Corey answered truthfully. When he realized his leg was bouncing again, Corey stopped it.

O'Brien shot forward in his chair. "In an effort to intimidate and threaten the residents of the town." It wasn't a question.

Corey straightened his spine. "No, sir."

"What other reason could you possibly have?" The lawyer was openly confrontational.

"Placing the dead bodies of enemy combatants inside of Humvees with live Marines, without placing them into body bags, is detrimental to the mental health of the Marines." Corey's reply was succinct. He tried to keep all emotion out of his voice.

"Staff Sergeant Yarwood," Hirata interrupted, "if your platoon had had sufficient number of body bags, would all of the bodies have been placed inside the Humvees?"

Relieved, Corey answered quickly. "Yes, sir."

"Why did the platoon RTB through the town of Ghazni?" the captain continued.

"It was the most secure, most direct route back to base." Some of Corey's tension eased as he answered, silently grateful to Hirata for rescuing him.

There was a protracted silence in the room as O'Brien and his partner glanced at one another, shuffled papers and made notes. Corey stared directly at Nygaard, daring him to make eye contact. Nygaard didn't even look in Corey's direction. Instead, he stared at the table and shifted uncomfortably in his chair.

"What purpose does it serve to desecrate the dead bodies before transport?" O'Brien asked abruptly.

If he was trying to throw Corey off balance, it failed. The silence had given Corey a chance to regroup, and now he was just baffled by the question. "None that I can name."

"And the relevance of this question?" Hirata demanded.

O'Brien produced two color photographs that he set on the table in front of Corey. They were graphic and sickening. "Do you recognize the subjects in these photos?"

As Corey looked at them, he could hear the chatter of gunfire and the blast of ordinance. He swallowed back the bile that rose in his throat. "Yes, sir."

"Well? What do the pictures show, Staff Sergeant?" the lawyer asked.

Corey could barely hear over the sound of his blood rushing in his ears. "The dead bodies of enemy combatants killed during the battle in Ghazni," Corey answered carefully. His leg started to bounce violently and he clenched both fists once again.

"That's not all the photos depict, is it?" O'Brien pressed, leaning his arms on the table as if ready to pounce.

"Ask a specific question, Counselor," Captain Hirata snapped, leaning to the side as if trying to enter O'Brien's line of sight.

"Whose hand is in those photographs?" O'Brien asked, pushing the offending pictures closer to Corey's place at the table.

Corey's stomach turned sour and his heart raced. His mouth flooded with spit and he clenched his jaw, swallowing rapidly to keep the bile down. "Corporal Tyler Howe's." His voice was strained and rough. Corey knew O'Brien was misinterpreting his distress.

"What is he holding in his hand in each of the photographs?" The lawyer nudged the pictures even closer to Corey.

"Human brains, sir." Corey couldn't even see the graphic images, anymore. He heard gunfire and felt the heat of an incendiary blast.

"I thought Marine Corps policy didn't include the desecration of enemy bodies." O'Brien was openly mocking him now.

Corey's palms were damp and he wiped them unthinkingly on his thighs. The room spun and something deep in the back of his skull buzzed. He struggled to take a deep breath so he could reply to the asshole lawyer.

"Ask a question, Mr. O'Brien," Hirata snapped. Corey vaguely wondered why the captain's anger had become real.

"If no disrespect was meant to the dead combatants, why did you and your Marines desecrate these two bodies?" O'Brien tapped his finger against one of the photos, again directing Corey's attention to the ugly images.

Corey's vision cleared and his stomach settled. He managed to focus on the photos. He suddenly wanted to put his fist through Nygaard's face. He wondered which one of them had made the error in judgment to use these specific pictures to try to rattle Corey.

Nygaard had been the one taking the photos that day. Obviously, he'd forwarded some for his personal use, in violation of Corps policy. Hell, he might have used his own fucking cell phone to take these particular pictures.

"There was no desecration committed that day," Corey replied stiffly, jaw stiff from being clenched for several minutes. He turned to Captain Hirata. "Sir, I'm concerned that official Marine Corps photos found their way into civilian hands."

"You and me, both, Staff Sergeant," the captain said dryly, making notes on his pad. "This, too, will be investigated."

"My source is confidential," O'Brien said quickly, almost smugly.

"Your source stole official Marine Corps documents, in a breach of national security," said Hirata without looking up, his choice of words indicating he also believed Nygaard was the guilty party in this. "Confidentiality is moot."

"So you admit the Marine Corps have committed war crimes and have documented their own actions?" O'Brien's smile had teeth. Corey wondered if he didn't realize, or just didn't care that Hirata seemed to be turning the tables on him.

"No war crimes have been committed," the captain barked. "Staff Sergeant, why does Corporal Howe have a brain in his hand in each of those photos?"

"Each of those men had taken a two-two-three round to the head, shattering his skull, sir," answered Corey, forcing his leg to be still. "Howe is documenting that as the cause of death and also showing that all body parts are accounted for, to be returned to the family."

"So, the very opposite of desecration and war crimes, correct, Staff Sergeant?" Hirata was openly derisive but not directed at Corey.

"Yes, sir," he replied.

Hirata heaved a heavy sigh. "Is that all?" he asked O'Brien, with exaggerated weariness.

O'Brien collected the photos and the last of the tension in Corey's body eased.

"No, it's not," the lawyer answered irritably. "Staff Sergeant, what orders did Lieutenant Adams give you, regarding events and details to include in your after action report?"

"Okay, we're done here," Hirata said abruptly, returning items to his briefcase. "Your line of questioning no longer pertains to the crimes with which your client has been charged. You're venturing into areas that are matters of national security and are currently under investigation."

"It's relevant if Marine Corps officers are covering up wrong doing that caused my client to develop PTSD." O'Brien's voice rose in agitation.

"The events as documented are sufficient to justify Staff Sergeant Yarwood's PTS diagnosis," Hirata countered. "Your client is at no disadvantage." He paused. "In point of fact, there is evidence that whatever diagnosis your client has received, his bad attitude and violent behavior pre-date the events of Ghazni."

"That is patently false," snapped O'Brien.

It was Hirata's turn to sport a predatory smile. He withdrew a file folder from his briefcase, opened it, and began to read. Nygaard's fitness reports reflected a lazy, aggressive, insubordinate Marine, even before Corey had been forced to deal with him.

As Hirata read, Corey openly watched Nygaard. As he had each time Corey had been forced to discipline him, Nygaard looked inconvenienced and at times disdainful. He rolled his eyes and shook his head, sometimes even smirking, as if amused by the memory of the behavior that had landed him in trouble.

Corey's anger unfurled inside of him like a tangible thing.

"Staff Sergeant?" Hirata startled him by suddenly asking. "Did you ever submit a fitrep for Sergeant Nygaard that was anything more than mediocre?"

"No, sir." Corey didn't hide his contempt.

Hirata leaned his arms on the table and looked directly at Corey. "How many incidents of fighting were you forced to deal with while deployed to Afghanistan?"

Corey counted back. "Seven, sir."

"And how many of those incidents involved Sergeant Nygaard?" The captain's tone told everyone in the room what Corey's answer would be.

"They all did, sir." When Corey glanced at Nygaard, the asshole had the temerity to look bored and disinterested.

Sitting back, Hirata asked, "Did you or your platoon commander ever have to discipline Nygaard for excessive violence directed toward civilians?"

Corey finally looked away from Nygaard. "Yes, sir."

Hirata closed the folder. "I think you get my point," he said to O'Brien as he replaced the folder in his briefcase. "We're leaving, Staff Sergeant."

Corey stood, grabbed his cover from off the table and followed Hirata out of the conference room. They strode quickly through the office, the two attorneys following them and demanding they return to finish the deposition. Hirata ignored them, and Corey followed his lead. At the elevators, the captain pressed the button.

"Don't say a word until we're in the parking lot," he whispered to Corey.

They were silent on the ride down to the lobby. As soon as they stepped outside, they both settled their covers on their heads. Corey stayed silent as they walked, despite not seeing anyone around them. Hirata took his cell phone from a pocket of his briefcase and placed a call. Corey turned his phone on, ignoring the nagging hope that Sean had tried to reach him from New York.

He shook his head at the pleasant warmth that flooded him when he saw a missed call and a text message.

Knock 'em dead, Devil Dog!

Corey smiled to himself. He called Sean's phone, unsurprisingly reaching his voicemail. He knew Sean had meetings with the play's producers and writer, as well as with his own agent. It was still mid-afternoon in New York.

He climbed into the passenger seat of the car, fastened his seat belt, and sent Sean a text as Hirata started to drive.

Think it went ok, but would rather b in firefite.

Corey pocketed his phone as Captain Hirata spoke. "Kellan wants to meet with us when we RTB."

"Yes, sir." He liked Kellan but he really didn't want to hash out any more of the fucked up details of that fucked up day in Ghazni.

The captain chuckled, but didn't seem to be mocking Corey, so he let it go. He tuned out the phone conversations Hirata had via the vehicle's Bluetooth. He was talking to staff at his J.A.S. office and Corey imagined he wouldn't understand any of it.

Captain Hirata parked the sedan directly in front of the HQ building on base. As they walked toward the door, he smiled at Corey. "Don't look so much like you're on your way to face the executioner. The hard part is over, for you."

"I wish I believed that, sir," Corey replied with a sigh.

The captain nodded to the receptionist who smiled in return and picked up her telephone handset. As they entered the back offices, Corey could hear more activity than he had during his previous visits. Jonah stepped out of an office, looking smug. Captain Evans and Agent Hoffman followed soon after.

As Corey and Captain Hirata reached the conference room where all of the interviews had been conducted, Kellan Reynolds appeared in the hallway, just in front of Jonah.

"Hail the conquering hero," he called, smiling broadly.

"I swear he missed his calling as a lawyer," Hirata said with a chuckle. "I was almost superfluous. I had to shoehorn the fitness reports in at the end! He left me no openings to introduce them."

Kellan slapped Corey on the shoulder. Corey glanced between Kellan and Hirata in confusion wondering who they were talking about.

Captain Hirata entered the conference room. "Let's get this over with so the Staff Sergeant can get out of here. He's practically vibrating with restlessness."

Kellan gestured for Corey to precede him. Surprised, Corey did. Jonah closed the door when everyone was inside the conference room.

"So, our staff sergeant held off the evil lawyers?" Kellan asked.

"He drove O'Brien nuts," Hirata replied, taking his notepad out of his briefcase. "He stuck to yes or no answers better than I've ever seen anyone do. At one point, O'Brien asked a question that was half right and half wrong and he gave an answer that addressed only half of the question. O'Brien about gave himself a stroke trying to drag clarification out of him."

"Too bad the sack of shit didn't stroke out," Kellan said heatedly. Jonah snorted a laugh which made Kellan smile.

Hirata turned to Corey. "Did you drop Nygaard's rank when referring to him just to be casual? Or were you trying to get a rise out of him?"

It took Corey several moments to realize the question was directed at him. "Using his rank is a sign of respect and he doesn't deserve any. And yeah, I wanted to fuck with him."

Everyone in the room laughed and Corey's face flamed.

"O'Brien severely underestimated the staff sergeant and he got his ass handed to him," Hirata continued. "He laid several verbal traps and Corey just stepped right around them without breaking a sweat."

"It's unwise to underestimate a Recon Marine," Kellan said. "That's where the smart ones seem to end up." He grew serious, crossing his arms over his chest. "So what did you learn?"

"I don't think they know the truth about the occupants of the vehicle, but it doesn't matter," replied Hirata, consulting his notes. "They need to perpetuate the cover-up, or their entire defense falls apart."

"Well, they can have him back after his Court Martial," said Kellan, "Because we're shining a light on this cover-up. Officers and enlisted alike will be held accountable."

"Because they're unaware of what happened with the vehicle occupants, I also believe they're unaware officers are involved in the cover-up," Hirata continued. "It seemed as though they believe the staff sergeant did the covering up."

Corey stiffened. He hadn't realized that.

"So they're going to try to say he was the only one who ordered Nygaard to enter the second structure and kill the occupants?" Kellan asked.

Corey couldn't suppress his gasp.

Everyone looked at him with concern.

"Corey, I know you don't have all of your memories back yet," Jonah said, narrowing his eyes as he watched Corey intently, "but you *are* aware of what it is you're remembering, aren't you?"

Was he? Corey nodded stiffly. "It's just the first time anyone has said it out loud."

"Has anyone talked with you about what was done to the occupants of the white car?" Kellan asked.

"I know they were executed and not killed in combat," Corey replied. "But no one has discussed details."

"Which reminds me," Hirata interrupted, "O'Brien is making the war crimes claim based on the treatment and transport of the bodies back to the base." Everyone looked confused. "Nygaard either took personal photos, or he forwarded official Marine Corps photos, used to document the deaths of the combatants that day. It's part of their defense that the bodies were desecrated and driven through the town on the hoods of the Humvees in a show of force and intimidation," explained Hirata.

"Do we have sufficient evidence that this was not the case?" Kellan asked.

Hirata nodded solemnly.

"How close are we to initiating Courts Martial?" Captain Evans asked.

"Pretty close," answered Hirata. "Chris wanted to make sure we understand just exactly who falsified documents."

Agent Hoffman said, "There were changes made to documents, and some documents were typed by enlisted that seem to have been acting on orders and were unaware the information was false. I'm gathering evidence on the officers who knew what they were doing, so the enlisted don't get caught up in the net."

"Good," Kellan replied. "And once we start the military legal proceedings, this mess with Nygaard goes away."

"It goes away as far as Corey is concerned," Hirata answered. "The D.A. isn't going to stop prosecution, but the PTS defense will be dead in the water."

"He can't claim PTS resulting from the events at Ghazni," Jonah summarized, "if he was the one perpetrating the atrocities. His violent behavior was already ingrained."

"Just because Nygaard's a violent asshole doesn't mean he doesn't really have PTS," Corey said in frustration.

"You *do* have PTS, Corey. Are you going to go beat someone you claim to care about to death with your bare hands?" Jonah asked challengingly.

"No one doubts he's got some level of PTS and TBI," Kellan said quietly, a restraining hand on Jonah's arm. "My final report will address the military's need to acknowledge the prevalence of these conditions and provide easily accessible treatment. But his PTS doesn't excuse anything he's done; all the harm he's caused."

Corey sighed heavily. "Yes, sir."

"Do we need the staff sergeant for anything else, today?" asked Kellan.

"No, he's done for the day," Hirata replied.

"Good. Thanks for your help, Corey," Kellan said, heading for the door. "Jonah, see the staff sergeant out."

As they headed for his Jeep, Corey said, "I don't need a fucking babysitter, Jonah."

"And I don't fucking babysit," Jonah replied snidely. "You gonna go see your new friend?"

"He's in New York for the next couple of days." Corey's disappointment was a dull ache. "I'll call him, but I'm sleeping alone tonight."

"I'm not offering to sleep with you, but we can go grab dinner later," Jonah said dryly.

Corey chuckled. "I've had the drinking under control for a couple of weeks now. The meds help with the sleep and the nightmares, so I don't need the booze."

"Glad to hear it," Jonah said.

"I think I might see if Tyler Howe wants to get dinner," Corey mused. "Since Nygaard has sucked both of us into his fucked up mess."

"Sounds like a plan," Jonah replied. "But call if you need me."

§ § §

Corey flopped down in his rack, feeling serene and relaxed. He and Tyler each had two beers with dinner. Corey hadn't felt the need for more. Even now, he knew he could sleep easily. He even doubted he'd have a nightmare.

Again, he read Sean's last text message, received during his dinner with Tyler.

Bed still 2 big w/o u in it. Call when u & Tyler dun causing trbl

That warm feeling that twisted in his gut pleasantly was back. He pulled up Sean's number and hit call.

"Did you have fun?" Sean asked in greeting.

"Yeah, we did," Corey answered. "We also talked about the shit that's going on. It was good."

"How'd the deposition go?" Sean asked.

Soft strains of guitar music drifted over the connection and Corey closed his eyes with a sigh. The last of the day's tension fled his body. "They said I did really well. Better than they'd expected me to, I guess. I don't know what I did right, I just followed orders, like a good Marine."

"Don't sell yourself short, Corey," Sean said firmly. "You're smart, you understood the intent behind the orders. You understood the overall goal and you acted accordingly."

"I guess," he answered, pleased at Sean's praise. Corey told him about the day's events, the things he'd learned and what he was allowed to share about the investigation.

"I'm thankful none of this is going to fall out on you," Sean said heatedly. "It'll be over some day and you can move on. You won't have the cloud of it hanging over your head."

"I hope that day is soon," Corey murmured. He listened to Sean strum the guitar for a time before he asked, "Are you still coming home tomorrow?"

"Yes! I'll be home tomorrow night." Sean paused. "Any chance of a welcome home?"

It was like Sean had read his mind. "Tomorrow is a long day for me, but if I can swing it, I'll come over and welcome you home."

"I'd like that. Speaking of which, thanks for not being an asshole about this trip."

Something in Sean's tone had Corey on high alert. "Why would I be an asshole about it?" What was there to even be an asshole about?

"Because you weren't able to come with me, I've been gone for nearly a week, I've been too busy to answer all your calls and texts right away, and I've been spending time with people you don't know." Sean said that last one on a heavy sigh.

"It's your career, you gotta do what you gotta do." Corey shrugged, even knowing Sean couldn't see. "I can't always take your calls and answer texts right away either and you're not a dick about it. You don't know *anybody* I work with, except Tyler. You've got a goddamn life, so do I."

Sean laughed. "I love that you know how big your dick is and don't have to prove it."

It was Corey's turn to laugh. He really didn't know how to answer. "Text me when you get on the plane and then let me know when you've landed, just so I know."

"You got it." Sean sounded pleased with Corey's request.

Corey was asleep almost as soon as they ended the call.

CHAPTER SIXTEEN

Corey and his team of five Marines crouched in the tall grass, deep inside of Camp Pendleton. This was a training mission, so Corey was Team Leader. They had all passed the classroom portion of executing successful recon missions. Now, Corey had the job of showing them how to apply those lessons in a practical manner.

He was just glad they hadn't had Zodiac training yet. He wasn't in the mood for an amphibious operation. Tonight, there were three teams, all with different objectives and approaching from different directions. The rest of the class and instructors had established a base camp and were keeping watch. There was no hunting going on tonight.

All Corey and his team had to do was execute their mission without detection. There would be no patrols to evade. If these Marines applied their lessons and did as Corey ordered, they'd be done in several hours, mission successful. If they fucked up and gave away their position to the Marines standing watch, a mock firefight might ensue and Corey would be stuck doing an extensive after-action all night.

He'd much rather be welcoming Sean home.

Their mission was to get past the Marine encampment, locate a small village several klicks out, and observe it for an hour. During that time they were required to determine if the village was occupied, sketch the layout, and establish dimensions and distances. Once their mission was complete, they had to get past the Marines once again, without being detected. At a predetermined location, they would uplink their intel, then use chemlights to signal for extraction.

Oceanside was cool at night, even this far inland. They all wore their fleece shirts under their armor. As Team Leader, Corey wore a radio headset beneath his Kevlar. Each student wore a sensor on his vest that would react if hit with the beam of a laser mounted on top of the M16s they'd all been issued for the night. Everyone was loaded with blank ammunition. A firefight would make a hell of a lot of loud noise, but casualties would be determined by a hit with a laser.

Corey looked at his team and issued silent orders using hand signals. They would proceed single file, Corey in the lead. He indicated the order in which his team members would follow him in. Next, he signaled the preliminary information he'd been prepped with to start the mission. From this point on, they would rely their own skills to gather intel and execute the mission.

When all five men had acknowledged Corey's orders, he signaled for them to step off. Rising cautiously to his feet, he took careful, silent steps. He held his weapon to his shoulder, muzzle down, finger on the trigger guard. He dropped his night vision goggles down over his eyes and slowly scanned their surroundings.

He knew the Marine encampment was two and half klicks directly ahead. His orders were to lead his team straight at the encampment so the Marines would have to devise a plan for skirting it, and implement that plan without detection.

Corey's fingerless gloves kept his hands relatively warm, still allowing him the dexterity he needed to manage all of his gear. Still moving silently, he stepped over foliage instead of through it. He avoided loose gravel and rocks that could shift underfoot, as well as sticks and twigs that might fracture. Corey moved forward steadily, not looking back to check the team. He was listening to see if he could hear any one of them and was pleased that he couldn't.

Then again, that could be because they'd all lost sight of him and were now lost. Corey still didn't look backward. If they lost sight of him, they failed the exercise. For some of them, that would be the end of their time in BRC.

Corey flipped his goggles up and looked at the sky. The night was clear, probably why it was chilly. He scanned the stars and identified his direction of travel and the approximate time. With his red penlight, Corey glanced at his watch and compass to verify that he'd read the sky correctly.

Adjusting their direction slightly, more northerly, Corey dropped his goggles back into place and kept moving forward silently. He smiled to himself in triumph when he caught his first glimpse of a parked, manned Humvee. He'd led his team right to the encampment, well within the time he'd been given.

Now the fun began. Corey loved this shit.

He gave an abrupt hand signal, ordering his team to drop to their stomachs in the tall foliage. Corey thought he heard movement behind him, but it was no louder than a breeze through grass and wouldn't carry to the encampment. Good. Very good. He signaled for his team to crawl forward, one at a time, and join him in his observation of the enemy encampment. If his team did things correctly, they would relay the order down the line and would spend the next several minutes making their way to Corey's position.

As he waited, Corey lay silently on his belly, watching the encampment through his night vision. One by one, five Marines materialized from the darkness and ranged themselves in the tall grass on either side of him.

Corey signaled for his team to pull back a safe distance so they could formulate a plan for evading the encampment. He would provide no guidance or input. They had to decide for themselves. Pass too close to the camp and risk detection. Swing too wide around and risk not completing the mission in the allotted time.

To Corey's pleasure and surprise, his team decided to creep forward for a better look. They wanted more intel before they finalized their plan. Corey ordered them forward and he brought up the rear.

The team came to a stop close enough to see the entire size of the encampment. It gave them a clear idea of how many troops they were up against and what resources they had. Corey watched them communicate as they gathered intel. Very quickly, they settled on a plan for evasion. He ordered them to execute it, as he continued to follow in their wake.

The team belly-crawled west to the edge of the camp. Corey followed them, wondering if they would turn back north in time. One of the team determined they were far enough out of sight that it was safe to get to their feet. Their pace picked up, but still, the team didn't turn north as soon as Corey would have.

Flipping up his night vision, he gauged the time. Maybe they weren't that far behind after all.

They quickly and quietly traversed the five klicks Corey knew were between the encampment and the village. Wisely, the team dropped low and belly-crawled into observational position. Corey watched as the Marines divided up the duties of the mission between themselves and went to work.

Monitoring the time, Corey waited for the team to finish gathering the required intel. He wasn't paying particular attention when his radio went live. "Eagle-two-one, if you copy this transmission, key your mic times two."

Surreptitiously, Corey pressed the button in the center of his chest twice in rapid succession.

"Roger that. Eagle-two-one, has your team reached the target village?"

Corey keyed his mic twice more.

"Solid copy. Carry on. Base out."

Corey thought the master sergeant might have sounded impressed. He didn't have a chance to dwell on that thought, though. Weapons fire suddenly echoed through the previously quiet night.

Resisting the urge to take back command of the team, Corey watched their startled reactions and how they dealt with the change in circumstances. He was proud of them when they almost immediately settled down, refocused on the task at hand, and got back to work.

When the Marines had secured their gear, they silently backed away from their vantage point over the village. It was unoccupied and Corey assumed they'd determined that, but they were still cautious enough to crawl away on their stomachs.

Several yards out, the team climbed to their feet. They resumed their single file trek back the way they had come. Corey watched as they increased their situational awareness the closer they drew to the Marine encampment.

Gunfire erupted once more. The team stopped all movement as they each listened, gauging direction and distance, trying to determine if they were at risk. The sounds of combat moved away from them, growing more distant. Tension bled from the team and they resumed their journey to the extraction point.

When the team dropped down to crawl through the scrub brush, Corey followed suit. The real risk now was that they would get over-confident and complacent. If that happened, they'd start to make mistakes and mistakes would get them detected.

When they cleared the encampment, Corey thought it had all been too easy. Flawless real-world missions were a good thing. Training missions were supposed to go wrong. That's how lessons were learned.

"Eagle-two-one, if you copy, key times two," the Master Sergeant's voice sounded in Corey's ear.

Corey pressed his mic button twice.

"Advise your current location via Morse."

It took some time but Corey clicked through their rough location.

"Outstanding, Eagle-two-one," replied the Master Sergeant. "Can't let your team off that easy. Be advised, you've got incoming. Let them handle it and observe how they adapt and overcome."

Corey clicked twice in acknowledgment and tightened his grip on his weapon.

The attack came from the right. Gunfire erupted, shattering the quiet of the night. Corey hit the deck, adrenaline flooding his blood stream. His hands tingled, a buzz started at the base of his skull. Even though it was fucking freezing, Corey was still drenched in sweat.

AK47s chattered. Rounds struck the ground all around him. Daring a glance over the tall grass, Corey saw several enemy combatants moving closer. The sounds of their weapons grew louder. If he didn't do something quickly, they would end up surrounded.

Corey rose up onto his knees. He picked a target and fired. One after the other, he aimed at movement and squeezed off two-round bursts. The urge was strong, to switch to full auto and just mow down his enemy. Corey had better discipline than that. He'd been trained to keep control of himself.

Marines nearby shouted. They had to complete their uplink, then make it to the extraction point. He was hopeful for a moment, his team was getting to their feet, returning fire. They moved forward again. Corey had the rear. It was his job to cover his team's six. They were outnumbered and had too far to go. Corey was going to die executing this mission.

His fear and dread gave way to acceptance. Corey was going to die, but he'd die making sure his Marines made it to the chopper safely. Round after round he fired, moving backward in the wake of his team. Bullets sang as they passed within inches of him. Men shouted all around him as they fell, wounded and dead. Corey kept moving, he kept firing his weapon.

His men shouted. They stopped moving and took cover. Corey ducked behind a small boulder surrounded by scrub brush. He rested his M16 on top of the boulder and fired at any target he could see. The enemy was almost on top of them. Soon, Corey and his team would be flanked. It wouldn't be long after that they'd be overrun.

They were on the move again. The rotors of the chopper grew louder than the gunfire. Corey felt the thump of the blades in his chest as they sliced through the air. The helicopter set down just a few yards away. His team had a chance. If Corey could cover their retreat, his Marines might live.

Corey broke cover, firing rapidly. He aimed at the targets he could identify. He backed quickly toward the chopper. Gunfire sounded from all around him. Cory knew he'd be dead before he got there. He fired relentlessly, covering the retreat of his Marines.

The sounds of AK47s were growing closer. He was being overrun. There were too many hostiles advancing on his position. Corey kept firing, backing toward the sound of rotors and the shouts of his men. He couldn't take his eyes off the hostiles to see if his Marines were safely on the bird.

Corey took a knee and continued to fire. He was going to die, this desert was going to be his grave. There were too many hostiles pressing toward him. It didn't matter. He'd defend his position until the chopper lifted off with all of his men secured inside.

There was a shout behind him. Fuck. One of his men must have gone down.

"Staff Sergeant Yarwood!"

He couldn't look back. If his attention wavered, his position would be overrun.

There was a tug on his armor. "Staff Sergeant! Our ride's here. Get on the bird, Sergeant."

The voice behind him was surprisingly calm, close to death as they all were. Another tug at his vest. Corey dared to glance behind himself.

"Come on, Staff Sergeant. We're waiting on you."

The Marine was a young corporal. Corey should recognize him. All he knew was that a Marine was urging him to his feet and into the chopper.

Standing up, Corey fell back to the open door of the bird. Several hands pulled him roughly into the chopper as it lifted off. He sat up and looked around. None of the faces were familiar, but they looked happy. They smiled at one another triumphantly.

Corey watched as a few of the Marines bumped fists. There were no wounded men inside the chopper. Had they left anyone behind? Corey couldn't remember seeing any bodies.

"Mission completed successfully and zero casualties," one of the Marines crowed over the roar of the chopper's engines and rotors.

Mission complete? What mission? Corey searched his memory. He looked out the chopper door. The landscape was familiar, but it wasn't Iraq or Afghanistan. It looked like fucking California.

"How'd we do, Staff Sergeant?"

Corey looked at the Marine who had addressed him. He blinked several times, recognizing the face and struggling to recall the name.

Training. This was a training mission.

"Did you complete the uplink?" he asked.

"Yes, Staff Sergeant," answered several Marines.

"Did any of you get dead?"

"Hell no!"

"Fuck, no!"

Corey shrugged. "Then you did your jobs."

He looked away, staring out the chopper door. He remembered the names of the Marines who had just spoken to him. They were his team, but he was their instructor. Corey remembered the Master Sergeant's radio transmission just before they'd been ambushed.

Corey breathed quick and shallow. The chopper seemed to tilt and he grew light headed. He wasn't entirely sure what had just happened. If his Marines had completed their intel uplink and made the extraction without taking any casualties, they had done a damn good job of adapting and overcoming.

Fuck. Corey had only the barest recollection of the ambush itself. He'd been convinced it was real. He'd been sure his team was being overrun and they were all going to die. It had looked and sounded and felt so fucking real.

Corey ran a trembling hand over his face, wishing he could get off the chopper. He needed space. He needed to breathe. He didn't want to talk to anyone, to pretend everything was normal and he wasn't totally fucked up.

Before the bird had even touched down, Corey leaped out the door. He strode several yards away, dragging in deep, shuddering breaths. He stripped off his Kevlar and scrubbed a hand over his sweat-damp hair. He walked in a circle, struggling to put his memories in order.

The chopper lifted off and the only sounds left were of celebrating Marines. Corey could breathe now. He wiped the back of his hand over his dry lips. He swallowed several times, trying to wet his parched throat.

"Mighty fucking impressive, Staff Sergeant," Master Sergeant Whitfield said, gripping Corey's shoulder firmly.

"Thank you, sir," Corey replied, standing straight.

"Not even that ambush rattled them," Whitfield continued. "And you are one hell of a dangerous shot."

"Every Marine is a rifleman, Master Sergeant," Corey quoted.

"How is it you haven't been sent to sniper school, yet?" Whitfield appeared genuinely baffled.

Because Corey had made jump school and dive school his priorities, because those were Jonah Carver's specialties. "I've been trying for dive school, sir. Nothing against sniper school, though." Maybe it was time Corey figured out what his own strengths were.

The master sergeant nodded at Corey's explanation. "If diving's what you want to do, by all means. But you shamed some good Marines today, dropping them like flies while moving backward." Whitfield grinned.

Corey huffed an awkward laugh. He wasn't used to such direct praise. "Had to get my team's backs."

"Well, everyone is talking about how you're a dead-eye shot with unnatural combat discipline, who had to be dragged onto the chopper by his students." Whitfield grew serious. "That's the story we're going to go with."

Corey froze, his stomach plummeting. He swallowed hard. "Yes, Master Sergeant."

Whitfield folded his arms over his chest and lowered his voice. "It says a lot about your character, Corey. You dug into a defensive position and protected your fellow Marines, instead of turning aggressive and excessively violent. For that reason, I'm not going to relieve you of duty."

Corey gave a single nod. His relief was so powerful he struggled for words. "I'm sorry to cause trouble, Master Sergeant."

Whitfield shook his head emphatically. "No trouble, Corey. I'm aware of what you have going on, and that you're actively seeking help for some issues. I expect you to continue to do so."

"Believe me, if it wasn't so late at night, I'd be calling my counselor right now," Corey said derisively.

"Is it that bad?" Whitfield's concern was obvious. "Do I need to make some calls?"

"No!" Corey took a deep breath. "No, Master Sergeant. The worst is past. I know what triggered my reaction. I'll just write it down in my journal and discuss it at my next appointment."

Whitfield chuckled. "You know, this asshole coward, Nygaard and his ambulance chasing lawyer are trying to sully the good name of our beloved Corps. I will not make their lies about how we treat our men with PTS into truths. I encourage you to keep getting help. I will facilitate you getting that help, and you will not be penalized for doing so."

Corey swallowed hard. "I appreciate that, Master Sergeant." Anything he could say wouldn't adequately express his gratitude.

"What do we need to do to get you safely through the night?" Whitfield asked.

Corey didn't understand at first. Whitfield's meaning finally registered. "Oh, I'll be fine now, Master Sergeant." He consulted his watch. It was 2200 hours and he didn't have to report back to class until 1800 hours tomorrow. "I have some meds I can take. I'll record what happened in that damn journal. And I'm going to call a friend who knows about what's been going on, so there is someone I can talk to."

"Good, good." Whitfield looked relieved. "You're too damn good a Marine to lose to something we actually know how to fix. We'll get you through this."

Corey swallowed past the lump in this throat. "Thank you, Master Sergeant," he said in an embarrassingly raw voice.

"Now get the fuck out of here and go be with your friend." The way Whitfield phrased it, Corey knew he understood just what kind of friend Corey was going to call.

Inside his Jeep, Corey headed for his quarters. He called Sean as he drove.

"I was hoping you'd get to call tonight," Sean answered, voice warm and friendly. "Are you done for the night?"

"Yeah," answered Corey. "I'm gonna throw some gear into a bag and come over. Is that all right?" He needed to shower and change out of his uniform but he needed to be with Sean even more.

"Corey, what's wrong?" Sean asked, fear lacing his voice.

"Nothing anymore, I'm fine," he quickly told Sean. "I'm fine now. I just…" Corey couldn't finish his sentence.

"Okay, I'm here," Sean assured him. "Get here as soon as you can, but be safe. Do you need anything special? Are you hungry?"

"No. Just wait for me." Corey's pleading tone made him wince.

"I'll get something ready in case you need to eat, and I'll turn down the bed." Sean's voice was low and calming.

Corey's frayed nerves already began to soothe. "I'll get there as soon as I can."

Corey grabbed his ruck and shoved a change of clothes, skivvies, sweats, and his dopp kit inside. He didn't take the time to pack neatly, despite his seven years in the Marines. His DI would be shitting himself if he could see. He paused in tossing all of his meds into a pocket to take a Xanax.

Corey flew out of the BEQ like he was being pursued. He sort of felt like he was.

He drove as fast as he dared, his leg bouncing the entire time. Corey fought for patience. Over and over, he eased his white-knuckled grip on the steering wheel. At some point during the journey, he realized his anxiety had eased slightly, and now he just really needed to see and touch Sean.

Sean's front door opened seconds after Corey rang the bell. He pushed into the condo as Sean reached to take his ruck from his shoulder. Corey let it go as he wrapped his arms around Sean's body and pushed him back against the wall. Sean let the ruck fall to the floor beside them, his own arms coming around Corey's shoulders.

Corey pressed the full length of his body against Sean's. He pushed his tongue past Sean's lips and swept it through his mouth. He licked into him deeply, Sean's lips slipping slickly against Corey's. Sean returned the kiss with equal fervor. Corey swallowed Sean's deep, guttural moan.

Sean's fingers dug deep into his shoulders. Sean smelled clean and fresh, the spice and musk of his shampoo and cologne assailed Corey's senses. His mouth held a hint of mint. Corey ground their hips together and felt Sean's hardness already growing against him. Corey's chest ached with need but his dick was still limp in his skivvies.

Shoving his hands under the hem of Sean's T-shirt, Corey ran his palms over every patch of warm, smooth skin he could find. Sean moaned again, pressing into Corey's hands. He hated that there was so much clothing between them.

Sean's hands slid down Corey's shoulders to his chest. Sean fisted his hands in Corey's fleece as if he was clinging to him. Breaking the kiss on a gasp, Sean pressed his hot, wet mouth to Corey's chin and jaw. His breath was hot against Corey's skin. Corey skimmed one palm along Sean's tight stomach. At the edge of his track pants, Corey reached lower and palmed Sean's erect cock through the slick fabric.

Sean gave a filthy groan and nuzzled Corey's ear. "You smell different," he murmured huskily.

That wasn't the mindless dirty talk Corey expected. "Yeah?" His voice was rough and breathless. Corey shivered as Sean skimmed his nose the length of Corey's throat.

"You're sweaty," Sean said. "I smell dirt. Leather. Something metallic."

Corey pulled back abruptly, feeling like he'd been doused with ice water. He lifted a hand and stared at it like he'd never seen it before. It was filthy. Corey's skin was dark with dirt, his nails encrusted black with the stuff. "Kevlar," he said thoughtlessly. "The metallic smell. Kevlar. From my helmet."

Sean took Corey's upraised hand and brought it to his own cheek. His eyes drifted shut as he nuzzled against Corey's palm, heedless of the dirt. "You got down and dirty like a real Marine today, didn't you?" He opened his eyes and they glinted with humor that was mirrored in his voice.

"I should have showered before I got here." Corey was ashamed. "I don't know what I was thinking. I must reek." How could Sean stand to be near him?

"I have a shower." Sean smiled playfully. "We can get you cleaned up together."

"You already showered," Corey said numbly.

Sean gave him a quelling look. "Getting clean is *not* why I want to shower with you."

Corey was struck dumb. He followed on leaden legs as Sean pushed off the wall and tugged him forward by his fleece.

"Grab your gear," Sean said as they stepped past his ruck.

Corey snagged it in mid-stride. Sean walked backward toward the bedroom, tugging Corey along by his uniform fleece. Inside the bedroom, Corey set his ruck on the foot of Sean's bed, vaguely aware the bedclothes were turned down.

"Get out what you need for your shower, I'll go start the water." Sean stripped off his own T-shirt as he crossed to the bathroom.

Corey watched hungrily as the muscles in Sean's shoulders and back shifted with his movements. Quickly, he unzipped the neck of his fleece before turning back to his ruck and pulling out skivvies, his own track pants, and dopp kit. In frustration, Corey palmed his aggravatingly soft cock through his utilities, squeezing and stroking, trying to get some life into the fucking thing.

He heard water begin to run in the bathroom just before Sean reemerged, wearing only his track pants and a smile.

"Seriously, Corey, you don't need *clothes* for your shower," Sean said with a laugh. He stepped in behind and pressed his chest to Corey's back. Sean reached around and put Corey's clothing back into the ruck. "If you don't want to smell like me, bring your soap and shampoo, otherwise you can use mine. Really, you probably only need your toothbrush."

Corey ran a palm over his shorn hair in agitation. He wanted nothing more than to lose himself in and with Sean's body. His fucking dick wouldn't cooperate. How fucking much patience was Sean going to have with Corey's traitorous body? "I like the way you smell." It seemed like the only safe thing to say.

"Thank you," Sean replied, kissing the back of Corey's neck. "I love the way you smell, too."

"I fucking stink, right now," Corey said scornfully. "I can't believe I came here without showering after all the shit I did tonight."

"I love the way you smell," Sean said with feeling. "Even now, you smell like a *man*; all man. You smell like you did something worthwhile today, like you were out there being all strong and competent and *dangerous*."

Corey didn't have a reply. He stood passively as Sean pulled his fleece and skivvy shirt over his head. He leaned back eagerly into Sean's chest, sighing in pleasure at the feel of skin and heat. Corey started to pull his dog tags over his head.

"Oh, do you have to do that?" Sean asked plaintively, pressing a kiss to Corey's shoulder blade.

"I'll put them back on after the shower," he replied with a smile.

"Good. Now sit on the bed so I can get your boots off," Sean said softly, giving Corey a nudge.

"I'm not helpless," Corey groused. Still, he complied, leaning over to unfasten his boot straps and toss them into his ruck.

"Oh, I know you're not," Sean said, grinning broadly. He dropped to his knees between Corey's legs. He leaned in and kissed Corey, licking lightly at his lips and tongue. Sean broke the kiss and began to unlace Corey's boots.

Sean climbed gracefully to his feet and held out a hand to pull Corey up as well. When Sean reached for the fly of his utilities, Corey tried to push his hands away. "I can do it."

"I know you can, but I want to." Sean whispered against Corey's throat, his breath warm and his lips soft. "It's okay. It's all right. Just relax and let me enjoy being with you again."

Corey stepped out of his utilities when they hit the floor. He didn't look down at his flaccid cock hanging uselessly between his legs. He wanted so badly to be with Sean, to show him how much Corey had missed him, and his fucking body was refusing to cooperate.

Sean stripped off his own track pants and reached for Corey's hand. He pulled him into the steamy bathroom, smiling wickedly the entire time. His hazel eyes were soft, and the way Sean looked at him made Corey's chest ache even more.

Opening the shower door, Sean pushed Corey into the cubicle. The heat was soothing and the stinging spray stimulating. Corey ducked his head and let the water course down over his entire body. He felt Sean moving in front of him so he opened his eyes and looked down. The water ran off of him, brown in color. Corey grimaced.

Sean's tanned skin glistened. His muscles rippled beneath the slick skin as he poured shampoo into his palm and returned it to the shelf. Sean's cock was semi-hard and growing. Corey's mouth watered, even as he silently cursed his own unresponsive dick.

Smiling, Sean reached up and washed Corey's hair. "You hardly have any hair. It doesn't take much shampoo."

Corey ran his hand over Sean's thick, damp hair. The mist and the steam made it fall over his forehead and frame his face handsomely. "Sorry. Gotta keep it regulation." Corey explained the reason for his shorn hair.

"I'm not complaining. It suits you. Rinse," Sean ordered. "It's easier to take care of than my unruly mop, I bet."

When the shampoo was rinsed from his hair, Corey opened his eyes. He fisted a hand in Sean's longer locks. "I love your hair. I love running my fingers through it."

Sean's eyes drifted closed, his expression blissful as he leaned into Corey's tugging hand. Corey leaned down and kissed Sean's full, pouty mouth. Sean moaned against Corey's lips, running his hands up the slick skin of Corey's arms. He wanted to step closer and pull their wet bodies together.

When Sean stepped away, Corey released him reluctantly. Sean turned back toward him, holding a bar of fragrant soap. He lathered his hands generously and began to run them over Corey's body. He was firm and thorough. Corey's eyelids grew heavy, as his muscles released their tension under Sean's ministrations.

He couldn't help but chuckle at how ridiculous he felt when Sean dropped down to wash Corey's legs and feet. He took a deep breath and pretended it was perfectly normal that his dick was still soft, despite Sean's hands touching him everywhere.

Sean stood and grinned at Corey, nibbling on his own lower lip at the same time. He built up the lather once again and this time, began to wash Corey in much more intimate areas.

Unable to stop his embarrassed sound, Corey shifted uncomfortably under Sean's hands.

"Relax and just let me be with you again," Sean said against

Corey's ear, over the rush of the flowing water.

Corey closed his eyes and pretended his dick wasn't hanging limply. Sean had to know Corey wanted him and wanted him badly, didn't he? He gave himself over to Sean's attentions, as he'd asked.

Sean's hands, slick with soap, skimmed over Corey's chest and teased at his nipples. It tickled slightly when the tips of Sean's fingers traced the lines of his tattoos. Gooseflesh pebbled Corey's skin. When Sean's other hand slid down the small of his back, Corey slid his feet slightly wider apart. He moaned when Sean gripped each of his ass cheeks in turn, immediately soothing them with gentle caresses. Corey snaked one arm around Sean's waist and pulled him closer. Sean obliged him by pressing their bodies together and rubbing his hard cock against Corey's hip.

Corey sucked in a harsh breath when Sean's fingers slid between his cheeks and teased his opening. One of Sean's wicked fingertips circled Corey's hole without seeking entrance. He added a second finger and still only teased around Corey's rim, not trying to go further. Sean's other hand roamed restlessly over Corey's chest and stomach. Occasionally, he plucked at Corey's nipples, thumbing them, rolling them between his fingers.

With excruciating slowness, two of Sean's fingers nudged at Corey's hole. Steadily, he pushed them up and in. Corey's ass stretched pleasantly. He groaned and turned his head blindly, eyes still shut against the sensation. He sought Sean's mouth and couldn't find it. Frustration nearly burst in his gut when Corey couldn't feel Sean's lips on his own.

"Kiss me," he demanded in a rough and frantic voice. "Please kiss me."

Sean's hot mouth was on Corey's an instant later. Corey opened his mouth and pushed his tongue into Sean's. It was too wet for their mouths to seal and they licked at each other, steam and spray splashing over them. Corey's desperate moans echoed off the tile and drifted over the sound of the cascading water.

The fingers in his ass mimicked the motions of Sean's tongue in Corey's mouth. Corey gripped Sean's ass with one hand and pressed their bodies tight together. They slid against each other, skin slick with water and soap.

Pulling out of the kiss, Sean gasped, "I need to get you into bed."

Corey reluctantly allowed Sean to rinse the soap from his skin. He opened his eyes when Sean shut off the water and painful reality slammed into him. Sean was moving them to the bed and Corey's cock was still limp and lifeless.

Pushing out of the shower stall, Corey quickly grabbed a towel and wrapped it around his hips. Sean followed at a slower pace, eyes heavy with desire and mouth swollen from their hard kisses. He grabbed a second towel and languorously swiped at his own chest and stomach. Corey couldn't miss the proof of Sean's virile desire. His cock was fully hard, standing proudly. It was dark red, filled with ridges and veins. Corey felt mocked.

"I can't do this," he blurted, fleeing the bathroom.

"What? What can't you do?" Sean asked, following Corey.

"This. I can't do this. I'm so fucked up, how can you want to be with me?" Corey demanded, dragging clothes out of his ruck, intending to dress and get the hell out of there.

Sean stood in the middle of the room, between Corey and doorway. He had a towel around his hips but it did nothing to hide his proud erection. "It's all right, I understand," Sean declared, palms out in supplication. "There's a reason this happens. It doesn't matter. We'll work around it. It's all right."

"It's not all right!" Corey shouted, turning on Sean, fists clenched at his sides. "Why do you keep saying that? It's not all right! I came here for sex. You're expecting to fuck. My dick is limp. I want you so bad my chest hurts, but my dick won't get hard. How the fuck is that all right?" Corey's heart thundered. He could barely hear over the sound of his blood rushing in his ears. Corey sucked desperate breaths through clenched teeth, each desperate inhalation loud in the quiet of Sean's bedroom.

Sean starred at Corey with wide, surprised eyes. His mouth

hung open slightly, his palms still raised as if entreating Corey to calm down. "Okay, you're right, it's not all right," Sean said. His voice was quiet but held a slight tremor. Corey thought he saw Sean's hands tremble. "You lived through some shit that's left you fucked up and that's not fair, but it's understandable. It can also be fixed. Do I wish that big dick of yours was rock hard and able to fuck me into the mattress? Hell yeah! So from that aspect, it's not all right. Am I disappointed? Fuck yes. But none of it is your fault. It's frustrating but it doesn't mean I care about you any less."

Sean looked surprised at his own words. His eyes were round and wide open. He closed his mouth with an audible click. Corey watched him swallow hard several times. Still, Sean stood his ground, blocking Corey's path to the door, meeting Corey's eyes, and not trying to take back anything he'd just said.

Corey unclenched his fists and took a step back. Sean's outburst had been honest. He'd stopped trying to placate Corey. He looked like his emotional confession had been accidental, but Sean wasn't trying to take it back.

Taking a deep breath, Corey gave Sean a confession of equal emotion. "I had a flashback tonight."

Sean's expression shifted to concern and Corey's chest loosened when he didn't see the pity he despised. Taking a careful step forward Sean asked, "Where? When? What happened?"

Corey rested his hands on his hips, shifting his weight awkwardly. He was suddenly very aware he wore nothing more than a towel. "Tonight's training was simulated combat. My brain decided it was real and I thought I was going to die making sure my men made it out alive."

"Jesus Christ, Corey! Why didn't you say something when you called me?" Sean demanded angrily. His posture changed dramatically as his shoulders tensed and he planted his feet firmly.

"Because I'm afraid you think I only want you when I've had a bad day," Corey blurted heatedly. "You shouldn't have to always take care of me."

Sean gave Corey a look that was both irate and incredulous. "Where are your fucking medications?" he asked sharply. "Did you at least remember to pack them?" Sean didn't let Corey answer. He stepped to the bed and reached for the ruck.

"Yeah, I brought them," Corey answered lamely, feeling like a chastised child and thinking he might deserve it.

Sean dug in the outer pocket and pulled out the amber bottles. "Did you take a Xanax?" At Corey's mute nod he asked, "When?"

"When I was packing to come here," Corey answered, subdued.

"Then you're fine for now." Sean handed Corey the prescriptions. "Did you take a Viagra at the same time?"

"I didn't take one at all," Corey confessed, bracing for the expected storm.

Sean looked at him in disbelief. "Why the hell not?"

Corey sighed explosively. "Because I shouldn't need a fucking pill to be with you! You deserve to be enough," Corey snapped in a raised voice. Christ that made no fucking sense to him and he knew what he was trying to say.

Sean's expression was furious. "I know the fucking pills don't affect your desire. They just make it possible to do something about what you feel." He took Corey's hand and placed the bottles in it. "Go put these on the nightstand. I'll be right back. Get out a Viagra so you can take it, you stubborn asshole."

Corey didn't dare defy Sean. He regretted upsetting him. Now that he'd said some of that shit out loud, he realized how stupid he was being. Corey took a blue tablet from the bottle and set all three on the nightstand as Sean had ordered him to do.

Sean appeared at Corey's side, bottle of water in hand. He removed the lid and took the Viagra from Corey's fingers. When Sean slid the pill between his lips, Corey took it onto his tongue. He licked at the pad of Sean's thumb when it too, pushed into his mouth. Sean lifted the water and Corey drank deeply, swallowing down the cool liquid and the medication.

Setting the water next to the prescriptions, Sean slid Corey's dog tags over Corey's head, letting them rest against his breastbone. Sean removed the towel from his own hips and dropped it to the floor. Corey tried to hold his towel in place when Sean reached for it.

"Just let it go. Stop thinking about it. Just relax and feel," Sean urged. "If you let yourself enjoy it, everything else will work itself out."

The last of Corey's resistance fell away. Sean removed Corey's towel and dropped it to the floor with his own. He smiled seductively at Corey, gripping Corey's dog tags and twisting the chain around his fist. Sean used the chain to pull Corey in for a searing kiss.

When Sean knelt on the bed, Corey followed him without resistance. Releasing Corey's tags, Sean twisted at the waist and reached behind himself to pull some items from the other bedside table. He set the lubricant bottle and condom strip on top of the nightstand.

Corey knelt admiring Sean's muscular body. His shoulders were broad and his waist and hips were narrow. He obviously spent a fair amount of time working out, which made sense given his profession. Muscles in his arms, shoulders, chest and legs flexed attractively. His erection was already returning, beginning to rise from the neatly trimmed nest of curls at Sean's groin. Corey realized there were things he could do to pleasure Sean despite his own lack of a hard-on.

As Sean turned back to face him, Corey wrapped his arms around Sean's body and picked him up. Sean made a loud sound of surprise which quickly became laughter. Corey tilted Sean and laid him down on the bed, quickly sliding between his legs.

"Corey, you don't have to…" Sean started to protest, coming up on his elbows.

"I want to," replied Corey, stroking Sean's lengthening cock.

"But I want to take care of you tonight," Sean said plaintively.

Corey ignored him and lowered his head. He took the tip of

Sean's cock into his mouth and pushed his lips down around the shaft.

"Fuck," Sean hissed, his head tipping backward and the muscles of his stomach clenching. His fists curled into the sheet beneath him.

That was the kind of reaction Corey was looking for. He gripped one of Sean's lean hips and held him steady. He wrapped his other hand around Sean's cock and stroked in time with his mouth. He sucked hard, flicking and swirling his tongue around the head. Sean flexed his hips against Corey's grip, his legs moving restlessly on either side of Corey.

"Christ, that feels good," Sean murmured. "Feels so fucking good. I love your mouth on me. God, you're fucking gorgeous."

Corey worked Sean's cock, trying to pull more of that needy, filthy talk from him. Sean's last mindless, senseless declaration managed to take him by surprise. Corey pulled off and licked at Sean's prick. He dragged his tongue along the shaft, pressed his closed lips to the thick underside vein. Corey licked at Sean's balls, nuzzling and mouthing them, before moving back up to take all of Sean's dick into his mouth.

"Fuck, you're killing me," Sean groaned. "I love it when you suck me. Christ, look at me, Corey. Fucking look at me. Let me see your beautiful eyes."

Startled, Corey looked up, met Sean's hazel eyes and held them. Sean's red, wet mouth hung open as he stared intently at Corey.

"That's it, that's it," Sean chanted in a whisper, never looking away from Corey's eyes. "You have such beautiful eyes. Your mouth feels so good on me."

Corey sucked hard and slowly dragged his mouth up the length of Sean's dick, feeling a fresh rush of blood under his lips. Sean's words touched something deep in Corey's chest. He redoubled his efforts to bring Sean pleasure.

"Oh, fuck," Sean groaned, eyes falling shut and head tipping back. His hand was suddenly grasping Corey's head. "Stop. Please stop. I don't wanna come like this."

Corey pulled off of Sean's cock with a wet pop. He smiled in triumph. Corey surged upward, capturing Sean's mouth in a sloppy kiss.

Sean lifted one hand to Corey's cheek, still propping himself on the other elbow. "I wanna take care of you. Will you let me take care of you?"

It seemed important to Sean and Corey wanted him to please him. "Yes. Whatever you want," he whispered against Sean's mouth.

"Turn around, okay?" Sean asked between teasing licks at Corey's lips. "Trust me?"

Corey didn't hesitate. He knelt up and when Sean extended his own legs, Corey straddled them, facing away. He settled down to rest back on his heels.

Sean laughed nervously. "No, that's…wait, hang on. I can work with this."

Corey didn't have time to question Sean's meaning. He moaned when Sean's hands gripped his ass firmly, massaging slowly. He arched his back at the feel of Sean's warm palms sliding up his spine.

Sean's hands left Corey's skin. He glanced over his shoulder to see Sean stacking pillows against the headboard. Next, he retrieved the lube and condoms from the nightstand and set them on the bed beside them.

"Lean forward," Sean urged, hands on Corey's ass.

Corey bent over, resting on his elbows on either side of Sean's legs. Sean's strong hands parted his ass cheeks, stretching him slightly and baring his hole to Sean's gaze. Small tendrils of pleasure wove their way up Corey's spine and he forgot to be embarrassed that he was so vulnerable and exposed.

When Sean's thumbs lightly circled Corey's opening, he moaned and pushed backward. Sean's touch was slight and teasing, leaving Corey aching for more contact. Heat was coursing through his groin now. There was finally a tingling at the very base of his cock.

Corey heard the snick of the lube bottle being opened just before the cool gel oozed between his cheeks and down the length of his crack. He hissed in surprise, then laughed reflexively. Sean's fingers smoothed through the slick, catching it as it ran down Corey's balls. One lubed finger pushed slowly into Corey's hole.

"Mmmm," he moaned, relaxing his lower back, the muscles of his stomach, and willing his entire body to open up for Sean.

"Damn, you're already loose and relaxed," Sean said with wonder, pushing a second finger firmly into Corey's ass.

"Uh huh," Corey answered distractedly, letting his head drop as Sean's fingers twisted inside of him.

More cool lube slid down Corey's crack and Sean pushed it into him with three fingers. "I thought I was going to have to really work to get you ready," said Sean.

Corey's brow furrowed. He looked over his own shoulder at Sean. "Did you think I was a nervous virgin?"

"You don't strike me as someone who does this very often." Sean fucked him with three fingers and Corey rocked into it rhythmically.

He made a scoffing sound. "If it feels good, I'm generally up for it." Sean pressed downward with his fingers and Corey's limbs turned to liquid. A frisson shot up the length of his spine. Corey dropped his head again with a low groan. "Oh, fuuuck. You can stop fucking around now."

Sean's fingers slid free of Corey's ass. Gripping Corey's hips, Sean urged, "Shift forward."

Corey came to his knees and moved forward slightly until he was straddling Sean's hips. Behind him, he heard foil tear and latex snap several times. Once more, the lube bottle opened and closed.

Sean's hands spread Corey's ass wide with a hard grip. "Okay, ease back onto me," Sean said breathlessly.

Corey eased himself backward, trusting Sean's hands to guide him. The blunt head of Sean's cock pressed against Corey's asshole and Sean's hands released him, moving to grasp his hips instead. Corey shifted his knees to get the angle right before he let his weight carry him down onto Sean's dick.

When the head of Sean's cock slid past the ring of muscle in Corey's hole, he gave a long, low moan. Sean's strong hands held him steady as Corey rocked backward, taking Sean's erection deeper.

"Christ, that's so fucking hot to see," Sean said, voice raw. "Your ass just opens up to take my cock."

Corey rose up and rocked back, groaning at the stretch of Sean's dick as it slid in deep. The only thing Corey had to hang on to was his own thighs, and his knuckles whitened against his own skin. When Corey's ass brushed against Sean's thighs, he knew he was nearly there.

"Fuck, you feel good," Corey gasped as he settled fully onto Sean's lap. He shuddered at the sense of being filled up and completed. It didn't matter that his own cock was still limp.

Sean slid his hands up Corey's back, then back down to his sides. Corey found a rhythm, rising and falling on Sean's dick. He rose up and the head of Sean's cock stretched the rim of his opening. When Corey sank down and took Sean deep, frissons ran the length of his spine. Shudders wracked Corey's body and he moaned loudly each time his ass met Sean's thighs.

Sean's fingers fluttered at the back of Corey's neck. The chain of his dog tags twisted against his throat, just before it was pulled snug. The tags themselves clinked against Corey's back.

"That's it, make yourself feel good," Sean murmured. His hand moved at the base of Corey's neck. "Use me to make yourself feel good."

Corey realized Sean was gripping his dog tags, his hand wrapped up in the chain. Corey leaned back slightly, when Sean used his tags to tug him backward. When Sean's other hand ran up the length of Corey's back, Corey arched into his touch. Fuck, this was nice. Sean's touch on his skin made Corey feel cared for.

Christ, Corey had never felt this way before. He even stopped caring that his own dick shifted limply against his thigh as he rode Sean's cock.

"Fuck me," Corey whispered, head tipped back and eyes closed. "Fuck me deeper, I wanna feel you deeper."

Sean's hips rose up to meet Corey's ass the next time he rocked back. Corey took Sean's cock deeper than he had previously. The stretch at his opening was more intense. Corey shouted, gripping his own thighs harder. Sean's hand rubbed at his shoulder soothingly.

"Like that?" Sean's voice was strained. "Is that what you needed?"

"Uh, yeah," Corey moaned, picking up his pace, grinding down hard onto Sean's hips. His own cock shifted against his thigh, a slight throb building in the base.

"You're so fucking sexy." Sean's voice strained with the effort of his thrusts and the force of Corey's body pressing down on him. "Broad, strong shoulders. Gorgeous ass."

Corey's cock lifted from its nest of curls. He pushed against the chain at his throat, feeling grounded by Sean's fist using it to hold him steady. Sean's palm slid over the skin of his ribs, his hip, coming to span Corey's belly. His rhythm faltered, afraid Sean was going to reach for his erection and find it only semi-hard.

He made a strangled sound, low in his throat, shifting in Sean's lap. "Sean…"

"Yeah, tell me what you want." Sean's hand moved back to Corey's hip. "Tell me what feels good."

Corey rocked back against Sean, driving his cock deep. He shouted when he shifted in a way that pushed Sean's dick against that sweet spot deep inside. Starbursts lit the backs of his eyelids and Corey's erection reached full hardness.

Sean's fingers traced Corey's bicep. The light touch made Corey shiver pleasantly.

"Fuck, I wish you had ink on your back," Sean said roughly, "so I could see it and touch when you're like this."

Corey didn't have the breath to say that he'd been thinking about it. A Celtic knot or a triskelion, in honor of Sean's name. Maybe they'd go to Corey's artist together. Those thoughts all faded into nothing when Corey curled forward against his dog tag chain at his throat and rocked down on Sean's cock. Stars blurred his vision as his gland was nailed once more.

Sean's hand suddenly gripped Corey's hip painfully. "Oh Christ, Corey," he cried out desperately. "You feel so good, gonna make me come."

Corey was rock hard now. The Viagra had kicked in fully and Sean's cock pressed firmly against that spot deep inside of Corey. His erection stood up straight, harder than Corey thought he'd ever been. His cock throbbed, the veins standing out along the length of the shaft. The head was deep red, clear liquid leaking from the tip. Corey resisted the urge to touch himself. He wanted Sean to see the full, proud evidence of his arousal.

Sean's legs moved restlessly beneath Corey, like he was trying to hold back his orgasm. Corey tightened the muscles deep inside and sped up his rocking motions on Sean's dick. "Come inside me, Sean," Corey demanded. "I want you to come."

"Not 'til you," Sean replied, voice broken.

Corey reached down and cradled Sean's sac in one hand. He gently rolled the firm balls in his palm. "I wanna feel you inside me," Corey said hoarsely.

"Ah, you fucker," Sean shouted, his body folding up behind Corey, the pressure on the dog tag chain growing tighter. "Son-of-a-bitch, I'm coming."

The bed rocked beneath them as Sean's body vibrated violently. One hand stayed twisted in Corey's chain, the other held on tightly to his hip. Sean shouted and swore, his cock pulsing, over and over, buried deep inside of Corey's ass. In Corey's palm, Sean's balls tightened and slipped up closer toward his body.

Sean fell back on the bed, breathing heavily. Corey stayed

where he was, eyes closed, feeling Sean's cock soften inside of him. His own erection ached painfully, but it felt good, after being so afraid he wasn't going to get hard at all.

"That wasn't fair," Sean gasped. "I wanted to wait until you could come with me."

Corey gripped the condom as he slid off of Sean's softened cock. He shifted off of Sean's body to remove the condom for disposal. When Corey knelt at his hip, Sean's smile was blinding.

He was caught by surprise when Sean leaned up and grasped him behind the neck. Corey's lips tingled when Sean pressed their mouths together. His other hand wrapped firmly around Corey's straining erection. When Corey gasped into their joined mouths, Sean swallowed it down.

Still smiling when he broke the kiss, Sean gave Corey's dick several firm strokes. "I know just what I want to do with this." Releasing Corey, Sean started to slide from the bed.

"You don't have to *do* anything with it," Corey protested. Sean had already done so much for him.

"Are you kidding? After all the angst we went through together to get that gorgeous hard-on, I'm not letting it go to waste." As he spoke, Sean disappeared into the bathroom. He returned with a condom in hand.

"I hadn't planned on wasting it," Corey said slowly. Sean's cock was obviously spent for the time being so there could only be one use for that condom.

"You're not the only one who knows a few tricks," Sean said, still smiling broadly. He searched the bedclothes until he located the lube bottle. "Besides, I want to give you the kind of pleasure you just gave me."

Corey started to protest again.

Sean tugged at his arm. "Just sit at the edge of the bed, dammit. Christ, you even have to make getting off difficult."

Corey barked a surprised laugh. He slid to the side of the bed and planted his feet in the floor. Quickly and efficiently,

Sean rolled the condom onto Corey's erection and doused it in lubricant.

Gently gripping Sean's hips, Corey held him steady as he knelt on the bed. Sean straddled Corey's thighs, settling carefully onto his lap. His chest and belly were warm and firm against the front of Corey's body. Sean ran his hands over Corey's hair and down his shoulders and arms. His hazel eyes held Corey's gaze steadily.

Corey ran his hands restlessly over Sean's well-muscled back, pulling him closer. Something in Sean's eyes made Corey's chest tighten. It was hard to breathe. One corner of Sean's mouth quirked up and he continued to watch Corey with humor and affection.

"You have the most beautiful eyes," Sean surprised Corey by saying. "They're such a clear, pale blue."

Corey flushed. "Thank you." What the hell else was he supposed to say to that?

Sean took Corey's face between his hands and lowered his head. Corey tilted his face eagerly, meeting Sean's full, warm lips with his own. He expected passion and hunger. Instead, Sean kissed him gently; light, slow flicks of his tongue. Corey dug his fingers into the dense muscles of Sean's back and moaned quietly.

Breaking the kiss, Sean left his mouth hovering just above Corey's. "Hold me open while I guide you in," he whispered.

Corey stared into Sean's smoldering hazel eyes. He didn't understand at first. Sean reached behind his own hip and skimmed his fingertips along Corey's thigh. Understanding dawned just as a shiver ran through Corey's body.

Lowering his hands to grasp Sean's ass cheeks, Corey parted them and held Sean open. Corey's hard cock was trapped between their bodies so Sean rose up slightly. Corey sucked a harsh breath in through his clenched teeth when Sean's fingers touched his dick. His hips moved reflexively at the slight stimulation.

Sean never looked away from Corey's eyes. Corey felt trapped by Sean's knowing gaze. He held his breath when Sean guided his erection into position. Corey felt the head of his cock press against the clenched opening of Sean's ass. His grip on Sean's ass cheeks tightened as he braced himself.

"Just hold onto me and I'll take care of the rest. Okay?" Sean murmured against Corey's lips.

"Yeah. Okay." Corey answered in a hoarse whisper. The anticipation of his cock being engulfed in Sean's tight heat had him trembling.

Sean wrapped his arms around Corey's shoulders and rocked back slightly. Corey's cock pushed up inexorably into Sean's hole. Corey held Sean open as the head of his dick slipped past his opening and into the heat of his body.

Corey watched Sean's expressive face closely. When Corey's cock breached his body, Sean's eyes tightened at the corners, he bit down on his lower lip and grunted softly.

"Okay?" Corey asked in a strained whisper, afraid he'd inadvertently hurt Sean.

"Mm hmm, yeah," Sean gasped. "Feels good." He rocked back with a little more force and Corey slid deeper into him. Sean moaned, his mouth falling open slightly but never looking away from Corey's eyes.

Sean's inner walls were tight, slick and hot. "Fuck," Corey sighed. He released Sean's ass and wrapped his arms around is chest, as much to ground himself as to steady Sean.

With three strong thrusts, Corey's cock was completely consumed by Sean's heat. A violent tremor had Sean's body trembling in Corey's arms. His ass settled snugly into Corey's lap, his ball sac resting against Corey's belly. Corey thrust up into Sean reflexively, trying to get even deeper.

Sean's muscles tensed and bunched as he rose up slightly then sat back down in Corey's lap. He found a rhythm, riding Corey's cock steadily. Sean's breathing was harsh, his chest heaved against Corey's arms. Corey tilted his face so he could feel Sean's hot breath against his lips.

He could feel it building. Heat spiraled through Corey's

system as Sean's ass clamped around his cock before sliding up to the tip. The friction was intense. Corey moved against him, almost unwillingly. He reached toward his orgasm, even as he wanted to draw this out, make it last.

Sean's face was flushed. His mouth was red and swollen and his pink tongue snaked out to wet his lower lip. "Are you close?" he gasped.

Corey moaned, straining for a kiss. "Yeah. Feels so good inside you, I'm so fucking close."

Sean stayed just out of his reach, hazel eyes luminous and never wavering from Corey's. "Just let go. I've got you, baby. Just let it all go."

What he saw in Sean's face made Corey's chest tighten painfully. He swallowed hard against a lump in his throat. Sean's open expression hit Corey like a punch to the gut. It scared the shit out of him because he knew Sean's emotions were reflected in Corey's own face.

He tightened his arms around Sean's straining body and pulled him closer. Corey hid his face in Sean's neck, breathing in his clean scent and the slightest hint of his sweat. Jesus Christ, he'd never felt like this before about anyone. Corey's sac tightened, heat pooling low in his belly. Sean left one arm around Corey's shoulders, his other hand came to rest on the back of Corey's head. The touch was filled with affection and comfort.

Their rhythm sped up, Sean moving hard and fast against him. Corey's balls lifted and his climax unspooled from deep inside. His chest hurt. He wanted to say something, make a joke that would have them both laughing and ease this intense ache. Instead, Sean kissed the top of Corey's head.

The tender touch was Corey's undoing. A shudder ran through him and Corey was mortified when he sobbed against Sean's neck.

"I know, baby. Me, too. Me, too." Sean whispered against Corey's hair, running his hands soothingly over Corey's back.

Corey's orgasm slammed into him like a storm driven wave.

He clung to Sean, his cock pulsing as his balls pumped hot spunk into the condom. Corey cried out desperately, pressing his forehead to Sean's collarbone as he helplessly rode out his climax. Sean's touch and his softly spoken words frightened Corey at the same time as he felt loved and cherished.

In the four years he was with Katherine, Corey had *never* felt this way.

As his body became his own again, Corey left his face pressed to the moist skin of Sean's shoulder. He breathed shakily against Sean's chest. Sean wrapped his arms around Corey, held him close and rocked them gently, side to side.

His breathing calmed and Corey could hear Sean's heart racing in his chest. He placed a soft kiss on Sean's shoulder and pulled back slowly. Sean exhaled harshly. Corey was afraid to look into Sean's face. He needed to see his own feelings reflected in Sean's expression and he was afraid he wouldn't anymore.

Corey swallowed hard. He chanced a glance at Sean's face and was surprised to find him looking hesitant and almost shy. Sean wet his lower lip nervously. Corey replayed the last few moments in his head and remembered Sean calling him 'baby'. He'd always hated that pet name; it made him *feel* like a baby and Corey was anything but a child. When Sean had said it, though, Corey had felt…*loved*.

Corey grasped Sean's face between both hands and kissed him. He didn't have words to say what he was feeling, or how strongly he felt it. So he took action. Corey had always been better at doing than at saying.

Sean kissed him back with just a hint of desperation. There was relief there, too. Corey told Sean everything in that kiss. He put everything he couldn't say into that kiss and hoped Sean would understand.

Me, too Sean had said. He'd said *me, too*, as if he already understood how Corey felt, and even felt the very same way.

When Corey finally broke the kiss, Sean looked dazed. He smiled lazily and flushed bright red.

"Let me get rid of the condom and we can get some sleep," Sean said, slurring slightly.

Corey got up and straightened the bed. When Sean emerged with a damp cloth, there was a small skirmish over which of them got to clean Corey. Pretending to surrender, Corey let Sean have his victory. Sean returned to the bathroom and Corey crawled beneath the covers. He lay back against the pillows and examined his prescription bottle that contained the sleep aid. He didn't think it would be necessary tonight, he felt strangely peaceful.

When Sean emerged from the bathroom, he shut out all the lights and crawled into bed beside Corey.

"Gonna take one of those?" Sean asked softly.

"No," Corey said, setting the bottle on the bedside table. He settled back onto the pillows next to Sean. He could feel the heat of Sean's body across the slight distance that separated them. His hands itched to touch but he couldn't tell if Sean wanted that. "I shouldn't have a problem falling asleep."

"Come 'ere," Sean whispered. He reached across Corey's body and tugged at his arm, urging him to turn over.

Corey's heart leapt. He rolled onto his side and pressed himself against Sean's side. With a gentle hand on his head, Sean guided Corey to use his chest as a pillow. Corey draped an arm over Sean and tried not to seem like he was clinging. Sean's heartbeat was strong and steady beneath Corey's ear.

"Is there something we should talk about?" Sean asked in a soft voice.

Corey tensed. Sean's words, *Me, too* echoed in Corey's memory. He wanted to know if Sean had meant what Corey thought he had, but he was afraid what the truth might be. Corey swallowed hard.

"No," Corey answered roughly, "I don't need to talk."

"Are you sure?" Sean pressed. "You had a flashback, tonight. Isn't there something you need to discuss?"

A chill ran the length of Corey's spine. Of course Sean meant the flashback. Fuck. Corey had almost humiliated himself.

"Oh—no, I'm fine now," Corey said hesitantly. "I know what caused it. I'll talk to my counselor at my next appointment, work on ways to prevent it from happening again."

Sean idly dragged his fingertips along Corey's spine. He pressed his lips to the top of Corey's head. "Let me know if you change your mind." Sean paused so long, Corey thought the conversation was over. "Did you think there was something else I wanted to talk about?"

"No," Corey answered quickly. Too quickly. He took a deep breath. "Is there anything *you* want to talk about?"

If it weren't for Sean's fingers on his back, Corey would have thought he'd fallen asleep. "You had an emotional night—the flashback, stressing about your body's reactions, our shouting match. Things happen in the heat of the moment." Sean sighed explosively. "I'm not making any assumptions, I guess is what I'm trying to say."

Corey thought his heart had stopped. He leaned up onto his elbow, straining to see Sean's eyes in the dim light from the window.

"What?" Sean asked, sounding worried.

"Me, too," Corey answered breathlessly.

"What?" This time Sean sounded confused.

"What did you mean when you said, 'me, too'?" Corey hoped Sean couldn't hear the quaver in his voice. His stomach plummeted when Sean didn't answer right away.

"What do you think I meant?" Sean finally asked.

The words stuck in Corey's throat.

Sean moved restlessly beneath him. "Nothing. I didn't mean anything. Heat of the moment."

Corey could hear the disappointment in Sean's voice. He stopped the painful words the only way he could think of. He pressed his mouth awkwardly to Sean's. For the first few moments, Sean didn't respond. Then, his hands grasped Corey's head and held him steady. His lips parted, his tongue snaking out and seeking Corey's.

Pulling back on a gasp, Corey whispered, "Me, too."

"Okay, good," Sean said brokenly, bringing their mouths together again.

Corey wrapped his arms around Sean and held him close as they kissed. Christ. He'd never felt like this before. If Sean felt even half as strongly as Corey did, shit just got complicated. There was so goddamn much going on in his life, how the hell could he be what Sean needed him to be?

When he finally broke the kiss, Corey hid his face in the sweaty hair behind Sean's ear.

"I'm so glad we had this talk," Sean said before he burst into giddy laughter.

Corey joined in, the pressure in his chest easing enough to let him sleep, nightmare free.

CHAPTER SEVENTEEN

Corey sat at the conference table, dressed in his olive green service uniform. His coat was neatly folded over the back of the chair beside him. Captain Hirata was seated on Corey's other side, removing documents from an accordion folder and spreading them out on the table.

"I don't understand, sir," Corey said, furrowing is brow in confusion. "I wasn't involved in the exchange of fire with the occupants of the hostile vehicle."

"We know, Corey." It was Agent Hoffman who answered. "But you dealt with the aftermath, so we need you to help us piece together what really happened."

Corey let his eyes move over the familiar photos, dread settling like a lead weight in his gut. "The lieutenant covered up what really happened. He covered up the actions of my fellow Marines." He felt like the whole world had gone insane when he wasn't looking.

"It's possible the lieutenant issued orders in a moment of confusion," said Captain Evans. "The Marines might have mistakenly opened fire. If there were errors in judgment, or panic and confusion, that would be understandable. Unfortunate, but understandable. If that was the case, the lieutenant should have owned up to it, as a man and as an officer."

"Covering up what happened destroys everyone's credibility, Corey," Hirata said quietly.

Corey ran an agitated hand over his forehead. "Is it possible the platoon didn't know the lieutenant covered everything up? Is it possible they don't even realize they did anything wrong?"

"It's possible," Hoffman replied. "That's the approach we took when we opened the investigation. But it's not looking like that's what happened."

Corey opened the bottle of water that was on the table in

front of him. He took a long swallow, washing down the rising bile.

"For what it's worth, Corey, we know this isn't easy for you," Hirata said. "We have no desire to scapegoat enlisted Marines. But we're not going to let anyone get away with dishonoring the Corps."

Corey nodded, reluctantly agreeing. "Anyone who acted without honor deserves to be punished, sir. I just really don't like the idea that Marines with whom I have served would behave this way."

"We understand that, Staff Sergeant." Captain Evans looked at Corey with compassion. "It's not lost on any of us."

Corey cleared his throat. "So, what do you need me to do?"

"Let's start with you leaving the structure and returning to the Humvees and the scene of the IED blast," replied Hoffman.

Hirata slid a copy of Corey's after-action across the table. It was heavily annotated, including Corey's own marks to show what had been altered. Corey recounted how he took three Marines with him when he headed back to where the rest of the platoon had secured the Humvees and engaged the hostile white vehicle.

Corey ran a hand over his suddenly dry lips. He took a sip of water so he could continue. His heart raced and sweat broke out along his hairline. The memory of his actions was more vivid than it had been since the day of the actual events. Unlike every other time he'd recalled his actions of that time, it had been like he was viewing things through a filter.

"I'm going to stop you here, Staff Sergeant." Captain Evans interrupted Corey's recollections. "Wouldn't it have been SOP to raise your lieutenant on comms, update your status, and request someone respond to your location with the appropriate number of body bags?"

"Yes, ma'am," Corey answered. "But I remember needing to advise the lieutenant of something that I didn't want to broadcast on comms. I needed more than body bags. I needed additional Marines and for my platoon commander to—" He couldn't remember what he needed from the LT but now, Corey remembered feeling like he was in way over his head.

He looked down to find his hands were trembling.

"Are you okay, Staff Sergeant?" Captain Hirata asked.

Corey cleared his throat. "I'm fine, sir."

"Resume your narrative, Staff Sergeant," said Captain Evans. "You needed to make contact with Lieutenant Adams. You and three of your Marines returned to the line of Humvees. What happened then?"

Captain Hirata slid a stack of photographs in front of Corey. Glancing through the photos, Corey recognized most of them. He could also conjure actual memories of the same scenes, now. Corey viewed the events of the remainder of that day with the additional knowledge of what had really happened to the vehicle occupants.

"A secure perimeter was in place," he recounted. "A team of Marines surrounded a white compact car. Lieutenant Adams and several more Marines stood over the corpses of four Afghan males."

"Do any of the photos before you accurately depict how those bodies were laid out when you first rejoined the platoon?" This question was from Agent Hoffman.

Corey went through the color photographs. He'd seen most of them before. He'd seen far worse things in reality, than were captured in those photos. He didn't know why bile rose in his throat this time.

He pulled out a few photos that showed the four men laid out on their backs, lined up side-by-side. Handing the pictures to Agent Hoffman, Corey blurted, "I should have noticed. I let my situational awareness slip."

Hoffman looked puzzled as he took the photos. If he noticed Corey's trembling hand, he gave no sign. "What do you mean, Staff Sergeant?" he asked.

"When the lieutenant said the occupants of the vehicle had

opened fire on the platoon and had been killed in the ensuing firefight, I didn't question his story." Corey clenched his fists on the table in front of him. "The bodies were laid out like they would have been if they'd been pulled from the vehicle after the battle. If I had paid attention to details like I should have, I would have noticed the corpses showed no combat wounds."

"What about the white car?" Hoffman asked. "Did you observe any damage that appeared to have occurred during a firefight?"

Corey glanced away and pictured the scene. "Bullet holes and shattered glass." He quickly thumbed through the stack of photos until he found one that matched his mental picture. "There shouldn't have been shattered glass. If the occupants had started a firefight, they would have had the windows rolled down." Why hadn't Corey noticed that before?

Hoffman nodded as he took the picture. "You have once again independently confirmed an important detail for us, Staff Sergeant."

That was a small consolation.

"What was on your mind at that moment, Staff Sergeant?" asked Captain Hirata. "What were you thinking about when Lieutenant Adams gave you his account of what had happened?"

"That I needed the LT to return to the residence with me. Something significant had to be handled." Corey stared at the table in front of him without seeing it. "I was pissed off," Corey caught himself. "I beg your pardon, ma'am," he said with contrition, glancing at Captain Evans, "I was angry. I was outraged. There was someone on my team I wanted to hurt, but I knew I couldn't do that. I had to hand this off to my platoon commander."

"Can you recall any of those details, yet?" Captain Evans asked.

"No, ma'am," Corey replied, meeting her eyes. "But this is the clearest my memory has ever been of that afternoon."

"We're making progress, then," she said. "So, when you

reached the platoon and made your initial observations, what did you do first?"

"I approached the lieutenant and told him I needed to speak in private," Corey recalled. "He was distracted and edgy. He told me he didn't have time. I chalked it up to post-combat reaction and told him it was critical I speak to him."

The events of the day played out vividly in his mind's eye. Corey relayed those events as they sprang into his memory. The lieutenant was visibly agitated. Corey told him about something that had happened during the execution of his mission and the LT's agitation had grown worse. He felt his own confusion and worry as if this had occurred just yesterday. He'd anticipated accompanying the LT back to the structure to deal with…what had happened, but the lieutenant surprised Corey by ordering him to stay behind and supervise the bagging of the four dead Afghanis.

He'd followed orders. The LT had taken a team and gone into the structure. Corey had made sure the bodies were bagged, not bothering with documenting the wounds.

Because the lieutenant had told him it had already been done.

As the bodies had been placed inside the Humvees, the LT had returned with all of Corey's team in tow. They carried only five body bags.

"I kept asking Corporal Howe where the other bodies were and he kept asking me what other bodies I meant." Corey scrounged through his memory for images that had been lost to him until this moment. "Howe and I documented the wounds of the five hostiles we had killed in the initial assault on the structure. No one knew what other bodies I was talking about, but I knew there should have been more."

"What was Lieutenant Adams doing while this was going on?" Evans asked.

"Standing with Nygaard and his team at the very last Humvee. They were talking." Corey hadn't remembered that detail before. "We secured the un-bagged bodies to the hoods of the Humvees and the LT came up to talk to the corporal and me."

"What was said?" asked Hoffman.

"Howe asked the LT what other bodies I was talking about. The lieutenant said he had no idea. I couldn't say anything. I couldn't tell anyone what bodies I meant, but I knew they should have…"

With a wordless shout, Corey stood up so fast he toppled his chair. All he could see was a room full of women and children in a blood soaked room, throats slit and left to die on the dirt floor.

§ § §

"Tyler, I can't raise Nygaard on comms. Have you heard anything?" Corey called across the room.

"No, Sergeant. Want me to go make contact?" Corporal Howe and several other Marines were inventorying the weapons cache they'd found in the house.

"I'll go. You guys just hurry it up so we can get out of here." Corey headed out the rear door of the structure in search of Sergeant Nygaard and the Marines he'd taken with him to secure the perimeter.

He walked slowly, his head on a swivel, weapon at the ready. They had heard no weapons fire so he didn't think Nygaard had engaged any hostiles, but he couldn't be sure.

Corey's headset crackled to life and he tuned out the short conversation between the LT and one of the teams still at the site of the IED blast. He vaguely noted that the lieutenant sounded more stressed than usual today, even having lost Marines.

The hairs on Corey's arms and neck lifted as he scanned his surroundings. He should have seen a Marine or two by now, holding down the perimeter. A sudden sound had him aiming his weapon toward the structure directly ahead as a door swung open.

"Sergeant." The private stared at Corey, wide-eyed in shock.

"Where the fuck is Sergeant Nygaard?" Corey demanded, lowering his M4 and striding forward.

"He's inside, Sergeant. Searching the house." The Marine's eyes darted around their sockets but never quite looked right at Corey.

"Searching for what?" Corey demanded, pushing the private out of the way so he could open the door. "You were supposed to be securing the perimeter."

The coppery scent of blood assailed Corey's nostrils as soon as he stepped inside. An eerie pall hung in the air. He could hear movement coming from deeper in the residence, male voices speaking English carried to him.

Stepping carefully through a small room, Corey reached a narrow doorway that opened into the main room of the residence. The scene that greeting him was horrific and the world spun around Corey. He gripped his M4 until his fingers ached. He swallowed back bile as the scents of blood, excrement and death overwhelmed him.

Slowly, Corey took several steps into the room. His LPCs made moist sucking sounds as he walked and he didn't dare look down. Corey knew how much blood it took to make that sound. He also knew he'd lose it if he looked down to see it. He wondered briefly if it was all fake. The blood splattered up the walls of the room looked like it belonged in a shitty horror flick.

"Yarwood, man, we found these bitches waiting to fucking ambush us!" Nygaard shouted from across the room.

Corey looked up into Nygaard's wild eyes. "What the fuck did you do?" he asked weakly.

"The fuckers who ambushed us didn't think we'd find their families hiding out in here." As he spoke, Nygaard kicked one of the corpses that lay at his feet. "They wouldn't tell us where they hid the weapons and explosives."

Corey's chest heaved as he dragged desperate breaths in through his open mouth. All five of the Marines who had accompanied Nygaard on his mission stood casually around the room, M16s leaned against a wall. Each one wore an expression that was part hate, part smug. Their uniforms were all heavily splattered with blood. Corey put the back of one hand to his nose and mouth in a futile attempt to block the nauseating smell that filled the room.

How the fuck was he going to handle this?

"They're fucking women and kids, Nygaard." Corey's horror abruptly morphed into outrage and no small amount of disgust. "How much of a threat could they be?"

"This is where they been hidin' their guns," Nygaard replied angrily, as if he didn't understand why Corey didn't get it. "This is where they put together those IEDs that kill *Marines*," he snarled.

Corey forced himself to look at the piles of bloody bodies scattered on the floor. His stomached churned and he swallowed repeatedly as his mouth flooded with bitter saliva. Despite that, Corey's lips were dry.

He focused on the gruesome scene before him. The bodies were in clusters, the clusters making up a rough circle. They were all face down in their own blood that was inches deep on the tiled floor.

"You had them all detained." Corey put the facts together even as he said them out loud. "They weren't armed. All you needed was to interrogate them about the cache."

"They lied, refused to tell us," Nygaard's response was filled with agitation.

Corey crossed to one of Nygaard's Marines. He gripped the Private by the throat. "Who made the first kill?"

"Sergeant Nygaard wouldn't let any of us do anything until he was done with his," the private replied with eagerness and pride that weakened Corey's knees.

He turned on Nygaard, careful not to slip in the still-wet blood. "You had them on their knees, didn't you?" demanded Corey. "Surrounded by armed Marines, they were no threat."

"None of them would give up any information." Nygaard again kicked the dead woman at his feet. "This one didn't believe I'd kill her daughter if she didn't talk so I had to show her I was serious."

Corey gripped Nygaard's armor and dragged him closer. Corey shoved his face right into Nygaard's, disturbed by the joyful gleam he saw in the Sergeant's eyes. "How many did you kill before you realized they had nothing to tell you?"

"What the fuck, Yarwood?" Nygaard clawed at Corey's fist in the front of his armor. "I was trying to save Marines. How many did you kill when we busted into the other house?"

"I killed armed men who were firing at me in a combat situation!" Corey shouted, his voice cracking at least once. "I didn't put women and children on their knees and make them watch me slit their throats." He gave Nygaard's vest a vicious yank and sent him sprawling to the floor amongst the corpses. Corey shouldered his M4 and turned back to aim at the remaining Marines. "Don't anyone reach for your weapon."

Nygaard slowly climbed to his feet, the front of his uniform covered in tacky blood. "Why do you care?" Nygaard seemed genuinely puzzled. "They're just the families of terrorists."

"All of you; back to the first structure. Leave your weapons where they are." Corey kept his weapon raised, genuinely ready to blow one of them away if they reached for their Ka-Bar or tried to make a run for it.

Corporal Howe and the rest of Corey's Marines looked shocked and confused when he brought his prisoners in at gunpoint. "Sergeant Yarwood?" Tyler questioned.

"Take their Ka-Bars," Corey ordered brusquely, pushing his prisoners up against a wall. "Restrain them."

"Sergeant?" Howe asked again. He looked stunned, even as he removed plastic cuffs from his leg pouch.

"You're in charge here, Corporal," Corey ordered as Nygaard and the other four Marines slid down to sit with their backs to the wall. "Don't talk to them, don't answer any questions. Don't anyone go into the next structure until I get back with the lieutenant."

"Yes, Sergeant," Tyler replied hastily. He quickly crossed the room to where Corey stood. "Shit, Corey, what the fuck happened out there?"

Corey swallowed against a tight throat. "You really don't want to know, Tyler," he replied just above a whisper, refusing to give in to the sudden wave of exhaustion and sadness. "I really need your help with this. Please."

"You got it, man, you know that," Tyler replied emphatically, keeping his voice low and calm. "But you're scaring me. Something bad happened, didn't it?"

"Really bad," Corey confirmed. "Just keep everything calm and secure here 'til I get back."

"Yeah, sure, of course." Tyler took a step back and scanned the room quickly. "Waters, Green, you're with Sergeant Yarwood."

Corey led the two Marines back to the site of the IED blast and they discovered there had been an engagement with the occupants of the white vehicle. By the time the lieutenant returned without the massacred bodies of the women and children, Corey's memories of the event were fuzzy and fading by the moment.

It was bad enough Marines had slaughtered innocent Afghanis. Corey's platoon commander had covered it up, letting five Marines get away with murder. Even as that thought settled over him, Corey realized that Lieutenant Adams had to cover up Nygaard's crime, because the investigation would probably uncover his own.

"He hid what Nygaard did 'cause he had to hide his own crime," Corey said on a sob.

"Hey, Corey, it's all right. You're safe. You're with friends. It's all okay." A calm, soothing voice cut through the fog of Corey's rage and despair. "Are you back with us now?"

Blinking several times to clear away the fog and the disturbing images of the slaughtered families, Corey struggled to focus on the figure in front of him. Kellan Reynolds, dressed in shirtsleeves and neatly knotted tie, crouched several feet away. His expression was calm but obviously concerned.

"Yes, sir." Corey was surprised by the raw sound of his own voice. He glanced around, recognizing the now-familiar conference room. He caught sight of Jonah Carver, crouched farther away, near the door.

"Take your time, get your bearings," Kellan said quietly.

Corey slowly became aware that he himself was crouched on the floor, his back pressed to the wall behind him. Like Kellan, Corey was in his shirtsleeves. Unlike Kellan, Corey was a disgrace to the grooming standard. His cuffs were unbuttoned, his tie was pulled away from his collar and was twisted askew. His back ached from curling inward on himself, his palms pressed over his ears.

"I remembered," Corey choked out.

"Yes, it seems that way," Kellan said calmly. "Are you ready to come up off the floor, yet? Jonah can bring you a chair."

Corey managed not to flinch when Jonah quietly appeared beside him with a guest chair. Jonah set the chair down and slowly backed away across the room.

With a shaky hand, Corey gripped the chair's arm rest and tried to get to his feet.

"Can I help you, Corey?" Kellan asked, rising to his feet. He held his palms outward in supplication. "If I can touch you, I can help you into the chair."

Corey nodded his consent. Kellan slowly stepped forward and took Corey's arm, easily helping him into the chair. Immediately, Kellan stepped back and resumed his crouch.

"You need to hydrate, Staff Sergeant." Jonah's soft voice alerted Corey to his proximity.

Taking the open bottle of water, Corey's hand trembled so violently he couldn't drink.

"Let me help," Jonah said, his hands closing over both of Corey's around the bottle.

Corey drank gratefully, not stopping until half the contents were gone. He managed to finish off the water without assistance. Jonah took the bottle and stepped away.

"I'm sorry," Corey said, clearing his throat awkwardly. He straightened his tie, then saw that his shirt tails were un-tucked so he shoved them into the waist of his uniform trousers.

"What are you sorry for?" Kellan asked. He was slowly moving a chair so he could sit while he talked.

Corey gave a self-deprecating snort. "I obviously lost my shit. Sir." He struggled and failed to fasten the cuffs of his shirt.

"Actually, I'd say you just got your shit back." Kellan gestured toward Corey's hands. "I can help you with that if you like."

Corey heaved a frustrated sigh. Kellan and Jonah both had seen him out of his fucking mind. There was no point pretending he didn't need help. Corey nodded and Kellan carefully moved his chair closer. He had Corey's cuffs fastened in seconds.

Murmuring his thanks, Corey shifted in his chair. He grimaced at the feel of his dress shirt clinging to his skin. He tried to straighten the fabric but it peeled away from his chest and back. At some point, he'd sweated through his shirt. Lifting his arms, Corey saw dark stains.

A square of white cloth appeared in his line of sight. Kellan was handing him a neatly folded handkerchief. Corey took it with grateful thanks. He blotted his sweat covered face and neck, saturating the fabric. What the fuck had he done when his memory had returned with such force?

"Where is everyone?" he asked, noting that only Kellan and Jonah were in the room with him.

"They're waiting in my office for us to give the all clear," Kellan answered.

Corey scraped his thumbnail over the embroidered monogram on a corner of the handkerchief. *JC* in a thick, bold font. "Did I hurt someone?" It hurt to ask that question.

"No. Why would you think that?" Kellan replied. His tone sounded genuinely puzzled.

"The two of you are walking on eggshells around me and everyone else is hiding out in your office." Was it strange that Corey wondered why Kellan was carrying a handkerchief bearing Jonah's monogram?

"No one's afraid of you, Corey. We're concerned." Kellan gestured between himself and Jonah. "We're here because none of the others have seen combat. They can only guess at the things we've seen and done, and how it all makes us feel."

Jonah dragged a chair closer and sat down. Corey noticed he had been careful not to get between Corey and the open door. He wanted to ask what he'd said and done when during his flashback, but he feared the answer. Corey continued to thumb Jonah's initials.

"When DADT was repealed, we stopped worrying about keeping the small things separate," Kellan said.

Corey looked up in confusion.

Kellan gestured at the handkerchief in Corey's hands. "It stopped mattering if Jonah showed up with something bearing my initials, and eventually a lot of things just ended up mixed together."

Corey wondered what it might be like to have Sean's possessions mixed in with his own. The idea sent warmth spreading through his chest. Thinking of Sean made Corey ashamed that he was avoiding the truth.

"So, what did I say and do during the flashback?" Corey blurted.

"Well…" Kellan spoke slowly, ask if carefully selecting his words. "You knocked over your chair standing up, which is what alerted Jonah and me to the fact something was going on. After that, you didn't do much more than put your back to the wall and crouch down. As for what you said…well…what is it you remembered?"

Corey took a ragged breath and clutched the handkerchief in his fist. He tried to speak but his mouth had turned dry as dust. "I need some more water." Before Corey could stand, Jonah was out of his own chair and across the room. Jonah handed him an open bottle. Corey took it gratefully. "Thank you, Jonah."

Jonah's hand rested briefly on Corey's shoulder, giving it a squeeze before he returned to his chair. As Corey drank, he remembered when even the most casual touch from Jonah made his heart race. This time was different. Now, all Corey felt was what Jonah had intended; comfort, reassurance and support.

He forced himself to meet Kellan's eyes. To his relief, Corey didn't see the expected pity. Instead, Kellan's expression was intense and interested, possibly even eager.

"When Nygaard didn't report in that the perimeter was secure and I couldn't raise him on comms, I went looking for him." Corey swallowed hard. "I went alone, Kellan. I deviated from the SOP and didn't take another Marine, almost like I knew I was going to find something bad and didn't want anyone else to have to deal with it."

"I doubt that's the case, Corey." Kellan shook his head and frowned. "You were only expecting to step a few feet away from the structure in order to locate one of your Marines. That's not a blatant deviation from standard operating procedure."

Corey dragged the back of one hand across his forehead. "I guess it doesn't matter now. I saw two of my men exit a structure directly behind the one we had secured. Their behavior was suspicious so I entered the residence." He exhaled a shaky breath. "Kellan, they put the women and children on their knees, circled up in family groups. They made them all watch as they slit their throats, one by one." Corey nearly sobbed the last word, but as soon as he said it out loud, his entire body felt lighter.

Kellan sat back in his chair and ran one hand over his mouth and chin. His features hardened and Corey realized he was angry. Surprisingly, Corey didn't think Kellan was mad at him.

"What reasons did they give for their actions?" Kellan asked tightly. Corey suspected he already knew the answer and was just waiting for confirmation.

"Nygaard claimed they were trying to force them to give

up the locations of weapons caches and plans for additional ambushes," Corey answered, breathing easier than he had since he'd returned from Afghanistan. "It was bullshit. All of it," he continued bitterly. "They enjoyed scaring and torturing those poor people. They did it for fun."

Kellan nodded and sat forward again. "You reported all of this to Lieutenant Adams, correct?"

"Yes, sir." Corey paused as the implication of that question sank in. "The lieutenant covered up what Nygaard and his team did because he had to hide his own crime. An inquiry into one incident might have uncovered the other."

"The evidence supports that supposition, yes," Kellan said as he stood. "It doesn't stop with the lieutenant, though. We need to record a brief statement from you, while your recall is fresh. We'll save the deposition for another day."

"Yes, sir." Corey finished his water as Kellan left the conference room. He looked over at Jonah and found him lost in thought. "Can I ask you something, Jonah?"

Jonah met Corey's eyes easily. "Of course."

"Does my old platoon believe I helped cover up what Nygaard did?" Corey thought Tyler would have told him if that was the case, but he needed to hear it from Jonah.

"From what we've gathered from search warrants and wire taps, no one involved in the white car incident thinks you know anything at all," Jonah replied. He stood and began to pace. "The only people who know about the incident inside the structure are the five who were involved, Lieutenant Adams, and Battalion command."

"Command?" Corey asked, incredulous.

"They assisted the lieutenant in his cover up, which is why no one made sure you received counseling for a traumatic experience." Jonah's reply was harsh. "Nygaard and his team mistakenly believe Adams ordered you to keep silent, and then you were bribed into silence with a promotion and transfer to BRC."

"Fuck!" Corey snapped. He'd earned his promotion and transfer. If telling the truth about Nygaard meant he had to give them both up, he would, without a second thought.

Jonah made a dismissive gesture. "No one cares what those assholes think. They're going to do time and be dishonorably discharged. Everyone else involved knows you suffered memory loss. They just don't know that command is using your memory loss to hide criminal behavior."

Before Corey could respond, Kellan returned with the rest of the investigative team. Corey stood and finished straightening his uniform. He was going to give his statement and call Sean. Now that he had his memory back, all Corey wanted to do was forget.

CHAPTER EIGHTEEN

When Captain Hirata declared Corey's statement complete, Agent Hoffman shut off the video camera. Corey's limbs felt leaden when he stood and started to pull on his uniform coat. He was exhausted. He wanted out of this building so he could call Sean.

"What's the name of the counselor you're seeing?"

Corey glanced up in surprise to find Jonah standing beside him, pen and notepad in hand. "Why?" he demanded suspiciously.

"Unlike the way you were treated after your previous traumatic experience, *I* am going to ensure you receive the assistance you require," Jonah replied with complete aplomb.

Corey shook his head emphatically. "I'm fine—"

"Oh, I'm sorry. Did you think this was optional?" Jonah asked dryly.

Corey nearly laughed before he realized Jonah was serious. "You're pulling rank? Are you kidding me?"

"Your emotional health is important to the investigation," replied Jonah. "I'm not taking any chances."

Corey should have known. He fastened the belt of his coat and tugged his cuffs straight. "All I need are my meds and some sleep. I'll be fine."

Kellan's soothing voice broke in. "What Jonah doesn't seem capable of communicating is, if you'd watched one of us go through what we just watched you endure, you'd be reacting just like he is."

Corey hadn't considered that. "Dr. Ingram." He watched as Jonah scrawled the name. "I have an appointment the day after tomorrow."

Jonah didn't reply, he just crossed to telephone on the table against the wall. "Yes, ma'am, can you connect me to the base medical clinic? Thank you, ma'am."

"What's he doing?" Corey asked Kellan in alarm.

"Making sure you're okay," Kellan replied simply.

Jonah asked to be connected to Doctor Ingram's office. He identified himself and asked to speak to the doctor regarding an emergency involving one of her patients. Corey could tell when Doctor Ingram began speaking to Jonah. "Good afternoon, ma'am. My name is First Sergeant Jonah Carver. I'm the Senior Enlisted Advisor for the Deputy Under Secretary of Defense for Strategy, Plans and Force Development…I need to speak with you regarding your patient, Staff Sergeant Corey Yarwood… I'm aware of that ma'am, I have no interest in obtaining any confidential information. I have information to provide to you… your patient suffered a severe flashback less than thirty minutes ago. He's recovered all of his missing memories. It's important that he meet with you as soon as possible, Doctor Ingram."

Kellan snorted and shook his head at Jonah's calm dialogue. "He even has to turn calling a doctor into a sit-rep."

Corey recalled Sean's annoyance with him for making the simplest things difficult. Maybe he'd begun to emulate Jonah more than he'd realized.

"Of course I won't allow him to drive himself…thirty minutes is acceptable…thank you, Doctor." Jonah hung up the handset. "Do you have your prescriptions with you?" he asked Corey as he turned.

"In my Jeep, Top," Corey said with resignation.

"Do you want to drive him in his Jeep and I'll follow?" Kellan asked.

Jonah nodded and gestured for Corey to precede them out of the conference room.

Corey always felt awkward when he sat in the passenger seat of his own Jeep. He knew it was futile to argue with Jonah so he just took the Xanax tablet. He rubbed his fingers over his forehead, wishing this day was over. Exhaustion was threatening to overwhelm him.

"Are you still seeing your new friend?" Jonah asked suddenly.

"Yeah." It felt good to tell Jonah the truth.

"Is he available for you to stay with tonight?" Jonah kept his eyes on the road.

Corey sighed. "He usually is. I was about to call him when you insisted on dragging me to my counselor," he said dubiously.

"Humor me, Corey," Jonah said quietly. "If you really are fine, this should be a quick conversation."

"Yeah, yeah." Corey turned to regard Jonah with narrowed eyes. "Let me ask you this, though; if you were in my place, would you rather be with your counselor? Or with Kellan?"

"Oh, I assure you, I'd be wanting to crawl naked into Kellan's arms and absolutely lose myself in him," Jonah said, one corner of his mouth lifting in humor. "I understand that desire. But Kellan would be the first one to tell me that that would be avoidance, not coping."

"Do you ever get tired of Kellan being so fucking smart?" It was the closest Corey could come to admitting Jonah was right.

Jonah chuckled. "I'm too busy being turned on by it."

Doctor Ingram was waiting for them, the inner door to her office standing open. As soon as they walked into reception, she came out to greet Corey.

"Well, you don't look any worse for wear," she said softly, giving Corey a smile.

Inside her office, Corey began to remove his uniform coat. Doctor Ingram surprised him by offering a wooden coat hanger. "Thank you, ma'am," Corey said, neatly hanging the olive-drab garment from the coat rack.

"You're welcome, Corey," she said brightly. "Those uniforms are entirely too nice for them to get rumpled." She paused and looked at him askance. "Has Sean seen you in that uniform yet?"

"No, ma'am," Corey answered as he sat on the love seat and

picked up the throw pillow. "Not yet."

"You should wear it for him. I'm sure he'd very much like to see you in it." Ingram didn't even try to suppress her smile.

Corey huffed an embarrassed laugh. His face warmed when he imagined Sean's appreciative reaction to seeing him in his uniform. At least that's how he hoped Sean would react.

"So, tell me about the circumstances leading up to this flashback," the doctor said. "And then I want to discuss the memories you recovered."

§ § §

When Corey and Doctor Ingram stepped out into reception, Jonah and Kellan both stood. They looked expectantly from Corey to the doctor.

"Everything is fine, gentlemen," Doctor Ingram said. "Thank you for thinking to bring Corey to see me. Now, he shouldn't be alone tonight. He's going to call a friend he thinks he can stay with. Can I trust one or both of you to look after him if his friend can't?"

Jonah held up Corey's cell phone. "Sean has already been made aware of today's events and he's waiting for Corey to arrive. Kellan also placed a call to Master Sergeant Whitfield."

"How the hell…" Corey broke off when he remembered Jonah relieving him of his cell phone as they entered Doctor Ingram's office.

"I didn't think Sean would have a problem looking after him," the doctor said with a smile. "Take the sleep aid, Corey," she admonished a final time. "That's what I prescribed them for."

"Yes, ma'am," Corey said docilely, knowing Sean would demand the same thing.

They left the clinic and Kellan followed as Jonah drove Corey's Jeep to the BEQ. Kellan waited in his car while Jonah helped Corey pack an overnight bag. He tossed his dopp kit and a uniform into his ruck and was ready to go.

"So, when are you going to move into a big boy house?"

Jonah asked dryly.

Corey chuckled as he zipped his ruck. "I had all I could deal with when I got back this last time." He locked the door to his room and followed Jonah to the elevator. "Lately, though, I been thinking it's time to grow up."

"Thinking about setting up house with Sean?" Jonah teased.

"No," Corey answered a little too quickly. "Well, I sometimes think about what it might be like but no, it's too early for that."

"Is it?" Jonah lifted a single eyebrow.

"I don't even know if this is going anywhere," Corey said as Jonah waved at Kellan and they climbed into the Jeep.

"Well, when I meet him, I'll have to ask him what his intentions are toward you," Jonah said casually.

"Don't you fucking dare, Jonah," Corey snapped. "You'll scare him off."

"And what if he can't be scared off?" Jonah asked.

Corey admitted to himself for the first time that he hoped Sean couldn't be scared off. He just wasn't ready yet to find out. To change the subject, Corey asked, "Now that I remember what happened, what's next with the investigation?"

"I don't know, that's Kellan's department," replied Jonah. "And you can afford to take an evening off from worrying about it."

Exhaustion swamped Corey with a startling suddenness. He didn't want to talk anymore. He just wanted to crawl into bed and curl up around Sean. He somehow managed to guide Jonah to the guest parking in front of Sean's condo.

Jonah helped Corey slowly climb the steps to Sean's front door while Kellan shouldered Corey's ruck. It seemed like only seconds after Kellan rang the bell that Sean abruptly opened the door. As soon as their eyes met, Corey breathed a little easier.

"Sorry to impose," Corey said as he crossed the threshold.

Sean wore a look of exasperation. "Shut up and get inside."

The hand that squeezed Corey's took the sting from Sean's words.

Corey headed for the sanctuary of the living room. He perched on the arm of the sofa as Sean asked Kellan and Jonah in.

"Kellan Reynolds." Kellan extended his hand as he stepped past Sean into the narrow foyer.

"Sean Chandler."

Jonah stepped into the condo as if he was surveying his own domain. He loomed over Sean as he extended his hand. "First Sergeant Jonah Carver."

Sean didn't flinch and he didn't back down, despite the several inches of height Jonah had on him. Sean was broader in the shoulders, though. He was thicker in the chest. Corey smiled to himself when he realized the two men were trying to stare one another down. He wasn't surprised to find he couldn't look away from Sean. For the first time since he'd met him, it was as if Jonah didn't exist for Corey.

"So you're Jonah Carver," Sean said tightly.

"I most definitely am." Jonah turned away and met Corey's eyes, one corner of his mouth lifted in humor. He was apparently amused that Corey had mentioned him.

"Jonah, behave," Kellan said quietly as he set down Corey's ruck.

"I am behaving," Jonah replied as he slowly walked the perimeter of Sean's home. "But I'm also not leaving a friend to be looked after by someone squirrely I can't trust."

Corey frowned at Jonah, surprised to be referred to as a friend and not just a witness in his boss' investigation.

Sean came to stand beside Corey, pressing a possessive hand to Corey's back. "You're concerned about your *friend* now? Where have you been these past weeks when I've taken his three a.m. phone calls when he's had a nightmare? Where were you when I was talking him down from anxiety attacks? Have you been making sure he sees his counselor and takes his meds? No, you haven't."

Jonah drew breath to respond but Kellan stopped him. "Jonah, you don't need to take your dick out and piss all over everything. It's Corey's choice to be here, you'll respect it."

"Yes, sir," Jonah muttered, turning to glance into Sean's bedroom.

"You might want to be aware that Jonah is very protective of Corey," Kellan told Sean with an amused shake of his head. "It's not like Corey has needed much protecting since about the time he made corporal, but that's Jonah for you."

It was after Corey had made corporal that he'd cleaned up his act. He'd always thought Jonah's assistance had been offered out of a sense of duty, not friendship or personal concern.

"It's good to know Corey has such loyal friends." Sean gripped the back of Corey's neck briefly before running his palm up the short bristles of his hair. "I'm just glad this is where he wanted to be tonight." Sean's tone was gentle and filled with affection.

Corey turned to look at Sean, surprised by what he heard. Sean's hazel eyes were soft and filled with a warm light. Corey's chest tightened, his own feelings mirrored in Sean's expression.

"I can see that," Kellan replied. He squeezed Corey's arm reassuringly. "We'll talk tomorrow. You take care of yourself and get some sleep." Turning toward the door, Kellan called over his shoulder, "Quit snooping, Jonah, we're leaving."

"I am *not* snooping," Jonah said indignantly. "I do not snoop. I'm performing recon."

"It was good to meet you, Sean," Kellan said as he opened the door. "I look forward to seeing you again under less stressful circumstances."

Jonah stopped several inches from Sean, who turned to face him fully.

Before Jonah could speak, Sean lifted a hand, palm out. "Whatever threat you're about to make, save your breath. His smile has more power than your tough guy act."

Corey's jaw fell open. He knew he should say something but no words came to mind.

Jonah grinned. "That might explain why he's been smiling a little more lately." He extended his hand to Sean. "It was a pleasure to meet you, Sean."

"And you, Jonah. Thank you for taking care of him until I could take over." Sean shook Jonah's hand.

Corey called his thanks and his goodbyes as Sean closed the door after them. He leaned back against it and regarded Corey.

"So *that* was Jonah Carver?" Sean asked.

Corey relaxed when he saw Sean's smile. "I told you."

Pushing off the door, Sean slowly walked toward him. "You look tired. Are you hungry? Can I ask what happened today? Or is it too soon?"

Corey reached out and pulled Sean to stand between his legs. Sean came easily, almost eagerly. Corey wrapped his arms around Sean's chest and pulled him close. Sean's arms went around Corey's shoulders and gripped him firmly. Corey pressed his face into the crook of Sean's neck and released a shaky breath.

"I've wanted to do this all afternoon," he murmured into Sean's warm, fragrant skin.

"With me?"

Corey tensed, even though he could hear the teasing in Sean's voice. He tightened his arms. "Don't. Not tonight."

"Okay," Sean said quickly. His hands moved up to cradle Corey's head.

Corey followed Sean's urging and leaned back slightly. Sean placed light kisses in a path from Corey's temple to his lips. Corey gripped Sean's chin and held him steady, placing a soft kiss on the tip of his ski-jump nose.

"As hot as you look in your uniform—and you do look hot—it can't be comfortable. Why don't you go change and I'll figure out something for dinner?" Sean pressed their foreheads together as he spoke.

Corey chuckled. "My counselor said you'd like my uniform."

"Someday, when it's more appropriate, I'd like to slowly get you out of your uniform."

"You got it." Core pressed a final kiss to Sean's full lips.

Sean started to assemble a simple dinner while Corey changed his clothes. He retrieved the track pants and tank top he'd begun leaving in the corner of a drawer in Sean's bureau. He hung his uniform at one end of Sean's closet, on the hangers that were always left empty just for him. Sean had volunteered the space without Corey having to ask or suggest. That meant something, didn't it?

Walking into the kitchen, Corey watched Sean for several moments. He moved gracefully, his back to Corey as he assembled a quick but substantial meal. Corey's heart swelled in his chest, thumping painfully against his ribs. Corey reflexively dragged in a ragged breath as he admired Sean's broad, muscled shoulders. His firm, rounded ass filled out his well-worn jeans. But that wasn't what made Corey's chest hurt, and it scared him shitless.

"Can I help with anything?" he asked, pressing himself lightly to Sean's back and resting his hands on Sean's hips.

"Nah, I got it, thanks." Sean tilted his head to give Corey access to the side of his neck.

Corey took advantage of the offer and pressed a gentle kiss to Sean's warm skin. "You know, I *do* know how to cook."

"I'm not surprised," Sean replied casually, almost distracted. "You're good at a lot of things."

"I can't say I'm good but I'm competent," Corey clarified. "I'm out of practice, though. I haven't had a kitchen of my own since I left for Afghanistan."

"You're free to cook here if you want." Sean's offer was given without restriction or a second thought.

"I should probably start doing that, at least until I get my own place." This was the first time Corey gave voice to the thought he'd been having more and more frequently. "You don't need to be taking care of me all the time."

Sean turned to look at him with a puzzled expression. "Is that what you think?"

Corey pulled back. "Well, we did meet during a pretty messed up time in my life."

Sean made a face as he turned back to the meal. "Which you are rapidly putting behind you. Can you get some drinks out of fridge?"

The request prevented Corey from arguing. He wondered if it had been intentional.

Sitting at the counter of Sean's kitchen, they made small talk as they ate the meal Sean had thrown together. Corey complimented him but Sean waved it off. He seemed so cheerful, so happy just to have Corey there, despite the imposition.

Setting down his fork, Corey finally asked, "Why do you keep taking care of me? Isn't it getting a little old yet?"

Sean looked stunned. "I don't think I understand."

Corey sighed. "My nightmares, the anxiety attacks, my trouble sleeping, all the times I've come here after some shit has happened to me. You cook for me, I've started leaving clothes here. What do you get out of knowing me? So far, I haven't been anything but a needy little whiner."

"Is that how you think I see you?" Sean laughed incredulously. "Jesus Christ, where do I start? You are the least needy man I have ever met in my life."

"You don't have to placate me," Corey said impatiently.

"For such a supremely confident Marine, you are a bafflingly insecure man!" Sean lifted his hands in frustration. "All the times I've had to go out of town for auditions or meetings, you've been disappointed enough to make me feel wanted, but you never pressured me not to go or to come back before I was finished."

"Of course not." Corey would never consider doing anything like that. "You've never bitched and moaned about me having duty or night trainings. You know it's my job."

"Exactly." Sean sat back and regarded Corey for several moments. "In all the time we've known each other, you have never asked me what my back up plan is, in case I can't make it as an actor. You've never told me I should get a real job with regular hours so I'd be more available to spend time with you."

Corey frowned. The words of his own parents echoed in his head, asking him when he would have this Marine thing out of his system so he could come home and get a real job.

"You like being an actor and you're good at it. Why would I expect you to do anything else?" He gestured around Sean's modest but clean and comfortable home. "And you make a decent living at it, obviously. I'll deal with your sometimes shitty hours if you'll deal with mine." He swallowed hard when he realized he was talking about the future, as if he and Sean had one together.

"It'll suck from time to time, but we'll make do."

Corey and Sean both laughed, mutually realizing Sean had used one of Corey's common phrases. Corey's chest eased and a wave of euphoria swept through him.

Sean sobered slightly. "Remember the night I told you that one of the things I like most about you is that you talk to me like I'm just another guy? That you don't obsess over my looks and don't always want to go out so you can be seen with me?"

Corey searched his memory. The words sounded familiar but he couldn't place when or where he'd heard Sean speak them. He shook his head. "No, I don't remember that. I just remember the night you were teasing me and saying I'm hot enough to make gorgeous guys notice me."

Corey froze in surprise when Sean's hands gripped his face and forced him to meet Sean's eyes.

"Why do you doubt yourself, Staff Sergeant?" Sean demanded. "Where's that sexy confidence you have about everything else? Where's that…what do you call it? PMA. Where's that positive mental attitude you have somehow managed to hang on to through all this shit other people have been causing you?"

Corey grasped Sean's wrists. "I can *do* something about the shit that's been going on. I can take action, make decisions. I can't *make* you like me or want to be with me."

A blinding smile split Sean's face. "You don't even try and I think that's why I do so much."

Corey's mouth fell open and words escaped him completely. His pulse thundered in his ears so loudly, he almost couldn't hear anything else. Suddenly, he knew just what to say. "Me, too," he rasped.

Sean burst out laughing, his entire face lighting up with delight. Then he kissed Corey. "Good," he whispered against Corey's lips, "good."

"So," Corey said shakily, clearing his throat, "we're officially in a relationship now?"

"Yeah, we are," Sean replied firmly. "I'm going to start referring to you as my boyfriend. And I'm monogamous." His last statement was almost a challenge.

"Good." Possessiveness unfurled inside of Corey like a living thing. "I don't want to have to kill other men for touching you. Except when you're working, of course."

"I'm not going to have to kill any other men, am I?" Sean asked, humor only thinly veiling his worry.

Corey shook his head emphatically. "No. I'm too lucky to have you. I'm not going to intentionally fuck it up."

Sean nodded. He closed his eyes when he pressed a gentle kiss to Corey lips. Corey suspected he saw tears just before Sean's lids settles over his hazel yes. It was miraculous that he could elicit such a reaction from a man like Sean. Corey was going to do his very best not to fuck this up.

CHAPTER NINETEEN

It was a cold day in Coronado, but then, most days were cold in Coronado, at least until the middle of a summer day. The south-facing beach of the submarine base, where both Marine Recon and Navy SEALs conducted their training and drills, was carved out of one of the most costly pieces of real estate on the western coast of North America. Its subtle beauty belied the treacherousness of its waters and the hell that cold water and rough surf could be.

The Marines were dressed in their utility uniforms and full deuce gear, right down to their LPCs. They were going to swim the surf in their full gear. Those who survived today would get to navigate a Zodiac through the ocean and surf tomorrow. They would just have to do it without an engine.

Corey had hated the cold and the exhaustion of this part of training when he'd gone through BRC, but it hadn't been particularly difficult for him. He was a strong swimmer and not afraid of the water. Corey's greatest challenge had been being stuck with a team that had struggled to perform. Some had lost their PMA and others struggled to just hack it at all.

"How you feeling this morning, Staff Sergeant?" Whitfield asked him suddenly.

"Fan-fucking-tastic, Master Sergeant," Corey replied eagerly. He hadn't felt this good since before Afghanistan. He was sleeping well, he and Sean were taking turns cooking so he was eating well, an end to the legal issues hanging over head was in view, and he was getting laid on a regular basis. "I've had my coffee and I'm good to go."

"Ooh-rah! Glad to hear it, Yarwood. I want you to take lead in this next series of training exercises." Whitfield wasn't wearing his Oakleys and Corey could see his eyes. He was completely fucking serious.

"I don't understand, Master Sergeant," Corey replied, heart

pounding in excitement as well as anxiety.

"Yes you do," Whitfield countered. "I want you taking over lead instructor responsibilities for the ocean Zodiac training."

"Roger that, Master Sergeant. I'm just not clear why the most junior instructor is being given this task." Corey knew he could do this and he wanted to prove it.

"I read your fit-rep from this set of exercises when you went through BRC," said Whitfield. He angled his body slightly so he could watch the class beginning to assemble in the soft sand just beyond the edge of the surf. "The way you rallied your team and motivated them to successfully complete the training was impressive. Your natural leadership ability was obvious and I want you to continue to develop that."

"Yes, Master Sergeant." Corey was determined to succeed at this mission. He knew what Whitfield was doing. "I'm honored." If Corey didn't fuck up, when his shot came to be promoted to Gunny, he'd probably make it.

He took the clipboard with the roster of Marines who remained in the class and held a quick briefing with his fellow instructors. Now came the cold, messy part.

Corey explained the point of this segment of training and what was expected from the Marines, for them to make it through successfully. Next, he ordered them into the surf for a short swim around a buoy. As each Marine came stumbling out of the rough water, Corey checked him off his list. If he didn't lay eyes on each student himself, rescue swimmers would be dispatched.

As each man hit the beach, chest heaving with exertion, Corey ordered him to roll in soft sand. It was natural camouflage. Recon Marines were stealthy motherfuckers. A mission was only considered successful if the objective was reached and the team remained undetected. Covering themselves in sand was a quick and easy way to blend in.

He sent the class back into the water. Recon Marines had to be able to stay alive in less than optimal circumstances, if a mission went tits up. Corey knew about missions that had ended with Marines having to swim into the open ocean and await extraction.

He watched the men drag themselves out of the surf. His fellow instructors gave words of encouragement and congratulations. Some gave out words of advice on how to make the task a little easier. Corey made a note of the Marines who encouraged fellow classmates or leant assistance when someone stumbled or struggled. He already suspected he knew who wasn't going to make it past this point.

As dark settled over them, Corey called an end to the day. They piled into the transport vans for the hour-long drive back to Oceanside. As they crossed the Coronado Bay Bridge back onto the main land, Corey's cell phone vibrated.

He expected it to be Sean but was surprised to see Jonah's name on the display.

"Yo, Top," Corey greeted.

"This is your heads up," Jonah said without preamble. "Kellan's report went to D.C. today. Hirata will make his arrests tomorrow. Kellan has given the Corps a chance to get in front of this and hold their own press conference, otherwise he'll do it himself on behalf of the DOD."

Corey's blood turned icy in his veins. "What does that mean for me, Jonah?"

"In the immediate future, be on the lookout for the press and direct them all to the J.A.S." Jonah answered. "You'll probably have to testify at the court martials."

"Everyone's been hinting it went pretty high up. You actually found enough proof to convene court martials?" Corey asked. Kellan was thorough and cautious. If action was being taken, he knew Kellan had the goods.

"Agent Hoffman is a scary fucking interrogator when he gets going." Jonah's tone held grudging respect. "Did you know he was an *Intelligence Analyst* for the Marine Corps?" Corey heard the implied air quotes. "I think that's just a cover 'cause the guy turned down a field agent position with the CIA to work for

NCIS. Anyway, Lieutenant Adams cried like a bitch."

"Is he getting off easy because of that?" Corey's stomach turned at the thought. Adams was the asshole who started this whole goat rodeo.

"Are you fucking kidding me? This is military justice, not civilian," replied Jonah smugly.

Corey chuckled in relief. "Does Hirata know anything about what's gonna happen with that civilian case?" He was careful of the curious ears he knew were listening in, even as they pretended not to.

"He's pretty sure this absolutely negates any use they may have for you as a witness," Jonah assured him. "But if not, he'll have your back all the way."

"Good," Corey sighed. "Thank him for me."

"That brings me to the second reason I called," Jonah said. "Kellan's report contains details that affect national security, so it won't be released publicly."

"Understood."

"If you want to come by the offices this evening, Kellan will let you read a hard copy. You have to leave it with us, but at least you'll know exactly what happened and who did what to whom."

Corey exhaled harshly. He was so close to putting all this shit behind him, did he really want to read all the gory details? When he considered all the rumor and speculation that he'd probably be faced with, Corey decided he wanted to know the truth. "Yeah. We're RTB now. I'll head over as soon as we're dismissed."

Corey ended the call and stared blindly out the van window. A heavy hand on his shoulder startled him. He glanced over to find the master sergeant watching him.

"Be proud of how you've conducted yourself, as a man and a Marine, in these last couple months," Whitfield said with a sharp nod.

The unexpected praise knocked Corey off balance. "Thank you, Master Sergeant."

Whitfield turned to look out the windscreen and Corey breathed a sigh of relief. He looked back over how things had changed since the first day of BRC and realized he *had* managed to get his shit together. He owed Sean a lot for his support and affection, but Corey had done the work and faced his demons.

When it had mattered most, Corey had been the man and the Marine he'd always wanted to be.

§ § §

Corey stared blindly at Kellan's bold, swirling signature on the final page of the summary of his investigation into the events of Ghazni, Afghanistan. Captains Hirata and Evans had also signed, as well as Agent Chris Hoffman. They all certified the information contained in the two-inch thick report had been obtained through their own efforts and was truthful to the best of their individual and collective knowledge.

With a heavy sigh, Corey closed the front cover of the folder and sat back in his chair.

Jonah looked up from the laptop he was working on. "Everything okay?"

Corey knew what Jonah was really asking. "Yeah. Everything is okay," he replied with conviction. And it was.

He was going to sit here and talk to Jonah about this shit. He'd go to Sean's place and vent for a little while. Then he'd let it go and move on. He felt what Doctor Ingram called a *reasonable level of justifiable anger* and now he had a set of appropriate coping skills. Corey was fine and getting better every day.

"Do you have any questions?" Jonah closed the lid of his laptop.

Corey ran both hands over his face. He was so tired, but it was a physical tired. His fatigue was well earned from a day of hard work. He folded his arms over his chest and regarded Jonah. "Are the charges going to stick?"

"On the ones who count, yes," Jonah replied. "The lieutenant colonel's aide might not do prison time and may keep his commission. The platoon gunny will probably walk but the company gunny will most likely be dishonorably discharged."

"What's gonna happen to Nygaard and his team?"

"Nygaard will face court martial. We'll let the civilian system have him and if he survives it, we'll take him back to serve his military sentence." Jonah shrugged. "The other four are as guilty as he is. They knew what they were doing was wrong. They showed cognizance of guilt. Nygaard didn't have to threaten any of them to get them to go along. Each one of them knew that all he had to do was walk out a door and go to you. To a man, they knew you could, and would, stop Nygaard, but they wanted to go along."

Corey leaned forward in his chair. "So, while my team and I were securing the hostile structure, a group of Afghan merchants rolled up on the platoon."

"That's correct," Jonah replied with a nod.

"The Marines extracted them from the victor and secured them." Corey struggled to form his next words. It was like none of this was real if he never spoke about it out loud. "But the lieutenant was still jacked up from the IED blast and ordered the men executed."

Jonah sighed and frowned. "He and two others double tapped them in the back of the head. The idiot thing is, it probably could have been dealt with if Adams hadn't covered it up. That made a stress reaction into a criminal act."

"And the two Marines who also fired shots?" Corey's anger gave way to sadness and disappointment. Adams might bear the most responsibility, but enlisted Marines were still culpable.

"Not enough evidence, but their careers are as good as over."

Corey stood and crossed to Jonah, handing him the file folder. "Fuckers took nearly a year of my life with their lying shit."

"Don't let them have any more," Jonah said fiercely as he slid the folder into a safe behind the desk.

"I'm not." Corey headed for the office door. "That's time and energy better spent on Sean."

"Good to see you've got your priorities straight once again," Jonah said with a grin. "I'm sure I don't have to tell you to have a good night."

CHAPTER TWENTY

Sean was about to empty his pockets and step through the metal detector at the Vista Court House. The deputies took one look at Corey in his olive green service uniform, barracks cover tucked under his arm, and pulled them both out of line. It took only seconds to pass the wand over each of them, determine they were unarmed, and send them on their way with reverently murmured thanks to Corey for his service.

He grinned at Sean as they crossed through a bustling line of foot traffic to where Captain Hirata stood waiting for them. Sean was dressed in a navy pinstripe suit, white dress shirt, and a navy tie accented with pale blue fleur de lis. He was a stunning sight and the heads of both men and women turned as they passed by.

"I see you made it, Staff Sergeant," Hirata said in greeting.

"Yes, sir," he replied with a smile. "Captain Hirata, may I present Sean Chandler. Sean, this is J.A.S. attorney Captain Mirai Hirata."

The two shook hands and exchanged the common instructions to use first names.

Corey had expected to be nervous this morning. To his surprise, he wasn't. Nygaard was evil, and Corey was on the side of the angels, and he realized he was ready for this.

"They've set aside a room for us to wait," Hirata said, leading them down the corridor. "There is no telling how long we'll be here. When they said you'd be first up this morning to testify, it was only an estimate."

"Yes, sir, I'm aware," Corey replied, setting his cover on the long table and moving to look out the wide windows. "That's why Sean's here; to keep me from getting too bored and getting myself into trouble."

"Nothing more dangerous than a bored Marine with time on his hands, is there?" Hirata chuckled.

Corey smiled. "That's no joke, sir."

They settled down around the table, resigned to wait until Corey was called to testify. He was a prosecution witness now. All the incidents he'd had to deal with involving Nygaard's fighting while in theater, the events in Ghazni, and Corey's visit to Vista Detention the night Nygaard was arrested, would be brought out.

The fallout from Kellan's report had been fierce, but the Corps had gotten ahead of it, held its own press conferences, and let military justice run its course. Several men were doing time in the Camp Pendleton Brig. A couple of them were serving their sentences in Leavenworth. Right up until the moment all of the officers were actually sentenced to prison time, Corey had been sure the enlisted Marines were going to be scapegoats.

Hirata worked on his laptop and spent a lot of time on his cell phone. Corey checked email and made a few phone calls. He read the news on his phone but he paid more attention to what Sean was up to. Sean trolled his own Facebook page, checking to see what his administrator was posting and reading some of the comments. He shared several of them with Corey and they laughed good naturedly at some of Sean's more ardent fans, male and female.

Corey was surprised when Sean consulted him regarding parts he should take and gigs he should play. Each time Sean accepted work, he'd reply to the deal memo and discuss the expected contracts with his agent. It was an entirely different world from what Corey knew and he found it fascinating. He liked that Sean wanted his input. Not that Sean always did what Corey wanted, but they at least discussed it.

Before Corey could broach the subject of his own professional opportunity, a deputy entered the room to offer them food or drink. Sean needed the men's room so the deputy escorted him down the hall.

Captain Hirata sighed, closed his laptop and sat back in his chair. "I got an email from Kellan," he said.

"And how are Mr. Reynolds and Top Carver?" Corey asked.

"Causing trouble as usual," Hirata replied. "He's pushing hard for more recognition of PTS, easier access to services, and a little more care in the number of times they rotate you guys through deployment."

"That sounds like Kellan," Core said with a snort.

"He said to give you a message. 'Give 'em hell, Devil Dog'." Hirata grinned.

With a smile, Corey said, "*That* sounds more like Jonah than Kellan."

Hirata nodded. "I think the words *are* Jonah's, but Kellan echoes the sentiment. He asked if you're ready for Scout Sniper School?"

"I still can't believe I was accepted after everything that's gone on," admitted Corey.

"You passed the quals with flying colors and those of us who wrote letters on your behalf couldn't make it more clear just how rock-solid you are."

Corey's face warmed. "I appreciate that, sir. And yes, I'm ready."

Sean returned at that moment, forestalling further conversation. Hirata went back to his laptop.

By mid-afternoon, not even Sean could keep Corey from going stir crazy. He paced the room, aware he was beginning to get on Sean's and the captain's nerves.

"It won't be much longer, Corey," Hirata said soothingly. "If the current witness isn't going to finish in the next hour, they'll release you until tomorrow."

"I'm gonna hit the head." Corey opened the door and got the attention of a deputy. "The walk down the hall will kill some time," he said, just as he stepped into the corridor.

Sean quickly chased after him. "I'm coming with."

"You just went," Corey said incredulously.

"You're not the only one getting bored in that room."

"You're probably gonna have to do this all again tomorrow," the deputy said apologetically. "This late in the day, even if the current witness finishes, the judge will likely adjourn."

"I just wish she'd do it soon," Corey groused. "I've been in this damn suit all day."

"We should hear something soon." The deputy stopped outside the door to the men's room.

"I'll wait here," Sean said, leaning against the sill across from the deputy. "I don't think you need your hand held in the john."

Corey drew breath to quip about which body part he'd like to have held, then remembered just where they were. He huffed a laugh instead.

No sooner did the door close behind him than Nygaard stumbled out of the second stall. Corey tensed. A quick glance at the stall doors hanging partway open told him there was no deputy or lawyer to keep Nygaard in check. Planting his feet and squaring his shoulders, Corey prepared for the confrontation to turn physical.

Nygaard leaned heavily against the wall at his back. He laughed mirthlessly when his eyes managed to focus on Corey. Nygaard looked and acted drunk. He wore a civilian suit since he'd been convicted at his Court Martial, had been dishonorably discharged and sentenced to life in a military prison.

"Pull yourself together, Nygaard," Corey snapped. "You're a fucking disgrace. Your family is standing behind you, and this is how you act in the middle of your murder trial? You don't deserve their love and support."

It was a low blow but Corey was so fucking sick of this coward. He wondered if it was too much to hope that someone had realized Nygaard had stepped beyond the wire, and would show up right about now, looking for him.

"You're right, I don't," Nygaard slurred. "I'm all fucked up. The Marine Corps fucked me up and then they set me up to take the fall."

"I'm not gonna listen to your crap," growled Corey. "You were a pain in my ass before you saw combat. *You* fucked *me* up, but I didn't murder innocent women and children. You do realize how much of a coward that makes you, right?" he demanded. "In Afghanistan and back home, you get your jollies murdering women and children."

Nygaard looked unsteady on his feet. Despite leaning against a solid wall, he swayed slightly.

"It's so fuckin' easy for you," Nygaard muttered, barely intelligible. "Everything's so fuckin' easy for you." He abruptly slid down the wall, landing on his ass with a thump. "Didn't mean to hurt her. I loved her. She just made me so fuckin' *mad*."

As Nygaard slid down the wall, Corey darted forward. Nygaard was more than just drunk. "Sean! Sean!" Corey shouted as he eased Nygaard's limp body to lie supine on the cold, tile floor.

The deputy sheriff was the first to burst through the restroom door, Sean right on his six and struggling to get to Corey.

"Jesus Christ!" Sean blurted. "How the fuck did he get in here?"

"He was already in here when I came in," Corey replied as he loosened Nygaard's collar. He checked his pulse and respiration and found it wasn't good.

"Where the hell are his attorney and his escort?" the deputy demanded.

"No idea, he's the only one in here," Corey barked out. "Call an ambulance. His pulse is weak and he's barely breathing."

The deputy finally let Sean pass and began to speak into the mic clipped to his shoulder. The outer door opened again and Captain Hirata burst in.

"Corey, are you okay?" he demanded.

"I'm fine, sir," Corey answered as he searched Nygaard's pockets. He wasn't drunk. This was something else altogether.

Hirata took a knee on Nygaard's other side.

"I'll make sure everyone stays out until the FD arrives," the deputy announced and turned toward the door.

Sean stood in the center of the room looking stunned.

"He was in here when I came in," Corey told Hirata. "At first I thought he was drunk, but he looks like he's dying." Even as he spoke, Corey pulled multiple prescription bottles out of the inner pockets of Nygaard's suit jacket. The bottles were all empty. Corey read the labels. Valium, muscle relaxants, two different narcotic pain killers. "Oh shit, I think he OD'd."

Nygaard looked unnaturally still. His skin was pale and waxy, his lips beginning to take on a blue tint. Corey pressed two fingers to Nygaard's throat. Captain Hirata leaned over and used his cheek to test for breath at Nygaard's mouth and nose.

"I don't think he's breathing," Hirata declared.

"His heart stopped," Corey announced at the same time. "Nygaard! Michael! Can you hear me? Michael, wake up." Corey shook Nygaard violently by the shoulders and received no response. "Sergeant Nygaard, wake the fuck up!" He slapped Nygaard sharply on both cheeks several times. There was still no response.

With one hand on Nygaard's forehead and the other on his chin, Corey tilted Nygaard's head back and opened his mouth. Pinching Nygaard's nose closed, Corey covered his mouth with his own and blew hard, watching from the corner of one eye as Nygaard's chest rose. He blew several times, filling Nygaard's lungs.

As Corey breathed for Nygaard, Hirata opened Nygaard's jacket and stripped off his tie. Buttons clacked against the walls and floor when the captain tore open Nygaard's shirt. Rising up, Corey placed his fingers on Nygaard's sternum and felt for the end of his breastbone between his last ribs. Measuring upward with two parallel fingers, Corey covered the heel of one hand with the palm of the other and began compressions.

"One, two, three, four, five," he muttered quietly. On five, Hirata blew air into Nygaard's lungs. "One, two, three, four, five,"

Corey repeated and Hirata once against breathed for their victim.

"Call it when you're ready to switch," Hirata said quietly.

Corey acknowledged with a single nod as he rocked on his knees, elbows and shoulders locked, and compressed Nygaard's chest. He counted out his five compressions breathlessly. The heat of his body built up in his uniform and Corey started to sweat. He ignored it.

The deputy re-entered the restroom and spoke into his shoulder mic. "CPR is in progress," he said. "Vic has been down about ten minutes."

Corey forgot Sean was there until he felt someone kneel behind him. Confident fingers unfastened the belt of his uniform coat and pushed the buttons through their holes. This time when Corey reached his five-count, Sean tugged his uniform coat over his shoulders and down his arms. As Corey placed his hands back on Nygaard's chest, Sean pulled his tie from around his collar.

Immediately, Corey was cooler and it easier to move. He'd have to remember to thank Sean for his cleverness.

When Hirata completed his next rescue breath, Sean quickly helped him out of his uniform coat. They easily fell back into their rhythm. Corey couldn't help thinking this wasn't going to end well.

Long minutes later, Corey was fatigued. His arms and knees ached. He was flushed, sweat beading on his face and rolling freely down his temples and neck, into his uniform shirt.

"Switch," Corey gasped as he started his next set of five compressions.

Hirata completed the rescue breath and knelt up to shift positions. He measured the right spot on Nygaard's sternum and took over compressions. When he reached five, Corey inhaled and blew a rescue breath into Nygaard's lungs.

Chaos erupted as the restroom door burst open and paramedics dressed in blue BDUs entered, heavily laden with equipment.

They were taught not to stop CPR until they could hand off the victim to a doctor, but Corey and Hirata were exhausted and let the paramedics take over. When Nygaard's pulse didn't resume after they used the defibrillator, Corey was convinced this was the end.

Together, Sean and Hirata pushed and pulled Corey out of the men's room. He couldn't stop staring at Nygaard as the paramedics continued to work on him. Corey was fucking pissed. The coward Nygaard had found a way to avoid punishment for all of his crimes. Corey should have seen it coming.

The rest of the night passed in a blur. Sean helped Corey back into his uniform, hiding the sweat stains on his shirt. He felt disgusting and wanted a shower badly. The paramedics transported Nygaard to the hospital. Corey answered questions for the deputies. Hirata demanded to know how Nygaard had slipped his escort and his attorneys. He was outraged on Corey's behalf.

Sean never left Corey's side. He gave his own statement but he hadn't seen much. He simply stood beside Corey, quietly reassuring him, touching his hand from time to time. Sean made sure Corey drank water and offered to bring him food. Corey couldn't eat, though.

When they got word that Nygaard had died, Corey snorted derisively. "Fucking coward, took the easy way out," he said angrily. "Couldn't face the consequences of his actions."

Hirata called a halt to everything and announced that he was taking Corey home. The homicide detectives tried to protest, but Corey was only a witness and he'd been cooperative. The captain told them to contact him to schedule a time for follow up questions, and with that, the three of them left.

Corey didn't remember the drive home. He followed Sean up the stairs and through the front door.

"Corey, you're scaring me," Sean said as he pulled off his own tie and unbuttoned the collar of his shirt. "Are you okay?"

Corey focused on him. He didn't like the concerned expression on Sean's face. "Yeah, I am. Don't worry. I'm just trying to absorb the fact that it's over. It's all over. Finally."

Sean crossed to him and drew Corey into his arms. "Yeah, baby, it is. Finally."

Corey pressed a kiss to Sean's temple. "I'm gonna shower."

"Maybe I'll start dinner while you're doing that." Sean looked around the room, seeming lost, his expression almost confused.

Corey supposed that Sean was still processing the unexpected turn of events from that day. "Just something simple. Don't go to a lot of trouble, I'm seriously not very hungry," Corey told him, heading for the bedroom.

"Are you sure?" There was something hesitant in Sean's voice.

Corey turned back. "It's because they fed us so well at the courthouse today, that's all." He tried to reassure Sean with a smile.

"All right," Sean said dubiously.

It surprised Corey how easily they settled into their evening routine, despite the horror of the day. It was comforting. He showered quickly and slid on nothing but a pair of well-worn jeans. He replayed the day's events over and over, waiting to feel something. It had been an awful experience, but he'd been through worse. Corey kept thinking he should be having a stronger reaction than he was.

As he quietly padded through Sean's condo on his way to the kitchen, it struck him; Corey felt extraordinary sadness for Nygaard's family. His father and his brother loved him unconditionally. He'd seen their faces when they had thanked Corey and Hirata for trying to save Nygaard, in spite of everything. Corey was saddened by the destruction that Nygaard had left in his wake, including the waste of his own life and family.

As soon as Corey realized what it was he was feeling and that it was, for once, completely appropriate to the situation, he relaxed and just let it go.

Sean moved around the kitchen barefoot, dressed only in

jeans and a tank top. He assembled simple sandwiches for them both. Afterward, Corey helped clean up.

They lay entwined on the couch catching up on television shows they had DVR'd. Corey stretched out on the sofa, settling Sean between his legs and back against him. At some point, the skin of his arms wasn't enough and Corey stripped off Sean's shirt so his naked back was warm against the flesh of Corey's chest and stomach. He ran his hands idly over Sean's body, in no hurry to take things further quite yet. They had all night and that thought settled peacefully over Corey. Still, each time he skimmed his fingertips just below the waist of Sean's jeans, he felt the burgeoning hardness.

As one of their shows ended, Sean snatched the remote and shut the television down completely. Corey watched in confusion as Sean turned in his arms until he lay with his chest pressed to Corey's belly.

"Godammit, Corey, you're too quiet and you're scaring me." Sean's fear and worry were starkly written on his features. His hazel eyes searched Corey's face, his lush mouth turned down at the corners. Corey watched the muscles in his jaw clench and could feel his rapid breathing.

"There's nothing for you to be afraid of," Corey said emphatically. Christ, he had no idea he could evoke such a strong response in Sean. It was satisfying at the same time he ached to reassure Sean that everything—*absolutely everything*—was perfect. "You have nothing to be worried about. Really."

"Please don't avoid this, Corey, please," Sean's voice was raw and pleading. "That was some serious shit today. You have to feel something, but you're acting like it was just another day."

Corey abruptly remembered Sean didn't have his same experience with death. Corey may not need to talk about what had happened, but maybe Sean did. He grasped Sean's face gently between both palms, running the pads of his thumbs over Sean's sharp cheekbones. "Sshh, sshh. Sean, remember what I do for a living and where I've been. That's one of the more peaceful deaths I've witnessed. That wasn't the first time I've performed

CPR. It wasn't the first time it didn't work, either. Except for *who* died, it was sort of just another day for me." As the words left his mouth, Corey wondered if he didn't sound too cold and callous; too jaded and dismissive of human life.

"You really don't have any problem with the guy who's made your life miserable for nearly a year dying under your hands?" Sean asked, brows knitting together.

Corey snorted. "I think he's a pathetic coward and I don't think the overdose was an accident," he replied. "I'm angry about how he checked out for good. I'm pissed at him for all the harm he caused innocent women and children. But he brought all of his problems on himself, despite what his lawyers were saying." Corey ran his palms down the length of Sean's muscular back. "Most of what I feel is pity and sadness for his father and brother. They lost someone they loved, after having to watch him spiral out of control. I wish I could have saved Nygaard just to save his family the additional agony."

Sean leaned up and kissed Corey softly. "That's very compassionate of you. I admire that," he said against Corey's lips.

"See? Not just a mindless killing machine." Corey grinned, meaning it as a joke.

"I never thought that about you," Sean said, almost angrily. "I've always known there was a big heart beneath the sexy tattoo."

"What about you?" Corey asked. "First death you've ever seen?"

Sean's exhale was shaky. "Yeah. I knew Hollywood wasn't realistic, but nothing can prepare you, can it?"

Corey shook his head in answer.

"I was so fucking angry at Nygaard for what he'd put you through, but I wanted you and the captain to save him today," Sean said, his gaze distant as if remembering. "Because I was afraid you'd have a stress reaction if he died, and because I didn't want you to feel responsible."

"No worries, I feel fine." Corey placed a reassuring kiss on

Sean's full lips.

"But I didn't give his family a single thought, like you did." Sean lay his head down on Corey's chest. "I only thought about how his death would affect you. I never considered how his family would grieve."

"I'm honored that someone like you cares about my well-being," Corey whispered into Sean's fragrant hair. "Have I told you that?"

"No. Of course I care," Sean replied. "I just feel badly that I didn't give Nygaard's family much thought. I was almost angry at them today when they came up to talk to you. I mean, he'd caused us so many sleepless nights and other problems. I nearly thought 'good riddance' before I stopped myself."

"I realize that it's over now." Corey held Sean close and running his hands up and down his back. "I can afford—*we* can afford—to be gracious."

Sean lifted his head and this time, his kiss was searing. Corey held him close and opened to him, letting Sean set the pace and the intensity. Sean shifted against Corey, coming to his knees. Sean's hardening dick pressed against Corey's and he circled his hips, getting a little teasing friction. Sean's hands glided over Corey's exposed skin. One twisted in the chain of his dog tags as if to hold him steady.

Corey surprised himself with the needy sound he made in protest when Sean abruptly broke their kiss. He tried to follow but Sean shifted out of reach. Corey didn't resist when Sean grabbed his hips and dragged him down to lay flat on the sofa. He wrapped his arms and legs around Sean and settled back to enjoy the hot, wet kisses being pressed to his throat and chest.

Gripping Corey's tags, Sean took one of Corey's nipples into his mouth and flicked it with his tongue. Corey arched up into Sean, closing his eyes and tilting his head back. He buried one hand in Sean's soft hair and gripped his bicep with the other. Corey moaned as Sean sucked at his nipple, dragging his teeth along it before flicking it again with his tongue.

Sliding across to Corey's second nipple, Sean teased it the same way. His teeth were exquisite as they sent stinging pain tingling through his system. Corey gripped Sean's hair and pulled him closer, encouraging him to keep up the attention.

When Sean pulled off his nipple, Corey growled in protest. He glanced down to watch as Sean traced the tip of his tongue over the colored ink on Corey's chest. Releasing Sean's bicep, Corey propped up his own head so he could continue to watch Sean's pink tongue drag along his skin.

Corey sighed harshly as gooseflesh rose and a shiver of pleasure ran the length of his body.

"You like that?" Sean asked breathlessly, swiping the flat of his tongue the length of Corey's tat.

"I like when you do it." Corey's reply was rough.

Sean licked a wet path down the center of Corey's stomach. Corey tightened his abs in response. He shivered again when Sean flicked his tongue into his navel. Corey hissed when Sean sank his teeth lightly into one of the ridged muscles of Corey's stomach. He soothed it with his tongue before moving on to another. Corey moaned, pushing upward slightly into the pleasant sensation.

When Sean's hands fumbled at the fly of Corey's jeans, he reached his free hand down to try to help. He couldn't bring himself to let go of Sean's hair, the feel of the strands between his fingers was turning him on.

Sean finally opened Corey's jeans. He tugged them roughly over Corey's hips and down his legs, tossing them aside. Corey let his thighs fall open so Sean could rest between them. He left himself open and accessible for whatever Sean wanted to do.

To Corey's immense pleasure, Sean apparently wanted to suck his cock. Corey was already fully hard and leaking when Sean swallowed him down.

"Oh, fuck yeah," Corey moaned when the wet heat of Sean's luscious mouth surrounded him.

Corey flexed his hips, trying to push deeper into Sean's throat. He used his hand in Sean's hair to push him down at the same time. One of Sean's hands cradled Corey's sac, the other rubbed up and down the inside of one of Corey's thighs. He took Corey's cock easily, breathing harshly through his nose, humming as he sucked hard.

Keeping his head propped up so he could watch, Corey stared in fascination as Sean's full lips slid up and down his shaft. Corey's cock glistened wetly each time Sean pulled off, the heat intense as it re-enveloped him. He muttered dirty things to Sean as he fucked up into his mouth. It felt so fucking good, he was damn near ready to come.

Sean looked up suddenly. His hazel eyes snagged Corey's and held. There was lust there, like always, but this time, something more as well. Corey eased his grip on Sean's hair and stilled his hips. He realized Sean wanted him to enjoy this. Sean seemed invested in Corey's pleasure at his hands and mouth. It was like it *mattered* to him.

Pain burst in Corey's chest, but it was a different pain than he'd ever felt before. It was a sharp ache and it was tied directly to Sean. Corey stared back into Sean's eyes, letting him see everything he'd been hiding. It was time to stop running.

This wasn't about fucking Sean's mouth, this was about enjoying the pleasure Sean wanted to give him. "That feels so good. You make me feel so good," he murmured.

Sean's fingers on his sac caressed more firmly, giving a light tug. Corey groaned and bit his lower lip. He grinned playfully at Sean. The hand on Corey's leg moved as Sean slid it upward. His palm skimmed Corey's belly and up over his chest. As Sean sucked on Corey's dick, his fingers traced over Corey's lips.

Corey licked at Sean's fingers, tonguing them, drawing them into his mouth and sucking on them in the same way Sean was sucking his cock. Sean moaned, the vibrations rocketing their way to the base of Corey's spine.

With his free hand, Corey gripped Sean's and held it against his chest. He twined their fingers and held tight as Sean's mouth moved faster. Corey's chest heaved as his breathing sped up, his orgasm building deep inside.

"I love watching you sucking me," he whispered to Sean, still holding his gaze unwaveringly. "You're so fucking gorgeous. I love the feel of you against me."

Sean's eyes warmed, his fingers tightened against Corey's. He moved faster on Corey's cock, taking him deeper down his throat.

"You're gonna make me come," Corey gasped. "I'm gonna come for you. Is that what you want? You want me to come for you?"

Sean pulled off with a gasp. "Yeah, but not like this." He wiped his swollen mouth with the back of one hand. He collapsed down on top of Corey, the skin of his chest scalding. Corey's mouth was captured in a wet, off-center kiss. It was hot and dirty and Corey loved it. He released Sean's hair and ran his palm down Sean's back. He kept their fingers twined against his chest.

When Sean circled his hips against Corey, the denim of his jeans was coarse and stimulating. Corey pushed back against him, his sensitive cock grazing across the seam of Sean's fly. He rubbed his tongue against Sean's as it delved into his mouth, seeking and teasing and demanding. His senses were overloaded but it still wasn't what he wanted or needed.

"Why are you still dressed?" Corey said between quick, sipping kisses. "You need to be naked. I can't touch you if you're not naked, you need to be naked."

"You are touching me," Sean replied, nipping at Corey's lip.

"No. Here." Corey reached between them and cupped Sean's hard cock through his jeans.

"Fuck. I need supplies," Sean gasped. He stumbled off of the sofa, nearly toppling, as he fumbled with the fly of his jeans. He disappeared into the bedroom.

Corey craned his neck, confused. He chuckled when Sean emerged from the bedroom, struggling to walk and shove his jeans over his hips with one hand while holding items in his other.

Finally, he succeeded in kicking away his jeans and kneeling once again between Corey's spread thighs. His laugh was embarrassed. "I want you so bad my hands are shaking."

Corey took the bottle of lubricant from Sean's trembling hand. "Are you gonna fuck me tonight?"

Sean paused in opening the condom, his face registering worry. "Is that okay?"

Corey let him stew for several seconds while he just admired. Sean was absolutely stunning. His tan skin was flushed and covered in a light sheen of sweat. His firm muscles were well defined, his hard cock standing proudly upright. "Fuck yeah, it's okay," he finally replied with a grin.

Sean smiled in relief. "Asshole," he muttered, going back to struggling with the condom wrapper.

Corey opened the slick and coated two fingers. "Yeah, I have one and I want your cock in it."

Sean made a choking sound. "Keep talking like that and I'm gonna come in my own hand."

Lifting his knees, Corey pushed one lubed finger into his own hole. He spread the slick around thickly.

"Impatient fucker," Sean groused as he rolled the condom down the length of his shaft. "I wanted to do that."

"Next time," Corey replied. "I just want you in me now. No fucking around with the fucking lube." He pushed two slick fingers inside himself and moaned. Smearing more lube around the rim of his hole, Corey tossed the bottle aside. "Come here," he said on a sigh, holding his arms open for Sean.

Settling his thighs against Corey's ass, Sean wrapped Corey's legs around his hips. He braced one hand on the cushion beside Corey's head. Corey watched as Sean positioned his latex sheathed cock against Corey's opening and began to push.

Corey wrapped his arms around Sean's chest and dug his fingers into the thick muscles in his back. He tugged at him, encouraging him to move faster, to get deeper. Breathing heavily, Sean obliged him. With slow, steady thrusts of his hips, he moved against Corey, pushing into him.

Corey grunted when the head of Sean's cock slipped past his rim. Sean gasped. With his legs and his hands, Corey urged Sean deeper. With each thrust of his hips, Sean slid in deeper. Corey felt fuller. The stretch of his hole sent frissons up his spine. His body took Sean easily, molding around him, clutching him, as if they were made to fit together.

Sean braced one hand above Corey's shoulder and the other on the arm of the sofa. Corey looked up into his face, watching his open and emotional expression. Sean's eyes glowed. His full lips were wet and parted as he breathed rapidly through them. Corey stayed wrapped around Sean, holding him steady and clinging to him at the same time.

He met Sean's steady pace. Corey lifted his hips into each slow, steady stroke of Sean's cock. It felt good. Sean felt good in and against him. The pressure on Corey's gland was perfect; just enough to make him feel good, warm him up, get him ready.

"Is this good?" Sean asked between gasping breaths. "Does it feel good? Do I make you feel good?"

"Yeah, you know you do," Corey told him truthfully. "You're perfect."

Sean chewed on his own lower lip as he focused intently on Corey's face. "You're clean, right?" he asked suddenly. "I mean, the Marines make sure you're healthy, right?"

Corey was confused at first. The desperate, needy look on Sean's face brought clarity. "Yeah. Yeah. I'm clean."

"So, if I get checked, we can get rid of the rubbers, right?"

Corey nodded sharply. "Yeah, we can. If you want to."

"Do you want to?" Sean's jaw clenched but Corey didn't miss it.

"Yeah, I do," Corey said without hesitation. "When we know we're both clean, we'll ditch the condoms."

Sean changed the angle of his thrusts and the head of his cock brushed more firmly against Corey's gland. He squeezed his eyes shut as a light show exploded behind his lids. He swore mindlessly as his orgasm built inside of him, his balls tightening.

Sean slowed his thrusts. Corey eased back against the sofa, relaxing and enjoying the slide of Sean's cock in and out of him.

"Christ, I'm so fucking close," Sean panted. "I wanna make you come first, though."

Corey wrapped a hand around his own erection and stroked. "Fuck me. Just keep fucking me. Let me feel you."

Sean sped up his hips and adjusted his angle once last time. He nailed that spot deep inside of Corey, over and over again. Corey jacked himself quickly, already close to coming. Sean was relentless, just like Corey had asked him to be.

"Like that?" Sean asked, watching Corey intently. "Is that good?"

"Yeah, that's good," replied Corey. "Just like that. Don't stop."

Corey's climax slammed into him violently. His back bowed and his ass clenched tight around Sean's cock. He shouted obscenities and praise. He might have begged Sean not to stop fucking him.

"That's it baby, come for me." Sean's loving words of encouragement only just registered with Corey. "Want you to feel good. Yeah, like that. Just like that. Come for me, baby."

"Fuck!" Corey shouted as his orgasm finally released him. He reached up and dragged Sean down on top of him. He kissed him hard, saying all the things he didn't have the words for. Corey dug his fingers into Sean's ass and encouraged him to move. He moaned into Sean's mouth with each rough thrust.

Sean tore his mouth away with a shout. He slid his hands beneath Corey's back and gripped his shoulders. His breath was hot against Corey's neck as he buried his face there and panted heavily. His body slammed into Corey's.

"Your turn, baby," Corey whispered against Sean's ear. "Your turn to feel good and come inside me."

"Oh my God," Sean sobbed brokenly as his body shuddered violently against Corey.

Corey could feel Sean's cock pulse inside his ass. He felt every tremor roll through Sean's body, felt his chest heaving against his own. He held Sean tightly against him, holding him steady through his orgasm.

When Sean finally pulled out and stumbled away to dispose of the condom, Corey actually nodded off. He startled awake at the feel of Sean wiping his chest and belly clean. Tossing the towel to the floor, Sean settled himself between Corey's legs again, resting his chin on Corey's chest. They were silent for several long minutes. Corey twisted strands of Sean's hair around his fingers. Sean toyed with Corey's dog tags.

"I didn't mean to put you on the spot again," Sean finally murmured. "I need to stop asking for emotional commitments just before you're ready to come."

Corey didn't even wonder what Sean was talking about. "I want to get tested. I want to stop using condoms. We'll do it this week."

Sean snorted. "Okay. Good." There was another long pause. "You know that means monogamy, right?"

"I thought we covered that already," Corey said. "I'm not fucking around. I don't fuck around."

"I just want to be clear about it all," Sean said around yawn. "And only if you want to. We don't have to—"

"Shut up, Sean," Corey said quietly. "I'm the one who's supposed to over think everything. Not you."

Sean chuckled, the sound vibrating through Corey. "Is there any reason you need to live on base?"

The question sounded casual but Corey knew it was anything but. It never ceased to amaze him that Sean seemed able to read his mind. "No, not anymore. In fact, I've been thinking lately that it's time to move into a real home."

"You can just move in here, you know," Sean said, looking everywhere but at Corey's face. "You're here so much of the time, anyway."

"That's one option," replied Corey.

"You have another?" Now Sean looked him in the eye.

"This is a nice place, it really is," said Corey. "But it's *your* place. I have a pretty good amount of money saved up and I thought maybe you could sell it, and we could buy a house together. Someplace that would be *ours*."

Sean's silence sickened Corey. He'd obviously miscalculated.

"It was just an idea," he said hastily. "I'll probably just find a little place to rent."

"No," Sean blurted. "No, I want to find some place together. I do."

"I don't want you to feel pressured," said Corey. "It was just one idea."

"You're not listening again." Sean sounded exasperated. "You surprised me is all. I didn't think you were ready, or even wanted to buy a place together."

Corey met Sean's eyes steadily. "When we met, I felt like I was dug in to a final protective line and was just waiting for hostiles to overrun my position. I don't feel that way anymore. Instead, reinforcement forces arrived."

Sean smiled. "Am I the reinforcements in this analogy?"

Corey chuckled. "Yes. I was your rescue mission."

They lay silently for long enough that Corey dozed. He awoke to the sound of his name softly spoken.

"Corey?" Sean whispered again.

"Mm hmm." He cracked one heavy eyelid to find Sean watching him closely.

"I just need to say it. Just this one time." Sean swallowed hard. "I love you."

Corey opened both eyes. He cupped Sean's cheek with one hand. "I hope it's not just this one time, because I love you, too."

He barely felt the touch of Sean's lips to his own as Corey slid into sleep, knowing there was no chance of a nightmare tonight.

Kendall McKenna's first work of fiction was written at the worldly age of nine, and was a transformative work that expanded on the story told in a popular song of the time.

She tried her hand at vampire and cowboy fiction, winning high school poetry and short story contests along the way. It wasn't until she discovered the world of m/m erotic fiction and found her stride with cops, Marines and muscle cars, that she felt inspired to share her stories with readers who enjoy the same things.

Putting herself through college by working in a newly-created HIV testing clinic in her local Department of Health, introduced Kendall to the gay and lesbian community. Understanding and empathy has made her a lifetime advocate of GLBT issues.

A brief bout of unemployment gave Kendall the time and focus she needed to finally produce a novel worth submitting for publication. Her first novel, Brothers In Arms, introduced the world to her authentic military stories and characters.

Kendall was born and raised in Southern California, where she still lives and works. A non-conventional relationship has kept her happy for the last decade. Her four dogs enjoy it when she writes, as she sits still long enough for them to curl up around her.

You can find Kendall on the internet at:

Website/Blog: www.kendallmckenna.com

Facebook: www.facebook.com/kendallmckenna

Twitter: @kendallmckenna

Email: kendall.mckenna3@gmail.com

TRADEMARKS ACKNOWLEDGMENT

CPSIA information can be obtained
at www.ICGtesting.com
Printed in the USA
BVHW072134020221
599232BV00010B/77